# The Predator

# The Predator
## *Dark Verse - Book 1*

# RuNyx

The Predator
Dark Verse #1
RuNyx
Copyright © 2020 by RuNyx
runyxwrites.com

All rights reserved.

Cover Design by Nelly R.
Proofreading by M. T. Smith.
Editing by M.T. Smith.

ISBN-13: 9781653678426
First Edition

# Table of Content

*To the fandom.*
*To the readers who have been with me through the years.*
*I am here because of you.*

# Acknowledgements

I want to thank many people for making this book, and me, possible. This book has been a labor of love spanning many years. Owing to that, I would first and foremost like to thank each and every one of my readers who have stuck with me through the years. Every single comment, ask, tweet, kudos, message, all of it. I can never put into words how much your love and support means to me. You all have helped me go through some of the darkest times of my life, and every day you inspire me. Thank you will never be enough to convey all of what I feel for you. All I hope is to continue telling stories you will enjoy.

Secondly, I want to thank my parents for always encouraging me to thrive and for believing in me, even when times were hard and there were bumps along the way. Your love shows me the way every day. Thank you for loving me so unconditionally.

I also want to thank Nelly for being the absolute superstar that you are. I've said this countless times, and I will again – your vision and your talent just blow my mind. Thank you for giving this story such a beautiful cover, something even beyond my wildest dreams.

On the same note, I want to thank my editor and proofreader, M.T. Smith (who's asked me not to mention her full name). Thank you for your enthusiasm and for respecting my writing style, as odd as it seemed to you in the beginning.

And last, but not the least, I want to thank you, T. Chances of you reading this are slim, but if you are, you know what you mean to me. Thank you for making me realize that soulmates exist. Keep believing.

And to you, my new readers. I hope this book gave you a great escape for a few hours. Thank you for choosing to read me.

## Author's Note

This is the first book of the *Dark Verse* series. As the name suggests, everything about this world is going to be dark, brutal and raw. The characters, their behaviors, and circumstances are all a direct result of their world. Morality is grey and humanity is questionable. This is not a world of rainbows and butterflies. With each book, I will be exploring more of the darkness and the good that can still exist in it. However, if you have certain expectations of how a character ought to behave, certain ideas that are cemented about the good and bad, or if you aren't fully ready to immerse yourself into this verse, this book might not be for you. It is dark and it is ugly. If you are not going to be comfortable with that, I sincerely urge you to pause. There are adult situations, explicit content, brutal imagery, and questionable actions. I have written this verse with a lot of love, and if you are taking this ride with me, I hope you enjoy diving into it.

*When you gaze into the abyss,*
*the abyss also gazes into you.*

*-  Friedrich Nietzsche*

# *the alliance*

*Tenebrae City, 1985*

On a cold, dark night in winter, with the wind howling and the skies crying in sleet, two men from the Tenebrae Outfit met the two men from Shadow Port in the middle of nowhere. Though the two families had been rivals for over a decade, it was becoming bad for business. Theirs was a small world and they could not keep biting each other's heads off when there were bigger, more lucrative ventures that could benefit them both. It was time to end the rivalry of a decade and begin a partnership for the future.

The leader of Shadow Port shivered under his heavy coat, not used to the freezing temperatures in his city in the west. The leader of the Ten Outfit laughed. They saw the sun even less than he saw his wife. Jovial conversation was exchanged. The man with each leader stayed a silent observant.

And then, the business was discussed. Weapons and alcohol - they were the face of the operation. It was time to begin a new venture, a first with the family. The leader of Tenebrae suggested the idea. It was a new trade, not common in the world yet, but had a great future and more money than they had dreamed of. The leader of Shadow agreed. The men vowed to keep it quiet, keep it a hidden trade, to let everyone think of arms and booze as their main business.

The Tenebrae leader opened up the trunk of his car. Two young girls, not more than eight years of age, lay there unconscious, unaware of what awaited them.

The leaders exchanged a small smile and shook hands.

"To the future," one said.

"To the future", the other echoed.

And thus, began the Alliance.

# scenting

*Present Day*

T he knife was digging into her thigh.
*She was not supposed to be here.*
The thought kept ringing through Morana's head on repeat, her nerves stretched taut even as she tried to appear aloof. Holding her full champagne glass aloft, she pretended to sip from it, her eyes constantly scanning the crowd. While she knew taking a few sips of the bubbly would do wonders to calm her frazzled nerves, Morana refrained. She needed a clear head more than liquid courage for tonight. Maybe. *Hopefully.*

The party was in full swing, hosted in the sprawling lawns of the home of someone in the Maroni family. Damn Outfit. It was a good thing she had done as much research as she could in the last few days.

Morana glanced around the well-lit garden from the shadows, seeing the faces she had seen in the news over the years. A few she had seen in her own house growing up. She saw the soldiers of the Outfit, milling around with stoic faces. She saw the women, mostly decorating the arms of the men they were there with. She saw the enemies.

Ignoring the itch from her wig, Morana just observed. She had taken great care to look like someone else tonight. The long black gown she wore hid the knives on her thighs, one of which had somehow twisted and was trying to dig into her. The bracelet on her hand had been

3

a purchase from the dark web, with a hidden slot for an aerosol poison that wasn't available in the market. And she'd tied her dark hair tightly to her head, donning a silky wig of strawberry blonde hair, her lips siren red. It wasn't her. But it was necessary. She'd been planning this night for days. She'd been relying on this plan to work for days. She couldn't screw it up. Not after being so close.

She looked at the mansion, looming behind the crowd. It was a beast. There was no other way to describe it. Like an ancient castle buried in the hills of Scotland, the house – an odd hybrid of modern mansion and primeval castle - was a beast. A beast with something of hers in its belly.

The cool air fragrant with the night blooms, Morana surreptitiously shook off the chills trying to lick at her skin.

The sound of a man's boisterous laughter drew her attention. Eyes lingering on the built, grey-haired man laughing with other men in the north corner of the property, Morana studied him. His face was wrinkled with age, hands clean from where she could see.

Oh, how he had blood on those hands. So, so much blood. Not that anyone in their world didn't. But he had carved a niche for himself as the bloodiest of them all, including her father.

Lorenzo 'Bloodhound' Maroni was the boss of the Tenebrae Outfit, his career longer than four decades, his rap sheet longer than her arm, his cold-blooded attitude a thing of admiration in their world. Morana had been around people like him long enough to not let that shake her. Or rather, not let it show.

Beside Lorenzo stood his older son Dante 'The Wall' Maroni. While his pretty face could fool some, Morana had done enough research not to underestimate him. Built like a wall, the man towered over almost everyone, his physique solid. If rumors were to be believed, he had taken up a key role in the organization almost a decade ago.

Morana pretended to sip her champagne. Exchanging a polite smile with a woman who glanced her way, she finally let her eyes wander to the man who stood silently beside Dante.

Tristan Caine.

He was an anomaly. The only non-blood member to have taken the oath with blood in the family. The only non-blood member to be that high up in the Outfit. No one knew exactly where he was placed in the hierarchy, but people knew he was very high up. Everyone had theories as to why, but no one really knew for sure.

Morana took him in. He stood tall, just an inch or so shorter than Dante, in a casual three-piece black suit sans the tie. His dark blonde hair was almost a dark brown, sheared close to his head, his eyes a light color from the distance.

Morana knew they were blue. A striking blue. She'd seen pictures of him, always candid shots in which he looked surprisingly blank. Morana was used to expressionless faces in their world, but he took it up a notch.

While his muscular frame was attractive, it wasn't the reason Morana couldn't look away. It was because of the stories she'd heard about him in the last few years, mostly by eavesdropping on conversations, especially her father's.

As the stories went, Tristan Caine had been the son of Lorenzo Maroni's personal bodyguard, who had died while protecting the boss almost twenty years ago. Tristan had been young, with a mother who had taken off after her husband's death.

Lorenzo, for reasons unknown, had taken the young boy under his wing and personally trained him in skills of the trade. And today, Tristan Caine was a son to Bloodhound Maroni. Some said Maroni favored him more over his own blood. In fact, word was, after Maroni's retirement, Tristan would be the boss of the Outfit, not Dante.

Tristan 'The Predator' Caine.

They called him the predator. His reputation preceded him. He rarely went on the hunt but when he did, it was over. When he did, he went straight for the jugular. No distractions. No playing around. For all his unruffled attitude, the man was more lethal than the knife cutting into her thigh.

He was also the reason she had come to the party.

She was going to kill Tristan Caine.

Life as the daughter of the boss of the Shadow Port family had prepared her for a lot of things. Not this. Despite growing up surrounded by crime, Morana had been surprisingly sheltered from the ugliness of their world. She had been home-schooled, gone to university, and now freelanced as a developer. All very plain.

That was exactly why she was so *not* equipped to handle this. She'd not been prepared to infiltrate the house of her father's enemies and by extension hers. And she'd definitely not been prepared to murder that said enemy.

Maybe she didn't really have to kill him. Perhaps, kidnapping would work just as well.

*As if.*

For over an hour, Morana watched Tristan Caine carefully without being too obvious, waiting for him to just move. Finally, after staying glued to Maroni's side with a dark scowl on his handsome face, he detached himself and moved to the bar.

Morana debated whether to approach him out in the open or wait for him to head into the house. After a split second of indecision, she decided on the latter. The first option was way too dangerous and was she exposed, it would not only mean her death sentence but a war between the two families. A mob war. She shuddered, just thinking of all the morbid tales she'd heard over the years.

She also wondered if she was being logical in wanting to kill the man.

Maybe not, but she did need to get into the house and find where he was hiding her codes.

It has all started as a dare from her ex-boyfriend (not that anyone knew about him). Being a developer himself, he had challenged her to create the most complex set of codes she could. Being a suck for dares that she was, she had succumbed.

Those codes were her Frankenstein. A powerful monster that went wrong, out of her control. They could digitally deface anyone, extract out every dirty secret from the deepest parts of the web, and destroy entire governments, entire mobs if it were to fall into the wrong hands.

They had fallen into the worst hands possible. Her asshole of an ex – Jackson – had stolen the codes when she was done three weeks ago, and disappeared.

It was when she'd started to track him that she'd discovered Jackson had actually been sent to get close to her by the Outfit. More specifically, Tristan Caine. How he'd learned about her skills and the codes, she didn't know.

She was screwed. So, so screwed.

There was no way she could tell her father. *None.* The offenses against her were too high. Dating an outsider, writing a time bomb of codes without any protection, but worst of all, knowing where the codes had ended up – her father would kill her without batting an eye. She knew it, and frankly, she didn't care. But innocent people and bystanders didn't deserve to have their lives destroyed by her mistakes.

So, after weeks of researching and stalking, she'd finally faked herself an invitation to the party in Tenebrae. Her father thought she was there meeting her non-existent friends from college. Her protective detail thought she was drunk and sleeping in her locked hotel suite.

She'd escaped. Come this deep into the den. She had to get those codes and get the hell out of there. And she had to do all that while silencing Tristan Caine. The only way to do that was to kill him.

Thinking of how he'd masterminded everything with Jackson, her blood boiled.

Oh yes, killing him won't be a problem. The urge intensified every time she thought of the sick bastard. Morana grit her teeth.

Finally, after throwing back a shot of scotch, Tristan Caine moved towards the mansion.

Showtime.

Nodding to herself, Morana put her glass on a tray of one of the many waiters and quietly made her way towards the secluded path he was taking. Sticking to the shadows, her dark dress ascertained she wouldn't stand out. A few steps on to the path, she saw the party disappearing behind her, as the bushes that shrouded the way grew thicker around her.

Up ahead, she saw Caine's tall, broad figure striding agilely towards the steps of the house. He climbed them two at a time, and she rushed on her heels, trying to keep him in her line of vision.

Her eyes darting around the area, she bent low and climbed the steps. Over to her left, she could see the party and the guards stationed around the lawns.

Frowning at the lack of security around the house itself, Morana entered the house through the space between the huge double doors.

And saw a guard heading straight in her direction through the lobby.

Adrenaline hitting hard, she ducked behind the first pillar she saw, her eyes darting around the huge entrance with an over-the-top chandelier. Her gaze tracked Caine taking a corridor to the left of the lobby, his back disappearing from view at the end.

She suddenly felt a hand pull on her arm.

The large guard frowned down at her.

"Are you lost, miss?" he asked, his eyes suspicious, and before she could rethink, Morana picked up the vase beside her and smashed it over his head. The guard's eyes widened before he crumpled down and Morana escaped, berating herself.

*Fuck, fuck, fuck.*

That had been sloppier than she would have liked.

Taking a deep breath, focusing on the task at hand, Morana crouched low, heading towards the hallway. Once inside, she made a run for it, stopping to pick her heels up in her hands to avoid making any noise. Within seconds, she was at the turn somewhere in the back of the house, looking at a set of stairs leading up to a single door.

Swallowing, her heart pounding, she climbed up.

Reaching the landing, she tiptoed her way to the door. Taking in a deep, quick breath, she pulled the knife out of its sheath from her thigh, aware of the little bruise it had left there. She reached for the knob, donning her heels, and turned it open.

Leaning her neck inside, she looked around the semi-dark guest room of sorts.

It was empty.

Frowning, she stepped inside, shutting the door behind her quietly.

The door on the other side of the large room opened before she even had a chance to take in her surroundings. Heart hammering, she crouched in the corner, seeing Tristan Caine step back out of the bathroom, throwing his suit jacket on the bed. Morana observed the suspenders stark against his white shirt, the crisp fabric unbuttoned at the collar, stretched taut across the broad expanse of his chest. A very muscular chest. She bet he had abs too.

Although she hated herself for noticing, she couldn't deny the man was very, very attractive. Too bad he was a bastard to match.

She saw him take his phone out from the pocket of his slacks, scrolling through the screen, his concentration entirely on whatever he was seeing. Watching his muscular back towards her, she straightened from her crouch in the shadows.

It was now or never.

Walking behind him, her hand slightly trembling with the knife gripped in her paling knuckles, she inched forward, not even daring to breathe lest she alert him. Almost two steps behind him, she placed the knife on his back, right above where his heart was supposed to be, and uttered as coldly as she could.

"You twitch and you die."

She saw the muscles in his back stiffen, one by one, even before she had spoken. It would have fascinated her had she not been so shit scared and raving mad.

"Interesting," he remarked evenly, as though his life wasn't two inches of flesh away in her trembling hands. She steadied her grip.

"Drop the phone and raise your hands," she ordered, watching him comply without hesitation.

His voice broke the tense silence. "Since I'm not already dead, I assume you want something."

The completely unruffled tone of voice did nothing to soothe her nerves. Why wasn't he even slightly bothered by this? She could carve him open. Was she missing something?

Sweat broke out over her back, her wig itching on her scalp, but she focused on his back. Pulling out a second knife from her other thigh, she shoved it against his side, right against his kidney. His back tensed slightly more but his hands didn't waver, staying completely upright.

"What do you want?" he asked, the tone unwavering like his hands.

Morana inhaled deeply, gulped, and spoke. "The thumb drive Jackson gave you."

"Jackson, who?"

Morana dug her blades a fraction deeper in warning. "Don't pretend you don't know shit, Mr. Caine. I know everything about your dealings with Jackson Miller."

His back stayed rigid, her knives a second away from breaking skin. "Now, where is the drive?"

There was silence for a few beats before he tilted his head towards the left. "My jacket. Inner pocket."

Morana blinked in surprise. She hadn't expected him to give it up so easily. Maybe he was actually a wuss under all that macho crap. Maybe the rumors and stories were all fabricated.

She looked at the black jacket, and it happened in the split second of her distraction.

Her back slammed into the wall beside the door, her right hand holding the knife up the wall, restrained by a tight grip. Her left hand with the knife came against her own throat, controlled by a much stronger, and much angrier Tristan Caine.

Morana blinked up into his eyes – his very blue, very pissed off eyes – stunned at the turn of events. She wasn't prepared for this. Shit, she was *so not* prepared for this.

Morana gulped. The blade of her own knife clutched in her own hand was gripped by his, right against her neck. She felt the cool metal threaten her tan skin. His second hand, large, rough, held her other hand above her head, his fingers wrapped like manacles around her wrist. She felt his much larger, muscular body press into hers, his chest warm against her heaving breasts, the musky scent of his cologne invading her senses, his legs retraining hers, rendering her completely immobile.

Swallowing, she looked up into his eyes, straightening her spine. If she had to die, she wasn't going to die like a coward, especially not at the hands of someone like him.

He leaned closer, his face just inches from hers, his eyes cold and voice brutal as he spoke. "This spot, right here," he spoke quietly, pressing the tip of the knife against a spot right under her jaw on her tilted neck. "It's an easy spot. I nick you here, and you die before you can blink."

Her stomach churned but she grit her teeth, refusing to show fear, silently listening as he moved the knife to her fluttering pulse near the center of her neck. "This spot. You die but it won't be clean."

Her heart thundered with vengeance in her chest, her palms sweating at the look in his eyes. He moved the knife again to a spot near the base of her neck. "And this... You know what happens if I cut you here?"

Morana stayed silent, just watching him, his voice taunting, almost seductive with the temptation of death.

"You'll feel pain," he continued, undaunted. "Bleeding to death. You will feel every drop of blood that leaves your body." His voice rolled over her skin. "Death will come, but much, much later. And the pain will be excruciating."

He held the knife steady to the spot, his voice suddenly chilling. "Now, if you don't want that, tell me who sent you and what drive you are talking about."

Morana blinked at him in confusion, before realization dawned. He didn't recognize her. Of course, he didn't. They had never really met, and as first meetings went, this one left a lot to be desired. He'd probably just seen her pictures in passing like she had his.

Wetting her dry lips, Morana whispered. "The drive is mine."

She saw his eyes narrow slightly. "Is it?"

Her own narrowed as well, the anger that had fled in the face of fear returning with a vengeance. "Yes, it is, you bastard. I worked my ass off on those codes and I'll be damned if I'll let you use it. Jackson stole it from me and I've traveled all the way from Shadow Port because I need it back."

There was a beat of silence, his eyes hovering over her features before surprise flared in them. "Morana Vitalio?"

Morana gave a sharp nod, careful of the blade at her throat. He looked her up and down, his eyes lingering on her wig and her lips, taking in every inch of her that he could before his gaze returned to hers.

"Well, well, well," he murmured, almost to himself as he pulled the blade away an inch, his scruffy jaw loosening now that he knew her identity.

She opened her mouth to ask him to take the knife away just as the door beside them banged loudly. Morana yelped a little in surprise and he let go of the hand above her head, putting his free hand over her mouth.

Seriously? What did he think she was going to do? Scream for help in the Outfit household?

"Tristan, have you seen anyone in the house? Someone knocked out Matteo downstairs," a heavy voice spoke from the other side, a slight accent deep in it.

Morana felt lead settle in her gut, her eyes widening as his gaze locked with hers, his right eyebrow rising as he answered back.

"No, I haven't." His eyes never moved from hers. "I'll be down in a few minutes."

Morana heard the steps shuffling away and after a few seconds, the hand from her mouth retreated. His body didn't.

"Would you mind removing the knife?" she asked quietly, her eyes pinning holes into him.

That raised eyebrow notched even higher before he leaned back in, the knife never moving an inch from the place. "You should know not to come into the house of the enemy, all alone, unprotected. And you should know never to sneak up on a predator. Once we catch the scent of your blood, it's a matter of the hunt."

Morana clenched her jaw, her palm itching to lay one on him and his patronizing attitude. "I want that drive back."

He stayed silent for one long second, before stepping back, releasing her arms but swiping the knives from her, checking them.

"Coming here was foolish, Miss Vitalio," he spoke quietly, looking at her. "Had my people found you, you'd be dead. If your people found out, you'd be dead. Did you want to start a war?"

Hypocrite much? Morana took a step closer to him, inches of space between their frames, glaring. "I'll be dead anyway, so it doesn't seem foolish. Do you have any idea what the contents of that drive can do? This hypothetical war you are accusing me of starting- imagine that but ten times worse." She inhaled deeply, trying to reason with him. "Look, just give me the codes so I'll destroy them and be on my merry way."

There was a heavy silence for long minutes, his eyes contemplating her, making her squirm a bit under the scrutiny. Handing her the knife after minutes that seemed to stretch, he spoke. "Under the stairs, there is a door. It'll lead you to the gates. Get out of here before someone sees you and chaos breaks. I'm having a quiet night after months and the last thing I want to do is clean up your blood."

Morana inhaled deeply, taking the knives from him. "Please."

For the first time, Morana saw something else flicker in his eyes. He just crossed his arms over his chest, tilting his head to look at her.

"Take the door."

Sighing, she knew she was beaten. There was nothing else she could do. And going back home meant telling her father. Which meant either death or exile. *Fuck.*

Nodding, accepting the sour taste in her mouth, she turned on her heel, hand going to the knob on the door, feeling his eyes on her back.

"Miss Vitalio?"

She turned her neck to look back at him, to see his eyes glittering with something that made her heart skip and stomach flutter. He pinned her with the look for a long moment, before speaking.

"You owe me."

Morana blinked in surprise, not understanding. "Excuse me?"

His gaze got even more intense, his blue eyes searing her. "You owe me," he repeated.

Her lips twisted. "What the hell for?"

"For your life," he stated. "Anyone but me and you would not have been breathing."

Morana frowned in confusion and saw his lips twitch at that, even as his eyes stared at her with that look she couldn't explain.

"I'm no gentleman to give you a free pass," he spoke quietly. "You are in my debt."

And then, he closed the space between them. Morana swallowed, her hand tightening on the doorknob even as her heart pounded, and she tilted her head back to keep their eyes locked. He stared down at her for long moments, before leaning in, their gazes never moving, and whispered, his breath ghosting over her face, his musky scent acute in her nose.

"And I will collect it one day."

Morana felt her breath hitch.

And then she ran out of the room.

# colliding

G od, she was seriously not supposed to be here.
It could be the title of her autobiography, given how she
kept finding herself in these situations. If she ever were to
write one, she was pretty sure a lot of people would be interested in
reading it. After all, how many genius mob daughters lay their lives out
in print for mass public consumption? It could even be a bestseller if she
actually lived long enough to write it. With the way things were going
through, she doubted she was even going to make it back home safely.

Dread was settling in the pit of her stomach like a heavy weight,
threatening to buckle her knees as she walked on shaky legs towards the
abandoned building. She was a genius but god, she was an *idiot*. A
world-class, stupid idiot. An idiot who didn't block her cheating ex-
boyfriend's number from her phone. An idiot who had let the said jackass
ex-boyfriend leave a message for her. An idiot who, for some stupid
reason, had listened to it.

She had been sitting in her room, working on her laptop, trying to
undo the disastrous effects of her code when Jackson had left a message
for her.

She could still hear the panic in his voice, as he'd whispered the
words out in a rush. She could still feel the whispered words making her
skin claw. She could still recall the entire message, word for word

because she had listened to it ten times. No, not out of any lost love whatsoever, but because she had been debating her course of action.

She was an idiot.

His frantic voice was stamped on her brain.

*"Morana! Morana, please you have to listen to me. I need your help. It's life or death. The codes... the codes are... I'm so sorry. Please meet me at Huntington and the 8th. There is a construction site there. 6 PM. I'll be hiding in the building, waiting for you. I promise I'll explain everything, just come alone. Please. I swear they'll kill me. Please, I beg you. The codes are..."*

And the message had gone blank.

Morana had sat for an hour, staring at her phone, debating the possibilities. The possibilities being very simple.

Possibility One - It was a trap.

Possibility Two - It wasn't a trap.

Simple, yet utterly confounding. Jackson was a snake of the highest order, she knew. There was a possibility that he had been paid to make the call, just as he had been paid to spy on her. He had faked his affection for her for weeks. What was a panicked phone call of mere seconds in the light of that? He had fooled her once. But was he trying to fool her again? Could this be a trap?

But that was what trumped her. Who would lay a trap for her? The Outfit? She had just been in their lair last week. She had gone into the den of the lion, had a face-to-face with the notorious *Predator*, and come out unscathed. She knew they didn't want to start a mob war at all, or Tristan Caine would have exposed her little stunt that night itself. But he hadn't. He'd let her go. It didn't make sense for them to lay any trap for her.

But if not the Outfit, then who would want to have Jackson fake a frantic phone call to her? Was it even a trap? Could it be possible that she was being overcautious? Was he really scared or faking it?

Morana, unfortunately, didn't have the luxury of not taking a chance. Because if he was scared, and if he really knew something about the codes, then she had to meet him. She had to let him talk. She had to get the codes back, by hook or by crook.

Not that the last time she'd taken that approach had worked out so well.

It still stunned her that she had been at Tristan Caine's mercy. *The* Tristan Caine. The man notorious for his ruthlessness. He'd had her pinned against the wall with her own knives at her throat. And he had let her go. In fact, he had directed her to the door to her freedom, her undiscovered escape from the beast of the Maroni house, smack in the middle of a party.

She remembered the disbelief she had felt hitching a ride back to the hotel. Disbelief at her own guts. Disbelief at her failed attempt. Disbelief at how close she'd come. Disbelief at Tristan Caine.

The meeting, though fleeting, had been pulsating with something that had left Tenebrae with her. It had been a week since her return home, a week since she'd infiltrated the Maroni premises, a week since her failure of retrieving the drive. A week of keeping the truth from her father. If he found out, when he found out, there'd be hell to pay...

Shaking off the distracting thoughts, Morana squared her shoulders, feeling the reassuring cool of the metal against her waistband where she'd tucked in her small Beretta and covered it with a simple yellow top. Besides the keys to her red convertible Mustang, she carried nothing, keeping her hands free and her phone in the pocket of her loose black trousers.

After the last week, she'd dyed her previously blonde hair to chestnut, trying to shake off the grim remnants of the meeting. She did that often – change her hair color. With so much in her life she couldn't seem to control, she liked calling the shots when it came to her appearance. Her new dark locks were bound in a high ponytail and her glasses were perched on her nose. She'd even worn ballet flats in case she needed to run.

Having told her father she was going to the city to shop, she'd left before her father's goons could catch up with her. She'd done it enough times in the past to garner nothing but admonishing looks from him.

With her father, it was less about her safety and more about his control. His control of his men, of her movements, of controlling the enemy's bargaining chip. They both had stopped pretending like they didn't know the truth a long time ago. She'd stopped feeling the disappointment a long time ago. It had left her somewhere between fearless and reckless.

Coming here was smack in the middle of that territory.

Stepping onto the construction site, inside the wrought iron gates that manned the single, incomplete building from the abandoned street, Morana looked around, taking the area in. The sun hung low in the sky, ready to jump below the horizon at a moment's notice, throwing just enough light to let the building cast long, creepy shadows on the ground, the sky slowly burnishing itself from purple to a cold grey as the moon waited to come out.

Morana could feel the wind cooling against her skin, making a small shiver travel down her bare arms in the chill, goosebumps erupting across her skin like small soldiers readying themselves for battle. But it was something else that truly creeped her out.

Eagles. Dozens of them. Circling the building, again and again, calling to each other, the cacophony of their voices lost in the flap of their wings against the wind.

Dusk was setting in, and they kept circling the tall building, telling Morana one thing about the structure. It was no ordinary construction site. Somewhere on the premises was a corpse – she looked up at the birds, at their number – more than one corpse.

She should so not be here.

Tamping down the sudden attack of nerves, Morana looked down at her watch.

6 P.M. It was time.

Where the hell was Jackson?

The sudden buzzing of her phone in her pocket startled her. Exhaling to calm her racing heart, she quickly pulled it out and looked down at the number. Jackson. Putting it to her ear, she accepted the call.

"Morana?" she heard Jackson's familiar voice whisper into the phone and frowned. Why was he whispering?

"Where are you?" she asked quietly, glancing around, looking for anything unusual. Anything unusual except the damn eagles, that is.

"Did you come alone?" Jackson asked.

Morana scowled, her senses on alert. "Yes. Now, will you tell me what's going on?"

She saw Jackson's head peek out from behind the building's door. He waved her forward. "Come inside quickly," she heard on the phone.

Morana's eyes wandered to the unfinished building, rising high up in the sky like a dilapidated monster surrounded by birds of death. She would have been laughing her ass off at the clichéd obviousness of the setting had this been a movie she'd been watching. The last thing she felt like doing now was laugh. This was some really creepy shit. And something was totally off.

"I'm not moving an inch till you tell me what this is about," Morana stated firmly, standing her ground outside the building, watching Jackson peek around the door again.

"Damn it, Morana!" Jackson cursed loudly for the first time, agitation evident in his tone. "She won't come in!"

Morana stilled, hearing Jackson shout to someone behind him, and the certainty of his second betrayal settled itself in her gut. The fucking asshole! He'd set a trap for her.

Without waiting for another second, she crouched down on the ground behind some rubble and pulled the gun out from her waistband. Readying it, straightening her arms, she got ready to aim and fire at the drop of a hat. Her heart thundered in her chest, her breathing laborious as adrenaline surged through her bloodstream, everything but the sound of her own breathing too quiet. Except for the eagles. They kept making their own noises, right above her head in the sky, surrounding the building that reeked of death.

She had to get back to her car.

Eyes darting to the gate, she gauged the distance between the stack of rubble and realized it was a few hundred feet away. Damn. There was no way she could run through the open space without being shot if someone was aiming for her already.

Think. She had to think.

"Morana!"

She stayed down, listening to Jackson calling out her name, his voice coming from the direction of the building.

"We won't hurt you! We just want to talk!"

Yeah, and she was a monkey's uncle.

She grit her teeth, anger filling her, the urge to punch his teeth hard enough to make him bleed surging through her. Oh, how she'd love punching him.

"I know you like playing games, babe, but this isn't one!"

She hated, absolutely detested, when he called her 'babe'. It made her feel like one of those floozies who surrounded men in their world. She should have knocked him down.

"Look, I know," Jackson continued talking, his voice inching closer to where she hid. "I know you hate me for taking the codes but it was all money, babe. I did like you. We can help you if you help us."

Was he high?

Her grip tightened on the gun.

A shot fired. The eagles went wild.

Morana flinched at the noise, her gaze sliding upwards to see the eagles flying haphazardly in chaos, completely frantic, and felt her heart beat in tandem with their wings. She waited for Jackson to speak again, but he didn't. The dread in her stomach tightened.

"I prefer you blonde."

Her breath seized in her throat at the voice coming from behind her. The voice she hadn't been able to forget for a week. The voice that had whispered the ways of murder into her skin like a lover's caress. The voice of hard whiskey and sin.

She swung her gaze up, her eyes leveling with the barrel of a Glock pointed right at her head. She slowly let her gaze travel up to the sure, steady fingers, up the forearms exposed under folded sleeves of a black shirt, roped with muscles, up the shoulders she knew possessed the strength to pin her useless against a wall, up that scruff littering his square jaw, and finally to his eyes. His blue, *blue* eyes. His blue, wiped-clean-of-every-expression eyes.

It was just a second of these observations, a second of feminine appreciation before she let herself remember who he was.

And swung her arm up, pointing her gun right at his heart with his own pointed at her head, in a silent standoff.

Standing up, her eyes not wavering from his, her arm not wavering in her hold, Morana tilted her head.

"I prefer you gone."

His face retained the stoic expression, his eyes narrowing slightly. They stood silently for a few minutes, just with their guns pointed at each other, and Morana realized it was rather pointless. She knew he wasn't going to kill her. He had ample opportunity just last week and he hadn't. He wouldn't do so again.

"We both know you won't shoot me, so let's remove the guns, shall we?" she suggested conversationally, never blinking once to give him any opportunity.

His lips curled but the amusement never reached his eyes. He raised his arm, pulling it back, waving the white flag, and she dropped her own, keeping him in his sights. The moment her gun was down, he stepped into her personal space, placing his gun right between her breasts, his face inches from her own, the scent of his sweat and cologne mingling in the air around her, every fleck of blue in his eyes somehow highlighted even in the darkness that had descended around them.

He leaned in slowly, speaking softly, his eyes hard, never moving from hers, his words making her breath hitch a little in her chest. "There are places on your body that I know," he spoke, his free hand wrapping around the back of her neck, his grip strong, just on the periphery of threatening, as the gun stayed right above her racing heart. "Places that you don't know. Places where I can shoot and harm and you won't die."

He leaned even closer, his whisper just a ghost across her skin as her neck craned to keep their gazes locked, his hand cradling her nape, his height looming above her, his eyes never moving from hers. "Death isn't the main course, sweetheart. It's the dessert."

His eyes hardened even more, his tone frigid, his fingers flexing on her neck in warning. "Never make the mistake of thinking you know me. It might just prove to be your last."

Her heart beat in her chest like a wild animal running for life. Even though her chest heaved with something she so did not want to look at, Morana grit her teeth at the sheer audacity of the man, the sheer arrogance of him. Why did all men around her behave like nominees for Asshole of the Year?

Steeling her spine, she flashed her arm out before she could stop it, her leg hooking around his knee, classic self-defense training overtaking her senses for a moment. She tugged with her leg just as she pushed his

21

weight with her arm, knocking him down on the hard ground, her triumph flaring at watching the brief surprise cross his face. Within a heartbeat, he was back on his feet again, in a lithe movement that would have awed her had he been anyone else. But she wasn't done.

Morana stepped into his personal space this time, her finger going to his hard pecs under the open collar black shirt, poking him once as she spoke, her head tilted back to keep their eyes locked, her voice colder than his had been.

"Never make the mistake of thinking you scare me. It will be your last."

His jaw clenched, his eyes trained on hers, the tension so thick between them she could have cut it with a butter knife. His stance remained icy. She felt fire flooding her veins as her chest heaved.

Another voice interrupted their tense moment.

"I must say, it is rare to find a person, let alone a woman, fearless of Tristan."

Morana turned on the spot, her eyes finding Dante Maroni standing a few feet away, his huge frame encased in a suit that was completely out of place at this construction site and rather belonged to the party she'd seen him in last week. His dark hair was perfectly styled, slicked back on his head, exposing high cheekbones models around the world would weep for. His jaw was shaven clean, two big silver rings adorning his right index finger and left middle finger. With a smooth smile on his face that Morana didn't trust one bit, she observed the Mediterranean heritage obvious in the bronze of his skin, and could not deny that Dante Maroni was one beautiful man.

He came forward, extending his hand, flashing an easy smile Morana would bet her degree on was paid for every month.

"Dante Maroni," he spoke in a soft, polite tone by the way of introduction, taking her hand in his big, smooth ones, clasping it. His brown eyes betrayed his smile though. "It is a pleasure to make your acquaintance, Ms. Vitalio. I rather wish it were under different circumstances."

"I rather wish it weren't at all," Morana shot back before she could help herself, years of enmity boiling in her blood, along with the knowledge that this man possibly had the drive and the power to destroy her. And that he'd possibly shot Jackson. She was pretty certain he was dead.

Dante Maroni flashed another smile, even as his dark eyes regarded her. "Fearless, as I said. It can be a dangerous thing."

She should get that tattooed on her forehead. Maybe she'd pay heed to it then.

Running out of patience, she looked around the area, noticing no other living soul in the vicinity. Okay. So, she was at an abandoned construction site with two reputed, super reputed, men of a mob family, who happened to be her family's enemies and who had lured her out here for a reason. Not the safest place but they hadn't killed her. Yet. Had to count, right?

"Why am I here, Mr. Maroni?" she asked, exasperated and really wanting to make sense of everything. "And where is Jackson?"

"Dante, please," he corrected her with another smile. Tristan Caine stepped out from behind her and joined his blood brother at his side, his muscular arms crossed across his muscular chest, no hint of a smile anywhere on his face. A tattoo peeked out from under his sleeves.

She looked at the two men, both reputed, both ruthless, and saw the stark contrast between them. It wasn't anything she could pinpoint, except this intensity around Tristan Caine that the other man did not possess. The intensity with which he was watching her, with a handsome face devoid of all expression.

She broke away from the intensity, looking back at Dante. She could feel the intensity searing itself upon her skin where Tristan Caine's eyes touched her. Dante's gaze was tame in comparison.

Focusing, she grit her teeth. "Dante."

The man sighed, her hand still clasped in his. "Jackson is dead."

Morana felt a twinge in her gut, but nothing more. She didn't know what that said about her as a person. She wanted to feel bad. But for some reason, she didn't.

She just nodded, not saying anything, not knowing what to say without exposing her own lack of reaction to the death of her ex-boyfriend.

Dante nodded, speaking, squeezing her hand while Tristan Caine stayed silent beside him, and simply watched them like a hawk.

23

"We needed to meet you without setting off any alarms," Dante began. "And the only way to do that was to have Jackson bring you out here."

"Why did you need to meet me?" Morana asked, studiously avoiding looking at the other, silent man.

Dante hesitated for a moment, and for the first time since the appearance of his blood brother, Tristan Caine spoke, in that rough, low tone.

"Because of the codes."

Her heart stilled, as she looked at him, raising her eyebrows. "Explain," she demanded.

Tristan Caine gazed back at her evenly, or as evenly as he could with those eyes that were constantly X-raying her. "You are under the impression that I have this drive of codes," he stated.

Morana felt her brows furrow. "I know you have them."

"Why?" Dante asked, making her turn towards him. Morana considered the two men for a second, confusion making her blink repeatedly, before speaking, addressing them both.

"When Jackson stole the codes from me," she began, her head swiveling between the two men. "I tracked his cell phone records and his movements since he met me. They traced back to you," she finished, gesturing towards Tristan Caine.

There was silence for a heartbeat before Dante spoke. "And you assumed Tristan hired Jackson to spy on you?"

Morana nodded, uncertainty taking hold. "I had no reason to believe otherwise."

"Except the fact that I didn't even know you existed," Tristan Caine chimed in a dry tone. Liar. Her eyes flew to his, narrowing, the memory of his recognition of her name sparking inside her. Oh, he'd known of her existence, alright. But he was lying for some reason.

His blue eyes challenged her openly to call him out on it, to dare and mention that she had been on Maroni property uninvited, in that bedroom, alone with him.

She turned back to Dante, her hands curling into fists and jaw clenching. "You're telling me you didn't hire Jackson?"

Dante nodded, his face serious. "We didn't even know these codes even existed. They have a lot of power, and if they fall in the wrong hands, both our families are screwed. That's why we flew out west to your city. Meeting you was important."

"And how did you come to know of the codes?"

Dante gestured to the man beside him. "Tristan told me about them after you called him last week, demanding its return. We felt we should pay you a visit under the circumstances."

She had called him? She looked at him, trying to ascertain exactly why he was hiding the truth from his blood brother. She found nothing.

Morana scoffed, looking at both the men. "You really expect me to believe you? After you killed Jackson?"

"We haven't killed you," Tristan Caine spoke softly, his eyes hard, dangerous, the look in them sending a shiver down her spine.

Morana steeled it. "Yet. What's to tell me you won't kill me now?"

"Because we don't want to start a war," Dante finally let go of her hand, shaking his head. "As much as our families hate each other, fact is neither of us can afford a war right now, not with outside forces closing in on us. Killing Jackson was to silence him. He was genuinely under the impression that he had been dealing with Tristan. Killing you, on the other hand, will create unnecessary friction."

The logic made sense. But she didn't trust them worth her pinkie. Her eyes latched back onto the blue ones watching her.

"So you're saying someone went to the trouble of elaborately framing you, down to the detail of hiring Jackson, knowing I will uncover their tracks?"

He shrugged his broad shoulders, his eyes fixed on her. "I didn't say anything."

Where did all his eloquence of murder and mayhem go before an audience? Infuriated, Morana crossed her arms over her chest, watching as Dante's eyes flickered at the action. Tristan Caine never looked away from her eyes, not once.

Out of habit, she pushed her glasses up her nose. "So now what? You want us to team up or something?"

"Or something," came his very helpful input.

25

The chime of a phone ringing startled the sudden quiet of the area, making her jump slightly. Dante pulled his phone out, exchanging a look with the silent man, before excusing himself and walking off towards the back. The moment he turned the corner, Morana headed towards the gates where her car waited, ignoring the man standing behind her.

"You really shouldn't walk out without hearing our side," he remarked as she neared the gate.

"Not if you pay me a million bucks," she threw back without breaking her stride, her entire body buzzing with tension. She was almost to her car when suddenly, without any warning, she was pinned flat on the hood, the world tilting as the night sky came into view, and along with it, the face of Tristan Caine. His hand gripped both of hers, holding them above her head as his other one pushed on her stomach, keeping her flat in place.

She bucked. He didn't budge.

She squirmed. He didn't budge.

She struggled. He didn't budge.

Trying to escape the manacles around her wrists, she thrashed against the hood of her own car, kicking her legs out, trying to bite his arms, but he hovered above her, not moving, not speaking, his jaw clenched.

"I don't want to touch you any more than you want to be touched," he grit out roughly, his breath fanning her face, his eyes hard.

"Oh please," Morana rolled her eyes, sarcasm heavy in her tone. "In the two times we have met, I can see how much you detest touching me. Pinning me to flat surfaces is loathsome."

His eyes flared, a snarl curling his mouth, bringing the scar right at the corner of his lower lip into focus. "You are nothing like the women I like to pin. I certainly don't hate them."

"You don't hate me," Morana pointed out.

"No," he shook his head, his eyes hardening by the second, resolve entering them as she saw him inhale heavily. "I despise you."

Morana blinked in surprise at the hatred in his voice, her brows furrowing. She knew they weren't fans of each other, but she didn't warrant this hatred from him. He didn't even know her.

"Why?" she voiced the question in her head.

26

He ignored it, leaning closer, his blue eyes icy, sending a shiver of fear down her body even as her arms stayed above her head, speaking in a low, forceful voice.

"I am not killing you only because I don't want that fucking war." His tone made her flinch. The look in his eyes made her stomach drop. "Just because I cannot harm you doesn't mean I won't."

Morana looked at him, stunned at the ferocity of his hatred. "You don't even know me!"

He stayed silent for a long minute, the hand on his stomach going lower, her heart pounding as panic set in. She struggled and his hand stopped, just below her navel, the gesture of a lover and not the foe, his eyes hard on her.

"I have people who are mine. Territory that's mine. Don't ever invade it," his hand bent a little lower to her hipbone, the threat clear, making her pulse skitter, his eyes glued to her, his voice a whisper right against her skin. "Remember that."

The fucking audacity of him! Stunned, Morana struggled harder against him, kicking her legs out. "You asshole!"

He leaned closer, his lips almost at her ear. "Wildcat."

The sound of footsteps had him releasing her. He straightened, his face donning that blank mask like it had never left, like he'd not been on top of her threatening, like he wasn't the detestable human that he was. Morana stood on slightly shaky legs, her chest heaving, her eyes glaring daggers at him as her hands curled into fists, her body shaking with the rage she could barely contain.

Dante stepped into the area, looking her up and down, frowning. "Are you okay?"

Morana felt her jaw tremble, her heart not even close to calm. The urge to pull her gun out and shoot him was so profound it almost knocked her to her knees. Shaking her head, she lifted her chin higher, steeling her spine and looked right at him, a snarl curving her mouth.

"The two of you can bleed to death for all I care."

Opening her car door, she looked back at the man who had turned her to this mess in seconds, her eyes locking with his.

"Stay the fuck away from me."

She saw something flicker in his eyes while nothing crossed his face, something he masked before she could see it, and she turned away, getting into her car, reversing out of the street. She never looked back in the rearview mirror. Never let herself focus on anything but the way she gripped the steering wheel. Never let herself feel anything but the blood pounding in her ears.

Everything had its time. She would have hers.

Maybe not tomorrow. Maybe not the day after. But the day after that. Or the day after that.

One day, someday, she vowed, with all the rage pulsating in her body, making her shake till she couldn't feel her fingers from gripping the wheel so hard, the rage making her body heated like never before, the rage making her whimper for an outlet.

One day, she vowed, she would kill Tristan Caine.

# *sauntering*

She had to tell her father. There was no other way now. Morana saw the metal gates of the mansion open up ahead, the house itself looming stark white against the cloudy, grey sky, hiding the layers of red that coated it. No matter how many times her father got the house painted, she knew of the blood that remained splattered underneath the coats, knew of the horrors the pristine white hid beneath them. She had grown up in this house, as had her father, and his father before him. The house had been in their family for three generations, every owner adding something more to the sprawling property.

Her family had been the first in the organized business. Shadow Port, back then, had been known as the city of docks. Located right on the West coast of the country, connected to international waters through the sea and locally through the river than bisected it, Shadow Port had been and still was one of the hotspots for trade. Her ancestors had seen the kind of profit that could be made, and made the city their own, slowly expanding over the years to the entire region.

This residential property that housed her had originally been only one building. Her deceased grandfather, and later her father, had expanded it to the sprawling mansion that set a knot in her gut. Especially the extra wing her father had added, where he handled

29

'sensitive' business matters. She never ventured into that wing, not unless absolutely necessary. Like it was today.

Swallowing, she slowly drove up the driveway, watching the lush green grass in the lawns roll by, watching her own bedroom window on the second floor. She had an entire suite to herself, with her own bedroom and a small study where she worked, her own walk-in closet, her own everything. She always had.

Morana had not grown up wanting for anything, not materially at least. If she'd wanted a new computer, she'd had one within hours. If she'd wanted a new dress, she'd had a whole selection of them. She used to think it was a sign of her father's affections - giving her whatever she'd wanted. She'd been corrected of that notion pretty early in life.

He'd kept her on the top floor above his own to keep an eye on her movements. Her wishes had been fulfilled so she wouldn't go out looking to fulfill them herself. She'd stopped wishing the moment she'd realized this, and taken her own choices into her own hands. At least as much as she could have.

Morana wondered, as she pulled up in front of the house manned by two guards, what it would have been like to have her mother while she'd grown up. Would the house have been home then?

Her mother had left her father and this life when a few years after Morana had been born. The marriage of Alice and Gabriel Vitalio had been made for the one reason older than love - business.

Alice's father had been a shady businessman working with Gabriel and they had sealed a lifelong deal with an arranged marriage. Her mother had tried to adapt to this life, this world. She really had. But in the end, after almost two years of trying, she'd decided to leave. From what Morana had heard, she'd tried to take her as well, but her father had put his foot down and given her an ultimatum - either leave alone or never leave at all. But Morana didn't know how true these stories were.

She didn't remember much from her childhood. Morana didn't know where her mother was anymore. She had tried to track on more than one occasion, without the knowledge of her father. It had yielded no results. Her mother clearly didn't want to be found, and after marriage to Gabriel Vitalio, she couldn't really blame her.

Her father had never tried to shield her, protect her or cajole her into a false sense of security. Since she'd understood things, she'd known every gruesome and bloody thing there was to know about their world - things that fathers were supposed to hold back from their daughters.

Ironically, she admired and detested that about him. She knew because of that very reason that he would see the codes as a betrayal and have her killed for it. That would be his form of mercy for his daughter. He'd pick an expert to kill her and he'd ask him to make it painless. After all, there was an example to be made for treason against Gabriel Vitalio, Boss of Shadow Port.

Parking the car in her open slot, Morana got out to the sound of thunder rumbling in the sky and looked up at the arched doorway above the low stairs that led inside the house. One of her father's many goons stood against the door and she sighed, ignoring them like she had most of her life, and walked inside. Except for a few staff, she'd never spoken to her father's men, much less be friendly. They had ignored her and she had returned the favor.

The inside of the house was tasteful, with the foyer leading to the stairs upstairs and the corridor on the left leading to the other wing. Morana closed her eyes for a second, aware she was walking to her own certain death, but knowing that she had to. Keeping her father in the dark could cost way more lives, innocent lives. With his connections and his knowledge, he might be able to retrieve the codes and destroy them.

Slowly, she ambled towards the one section of the house she'd rarely visited. Focusing on keeping her breathing even and her head clear, she kept her palms curled into fists by her side. Whatever happened, she would not beg. She would not beg for her life, or for the codes, or for anything.

She let her mind run over the meeting she'd just had in town. After ditching her bodyguards again, she had gone to the city to meet up with a college classmate, a highly intelligent man, for some advice, hoping that he'd be able to help her track the code. After a week of trying herself until her eyes burned and her fingers hurt, that had been her last resort.

So, she'd vaguely explained the problem to the guy, hoping for some miraculous solution that had escaped her. There hadn't been any. Due to the very nature of the codes, he had remarked that retrieving them

31

wouldn't be possible unless she happened to be in the proximity of fifty feet. And that was impossible because A. she didn't have the codes, and B. she didn't know where they were. Jackson had thought they were with the Outfit. And since The Outfit sons had come to her for help, she was pretty sure they didn't have it either.

Or maybe they did.

Maybe Tristan Caine did.

What if he did have the codes and was keeping it to himself for some reason? She'd seen him lie without batting an eyelash to his blood brother, and seen him try to scare her. What if he had, in fact, hired Jackson and falsely framed himself? What did she even know about the man to take his word for anything? From what she'd seen and heard, he was not what he seemed, besides an asshole.

The more she thought about it, the more certain Morana became that something was off with him. His entire threat to her had been for one reason and one reason only - he'd been trying to drive her away, and by running off, she'd given him exactly what he'd wanted. But the question was why? Why had he let her go from the Outfit party undiscovered? Why had he later found her with Dante, only to lie to him and kill Jackson? Why had he threatened her off if he hadn't wanted her help at all? What was his angle? What was he up to? And god forbid if he did have the codes, why pretend not to have them? Why send her and his own family on a wild goose chase? What could the codes even mean to him?

And, devil's advocate, if he didn't have the codes, then why run her off since she was his best chance of finding it?

What the hell did he want?

Damn it, the man was a book of blank pages written in invisible ink that she had no idea how to discover. So much information, so many answers in the book, and all she got was frustrated.

Sighing, Morana shook her head, removing the aggravating male who was number one on her hit list if she did live long enough to kill him. But she didn't have the luxury of focusing on him or his confounding hatred for her right now.

She had other things to focus on.

Like knocking on her father's door.

"Just get this over with," she muttered to herself, calling upon her courage. "You're not a coward. You are a genius who's created something equally amazing and terrifying. Just own up to it."

Thunder crackled outside, almost as though the skies were having a laugh at her expense. Her palms sweating as she raised her hand but stopped, hearing the voices inside.

"Does she know?" she recognized the accented voice of her father's right-hand man, Tomas.

"No," her father's deep baritone replied. "And she never will."

Who were they talking about?

"It's for your daughter's protection, I understand–"

Her father interrupted whatever Tomas had been about to say. "It's not her protection that concerns me. It's ours."

So, they were talking about her. But what wasn't she ever supposed to know?

"What do you mean?" Tomas voiced her own question.

There was a long pause before her father spoke again. "She's dangerous but she has no idea how much. It's best if we keep it between us."

Tomas must have given some sort of assent because the next thing she knew, the door opened. Tomas saw her upraised arm, ready to knock, and nodded at her. His short, stocky frame walked away from her without a word, moving with a grace she'd witnessed was lethal.

Morana turned back and saw her father speaking to someone on the phone, his tall frame pacing in front of the window. His black hair, the shade of her own original locks (also the reason she'd originally started dyeing hers), was highlighted with a single streak of grey above his broad forehead, that somehow added heaviness to his face, to make people take him more seriously. His beard was French-cut and groomed, just like it had always been, and only the small lines beside his eyes indicated to his aging. From afar, he looked no older than his late thirties.

His dark eyes swung up to where she stood. The lack of delight in his gaze at seeing her, the lack of displeasure, the lack of any reaction at all was something that didn't even pinch anymore. But her curiosity was fully flared.

33

"Hold on," he muttered into the phone, his voice grave and retaining hints of his slight accent, as he raised his eyebrows at her.

"I need to speak with you," Morana stated vaguely, the wheels in her brain spinning as she stood in the doorway of the plush area.

He nodded. "After dinner. We are dining out tonight at the *Crimson*. 7.30. I expect to see you there."

He turned back to the phone.

Confused by the eavesdropped conversation, Morana closed the door behind her as she left, looking down at the time on her phone. It was already 6.

Sighing, Morana started towards the stairs, towards her suite, keeping her breath steady.

She was going to find out.

*Crimson* was one the most expensive, beautiful and elitist restaurants in Shadow Port, located smack in the heart of the city. It was also frequented by the mob families. One of her father's favorites, it oozed class and taste from every wall, the interior designed in various shades of red, muted yellow lights creating a dim, intimate ambiance.

Morana hated it.

The entirety of it – the ambiance, the clientele, everything. One would think that people with too much red in their lives would avoid that color. Instead, they seemed to bask in it.

She hated it. She hated the way men her father did business with would sometimes look her up and down like she was a mannequin on display. She hated how she was expected to stay silent and just look good without having an opinion when she had more IQ than the entire table combined. And she hated how her father remained unaffected by it all.

There was only one saving grace. She didn't smile if she didn't feel like it, and thankfully that was something her father never forced her to do. Mostly, she just sat there listening to the men talk and scowled.

Sometimes, she played on her phone. Other times, she just stared out the window, watching laughing couples stroll by hand in hand, observing happy families with not much besides each other.

And while their table companions had commented on her behavior previously, her father never paid heed to it. It was a simple understanding between them. She would come to the said restaurant in her own car, sit and eat silently, play the dutiful daughter, and leave in her own car. And in her twenty-four years, the arrangement had never changed.

Sitting at their regular table for six, Morana closed her eyes, listening to the rumbling clouds and the mumbling crowd. The sky had been threatening to pour throughout the day but never really crossed the threshold since the afternoon. The chilled wind outside called to her though. Instead, she was stuck inside with the cool, conditioned air that was making goosebumps erupt over her bare arms.

She had arrived half an hour ago in her simple, sleeveless blue dress that fell to her knees in waves from her waist and hugged her torso, the straps on her shoulders baring half her back and just the hint of her breasts, with her favorite pair of nude high heels. Since she really didn't care much about the impression she made on whomever her father was meeting, she'd worn her hair loose and foregone her contact lenses, with minimal make-up. And half an hour had passed. The crowd in the restaurant was buzzing and her dinner companions kept talking about some new shipping venture.

But Morana was distracted by the impending conversation she needed to have with her father.

Sighing, she looked around at the restaurant, at the bustling waiters and the chattering crowd, letting her eyes rove over them, letting her mind roam as well.

And suddenly, she sat up straight.

Dante Maroni sat a few tables down with two other men she didn't recognize but was certain was the Outfit, engrossed in whatever conversation they were having.

Morana looked away quickly, her brows furrowing. It had been a week since she'd cursed him and his blood brother, and left them standing at the abandoned building. A week. What was he still doing in

35

town? And what were the odds of her father having dinner at *Crimson* the same night a Maroni was there?

And then her blood rushed, the memory of stark blue eyes invading her.

Was Tristan Caine still in town as well?

Her stomach sank.

Discreetly, Morana excused herself from the table, nodding at her companions, and stood up. Her father settled his dark eyes on her briefly, before turning back to his companion.

Avoiding as much attention as she could, she quietly glanced at the Maroni table, relieved to realize Dante Maroni hadn't spotted her. Or if he had, he gave no indication of it. Neither did his dinner companions. None of whom were blue-eyed men with a penchant for pinning her across flat surfaces.

Silently narrowing her eyes, Morana ducked behind a darkened alcove with a view of the entire restaurant, and stood in the shadows, letting her eyes wander through the place, and more importantly, the people.

Nowhere.

He was nowhere.

A loud exhale left her just as her tensed body relaxed.

And then, her heart stopped.

He was there. Right there.

Walking, no sauntering, towards the table like he owned the restaurant, like he owned every ounce of air in that room, as though he commanded it to will. A small part of Morana could not help but admire that lethal, powerful grace. The bigger part of her could not help push her defenses on alert.

He saw down, right next to Dante.

And his eyes came right up to her like he'd known exactly where she was hiding in the alcove the whole time.

Morana did not look away. Not this time.

She wasn't intimidated. Not by the complete focus of that intensity directed straight at her, not by the way her heart kept pounding so loudly she was sure everyone could hear it, not by the way Dante and the other two men followed his gaze and looked at her. Morana didn't spare them a glance, not breaking his stare, not backing down, not willing to admit defeat. She didn't even blink.

Straightening her spine, keeping their gazes locked, she walked quietly back to her table, aware of the way his eyes held her and hers held his with each step, aware of the way her blood was thrumming in her ears. The sounds of the restaurant dimmed to nothing but a distant buzz as he leaned back in his chair like he had a fucking right to even glance her way, much less stare.

It was an invasion. She retaliated in kind, sitting down.

She could feel his hands keeping her captive in that gaze. She could feel his hard body pressing into hers in that gaze. She could feel the coldness of his deliberate threats in that gaze.

Her chest almost heaved. She controlled it.

A bead of sweat rolled down her spine, chilling in the cool air, and making a small shiver go through her body. A shiver that apparently he detected from three tables down, because the moment she trembled, his eyes flared with *something,* something she couldn't place, something that wasn't triumph, something that wasn't gloating. She'd never seen that *something* be directed right at her before with that intensity.

She could suddenly feel the presence of her father and her dinner companions profoundly, suddenly realizing that one wrong move on either of their parts and chaos could paint *Crimson* red.

"Morana."

Broken out of her thoughts, she turned to see her father standing with the rest of the party, waiting to leave. Flushing slightly, she stood up, nodding a farewell to people she probably wouldn't even remember the faces of, acutely aware of that intense gaze boring into her. One of the dinner companions, a man in his late thirties from the looks of him, picked up her hand and brushed a kiss across her knuckles, locking his bland blue eyes with hers.

"It was a pleasure meeting you."

Yeah right. She doubted he even knew her name.

She nodded nonetheless, pulling her hand back, restraining the urge to wipe it on her dress, and turned to her father.

"I'll see you at the house in a few minutes. We can talk then."

"Your guard will follow you."

37

Nodding, he escorted his companions outside, his security team following after him, only one of them remaining behind to tail her as she stood at the same spot, breathing in heavily, that gaze never having left her the entire time. The truth weighed down on her.

Shaking her head, she turned, her eyes locking again with those intense blue ones, right before she picked up her purse, and headed to the back entrance.

"Miss Vitalio," the manager nodded at her respectfully. Morana nodded back, used to the staff knowing who she was here.

With a few more nods, she reached the back entrance and exited into the alley behind the restaurant, ready to take the short cut to her parked car. The moment she stepped into the alley with her father's man on her heels, thunder split the sky. Hurrying on her heels as they clicked on the pavement, she was almost at the end of the dark alley when another set of footsteps joined the ones following her.

Halting in her tracks, she turned to see Tristan Caine striding towards her purposefully, his huge frame clothed casually in a brown leather jacket and dark jeans. His long, sure strides were aimed right for her. She stayed still even as a small part of her urged her to run. She quelled it, standing her ground, watching him as he stopped a few feet away, just as her father's man pointed a gun at him.

"Step back, or I'll shoot you."

Tristan Caine raised one eyebrow at him, not even sparing the gun pointed at his heart a glance. Almost casually, he gripped her guard's wrist. And then, in a move that almost had Morana's jaw dropping, he twisted the wrist, applying pressure and bending it back, making the man fall to his knees with a sharp cry, the gun now pointed back at him, like he'd pointed her own knives at her that first night, tables turned.

All without blinking away from her.

Message delivered.

Morana curled her fingers into her palms, willing her heart to calm down, as another realization dawned upon her, watching him take the gun out of the man's grasp. She was unarmed. Fuck.

Heart pounding, she kept her eyes carefully on him, waiting to see what he would do, the darkness in the alley casting shadows over half his body, making him seem even more lethal.

Tristan Caine took the gun from her father's man, unloaded it, and punched the guy in the face once, knocking him out cold. Impressive. Had she not known better, she'd have called him a show-off. But she knew better. Watching the ease with which he did all this, Morana suddenly realized how easy it must have been for him to kill her at any moment. And that was not a knowledge she liked having.

She crossed her arms over her chest, silently appraising him, unwilling to break either eye contact or the silence first.

He seemed to be on the same page.

His actions confused her, just as he did. She knew there was no love lost between them, and knew they'd see each other at the bottom of the ocean the moment they could.

She just didn't know what he wanted as of now, following her like he had and knocking out her protective detail as he had, but it sure as hell wasn't to just stare at her across five feet of space with a thunderstorm coming. And she sure as hell wasn't going to stick around for it. Driving in the rain was a bitch.

Sighing, she turned to head towards her car, only to stop cold in her tracks, seeing the alley blocked by Dante and the other two men, standing far enough away not to hear her but close enough to not let her escape. A frisson of fear traveled down her body before she tamped it down.

"I didn't know your father pimped you out to his friends, Ms. Vitalio," Tristan Caine said quietly from behind her.

Morana felt the fear slowly be replaced by fury just at the sound of his voice, the same voice that had tried to scare her last week, the same voice which had recited murder across her skin that first time. The fury magnified at his words but she leashed it. She turned to face him, keeping her voice cool.

"Why the formality, especially with the kind of liberties you take?" she spoke in a conversational tone.

His eyes narrowed slightly, his face remaining clear of any expression otherwise. "I haven't taken any liberties," he replied in the same conversational tone she was using. "Yet."

Lightning split the sky, illuminating the entire alley in bright light to her eyes, showing her the man standing before her.

Morana studied him for a second, willing herself to remain calm and objective. Tristan Caine had an angle. She'd be damned if she couldn't figure it out.

She took a step towards him, almost into his personal space, their height difference a disadvantage. Even in her heels, she barely reached his chin. Her head tilted back to keep their eyes together, her heart thundering in her chest, watching him closely for any reaction at all. There was none.

"I wonder," Morana deliberately smiled at him, her body burning with anger. "Is that supposed to intimidate me?"

And that got her a reaction. One raised eyebrow. Blue eyes that pierced hers. "You're stupid if it doesn't."

She let herself sneer at that. "I'm many things, Mr. Caine. Stupid I am not. Which is exactly why I know your threats don't mean shit."

His eyes suddenly burned with that same undefinable *something* she'd seen in the restaurant, his head tilting to the side. He stayed silent, waiting.

Morana took another step closer, not knowing where the bravado of provoking him was coming from, not caring, just needing to. Her neck craned even with her heels, but she never broke their gaze.

"Oh yes," she spoke softly, leaning closer, her chin almost touching his chest, "did you honestly think that that entire 'Don't invade my territory' thing on the car scared me? Not a bit. It only pissed me off."

He didn't utter a word, didn't move a muscle. He just looked at her, with those eyes, and her heart hammered even as she went on.

"Why don't you just get it over with?" she challenged, calling his bluff, her gaze right on him. "There is a wall right there. There is even a car. Pin me down and 'invade my territory'. Or if you hate me as you say, hurt me. Kill me. Why don't you?"

Morana felt her body trembling by the end of her tirade while he stood stone-still, their gazes locked, their bodies almost touching. For long moments, he just looked at her with those icy eyes, something burning inside him, and her heart beat in a wild staccato against her ribs, thumping with a vengeance, almost chiding her for her words even as she controlled her breathing and kept her chest from heaving. He would pounce on a single sign of vulnerability.

Slowly, after long, long seconds, his hand came up to cup the back of her neck, almost like a lover's, his huge hand cocooning the entire nape in its grip. Morana froze, her muscles stilling, suddenly realizing that this had been very foolish. What if he hadn't been bluffing and she'd provoked the beast? He could kill her right then and make her disappear from the face of the earth and no one would know.

His thumb slowly traced her jaw while his hand held the back of her neck, keeping her head tilted back and their eyes locked, the rough pad of his thumb stroking her soft skin almost like a caress. A shiver wracked her body under his hawk-like gaze, a shiver she couldn't control as her body reacted, and his unsmiling mouth twisted a little, the scruff on his jaw seeming even more virile this close, the little scar at the corner of his lip peeking out. His thumb settled upon her racing pulse, and her heart started pounding even harder, pulse spiking even more, as she pursed her lips.

"Your heart is beating way too fast for someone so in control," he murmured softly, the words ghosting over her face, the faint smell of scotch he must have had on his breath, his own scent, an odd mix of sweat and cologne and something musky invading her senses. She kept those senses on alert, seeing the rings of blue in his eyes, the long lashes as he blinked once, noticing every single thing.

He leaned in closer, his mouth almost inches away, and he spoke softly, lethally. "I warned you not to think, for one second, that you know me."

"And I warned you not to think, for one second, that you scare me," she reminded him in the same whisper.

"Don't think," he started, his eyes hardening, "that if I have the chance, I won't kill you."

"But that's the thing, Mr. Caine. You don't have the chance."

Straightening her spine, she stepped back, removing his hand from her skin, ignoring the tingling sensation as she felt the muscle of his forearms, and grit her teeth. "So, for now, you understand one thing. This is my territory, my city, my house. And you've overstayed your welcome. Leave before you are thrown out with broken bones."

Tristan Caine pinned her with his eyes once again, just as the wind picked up, swirling her dress around her legs.

41

"One day, Ms. Vitalio," he spoke quietly, "I am going to enjoy collecting that debt very much."

He leaned in, lining his mouth with her ear, his scruff rasping against her skin as her hands fisted to keep another shiver down. "And you know what? You're going to enjoy repaying it."

Of all the...

Before she could utter a single word, he was striding away from her towards the car where the entourage waited, leaving her standing alone in the alley, the hard lines of his body moving quickly over to the car, as he addressed his people.

"We are done here."

Oh, they were not done. They were so not done.

But why had they intercepted her in the alley? If it had been about codes, why leave before talking about them? And if not, then why meet her at all?

What the hell did this man want?

Morana didn't know what he wanted from her, why he seemed intent on collecting a debt she didn't even consider one at all. He was still that book of invisible ink she couldn't decipher. A book she absolutely did not want to read. No. She wanted to burn the book and blow the ashes in the wind. She wanted to tear the pages and melt them in the rain.

But as everyone got in the car and she stood in the alley, as lightning lit the sky once again just as he opened the car door, he turned one last time to see her. She locked eyes with him one last time and saw that same something simmer in that intense gaze.

As her heart beat like a bird frantically flapping its wings against the cage to get free, Morana saw him for what he was.

A predator in the skin of a man.

And she knew one thing undeniably, deep in her bones.

They were not done.

# *bleeding*

Morana groaned at the laptop screen, ignoring the crick in her neck from staring at it for too long. She was trying every possible combination and permutation of ideas to track the codes, and hitting a wall every single time. Biting her lips, her fingers flying over the keyboards, Morana typed the latest codes and pressed the escape button, checking to see if the failsafe would work, and saw the screen go blank.

Again.

Damn it!

Frustrated beyond belief, she hit her palms down on the table and shoved away, pacing towards her bedroom window, pulling her glasses down, a small throb starting to pound right under her temples. It was past midnight and she was nowhere close to working any kind of solution out. Though that wasn't her only source of frustration. She'd wanted to speak to her father after dinner two nights ago, and the moment she had returned back to the mansion after being held up by Tristan Caine, she'd been told by her father's man that he'd had to go out of town on something extremely urgent, and it was unclear when he would return. Though a part of Morana had been relieved at the delay in that inevitable conversation, another had tensed, wanting to face whatever wrath and just be done with it.

For two days Morana had tried and failed, only fuelling her frustration higher.

What had added gasoline to that fire, though, had been stray thoughts of Tristan Caine, popping completely out of the blue at the most random of times. Not his rugged looks or his reputation. No. His intensity. For some reason, he had caught her off guard, his burning hatred for her, his constant aura of threat something she had never experienced before, and something that only fed her own loathing of the man.

She grit her teeth, turning her face towards the window, looking out into the dark garden below. A huge elm tree shadowed her suite from the driveway, enough to give her a view of the visitors but not let them see her.

The property was sleeping, only a slight breeze blowing in the gentle night, the moon an incomplete oval shape in the dark sky littered with stars.

And she was tired. So tired. The constant responsibility of her actions had been chipping away at her slowly from the inside, her own failed desperate efforts only aiding in that. She just wanted to disclose the entire thing to her father and face whatever punishment he deemed necessary. She just wanted to be done with it, one way or another, so she could focus on getting the codes before they fell into wrong hands. That is assuming she would be alive to do so. Haunting the thief from beyond the grave was really not her style.

She also needed to come clean for another reason. For whatever intents and purposes, the Outfit sons had knowledge and interest in the codes. What she didn't know was whether Tristan Caine did have the codes and was pretending not to have them, or if he was genuinely searching for them. Nothing about the man was genuine. Layers buried beneath layers. He kept her from being discovered and killed one instant and threatened her life the next. What was his game? A man who could lie to his own blood brother as easily as he had, could he be honest about anything? And even if he was, she had no reason to believe him.

But intent on playing the devil's advocate, her brain came up with the other very glaring, very dangerous possibility. If, for some reason, Tristan Caine was indeed being truthful, then that implied someone else had hired Jackson to shadow her and gather intel, someone who could be in the Outfit but not likely, since Dante Maroni and Tristan Caine would be in the clear. And unless Bloodhound Maroni himself had an interest in her, which was highly doubtful, she couldn't think of another person in the Outfit who even knew about her skills.

Which meant there could be a possible third party involved. A mysterious third party, which was never a good thing. Who were they and how could they know about her work?

And staring at the moon, another possibility knocked her brain. Could it be someone from her own side? Someone looking to start a war, using her as the pawn? There was no shortage of people this side who would love to see the Outfit fall, but could anyone really be brazen enough to go after her?

The sudden vibration of her phone broke the silence, startling her, an embarrassing yelp leaving her mouth before she could stop it. Her heart racing, Morana took a deep breath, shaking her head at herself. Walking back to the table where her phone continued to vibrate, she glanced at the caller id. It was unknown.

Hesitant, she picked it up, pressing the answer icon, and stayed silent, waiting for the person to speak.

There was silence for a few beats.

"Ms. Vitalio."

Stunned, she inhaled deeply, ignoring the slight shiver that ran down her spine, ignoring the way her heart started to pound, her eyes closing as the memory of his thumb stroking her jaw washed over her, her muscles clenching. She hated it. She hated her traitorous flesh reacting to that low, husky voice. She hated the extra breath she took because of the way it washed over her. She hated that he'd caught her off guard again.

But she had learned this game in her cradle.

"Who is this?" she asked, keeping her tone flat, bored.

There was a pause for a few seconds, and Morana could feel the tension across the line. She sat down on the chair, glancing at the number, and quickly typed it into her laptop, running it for details.

"Good to see your sharp tongue doesn't follow a clock," said the voice, laced with nothing, absolutely nothing, the tone as deliberately flat as hers had been. The result on the laptop was scrambled. Sneaky bastard.

"Says the man calling me at midnight," she retorted, typing in another command to overrule the older one, tracking the number. "How did you get my number?"

Something entered his voice. "You really don't know who you are talking to, are you?"

Arrogant jerk. But resourceful. She knew that. The headache was pushed to the back of her mind as the trace progressed to 89%.

"The thing is..."

If voices could be drinks, his was a centuries-old vintage whiskey, rolling off the tongue, down the throat, leaving a trail of fire inside, making every cell in the body aware that it had been consumed. Morana closed her eyes, taking a sip of the whiskey, before suddenly realizing what she was doing. She was on the phone, at midnight, with the enemy, savoring his voice. What the hell was wrong with her?

Before he could utter another word, she cut the call, putting her phone on the table, exhaling loudly. Control. This was ridiculous. She needed to stop letting him throw her in the wind. Or next, he'd be throwing her to the wolves.

Her laptop pinged with the completed trace results. She opened her eyes.

And gasped in shock.

The call had originated from her property. From outside her wing, to be precise. What the fuck was he doing there?!

Scrambling to her feet before she could stop herself, Morana took out one of her knives from the drawer, the very knives he had turned on her. Picking up her phone in the other hand, she slowly slid next to the window where she had been standing moments ago. Peeking outside, Morana let herself glance around, trying to see into the shadows.

Her phone buzzed again, and she bit her lip, before picking up.

"Don't ever cut my call," he said, his voice menacing, hard.

Morana gulped but spoke lightly. "Sorry, I must have missed the memo. Did I bruise your gigantic ego?"

Hard pause. "As much as I detest this, I'm here to talk business."

"Since when does the Outfit does business with the daughter of the enemy?"

"Since she created codes that can destroy both sides."

Morana grit her teeth, anger flushing her system. "And you're here to what? Make me agree with your charming personality? Should have sent Dante for that."

She could feel the tense silence pulsating between them, the urge to cut the connection again acute.

"I would have but he can't do what I'm about to."

Before Morana could blink, the line went blank. Frowning, she put the phone in the pocket of her bunny shorts, gripping the knife hard with the other, and looked out again, confounded as to what he'd meant.

Seeing a shadow move slightly, Morana squinted through her glasses, barely able to make out his figure. There was no way he could ever come out of the shadows on the property. From her vantage point, she could see the guards patrolling at the far end, the security extra tight, especially with her father gone. They would turn and head towards her wing within two minutes.

Tristan Caine was toast.

But he was one smooth toast.

She saw the smoothness in his movements as he slinked away from the shadows, merging with new ones, barely visible even from her vantage. There was no way he was going to make it past the front door undetected. No way.

Except he didn't seem to be heading towards the front door to his left. With lithe grace she couldn't help but admire, even as she chided herself for it, Morana watched, confused, as he headed straight for the wall. What was he going to do - hulk his way through them?

He stopped towards the right, still in the shadows, but visible enough that she could roughly make out the black ensemble he was wearing. Puzzled, and more than curious to see what he would do next, Morana felt her jaw drop when he jumped on the windowsill of the ground floor study, taking a hold of the metal pipes that ran beside it, heaving his body up.

He was going to climb up.

He was going to climb up?

He was dying tonight, she was certain of it. Tristan Caine, the blood of the Outfit, was going to splat down on the ground beneath her window and die on her property and start a fucking war. Was he insane? She didn't give a fuck if he wanted to break his thick neck but couldn't he do it away from her city under someone else's window? It would be better if the guards caught him alive.

Even as her mind told her to alert the guards, her tongue stayed stuck to the roof of her mouth, her eyes transfixed on his form. For a big guy, he was very, very athletic. She didn't want to appreciate anything about him but watching him move, there was no way she could deny it. She was a bitch to him, not blind.

His hand grabbed the metal rail of the first-floor balcony, and he let go of his footing, hanging in the air by the strength of one arm. Then, he gripped the railing with the other hand and swung his feet up, jumping on the balcony with a grace he should not have been capable of, not with those many muscles on that body, muscles she knew were very hard and very much real from being pressed against them, repeatedly.

The timing of his jump coincided perfectly with the patrolling guards, who made their rounds, completely unaware of the intruder on the property. Tristan Caine stayed crouched on the balcony, silently observing the guards below as they walked away. That was supposed to be the best muscle in the city. Clearly, she needed to get them fired.

Shaking her head, she looked down the window, unable to see how he would reach her window from the balcony below since there were no pipes, no rails, nothing. Just wall. The area was clear again.

Just when she thought she couldn't be any more surprised, she saw him jump on the railing, his balance perfect. He didn't even take a breath before walking towards the side of the balcony, on the railing, on agile feet, coming to a stop as he faced the wall.

*Now what, hotshot?*

He looked around carefully, before taking something out from the pocket of his black cargo pants, and before Morana could even think 'bomb', he was swinging it up and hooking it on the sill of her window. And the next thing she knew, his hands were on her windowsill and he was heaving his entire body up, ready to get in the second window she was standing behind. A walking, talking Mission Impossible, that's what he was. And Morana's stomach was in knots, exactly as it had been every time she had watched the movies, her heart pounding in her ears like she had been the one to scale two floors of her building.

At least her undercover had been more covert, less show-off.

The moment he heaved his body inside, Morana stepped back, holding her knife beside her head, her stance combative just like her instructor had taught her.

He landed on the carpeted floor, rolling off his back in the same motion, and standing up on his feet, his black full-sleeved muscle shirt hugging every sinew and muscle of his torso, the loose cargo pants tucked into black army boots, a com attached to his ear. He looked ready to infiltrate a fortress. She should be flattered, she supposed.

Except she realized, in that precise moment that her own inventory was complete and his began, that she was dressed for the night, in her bunny shorts and loose university t-shirt that almost hung off one shoulder, and no bra.

Even as heat rushed to her face at her realization, she stayed in the same stance, threatening, keeping her face completely blank, watching him. His sharp blue eyes locked with hers, sending a frisson of tingles down her body before she tamped it down, her fingers flexing on the knife. He touched his earpiece, never removing his gaze from hers, and spoke quietly.

"I'm in. Muting."

How eloquent.

His eyes drifted to her knife, before coming back to hers, his scruffy jaw relaxed, his entire posture non-threatening. But she knew better. She'd learned how quickly he switched first-hand, and she had no intention of even breathing easy as long as he stood within five feet of her.

He didn't speak a word, just looking at her with those unnerving eyes. She knew what he was trying to do. Shake her. And even though it worked, she didn't let it show.

"The way you scaled the walls," she began, in a conversational tone that was so fake she could roll her eyes at it, "you just confirmed what I always knew you were."

He just raised a lone eyebrow.

49

"A reptile," she provided, smiling forcefully at him.

The side of his lip with the damn scar twitched, his eyes never losing the hardness. "Predator."

"Delusions of grandeur," she nodded, ignoring the way the intensity in the gaze made her want to stop breathing. Had she been a dog, this was the kind of gaze that would have made her want to roll over on her back and offer her warm belly up. She wasn't a dog, just a proverbial female equivalent to him. She had to keep it that way. Focus. "Does your psychiatrist know you suffer from them?"

He took a step closer, and she straightened, pointing her knife at him, keeping her hand steady. "Nuh-uh. You move an inch and you'll go back with a scar."

He stilled, his gaze intensifying. "And you call me the one with delusions."

Morana grit her teeth, the urge to just give him a plain old punch in the face and possibly break his nose acute. She stayed back. The sooner she get this over with, the better.

"I'm sure you aren't here to stare at me, as much as you seem to enjoy doing that," she began, never removing her eyes from his. "Why are you here?"

He blinked once, his body completely still, as though ready to pounce on the breath of a motion. "You broke into my house. I thought I'd return the favor."

Morana kept her mouth shut, waiting him out. Her blood was rushing way too fast in her body, her skin way too warm for comfort, her pulse way higher than normal. Adrenaline. She was flooded with adrenaline. Nothing more. Fight and flight. Instinct. Yup, that explained it.

He tilted his head to the side, his eyes never wavering, the motion making him look even more lethal in the muted lamp lights of the room.

"As I said," he began, in that voice that had made her put the phone down, the voice of whiskey, the voice that made her want to roll her eyes back into her head. She shook herself mentally, focusing on his words. "This is business. Dante and I are the only ones who know about the codes on our side. You are the only one on yours, I believe?"

She didn't respond, just waited. He continued. "We want to keep it that way, contained. Even the right information in the wrong hands can be disastrous."

Scoffing, she raised her eyebrows. "And I should just assume you are men of honor when, in fact, I've seen you lie to your own side without blinking. Tell me, Mr. Caine, why should I believe a word that comes out of your mouth?"

His eyes hardened, and he took another step. Morana swiped the knife in the air in warning. He stopped.

"I'd prefer if you didn't," he spoke, the coldness entering his eyes sending a shiver down her spine.

Before she could say another word, she heard the main gates to the mansion open, the sound of horns blaring in the night as cars entered the property. At this time of the night, it only meant her father had returned.

She kept her eyes on him, watching his every move, her heart started beating faster as she realized her father was in the house, along with Tristan Caine. If she was caught, her death was guaranteed.

Morana sighed, the headache from before returning with a vengeance. "How do I know you don't have the codes?"

"I don't," he simply said. She saw the conviction in his eyes. She saw the heat in them. She ignored them both.

"Okay," she nodded. "Assuming you don't have them, I've been trying to find a way to destroy them on my own for days. It's not working." Her frustration notched, remembering her futile efforts. "I infiltrated your house, for goodness' sake, as a last resort! Trust me, Mr. Caine, doing business with me is not a good option right now."

His eyes narrowed on her, assessing her. "That's not for you to decide. You've involved us in this and now you have to see it through."

"Or else?" she demanded, raising her eyebrows, her arm starting to ache where she held it up beside her.

A corner of his lips lifted. "Or I go downstairs right now to meet your father and tell him what's going on."

Morana rolled her eyes, calling his bluff. "You wouldn't do that. You said you want to keep it quiet. Plus, I was going to tell my father already."

"Were you, really?" he asked, and she felt her hackles rise at his tone.

Before she could even straighten her spine, his hand was suddenly on her wrist, twisting her arm as the other hand twirled her around. Morana brought her leg up, trying to hit him in the knee but he sidestepped, taking a hold of both her wrists in one huge hand, pressing his chest to her back, giving her no room to move, the other hand gripping her hair painlessly but firmly, tilting her head back so she could see him behind her, the knife in her hand clattering to the carpeted floor with a muffled thud. Morana struggled against his hold, but as was the trend with them, couldn't move.

"Don't play with toys you don't understand," his voice whispered right against her ear, his breath ghosting over the exposed shoulder where her t-shirt had fallen away, sending a shiver through her before she could stop it, a shiver she was certain he could feel, a shiver that made her breasts heave. But the condescension in his tone made her jaw clench.

Steeling her nerves, knowing his hands were occupied, Morana threw her head back into his face and missed as he ducked at the last minute, his grip on her hands loosening. That was all she needed. Dropping down to the ground, she swiped his feet from under him while picking up the knife at the same time. The moment he fell on his back, she climbed his chest, pressing the knife right under his Adam's apple, glaring at him.

He looked back at her, the muted lights in the room casting his face half in shadows, no hint of fear in his blue eyes, not fazed at all, his hands pinned down beside him by her thighs.

Morana leaned forward, keeping their eyes locked, and whispered, with all the anger and hatred coursing through her body. "One day, I'm going to carve your heart out and keep it as a souvenir. I promise."

She'd thought he would respond with silence, or with a clenched jaw, or with another jab at her. He didn't.

He chuckled.

Seriously?

"You assume I have a heart, wildcat."

But the amusement faded from his eyes as soon as it had entered. He stayed still under her, watching her, the silence between them tensing, the tension between them thickening. Awareness slithered down her spine, seeping into her bones. She could feel his heartbeat against her thigh where she straddled him, her shorts having ridden up in the struggle, exposing more of her skin than she was comfortable with. Her nipples hardened under the cotton, because of the struggle and not because of his warm muscles under her or his intense eyes piercing hers. Not because of that.

Now that she had him under her, she didn't know what to do. She couldn't sit on him for eternity, even though it was tempting. She couldn't kill him in her own house, even though that was more than tempting. She couldn't do anything. And the bastard that he was, he knew it. Hence, the relaxed posture.

Disgusted with herself, Morana stood up, removing the knife from his neck, and walked towards the window, frustration flooding her, replacing the heat now that she looked away from him. This was getting them nowhere. She closed her eyes once, before opening them, the decision made, and turned to face him, where he stood just a few feet away, watching her with that damned focused look of his.

"So, you basically want me to work with you to find the codes and destroy them, and keep it to myself?" she asked, keeping her voice even.

"Yes," he answered simply.

Morana nodded. "And how will we go about it?"

"However we have to," he replied, in that simple tone that brooked no arguments. "Wherever the leads take us."

Morana nodded again, taking a deep breath, her eyes watching him closely. "I have one condition."

The clock ticked. The lights flickered. They breathed.

He stayed silent, waiting her out. She hesitated, for some reason, before swallowing, speaking.

"I work with Dante, not you."

Silence.

His eyes flared with something before he tamped it down, the air between them crackling with tension, his gaze almost electric in its intensity. Morana's heart pounded, her stomach clenching, the awareness of herself, of everything around her, sizzling through her.

He started walking towards her with slow, measured steps of the predator he was called, his blue eyes blazing with a fire she couldn't place, his face hard, jaw clenched, muscles tense. Morana stood her ground in her bare feet, bringing the knife up to his throat just as he stepped into her personal space, the metal pressing into his neck, his other hand coming beside her head on the windowsill. He looked down at her, his throat working, his breaths warm against her face, that musky scent of his cologne faded and mixed with sweat, wrapping around her, making her skin tingle and her heart thunder as their eyes stayed locked.

Suddenly, he brought his free hand up, between the knife and his throat, and Morana's eyes widened, stunned, as she watched him push it away from his skin, the sharp blade cutting into his hand, blood suddenly trailing down his wrist to hers, the warm liquid traveling over her elbow. The entire time he never looked away, even as she gasped, even as she tried to pull the knife away, even as she gulped. He held the knife in his fist, his inflamed eyes on hers, his blood dripping on her skin, their faces inches away, eyes unwavering, blue on hazel.

Something was happening in that moment. Something her brain couldn't understand but her body was intuitively aware of. The rushing of blood in her ears didn't lessen. The pounding of her heart didn't decrease. The heaving of her chest didn't diminish. Her knees weakened, her stomach in knots, her disbelief coursing through her body, transforming into something else, something that had never occupied her body before.

He looked down at her like a force of nature, and she stared back, unable to look away, captured by his gaze - his hard, unrelenting gaze.

And suddenly, he let go of the knife.

"Done."

His hard, guttural tone reached her, and he sidestepped her without sparing her another glance, jumping out the window before she could take another breath.

Morana didn't look out to see if he'd made it out, didn't lean down to watch him merge with the shadows, didn't move from the spot at all.

She didn't breathe.

Her heart thundered away in her chest like an unleashed storm cloud, her breaths rapid as though she'd run a marathon. She was trembling. All over. Her hands shook, the knife falling once again to the floor, coated in blood.

Morana looked down at the fallen knife, feeling as though a sword had pierced her chest, the tightness in her throat inexplicable, logic nowhere in the vicinity of her scrambled thoughts as she just stood there, frozen, unable to move, unable to even breathe.

Her eyes moved from the knife to her trembling hands, seeing a lone red trail on the right one, starting at her wrist and ending on her forearm, almost as though her skin had cried and swallowed a bloody tear.

The blood of her enemy. The blood of the one man she hated.

His blood.

The sight of it should have filled her with satisfaction. That he had agreed to her terms should have filled her with satisfaction. That he had left without a fuss and not turned this night into a disaster should have filled her with satisfaction.

Bending, she picked up the knife, moving almost on auto-pilot, her thoughts scattered in the wake of the tsunami inside her body, her emotions jumbled into an unrecognizable mess, her body trembling like a stray leaf in the storm. Walking forward, she dropped the bloody knife into the trash can, gazing as the red swirled and seeped into the white paper around it, seeping into it, scarring it, changing it.

As she felt the wind blowing across her exposed skin, across her frayed nerves, across her clothed flesh, Morana felt herself be filled.

But it wasn't with satisfaction.

It was anything but satisfaction.

## *waiting*

**D**ante Maroni: *Let's meet at Cyanide tonight. 8 PM. I'll wait for you in the VIP lounge.*

*Cyanide* happened to be the most popular, most nocturnal nightclub in the city. It also happened to belong to the Outfit.

Morana had never been to a nightclub.

She remembered seeing one for the first time on TV when she'd been 12. The hypnotic lights, the gyrating bodies, the loud music – all a setup in the backdrop of the mating dance of the two leads, as they'd flirted with their eyes from across the club before dirty dancing on the floor, surrounded by bodies, so close she'd wanted to bash their heads together just to make them kiss. It had been an enlightening experience. An experience she'd known was not something meant for her.

Even as a child, she'd already known not to wish for things she couldn't have. Back then she'd been scared – of her father, of his enemies, of herself. She'd been terrified of all the things she knew she'd want if she stepped out of her bubble. Nightclubs had terrified her too. The news and reports of girls being exposed to spiked alcohols and date rape drugs had only made her more cautious.

More than a decade, and there she was, standing in front of her mirror at her dressing table. She studied her reflection for a long minute.

With her dyed chestnut locks tumbling free around her face in soft waves, she finished putting her clear contacts in.

She had a pretty face, nothing that anybody would write sonnets about, but pleasing to look at. Slightly rounded, with average-sized lips she'd painted a dark red, a straight albeit short nose she had pierced once upon a time, and clear hazel eyes with flecks of green.

Her frame was short, on the smaller side, with decent breasts, a good ass, and a stubborn little love handle around her tummy she couldn't get rid of. Smoothening the crease of her emerald green dress that bunched under her boobs and fell to her knees, she tilted her head to the side, wondering if she resembled her mother. Aside from her original hair color, she really couldn't see him in her.

The dress itself was something she'd never worn before. It had been a birthday gift she'd bought for herself, not really knowing when, if ever, she would wear it. Tonight seemed perfect for the occasion.

The soft fabric of the strapless dress clung to her torso, shaping her breasts perfectly, the material cinching together tightly right under them, before flaring out in shades of shadowed green, the waves of the skirt stopping just above the knee in an uneven hem. The back was deep but simple, and black block heels adorned her feet. She had never dressed like this. But then, she'd never really been to a club either.

She read the message on the phone again, checking the time.

*Cyanide* was an Outfit club in her father's city. She didn't get it.

Her side and the Outfit had apparently been allies once, long ago, from what people said. But something had changed, and the enmity had been born. And even though now the two sides hated each other with ferocity, they both had businesses in each other's territory, and it was a silent understanding that while the businesses wouldn't be harmed, any hint of hostility would take all bets off.

She was surprised to be invited, to say the least. She'd half expected another abandoned construction site with a bunch of eagles flying overhead. But that was apparently the location for murderous meetings. She supposed she should be relieved.

While the little girl inside her bubbled with excitement, the woman she'd become stayed wary. It was a public place, where she doubted anyone would try anything, but it was still their club.

Turning away from her reflection, she picked up her black clutch – which held a small Beretta – and her phone, and walked out of her room, closing the door behind her. Heading down the stairs, Morana felt her palms sweat slightly as nervousness assaulted her, her wing of the house empty except for a few guards here and there. Useless guards, given how easily they'd been thwarted two nights ago.

Shaking her head before she could let herself go down that road, she exited the house and headed for her car standing in the drive, the lawns beyond it shrouded in darkness, as her phone rang.

It was her father.

"Take the guards," his curt, clipped command came over the phone as soon as she picked up.

She stiffened, stopping in her tracks, her eyes swinging up towards the other wing where she knew his study was. No 'where are you going' or 'when will you be back' or 'be careful'.

"No," she replied in the same flat voice she'd been using with him for years, stopping the twinge before it could pinch. She disconnected the call before he could say anything, not that he would have, and walked briskly to her car. No. Her father didn't discuss and argue matters. He simply decided. Which meant she was going to have a tail.

Getting behind the wheel, she started the ignition and turned out of the drive, her darling baby purring under her control as she steered the car out from the gigantic gates. Leaving the house behind, her eyes flicked to the rearview mirror. Just as she'd suspected, she saw a black muscle vehicle pull out behind her.

Something akin to exasperation filled her veins. She'd been doing this for years, refusing protection and ditching the guards. She was an expert by now, and yet her father never stopped trying to get her under his watch.

Switching lanes expertly as soon as she hit the traffic, Morana pressed the accelerator to the floor and felt the speed crawl over her as she zipped past other vehicles. Bikes and cars honked around her, the cool conditioned air in the car keeping the sweat from beading on her skin even as a shot of adrenaline filled her. She knew her father's men would try to catch up. She also knew they would fail, because catching

Morana Vitalio when she didn't want to be caught was something a very rare few could do.

And that was also a reason why she hated him.

Because he'd somehow always put her at a disadvantage when she hadn't wanted to be, put her in positions that had underlined just how much control he'd had over their bodies while she had floundered for it.

Morana grit her teeth as her mind, unwittingly, drifted to Tristan Caine. Again.

She'd pushed the entire episode from two nights ago out of her mind, vowing not to think about it ever again. Because the mess who'd been standing in her room with his blood on her hand, the confused mass of limbs who hadn't dared breathe because everything had been so baffling - that wasn't her. Morana Vitalio did not behave like a pathetic little girl being thrown a bone. Morana Vitalio did not show vulnerabilities to anyone but herself. Morana Vitalio did not expose the jugular to a man who went straight for it.

She'd been raised around sharks. And she'd learned not to bleed.

But she hated him because he had bled. Because he'd thrown her off guard. Because he'd done something she'd never believed he would do. Because he made her react not like Morana Vitalio but someone else. And she loathed admitting that the relief she'd thought she'd feel at her simple condition had been obliterated by drops of blood, and she had no idea why. She didn't even want to examine why. That was one episode of her life she'd gladly put behind her.

Taking a left towards the club, Morana shook her head and pushed all the thoughts out, focusing only on the meeting and on enjoying her first experience in a club as much as possible. Not that she wanted to get drunk or dirty dance with some random douchebag. No, she just wanted to feel those lights slide over her skin, feel the music pulse in her throat, feel the scents wash over her body.

A few miles of secluded road ahead, she saw a tall, grey warehouse rise towards the sky. A huge, ice blue sign glowed on top of the building, telling her she was in the right place. Parking the car outside in a spot as a valet came to her, she got out, declining his offer but nodding her thanks. The chill in the wind sent shivers crawling over her bare back as she hurried towards the building, the muted noise getting louder with each step she took towards the tall metal doors.

A muscled bouncer almost thrice her size looked her up and down as she approached, his hand on the knob, the scar covering the right half of his face hidden half behind dark glasses. She never understood why people wore dark shades at night.

"Invitation only," he spoke in a gruff voice, not budging a single inch.

Morana raised her eyebrows. "Morana Vitalio. Guest of Dante Maroni."

The man's dark face betrayed no expression, but he opened the door, the sudden noise exploding in her ears, and let her pass. Taking a deep breath, Morana stepped into the club, aware of the door closing behind her. A small, wary part of her reminded her that she was the daughter of the enemy in an Outfit club, alone and without security, making her heart race as a sliver of fear traveled down her spine. Jerking out of it, she stood right at the entrance, taking in the entire area.

Done in chrome and ice blue, with blue lights dimming and flaring alternatively with the heavy beats of music that pumped from the DJ's booth on her extreme left, the entire converted warehouse floor was the dance area. The bar lined up the right, and bartenders catered to the heavy crowd. Bouncers littered the corners of the space inconspicuously, observing the bodies sliding against each other.

Watching the crowd, Morana did not feel underdressed at all. In fact, she was pretty sure the fabric of her dress could cover up at least five women there.

Eyebrows in her hairline even as a grin chased her lips, the sheer joy of being away from her house, from her life, so, so precious, even for a second. She breathed in the mixed scents of cologne and perfumes and sweat and alcohol. She tilted her head to the side as the music beat against her eardrums. She felt her heeled feet tap with the rhythm.

It was all a novelty.

She looked up to see Dante Maroni making his way towards her, dressed in a dark, casual button-up and trousers that screamed 'rich and loaded', his lips in a polite smile, his huge body moving with grace even as his dark eyes measured her. Morana looked around to make sure he'd come alone, as she'd demanded. He had. But that didn't relax her, despite the inviting smile on his handsome face.

Pointing to an area behind the bar, which she guessed was the VIP section, he gestured for her to follow him. She slowly did, taking note of his arm behind her, keeping the dancing crowd away from her moving body. As much as she didn't want to, she appreciated the gesture, especially as the dancing crowd pressed into her, and a few stray hands tried to cop a feel, making her want to gag.

By the time they reached the bar, her heart was pounding faster than the beats of the music, adrenaline spiking her system. Swallowing, she followed Dante to a secluded section separated by the bar, where the music wasn't so loud for some reason. Plush burgundy couches came into view, lining the walls, the dimmer lights creating intimate seating areas.

Morana entered the section he indicated, taking in the space, and suddenly came to a stop, her body stiffening.

Sitting on one of the couches towards her right was Tristan Caine, dressed in a suit jacket and a crisp white shirt that shone blue under the lights, with an open collar and no tie. There was nothing of the man from two nights ago in him. Her eyes drifted to the white gauze wrapped around his hand, a swift reminder that he was very much the same man. The same primitive being cloaked in civilization.

A woman sat beside him - a tall, raven-haired, absolutely stunning woman in a silver dress that was poured on her, her open body language a clear indication that she was friends with the man beside her.

Morana looked away before she could stare at either of them.

Dante led her towards the left, the opposite side, where the area was relatively empty, and motioned for her to take a seat. She deliberately took a seat facing the wall, with her back towards the other man, and saw Dante fold his huge body in the seat in front of her.

She waited for her nape to prickle with an awareness of his eyes on her, for the goosebumps to break out over her flesh, but neither happened. He wasn't burning a hole in her back with his eyes. *Good.*

"It's a coincidence he is here," Dante began. "I know you requested he not be present, so I did not tell him where we were meeting. He just came a few minutes ago with Amara." His tone was slightly apologetic even as his brown eyes moved behind her, a shadow flickering across his face as he watched whatever was happening in somber silence. Was the shadow because of his blood brother or because of the woman?

Morana cleared her throat, bringing his dark eyes back to her. The shadows cleared as his eyes shuttered, his expression one of polite interest, one she was sure he'd been donning for a long time. "Can we focus on the codes?"

"Of course," he nodded, leaning back against the cushions as a server brought up some appetizers. "Would you like anything to drink?"

Morana shook her head, crossing her ankles and folding her hands primly in her lap, slightly uncomfortable with the whole situation. A frisson of awareness slithered down her spine.

His eyes were on her.

Taking a deep breath, Morana stilled her body, not betraying any movements.

"Let me be honest with you, Morana," Dante spoke, stretching one arm over the back of the couch, his shirt pulling taut across his well-built chest. "I have nothing personal against you, so as long as you don't threaten or hurt me or my people, we can work along just fine."

Morana narrowed her eyes and nodded. "Same goes for you."

"Good," he nodded, the dark hair on his head catching the blue lights, his eyes flickering again to the scene behind her momentarily before coming back. And in that one flicker, Morana knew it was the woman – Amara – who had his attention. She had a feeling there was a lot more to his distraction than a hot woman in a great dress. Ignoring the twinge of compassion it elicited, she bit her lip.

"Mr. Maroni, as I told Mr. Caine," Morana grit out, still aware that the man was behind her, watching her sporadically, "I am at a loss. I created the codes and before I could install a failsafe in place, Jackson stole them. I don't have any hopes of finding it like this, much less destroying it without actually having it."

"Tristan told me," the man said, his voice suddenly extremely serious, the air of responsibility around him so strong it made her realize he was the older son of the Outfit. "Whatever hostility exists between our families, fact is that the code is lethal for both our sides, and we cannot afford any war between ourselves with the outside forces looking for a way in."

"Could it have been someone on the outside?" Morana asked, voicing her own apprehensions as she settled back into the cushions, her nape tingling.

Dante shook his head. "I don't believe so. Only someone who had known your family could have known what you were doing." He paused for a second. "I'm not entirely sure it's not someone from our side, framing Tristan for the fall."

"Why would anyone on your side frame him?" she asked, curious.

The man before her shrugged even as his face remained grave. "There can be many reasons. Jealousy over his skills, over my father's preference for him. Hell, he has enough enemies inside the Outfit that anyone could want retribution."

Morana's gut clenched as she remembered how smoothly the man in question had lied to his blood brother. She wasn't sure it wasn't him, faking his own accusations.

"We traced the transactions from Jackson," Dante's voice broke into her thoughts, making her frown.

"I told you, they all lead to Mr. Caine."

"They do, but there were anomalies when we looked at them carefully," he informed her. "We're running traces on them now, but since this is your area of expertise, perhaps you could hurry it up?"

It felt weird, this alliance. But she nodded regardless, holding her palm out for the flash drive he put there.

"Everything we've been able to gather so far, all the information, is here."

She placed the drive carefully in her clutch and stood up, as did he. Since he was being amicable so far, Morana quietly said, "I'll let you know if I get something."

Dante Maroni tilted his head slightly, eyes sharp on her. "May I ask why you refused to work with Tristan?"

Morana raised an eyebrow. "May I ask what's going on between you and Amara?"

The amicable man before her suddenly stiffened, anger flashing over his face before he donned the polite mask, his lips pursing, making her realize yet again that he was no wallflower. He was the actual blood of Bloodhound Maroni. He glared at her slightly, his eyes flickering to the woman in question, before swinging his eyes to her again, a grudging smile on his lips.

"Courage takes only a second to become foolishness," he said quietly, his dark eyes alert. "Keep that in mind."

Morana smiled. So, she'd found a nerve, had she?

"Heed your own advice," she replied in the same tone, before turning on her heels and heading towards the bar, looking absolutely straight ahead, not sparing a glance on either side but aware of Tristan Caine's eyes on her. Her throat worked, a bead of sweat rolling down her cleavage, her muscles stiff in her body.

Parched, she reached the counter, the music louder outside, and leaned over, trying to catch the attention of one of the bartenders.

A man in his late thirties, in a black t-shirt, looked over at her, his eyes cooling as he looked her up and down. Morana frowned at the reaction, not understanding.

"What can I get you?" he asked, his voice loud over the music.

She watched his eyes, the blandness in them, and felt a shiver go over her spine. Yeah, she wasn't taking alcohol from him. "Just some orange juice."

He turned away and Morana furrowed her brows, trying to remember if she'd ever met him before. She hadn't. But then maybe he knew she was the daughter of the enemy family.

Sighing, she took the glass of juice he pushed towards her and turned to face the dance floor, gulping down the cooling drink, quenching her thirst, her eyes on the mass of bodies moving to the beat in front of her.

"Anton, one JD, on the rocks."

The voice of whiskey and sin carried over from her left. Morana swallowed, but she refused to turn, refused to acknowledge him, clenching her teeth, her hand gripping the clutch and the glass as her eyes stayed glued to the gyrating bodies.

His eyes came to her. She was aware. But she didn't turn. Slowly sipping the leftover juice, she stood still, aware of his presence beside her, aware that he stood just inches away, all coiled muscles and strength, but not really acknowledging her. And that was absolutely fine.

She should have moved away. She should have put her glass on the counter and walked out the entrance, without a word, without a glance, without anything. But for some unfathomable reason, at that moment, it almost became as wrecking as a staring contest where neither of them blinked first. It became a collision of wills, where moving away, running away, at that moment would've been equivalent to blinking, and she'd be damned if she caved first.

The music wrapped around her, almost ensconcing her in a bubble where nothing but her pounding heart and her racing pulse existed. She kept standing there, mindlessly watching the dancers, her entire body just so aware of the presence beside her, a presence that neither left not moved nor did anything. He was just present and that, for some reason, was enough.

"Morana Vitalio?"

The moment was broken. Closing her eyes as the heaviness lifted, Morana turned to her other side at the feminine voice, to see the woman who'd been sitting next to Tristan Caine looking back at her with the oddest green eyes she had ever seen, the shade something close to a forest at midnight, her curvaceous body gorgeous in that sleek, little dress, her dark curls wild and free on her head. Amara.

"Yes," Morana said, cautious and confused as to why this woman wanted to talk to her.

Something akin to pity filled the woman's green eyes as she looked at her. Before she could utter a word though, her gaze flitted to where Morana knew Tristan Caine stood and she shook her head, pivoting on her heel. Completely confounded by the odd, abrupt meeting, Morana stood there, blinking at where the woman had been. What the hell had that been about?

Without turning around to face him, Morana finished her drink.

And swayed on her feet.

What the hell?

She looked down at her one empty glass of orange juice, frowning, as the lights before her eyes blurred a bit, the world spinning slightly.

Had someone spiked her drink? The weird bartender?

No. No. No. This could not be happening to her. Not here, and not now.

Shaking her head to clear the haze enough to walk, Morana turned towards the entrance. And tried to take a step.

She swayed hard, almost tipping over.

Hands on her arms steadied her from behind, rough hands on her soft skin.

Morana blinked, her tongue swollen, wool in her mouth as the world spun a little more, her knees turning to jelly. Tremors wracked her frame, the music pounding in her skull painfully. Her lids got heavier. Fear pooled in her stomach because if she fell over in this club, she would be dead if someone found her or when her father found out. That kind of cooled the wave of drowsiness sweeping over her, just as those hands turned her around.

Morana blinked up at the blue, blue eyes peering down into her face, the hands holding her arms rough and hard. Suddenly, one hand moved up to grip her chin as he leaned her against the counter of the bar, his eyes focused on hers, holding her focus for one clear second before her lashes drifted down.

"Fuck!"

The growled expletive made her open her eyes and look up at him again, only to stagger under the sheer force of the hatred she could see searing the blue, searing her skin. She had felt him watching her but she'd had no clue how he'd been watching her. Had his eyes been burning with this loathing the entire time? Was that why her skin had tingled?

Her breath hitched in her throat, the realization that nobody had ever hated her as he did dawning upon her. She tried to open her mouth, to ask him why he despised her, where it was rooted, but her lips refused to cooperate.

The hand on her chin jerked her head, bringing her focus back to those blazing eyes, her heart hammering in her chest as her skin turned hotter under his touch, drowsiness battling with unrelenting focus.

"I'm not saving you again," he muttered through clenched teeth, his gaze livid, his other hand pulling out his phone, the bandage wrapped around the palm where he had cut himself on her knife making her stomach twist.

"Dante," he spoke, his voice tight, controlled. "Someone spiked her drink."

Silence as Dante said something. And then. "I'm not going to stick around and play hero. Amara can babysit her while she recovers."

Before Morana could swallow the lump in her throat, hatred burned through her – at the fact that she was at his mercy and his blatant disregard, at the bastard who had spiked her drink, at the situation – he was roughly pushing her towards the VIP area, his hand gripping her arms. She could feel the rage contained in his body, feel herself tremble in the vicinity of that rage. He had never been like this, even the short time that she had known him.

What the hell had happened? What was happening? Her mind muddled even as the heat of his body pushed her forward.

The beautiful woman in the silver dress came forward, concern marring her brows. "What happened?"

"I don't care," came the sharp retort from beside her. "I have to go."

He let go of her almost as though she'd burned his hands.

The moment his grip on her slackened, her knees gave away and she sank into the plush cushions again, her sluggish eyes watching his muscular back retreat. Utter fury filled her, making her body shake with the sheer force of it, the urge to punch him in the face ardently coursing through her veins even as she knew she couldn't even lift a finger right then.

Amara sat beside her, rubbing her back in a soothing motion, sighing deeply, her green gaze soft on Morana's. "I'm sorry about him."

Morana blinked groggily, her throat working, head pounding as darkness crept along the edges of her vision, the world stilling as her breathing slowed.

"You have to understand why he...."

Morana wanted to. For some godforsaken reason, she wanted to understand the reason for his hatred, for the intensity of that hatred. But even as she tried, Amara's voice began to drift away, her lashes gluing to her cheeks, her muscles going limp as she leaned back into the cushions and completely succumbed to oblivion, not knowing if she would wake up to see another day.

## *tailing*

A jerk suddenly startled her.

Disoriented, Morana pried her heavy lids open slowly, her eyes burning, to see trees rushing by at speed in the darkness and long stretches of secluded road ahead. The sound of an engine whirring broke into her dazed consciousness a second later, along with the scent of car perfume, warm air, and leather against the back of her thighs and shoulder blades. All of it extremely familiar.

Blinking, she sat up suddenly, the quick motion sending a shot of dizziness through her system and the dull echo of pain through her skull, and looked around.

Suave cream interior, the little trinket – glasses and a gun - dangling from the rearview mirror, a mystery paperback tossed in the console, along with her black clutch.

She was in her own car.

And a woman was driving her car. A woman in a hot silver dress, glancing at her with concerned forest green eyes. Where had she seen her before...?

"How are you feeling?" the woman asked in a soft, soothing voice that was somehow raspy in the silence.

Something about her seemed familiar. Morana shook her head once to clear it, and thought about the question, even as her eyes checked the woman out for any weapons on her. How was she feeling?

"Dazed, I think," she muttered, a frown taking over her face. "Who are you?"

The woman flashed slightly alarmed eyes at her. "Amara. We just met an hour ago. In the club. You don't remember?"

Now that she mentioned it, pieces started coming back to her. Meeting with Dante. Putting the drive in her clutch. Going to the bar. The weird bartender. The woman coming up to meet her. And...

Her jaw clenched as everything rushed back into her mind. Hot, hot lava flooded her blood, her fingers curling into her palms as acid burned through her chest. The memories returned, and along with them the absolute rage that almost shook her frame, the urge to hit something hard violent inside her.

Taking a deep breath, she turned to the woman, pinning her with her eyes. "Why are you driving my car?"

Amara glanced at her swiftly before turning her eyes to the road again.

"Things happened after you passed out," she spoke in the same soft voice that Morana realized was her natural tone. "It wasn't safe for you there anymore, so I thought it'd be better if you got out."

Morana narrowed her eyes at her, trying to gauge how honest she was being. "And you did this out of the goodness of your heart?"

"A little," the woman replied quietly. "Mainly I did this because Tristan asked me to."

Okay.

Morana's heart started pounding the minute the words were comprehended in her brain. Before she could say anything though, Amara spoke again, in that raspy voice.

"He's following us right now."

What?

Morana swiveled her neck to look at the empty road behind them. Sure enough, there was a huge black SUV tailing them on the secluded path, making her realize they weren't that far from the club yet, miles from the mansion. The headlights shone brightly, the vehicle keeping a distance of at least ten cars between them, maintaining the same speed Amara was.

"What is his damage?" Morana muttered to herself, not understanding a thing about that man even as the urge to punch him in the nose prevailed. She grit her teeth.

"I'm not sure I'm the right person to tell you that," Amara replied, and Morana turned back to her, ignoring the headlights in her peripheral vision.

"But you were going to tell me something," she insisted, pressing on. "Before I passed out."

When the other woman didn't speak but pursed her lips together, Morana sighed, knowing she wouldn't be getting any answer. Curiosity assailing her about the woman, she asked. "Are you in the family?"

Amara's lips curved as she smiled slightly, shaking her head. "Not technically."

At Morana's waiting silence, she elaborated. "My mother was the head housekeeper in the Maroni household. I've grown up with the men when they were boys, but I was never family."

"You were adopted into it?" Morana asked, curious.

The other woman shook her head. "No. The only one to ever have been adopted into the family was Tristan."

Morana studied the woman, a heavy feeling deep in her gut for some reason. "But you know the family?"

Amara glanced at her, her eyes hard. "Yes. But if you think I'll spill any secrets, you're wrong. I didn't when I was fifteen, and I won't now."

Morana raised her eyebrows. "Fifteen?"

She saw the woman's hand clench on the steering wheel, her lips purse tightly for a moment before she sighed. "I was abducted and taken prisoner by another mob. They tried to get me to talk, and when I refused, they damaged my vocal cords."

Morana's heart clenched in pain for the woman even as a sort of admiration for her strength seeped in. A fifteen-year-old young girl facing horrors and refusing to succumb. Morana knew the cost of being strong in this world, and even though this woman was the enemy, Morana could respect that strength. So she did. Silently.

"Dante and Tristan found me after three days. Dante took me home but Tristan stayed behind to clean up," Amara spoke on quietly, in that voice that had been made permanent forcefully, only the humming of the car permeating the air. "They'd both been so angry, not just because I had been theirs but because violating a woman is something they both truly abhor. They've always been protective of women and children. Which is why what happened tonight was not ordinary."

Morana took in all that information for a moment then huffed out a skeptic laugh. "You mean Tristan Caine is ordinarily not an asshole?"

"Oh, he is," Amara replied without missing a beat. "But he's an honorable asshole. And what happened tonight wasn't anywhere near honorable."

Was that why he was following them? Out of some misbegotten sense of honor?

When pigs would fly with soft, pink wings perhaps.

He had an agenda. He always did. She just couldn't figure out what it was.

"I won't try to defend him or give excuses for his actions, because as much as I get why he's acting like this, he's the one who has to offer his own excuses to you."

Even though the woman refused to give answers, Morana was starting to like her for her loyalty. She didn't let it show.

"Then what are you saying?" Morana asked, her eyebrows raised.

Amara looked at her for a second before turning back. "The man who drugged you - the bartender of the club - has been working for the family for almost two decades. After Tristan dropped you with me, he went to deal with the man. It got... heated. So, he came over and carried you to the car and told me to drive you home. But he's been following us all the way. That's all I'm saying. Make of it what you will."

That was the issue. Morana had absolutely no freaking idea what to make of him.

Heart pounding, she looked out of the window and realized they were just a few miles out away from the mansion. She couldn't go back to the house. Not like this. Not half drugged and off-kilter, only to have her father suddenly demand a meeting in the middle of the night. Which he would because she'd ditched her security detail. No. She couldn't go back, not yet, not until she had her wits about her and some alone time.

Swallowing, she took a deep breath. "Please stop the car."

Amara glanced at her. "Why?"

Morana raised her eyebrows. "Because it's my car and I'm going to drive it."

"You were just drugged," she pointed out rationally.

"I'm fine now, and it's only a few miles away," Morana told her. Amara slowed the car a little but didn't stop, and Morana could feel her hesitation.

"Stop the car," she demanded this time, more firmly.

She saw the woman bite her lips but swerve to the edge of the almost empty road, and slowly hit the brakes. The sudden silence in the car, the quietness from the engine, the stillness as lines of trees stood on the edges of the road became eerie. Shaking off the shiver, Morana turned to the woman, giving her a light smile.

"Thank you," she spoke sincerely, "for taking care of me when I was vulnerable. I'll not forget this kindness."

Amara smiled slightly, removing her seat belt. "I know what it's like to be a woman alone on enemy grounds, and I wouldn't wish it on anybody. Don't thank me for it. Just do the same for me someday if I need it."

Morana nodded, a moment of understanding passing between the two. In another life, in another world, she could actually have been friends with Amara.

But she wasn't in another life or another world.

This was her reality.

And her reality was alone.

Which was why she got out from her side, standing in the pale moonlight as the chilly wind caressed her skin, checking her own balance on tottering heels. Apart from some lingering lazy inertia, everything seemed to be alright. She started walking towards the driver's side, just as the following vehicle braked a few feet behind them.

Morana nodded at Amara as the woman got out and turned to the other vehicle.

"Take care, Morana," she spoke, that soft voice of hers and the reason behind it making Morana's heart ached for her. "I hope we meet someday under better circumstances."

"So do I," Morana whispered as she watched the woman in the shining silver dress make her way towards the black SUV.

Without a glance at the tinted windows, Morana got inside her own car on the driver's side, buckling herself in and adjusting the rear-view mirror. She watched Amara get into the back of the vehicle, and saw it pull onto the road before it took a U-turn and drove away into the night.

So much for following her.

He'd been following for Amara.

Morana sat in the car, gripping the steering wheel without turning the key, just processing. She needed to process. To breathe. Alone.

So, someone had drugged her at the club, which was not really surprising because of who she was and where she'd been. She should have been more careful. She'd slipped and she could have died because of it. Except she hadn't. Tristan Caine had pushed her into the VIP area with the one woman who'd shown her kindness. And he must have known it. Morana hadn't, but he must have. And then he'd gone back to the bar, according to Amara, to deal with the bartender. And then when things had gotten heated, he'd picked her up and put her in her own car, and told Amara to drive her home.

Why?

Her fury had not faded, not even a little. Only her confusion had increased. He hated her, she had no doubt of that. She didn't know why, but he truly, deeply hated her.

He could've left her completely with the other woman. He'd called Dante and told him so. Yet, he hadn't. And she couldn't figure out why. People did those things out of kindness, and that was a word she'd never, not in a million years, associate with Tristan Caine, not where she was concerned. It wasn't the kindness of his heart.

*'You assume I have a heart.'*

Then why? What was the point of getting her out? Because she'd been in their territory? Because of the old we-don't-want-to-start-a-war song? Because of... She couldn't come up with any valid explanation at all. She'd not expected him to behave like a world-class jackass, at least not to that extremity, but he had and he'd left her alone, vulnerable, with a stranger to her even though he'd known her.

Why was she thinking like that?! She wasn't his responsibility! She wasn't anyone's responsibility but her own. She'd slipped up and by all means, she should be dead right now, now feeling this odd heaviness in her gut because that man owed her absolutely nothing.

But her curiosity, and something else, refused to rest, refused to let it go. She wanted a reason for his actions – something he would never give her (and shouldn't), and something she failed to decipher herself. And that was extremely frustrating. She was good at reading people and he was the one man she couldn't read. At all.

The sound of an approaching engine broke her out of her thoughts.

Her eyes drifted to the rearview mirror, to see a vehicle approaching.

A big vehicle, coming closer and closer.

An SUV.

Her heart stilled before it started to thrum. She watched with alert eyes as the vehicle pulled in behind her, a few feet between them, and the ignition switched off.

Erratic heartbeats and sweaty palms assaulted her as she waited for something to happen.

A nocturnal bird cooed somewhere in the trees, it's sound loud and melancholic amidst the vastness. The moon continued to glow and bathe the entire area in the moonlight. Her pulse skittered like the wings of a frantic bird.

What the hell?

Never removing her eyes from the rear-view mirror, making a mental note to get her windows tinted, she started counting in her breaths, trying to slow her heart down. At this rate, she'd get a stroke.

One breath.

Two breaths.

Three.

Nothing happened. The door never opened. The lights never came on. Her eyes never wavered from the rear-view.

And then, on the heels of the nothingness, another thought flashed across her mind.

Was that even him in the vehicle?

A glance at the number plate told her it was the same car, but who was behind the wheels? It could be possible that he'd taken the SUV back to the club and someone had taken it out for a spin.

If that was true, and whoever it was had known where she would be, she wasn't sure if starting the car was a good idea. While she could floor it and try to make it back to the house, the other vehicle was bigger, bulkier and faster. And it could skewer her car within minutes. She didn't want to prompt any hostile motions suddenly.

The feeling in her gut churned, making it sink lower and lower as she breathed, quietly opening her clutch and mentally thanking Amara for not removing the gun when she took out the keys. Readying it with a quick motion, she locked all the doors, grateful for the bulletproof glass and bit her lip, not knowing what to do.

Something in her told her it wasn't him. While he hated her, he was in her face about it. This wasn't like him. She didn't linger on when exactly she'd gotten to know the bastard. She just focused on the now.

It was someone else, just a few feet away, and someone willing to harm her. Her eyes glanced at the phone before coming back on the rear-view. She could call her security detail, but that would mean alerting her father to her meeting with the Outfit and the reasons for it, which just could not happen. The understanding between the two families was precarious at best. It could not be tested. Not like this. Not because of her own stupidity.

God, she should have let Amara drive her back.

She straightened her spine. No. No regrets. She'd done what she'd done and that was it.

Morana swallowed, taking a deep breath, her fingers hovering over the key in the ignition, and with a final look at the unmoving vehicle, she turned the ignition on.

The moment she did, the SUV whirred.

Heart in her throat, Morana gripped the steering wheel, and changed the gear, pulling out onto the road. The SUV pulled behind her, keeping a few feet between them, the threat of its speed evident. Goosebumps broke out over her skin, shivers crawling over her as she tried to speed up and slow down and drive haphazardly. She didn't lose the tail. At all.

Adrenaline buzzed through her body as her mind worked, trying to find a way out, her heart pounding frantically now. She would not be chased like a wild animal and murdered. No.

Gritting her teeth, she almost hit the accelerator again when a loud noise broke through the blood rushing in her ears. Morana glanced at the rearview mirror again, to see a bike careen on the road dangerously as the rider throttled. Morana pulled to the side, giving him the space to pass, to not involve an innocent stranger in whatever madness this was, and saw the SUV pull behind her too.

The bike got closer and closer to them, and the moment Morana thought it would pass, the most bizarre thing happened.

The bike swerved and inserted itself in the space between her car and the SUV.

What the hell?

She should just dub this entire night 'what the hell'.

Was the rider insane? This could be a catastrophe!

Morana pulled to the edge of the road again, just a few miles out of her property, and turned around to look at the disaster about to happen.

Except it didn't.

The rider pulled out a gun from his back with one hand while maintaining both the speed and balance with the other impressively. He did a total one-eighty completely on the empty road, facing the oncoming SUV. He raised his gun as Morana watched, enthralled, heart thundering, and pointed it to the front tire.

A shot fired and the SUV skidded, before braking suddenly.

The bike stopped too, facing away from her towards the beast of a vehicle like it was a beast in itself.

The rider kept his arm raised, pointed at the vehicle, his dark helmet on. Morana looked at the white shirt stretched taut across his muscular back and tucked into dark trousers. She looked at the sleeves rolled up sinews and muscles of his forearms with the hints of tattoos peeking out, the other free hand on the handle on the big bike.

Her neck started aching from being turned around but she didn't remove her eyes, didn't even blink, her heart racing at the scene.

Everything was still. The SUV. The bike. The rider. Completely. Almost as though in a silent duel, a showdown she didn't understand a thing of. But she could feel the tension rolling in the air, thick and heavy and ready to explode at a moment's notice.

Everything was still. Except for her heaving chest. Whoever the rider was, she was rooting for him. There was something dangerous about the way he'd held himself in motion, something even more dangerous about the way he held himself in this stillness.

The SUV whirred. The rider didn't twitch.

The vehicle reversed. Quickly. His back muscles tensed.

And with a bad tire, Morana saw, in complete and utter disbelief, as the vehicle turned and drove away at a breakneck speed.

If she had a dollar for every time she'd thought 'what the hell?'

The rider stayed still for a moment, until the SUV disappeared from sight, before revving his bike and turning it back towards her. Morana turned her neck back as he drove forward, stalling beside the car.

She looked up at the intimidating size of the bike and the man riding it, being cautious and never rolling the windows down. He might have interceded in between her would-be creepy maybe-murderer but she didn't know him. And she'd had enough 'what the hell' moments for one night.

The man raised his hand up to his helmet, and Morana's eyes moved to the ropes of muscles and veins running under his exposed forearms, the tattoo swirls familiar, something fluttery happening inside her stomach as she watched it flex, her chest slightly heaving.

He pulled up his helmet with one hand, the palm of which was wrapped in white gauze that she'd missed at the distance, and all fluttery feeling came to a crashing halt before a storm raged through her entire body.

She knew that bandaged hand. She knew those forearms. *Fuck.*

The helmet came down before him. Those magnetic blue eyes watched her through the glass, locked on hers, as he leaned back slightly, in a seemingly casual stance atop his beast of a bike, straddling it with the same grace with which he'd scaled her house walls. His finger tapped the comm on his ear once and a sudden vibration in the car startled her.

Barely containing her surprised yelp, Morana picked up her phone and looked at the caller id, before swinging her eyes back to him.

He was calling her, from less than a foot away, with glass between them, with him out in the open and her safe in her car. He was calling her. And she was letting it ring, never breaking their locked gaze, her heart thudding wildly in her chest as a bead of sweat rolled down her spine, tingling her skin.

His hand never moved from his ear. The buzzing never stopped. The gaze never wavered. Blue on hazel. In the middle of an empty road.

He kept calling, sitting right beside her on his bike, and she kept ignoring it, gripping the steering wheel with her free hand, her knuckles white.

After long, long minutes of neither of them backing down, Morana touched the green button on her phone, bringing it to her ear.

She could hear him breathing on the line, and her own breaths quickened, her chest heaving as she looked at his expanding chest. He inhaled, stretching the shirt tight, and she watched the contractions as he exhaled, the sound clear over the phone. She'd never felt anyone's breaths before, never like this. It was almost distant. It was almost intimate. She wanted to break this, whatever this was. She could still feel that hatred for him fill her body, but she could not utter one word to break that heavy silence.

She had things to demand of him – so many questions. Why hadn't he stayed away from the meeting? Why had he done what he'd done just then? How had he known to come there? She had answers to find out. She had anger to unleash.

Yet, she could not break that gaze, could not remove her eyes from his, could not even hum.

Just breathe. Quick, shallow breaths slowly transforming to slow, deep breaths. Right in sync with his.

It disturbed her.

It disturbed her enough to blink and turn away.

It disturbed her enough to start the car and pull out.

It disturbed her enough to hit the red icon on her phone.

She didn't understand this. She didn't like this. So, she ran. Being alone with him, when he always pushed her off her game, made her vulnerable. She would never willingly expose her jugular to the man who'd made a name in going for it. Her brain had a habit of not functioning properly in his vicinity.

Her phone buzzed again and she looked in the rear-view, to see him right behind her, on her tail.

She picked up.

"I told you to never cut my calls," the whiskey voice rolled off, the tone harsh, intimidating.

It broke the spell even as it weaved it.

"No point in staying on the line if all I get to hear is creepy breathing," she retorted, swallowing, grateful that her voice didn't sound as breathy as she felt.

Silence. But the line stayed open.

She wondered if she should thank him for intervening. That would be the polite thing to do. Screw polite.

"Who was in the SUV?" she asked quietly.

"I'll find out after I get back," he replied quietly, the sound of air loud in the background as he sped behind her.

Morana's eyes drifted to the rear-view again. "You don't have to escort me," she told him tartly.

His voice came back equally tart. "I told you I don't do that gentleman thing."

"Then what are you doing?" she demanded.

"Making sure the information in your little bag doesn't fall into the wrong hands."

Of course!

She'd completely forgotten about the evidence Dante had given her to look at. Things framing Tristan Caine. Of course, he'd want that safe. That explained so much. She cut the call again, that feeling of being connected to him unsettling and she'd had enough of that for a night.

She stayed silent the rest of the way, focusing on the road. The phone didn't buzz again, but he followed. Right till the mansion gates were in sight.

He stopped beside the car again as she paused.

She deliberately didn't look at him again, not wanting him to ensnare her, and felt the weight of his eyes on her as her nape prickled with awareness. Shaking her head, Morana drove forward and into the property as the gates opened. She saw him drive away and relaxed a little, going up the driveway and finally, after minutes of seeing the extensive lawns, parking in her regular spot.

She switched the car off, and sat inside silently, taking a few deep, relaxing breaths, just as her phone buzzed again.

She seriously needed to do more yoga.

She picked up. That husky, deep voice came on again, making her close her eyes.

"There was another reason why I followed you tonight."

The air stuck in her throat and her chest tightened, her heart pattering.

"What?"

There was silence for a few seconds, before the words came on, the dead tone in them, the rigid hatred in them turning her stomach.

"No one else gets to kill you, Ms. Vitalio," he spoke quietly. "The last face you see before you die will be mine. When it comes to death, you're mine."

And then, for the first time, he cut the call.

# *tussling*

Two guards stood beside the huge double doors of the house, their eyes passively watching her approach.

Morana kept her spine straight and chin up, her legs gratefully not wobbling on the heels, the pounding headache the only reminder of her drugged state. Moonlight and ground lights mingled in an erotic combination of white and gold, making the path in front of her feet seem almost ethereal. Had she been some stranger walking the same path at the moment, she would have thought of fairy lights and enchanted tales, of long walks under the pure moon, of warmth against the chill in the wind.

But she wasn't a stranger. She knew these stones that seemed ethereal were nothing but an illusion created to hide the blood and gore than ran under, nothing but a mirage created to charm and impress the outsiders and remind the insiders of how deep things could be buried if they had to be. Secrets were the stones that paved these roads. Threats were the truths that lay in this ground, morbid tales of lost men never to be seen again ringing around in the wind.

Morana walked that path to the place she slept in, the place she'd been sleeping in for decades. She was more attached to her appendix than she was to this house.

One of the guards raised his hand and clicked the comm in his ear, holding the other up to halt her in her tracks.

"Boss?" he spoke in an even tone, listening to whatever command he was being given before he turned to her.

"Your father is waiting for you in the study."

Oh jolly.

Rolling her eyes, Morana walked around the bulky man and into the house, her heels clicking loudly on the marble floors. The lights in the house were dim since it was already way past midnight, the lights in the corridor leading to her father's wing getting dimmer and dimmer through the endless space, artwork adorning both the walls as she kept walking forward, the door to her father's study in sight. Her breathing remained even, not a bead of sweat popped up anywhere, not a knot twisted in her stomach. The headache throbbed under her temples but was otherwise manageable.

After the night she'd had, she doubted there could be anything her father could do that would make her say 'what the hell' again.

Finally reaching the door, not an ounce of fear in her system, she knocked.

"Enter," her father's baritone answered immediately.

Pushing open the door, Morana entered the spacious study, not sparing a glance towards the floor to ceiling columns he had for books, or towards the beautiful French windows on the extreme right that opened into the lawns, or towards the gun that lay openly on his organized desk. No. She entered and glued her eyes to him, his own dark eyes watching her carefully, and she walked to the chair across from his and sat down.

Silence.

Morana stayed silent, adept at the mind games he played, even with his own daughter, and being the genius that she was, she'd learned them very, very early. The wind whistled outside the closed windows. The huge aquarium on the left wall bubbled. The large clock near the bookshelf ticked, one ominous second after the other.

Tick. Tock.

Tick. Tock.

Silence.

He watched her. She watched him.

He leaned back in his chair. She kept her face blank, her heart rate completely even.

And finally, he drew in a deep breath.

"You were at *Cyanide* tonight."

Morana just raised her eyebrows.

He studied her for another second, before speaking, his voice old and rough from too much use with his men. Only his men. She could count the words he'd spoken to her over the years on her hands.

"What were you doing at *Cyanide?*"

Morana played dumb. "Why do you want to know?"

He leaned forward, his jaw clenching, accenting his French-cut beard. "It's an Outfit club."

Morana felt amusement wash over her. "And?"

"You know we don't go into their property directly. They don't come into ours," his steely voice brooked no arguments. "And you wouldn't have made it home. Not unless someone had invited you."

Morana stayed silent, just watching him back neutrally.

"I want a name," he demanded.

Morana kept her face blank. He cursed loudly, smashing his fist on the table, his dark eyes flaring in fury. "You have a name, a reputation as my daughter. No child of mine forfeits that name. And this is the Outfit. I want to know who you've been pimping your name with."

Morana's jaw clenched, her hands fisting as fury filled her body. Her hands shook as she gripped them together, keeping her torso and her gaze still. Shark. Her father was a shark and she could not bleed. Not a single drop. But in learning not to bleed, she'd also learned how to draw blood.

Staying still, keeping her mask in place, a small sneer curling her lips, she spoke.

"Your men couldn't get within a mile of the place, could they?"

She saw the lines around his eyes tighten as his lips pressed together. "You are to remain chaste until your marriage. That's how this works, that's what I've always told you. If you deliberately set out to disobey me..."

Morana laughed. "You will what?"

"I choose your husband, Morana," he told her in an icy voice. "Remember that."

Morana grit her teeth and bit her tongue. She'd hit this stone wall and bruised herself so many times she'd lost count. She detested this world. She detested the way every man thought himself a self-entitled jackass. She hated how every woman either had to bend to their will or suffer for life. She despised this world. And yet, it was the only semblance of a home she'd ever known. She wondered sometimes why she hadn't run away. She had the money, she had the skills, she had it all. And she'd stayed for some reason she couldn't find anymore. And now, with the codes in the wind, she had to stay.

"Is that all you wanted to speak to me about?" she asked stiffly, keeping her voice as calm as she could.

"This conversation is not over."

"Yes, it is."

"I want a name."

"And I won't give you one."

They stared each other down, her head pounding dully, exhaustion seeping into her bones but she didn't even twitch. Morana stood up and turned to leave.

"More men will be on your tail from now on," her father's voice stopped her. "I've ordered them to detain you if you slip the leash."

Her body almost quivered in her rage before she locked it in place. Leash? She wasn't a fucking dog. She sure as hell wasn't a fucking daughter.

*'When it comes to death, you're mine.'*

As the words from minutes ago came to her, the wheels in her mind started to churn. She inhaled deeply. "Send your men after me at their own risk, father," she informed him coolly. "Any one of them lays a finger on me and I will shoot."

Her father paused, before speaking. "They will shoot back."

She remembered the blue eyes of the man who'd claimed his right to kill her. Nobody else would be killing her. She knew he'd been serious.

She shrugged. "Then they will die."

Before her father could utter another word, Morana walked out of the study and towards her own wing, quickening her steps once she was

84

out on her own. She hurried up to her room and once inside, she locked the door. Undressing and freshening up, she took the drive out of the clutch and placed it in her bedside drawer. Then, tired and numb, she slid into her soft brown sheets, settling into her pillows and sighing as she stared out the window.

Not for the first time in her life, it hit her how truly, truly alone she was.

Her father wanted a puppet he could control and parade around to his whims. She knew he'd been serious about the marriage. And she knew that she would never marry someone like that. She wondered sometimes what would have been better - having had his love before he turned cold, leaving her with some childhood memories, or this aloofness that had existed between them forever.

She remembered being snubbed again and again when she'd been a little girl, remembered how early on she'd promised herself to never allow anyone to snub her again, how quickly she had hardened herself. A string of nannies had raised her, women who'd never stayed long enough for her to form a bond with them, and by the time she'd hit adolescence, she'd known she wouldn't bond with anyone, not in this prison, not in this world. So, she'd turned to computers, and poured her heart into them. College had been a battle she'd won only by telling her father how profitable it would be to have a resource like her on his side. He'd eventually agreed, with guards on her tail every single day, limiting her contact with people. And then she'd met Jackson.

Asshole Jackson who'd led her to asshole Tristan Caine.

Morana exhaled loudly, blinking. She didn't understand him. Honestly, she didn't even want to, but since he kept showing up and since she had to deal with him anyways, she'd rather know what or who she was dealing with than be in the dark.

And with Tristan Caine, she always, always seemed to be in the dark. The man sprouted absolute nonsense one second, claiming his right to kill her like she was a prized gazelle on the run, his hate of her genuine. But he'd threatened her a little too many times for her to believe it. And even if he did intend to kill her, she really didn't care since she slept under the same roof as the man who could kill her any moment without flinching.

85

No. It wasn't his death claim-slash-threat-slash-words that bothered her. Much. It was his actions. He shoved her away like she singed him one second, and saved her life in a way the next. He cut himself on her one second and showed up at her meeting the next.

He was a pendulum. Swinging from one extreme to another within seconds. And that confounded her and irritated her because she couldn't get a read on him. At all. And she hated it.

There was something going on with him, she thought as she looked out the window.

It was time she found out.

Morana worked the next day from her study on the drive Dante had given her.

And it did puke out a truckload of information at her, mainly IP addresses that did not belong to Tristan Caine, as they'd been framed to look like. Either Tristan Caine happened to be one brilliant Machiavellian mastermind who'd framed himself so he could look clean –which she honestly wouldn't put past him, not from everything she'd heard and everything she'd seen.

And yet, staring at the screen, she could accept the possibility that he was, in fact, innocent of stealing the codes. But what else was he innocent of?

Shaking her head, she pulled her phone out and called Dante as she'd told him she would. The phone rang and she looked around her study, the scant sunlight filtering in through the window as clouds covered the sky, the wind speedy through the trees.

"Morana?" Dante Maroni's heavy voice came after the third ring. "You found something?" he asked, getting straight to business. Good.

"Yes," she told him, changing tabs on the screen and looking at all the details. "There's a list of IP addresses that I traced back to a warehouse in Tenebrae, and one here in Shadow Port. There is one though, that's popping up with an error every time I try to track it. It's a self-destructive virus basically."

"So whoever is behind this knows computers enough to create and install a self-destructive virus?" Dante asked quietly.

Morana shrugged. "Or they could've had Jackson do it. He was good with computers."

Dante sighed. "Okay. I'll call Tenebrae and have someone look at it. Send me the address."

"Okay."

"Also," he added. "Could you meet and return the drive? I don't want to risk any information leaking online. But I'd like all the decrypted information."

Morana frowned. "That's fine, but what after that?"

"We can discuss it later. I have to go right now."

With that, he disconnected and texted her the address. It was an apartment complex on the west side of the city, near the coast. That must be where they were holed up during their stay.

Morana got ready in record time, in loose black pants with multiple pockets and a loose sleeveless red top, simple but comfortable flats on her feet and hair in a ponytail. Hiking her black tote bag over one shoulder, with her phone and car keys in hands, the drive safely in the bag with her gun, Morana walked out of her wing towards the main gate.

Her phone rang just as she reached her car. She saw her father's name on the screen and rejected the call, sliding in her red Mustang and pulled out of the space. Two muscle cars pulled out behind her. Oh goody.

Morana looked in her rearview mirror and pulled into the traffic, switching lanes and speeding up, the rush, the hit, exactly the same as it always was. The traffic was light and allowed her to weave in between vehicles and she sped towards the coast, her attention completely on the road and on losing the damn cars.

She lost one, but the other stayed on her tail almost half the way and she realized, aggravated, that he couldn't be shaken. And she couldn't lead them to the meeting point. Fuck.

Gritting her teeth, she pulled her phone up and put it on speaker, calling the last dialed number. It rang. And rang some more, then disconnected with no answer.

She kept looking in the rear-view, noticing the other car hadn't moved at all, like a fly in the ointment, and just stayed on the trail.

It was getting very problematic because she was barely five minutes out.

Knowing she couldn't lose the tail before time irked, but she accepted it and slowed down considerably, redialling the number.

No answer.

She almost smashed her phone down in frustration, before taking a deep breath and cooling her mind. Dante wasn't picking up. Okay. Time to make the hard choice.

Scrolling through her contacts, she found the number she was looking for, her thumb hovering above the icon as her eyes drifted to the car again. And she pressed it down.

Her heart started to pound, stomach knotting.

And this, right here, she didn't understand. She'd faced her father with no reaction at all while he'd been interrogating her, and yet she'd barely heard the phone ring and her body had come to life, all responses functioning and alert. She needed to figure this out, for the sanity of her own mind. She also needed to figure out what the hell to do with her tail and where to go.

"Ms. Vitalio."

That voice. The voice of death threats and old whiskey. Morana swallowed, shaking herself out of it.

"Mr. Caine," she replied in an even voice, bringing her attention back to the road. "I'm supposed to meet Dante and my detail is still on the tail. He isn't answering."

Morana had half expected him to gloat that she was asking him for assistance. She definitely expected one scathing comment. What she hadn't expected was his somber tone speaking quietly.

"Dante is tied up in something important. Did he ask you to meet him at 462-"

"Yes," Morana interrupted.

There was a brief pause before he came on again. "Pull over wherever you are. Don't disconnect."

Heart picking up pace, Morana quietly pulled over, not knowing why she was even doing as he asked, and sat. She heard an engine thrum in the background and realized it was that damned bike. She did not need that right now.

She could hear him on the bike and a knot settled in her gut. He was quiet. Not the waiting-for-her-to-crack quiet. Just quiet. She didn't like that she was observing anything.

The sky rumbled loudly overhead, thunder crackling dangerously just as the engine's sound joined in the cacophony.

"Drive," he ordered curtly, and Morana looked in the rear-view, to see the bike come closer and closer to her tail. She pulled back into the traffic, her heart hammering with the weirdest sense of deja-vu hitting her. His bike smoothly inserted itself between the two cars again. She saw him slow down, saw the tailing car brake to avoid a collision, and he ground out again in a rough tone.

"Hit it."

Morana didn't hesitate this time, pushing her foot down and feeling the car zip straight ahead, adrenaline rushing through her system as the wind went wild around her. One last glance in the rear-view before she turned left showed her the other car far, far behind, and the bike zooming through the spaces in between cars and speeding towards hers.

Morana turned, going across the bridge, and sped towards the gate looming in front of her, guarding not a complex but one lone, tall building that almost touched the darkening sky. Quickly entering the parking lot as the guards waved her through, Morana looked for an empty spot and parked, turning the ignition off.

Just as she got out and locked the car, she saw the bike enter the parking lot, saw him insert the beast of a vehicle smoothly across from her car, a dark helmet on his head.

He wore tan cargo pants and a black t-shirt, his attire casual, telling her he'd not been meeting people. She'd always seen him in shirts and trousers when he was in public.

His back muscles flexed as he swung his muscled leg over it, his thigh bunching and releasing as he stood up, his tattooed biceps bulging as he pushed the helmet over his head.

Morana blinked.

Not at the scruff or the hair or the arresting blue eyes, but at the look on his face. For the first time since she'd seen him, she saw something akin to pleasure on his face, just a ghost of an expression but on a man like him, enough to be classified as an expression in itself. His eyes were on his bike, and Morana realized, surprised, that it had been the riding that had put that look on his face. She didn't know why that surprised her, but it did.

And then he looked up to where she stood, the expression fleeting now, and his eyes hardened, his face shutting down.

Morana held his gaze, her heart thundering as thunder roiled outside, the clap in the sky loud and high, her own pulse skittering for some reason. She didn't understand this, didn't know why she did this even. It was a game. A staredown. She didn't remove her eyes from his, and he didn't remove his from hers, neither willing to look away first.

The entire parking lot was empty, the sound of rain loud in the silence of the lot, like bullets pelting down on the ground from the sky.

Her phone rang, the noise startling in the quiet, and she looked down.

Dante.

"Yes?" she picked up, her eyes coming back to where he stood beside his bike, leaning against it with his arms crossed, his forearms thick, the sinews and veins and ink adding to the brutality of his form somehow, his eyes on hers. He would look relaxed to any casual observer, lounging against his vehicle. He was anything but. Morana could see the alert tilt of his head, see the focused look in his eyes, see the tensed muscles ready to jump.

"I apologize. An urgent matter came up. Have you reached?" Dante asked.

"Yes," she stayed still too.

"Great. Just give the drive to Tristan. He's in the penthouse," Dante informed her, while the man in question stood mere feet away, his intent gaze upon her.

"Okay, but next time, I'm setting the meeting," Morana said and after a pause, Dante agreed before disconnecting.

She slid the phone down into her pocket, breaking their locked gaze to rummage through her bag. Finding the drive, she stood where she was, and extended her hand.

"Dante asked me to give it to you."

He extended his own, and their fingers brushed. Tingles ran up her arms and down her spine from the one spot of contact.

He didn't remove his hand. She didn't remove hers. Within seconds, it became another game where neither backed down. The sensations thrummed through her body, pooling in her belly and spreading through her blood, making her a little heady as she kept her eyes locked on his sharp blue ones, unable to read a single thing in them. Had she not felt his flesh and blood pressed against her own body, she would have believed he was a cyborg. Unfeeling. Cold. Aloof.

And that doused ice on her hammering heart.

"Why do you hate me?" she asked him the only question she could not find an answer to, the one question that had bugged her more than she cared to admit.

His lips tightened infinitesimally, his eyes flickering away.

And suddenly he stilled, his eyes leaving hers and sweeping through the parking lot. Morana blinked, clearing her head, and looked around, trying to see something.

All she saw were vehicles and all she heard was the thunder and rain.

The hand that hand been touching hers at the tips suddenly jerked her forward, his other hand clamping down on her mouth and drowning the muffled shriek that would have escaped her otherwise. One second she was standing next to her car, the next she was behind a pillar, pressed into it with a very muscled man against her front, one of his hands on the pillar beside her head, the other still on her mouth.

Morana tried to bite his hand off and he looked at her once, his eyes alert and telling her to be quiet. Morana felt anger fill her but she nodded. He removed his hand and leaned over the pillar, his eyes scanning the entire area. His chest brushed against her breasts as they both inhaled. And though she noticed that, she didn't focus on it, keeping her own senses open as adrenaline filled her twice in half an hour and her heart pounded, her stomach knotting as she looked and tried-

Movement.

She shifted slightly to look better, and the man pressed to her followed her gaze. Three men, three burly looking men, jumped out from behind the car she'd been watching, attacking, their hands raised with knives in them.

Heart slamming against her chest, Morana watched, stunned, as before she could take a step, Tristan Caine had one man down on the ground and was fluidly moving towards the other. One of them broke off from the group and headed towards her. Morana had never fooled herself into believing she was a badass because of her strength. Nope. She was one because of her brain and using that very brain, she took out her gun, switching the safety off in the same motion, and shot the man right in the knee without blinking.

He fell down with a cry, whimpering in pain as he clutched his leg, and Morana turned to see two men down on the ground, unconscious or dead she didn't know, and Tristan Caine flat on his back as the last man stood above him. Morana raised her gun instinctively before she stopped herself. She wasn't going to save him. Not at all. If he couldn't save himself, then someone else had done her job for her.

But she watched with her heart in her throat as the two men exchanged kicks and swift moves faster than her eyes could catch before the man slammed Tristan Caine down on the ground so hard Morana's ribs would have cracked. But Tristan Caine raised his legs in the same movement, using the momentum, and wrapped his ankles around the guy's neck, before flipping him down and getting him in a chokehold.

"Who do you work for?" he asked the gasping man in a cold voice that didn't belay any exertion, even as his chest heaved with quick breaths.

"Who sent you?" he asked again, the same questions he'd asked her the first time he'd pinned her to a wall with her own knives.

The other man spit on the ground, shaking his head. And Tristan Caine snapped his neck.

Morana was no stranger to death and murder. It was as much a way of their world as women being controlled by men was. So she didn't flinch or gasp or betray any emotion. But her stomach fell to the ground, her hands trembling slightly, the gun shaking in her grip.

Tristan Caine stood up and walked to the guy she'd shot, his eyes surveying her body once, for injuries maybe, before going back to the man.

"Talk or you die."

The man grimaced. "I will die anyway."

Tristan Caine tilted his head. "But it can be painful or it can be painless. Your choice."

The man fainted.

Morana stood a few feet away from him, her eyes glued to his face as he turned to hers.

"You should leave," he told her quietly.

Morana nodded, her insides in shock, and turned towards her car, keeping her eyes peeled for any other jumpers with knives, her gun loose in her hand.

She walked towards her car, her eyes rising from the ground, and she came to a complete halt.

There, in the middle of the parking lot, stood her Mustang where she'd parked it, with all its tires slashed open. Morana stood in shock, staring at the car. She'd bought that car with her own money. Her first car. This was the only friend she had, the only friend that understood her thirst for freedom. This had been her companion in so many escapades and her partner in crime. She'd repaired it on her own, took care of it on her weekends. She loved it. And there it stood, with all the tires ripped open.

Morana had just seen a man be murdered, just shot a man herself, but it was now that she felt violated, now that her eyes moistened.

But she couldn't shiver, couldn't cry, couldn't show an inch of vulnerability.

He stood behind her.

Morana steeled her spine and cleared her face.

"Surely you have another car I can borrow?" she asked in a completely natural tone.

"Yes, but the storm outside is not feasible for driving."

That made Morana turn, her eyes locking with his blue ones, a streak of dirt across his one cheek where he'd tussled on the floor.

"You're worried about my safety?" she asked, disbelief thick in her voice.

He raised his eyebrows. "I'm worried about my car."

Of course. She could relate to worrying about the car. She nodded. "I'll just call a cab then."

His brows furrowed slightly. "Cabs don't come to this area."

Of course, they didn't. Morana looked at the water pouring at the entrance to the parking lot with a vengeance, her gut in knots and she bit her lip, trying to figure a way out. She couldn't call her father, or everything would be a disaster. Driving any of the cars was out of option because the visibility would be zero and the distance was long. Cabs were out. What option did she even have left?

Her heart hammered as realization dawned. She didn't.

Her gaze flew up to collide with his. His blue, blue eyes arrested hers, the intensity in them searing through her, humming in her blood as her pulse pounded in her ears.

He tilted his head to a side, almost considering her before he spoke, and her heart jumped out of her chest.

"Looks like you're staying, Ms. Vitalio."

# *turning*

M oments.
Surprising, surreal moments.
Had someone told her a few weeks ago that she would be
spending a night alone in the penthouse of the Outfit's blood son, she
would have smacked them over the head. But then, had someone told her
that she would ever infiltrate the Maroni household, she wouldn't have
believed it either. Or the confounding fact that he would save her life
while claiming her death for himself.

Surreal.

Morana walked towards the elevator in a daze, unable to believe, to
actually *believe*, that she was going to spend a night away from home in
the apartment of Tristan Caine. These things did not happen to her. And
yet, there she was, walking with sure steps that betrayed nothing of her
inner turmoil, her mind alert of the man striding beside her. Although
how a man that big could move so gracefully was beyond her. But she'd
seen him scale the walls of her house with that grace. She'd seen him tilt
his bike and fight men bigger than him with that grace. And that she
could appreciate it irked her.

Her eyes wandered to her car, her destroyed car in the periphery,
and her heart clenched again, rage coursing through her body on the

heels of pain, the need for vengeance against whoever had dared violate her burning through her. Whoever it was would get it. Big time.

She saw his hand from the corner of her eyes, pressing a code on a keypad beside the second elevator, telling her it was private.

His eyes glanced at her briefly, and Morana glanced back, with absolutely no idea of any of his thoughts. How reluctant was he to her into his space? She'd have been very reluctant. But then he'd invaded her bedroom the other night, so fair was fair.

The elevator pinged, the steel doors sliding back, revealing a spacious area that could probably accommodate ten people. Tristan Caine, the absolute gentleman that he was, entered first with smooth steps and turned around to look at her, no chivalry anywhere whatsoever.

Curious but alert, taking a deep breath, Morana stepped after him and entered. Once she was in, he pushed the only button on the dial, entering another set of codes, and the doors slid closed.

The doors slid closed, and the sight made her fist her hands for control.

They were mirrored.

Their eyes locked in the reflection, her heart pounding for some crazy reason, as the elevator began to move up.

He stood in the corner, leaning against the elevator wall, his ankles crossed and arms folded over his chest, his eyes watchful on her, seeming curious, lacking their normal hateful vibes. Morana raised her eyebrows and didn't move a muscle, her ears throbbing with the rush of blood, her entire body buzzing.

She needed to distract herself. Loath as she did to admit, the closed space, the reflections, the gaze was getting to her.

"Who were those men?" she asked, her voice even, betraying absolutely nothing.

He stayed silent for a beat. "I don't know. I think someone wants you dead, Ms. Vitalio."

"Besides you, you mean?" Morana scoffed, rolling her eyes.

She saw him tilt his head to a side, considering her. "You're not afraid of death?"

Morana felt her lips curl in a smile that didn't reach her eyes. "You learn not to be afraid when it sleeps under your roof every day."

96

Their gazes held for a tense moment, Morana's heart hammering as she saw his blue eyes study her.

"Indeed," he said quietly. Mercifully, the doors slid open at that moment, and Tristan Caine exited.

The moment he stepped outside, his back to her, Morana inhaled, realizing she'd been holding her breath the entire time. Shaking her head at herself, not understanding at all why her body betrayed her like this, hating these reactions even as a part of her, the part that had been comatose for as long as she could remember, came to life. She needed to understand this, understand how she could control this. Because these were uncharted waters, and she had no idea what lay beyond. She was honest enough to admit that it terrified a little part of her.

Swallowing, watching his back muscles flex as he walked, she stepped outside the elevator. It opened right into the penthouse and the sight that greeted her eyes made her bite back a gasp.

The far wall of the huge space was nothing but glass. Endless wall of glass.

Morana saw the dark clouds in the sky, the skyline of the city on one side and the sea on the other, the view absolutely stunning. She'd never, in her entire life, seen something so vivid, so raw, so beautiful. Her hungry eyes roved over the entire glass wall, but she didn't step towards it, aware of his eyes on her, watching her every move.

Pushing her shoulders back, she pried her eyes away from the spectacular view and turned towards the room.

The interior, huge and spacious, was surprisingly inviting. She didn't know what she had expected, but what she hadn't expected was the large living area with two seating arrangements, done in various tones of grey and blue, steel and chrome shining. The far end of the room had a long electric fireplace. Above it hung a large piece of abstract art in the shades of fire, hues of red and yellow erotically mixed together, the only point of bright color in the entire room.

The couches were plush, ice grey and deep blue, the tables all glass and steel set atop navy blue rugs that looked expensive. The marble floor was black streaked with strands of gold, contrasting beautifully with the entire decor. The glass wall took the entire space from the fireplace to the open kitchen that held a dining table for six, and high stools scattered around the island.

And beyond the kitchen was one black door, beside which a staircase curved to the level above.

Her eyes finally found Tristan Caine, and he tilted his head, indicating the door at the far end.

"That's a guest bedroom. You can stay there," he spoke, his voice sending a shiver over her that she barely controlled.

Before Morana could reply, he turned back towards the elevators. He was leaving? Leaving her, the woman he hated more than anything, alone in his apartment? What kind of an idiot was he?

"You think it's wise to leave me here alone?" she quipped, disbelieving. "In your territory?"

He paused, but entered the elevator, turning around to face her, his face a clear mask. "I have nothing worth stealing. Help yourself, Ms. Vitalio."

The doors closed.

Morana felt the disbelief warring with the strange emotion in her gut. She was in completely strange territory and she had no clue how to proceed. Did he have surveillance? Was she supposed to take him literally and help herself to anything? She didn't even know why she was hesitating, considering the complete bull he was about her personal space.

Her eyes watched the darkening sky split open over the city contemplatively, her breath hitching at the view. A pang of envy hit her. Tristan Caine had this view every day that he was in the city.

Shaking herself, Morana turned towards the guest bedroom, and started walking, taking in the entire space which was surprising. And confusing, as was everything about him.

Opening the door to the guest room, she entered, looking around. It was simple, with a comfortable looking double bed, a line of cupboards in one corner, a window, and a dresser. Sighing, Morana entered, and rummaged through the drawers, looking for any weapons. None. Then, the cupboards, looking for any spare clothes. There were none.

She entered the bathroom. It was comfortably-sized, like the guest room, with all the basics – shower, toilet, bathtub.

Not that it mattered. There was no way she was going to relax. Absolutely not. But she needed a feel for the area. After freshening up a little, washing away the dust from her face, she quietly left the room. Coming out into the open living area, she looked up the stairs that spiraled up, wondering what lay beyond.

Shrugging, she climbed, one step after another, her eyes wandering around. Damn, she'd kill him just for that view. Coming to a stop at the top of the stairs, Morana blinked in surprise yet again.

She'd expected a corridor, a set of doors, something. Instead, the stairs opened directly into a huge, and she meant *huge*, master of master bedrooms, almost like a hidden loft. What surprised her though were the colors.

While the living area was comfortable but icy, this was the exact opposite. There was not a splash of grey anywhere as far as she could see. Done in browns and tones of greens, the room boasted of wood-finished walls, oak-wood doors that she assumed led to a closet and the bathroom, and a King-sized bed that looked way too comfortable and inviting. That was what this room was – warm, inviting, inspiring thoughts of lazy mornings with tangled sheets.

Who the hell was this man?

Morana stood at the top of the stairs, her surprised eyes taking in the biggest bed she had ever seen in detail – brown sheets like her own, enough pillows to make a fort. Black marble flooring added to the den-like feel of the place, another wall of glass with the gorgeous view of the sea at the far end.

The room looked welcoming. Homey.

Morana felt a sad tug in her chest, and turned to leave, just as the door across her, in the corner of the room opened, steam blowing out.

Her heart stopped.

Tristan Caine walked out, with nothing but a towel hitched low on his hips, his back to her.

Morana blinked, gaped, then ogled.

She should have left while he was unaware. She should have quietly made her way down and pretended she'd never seen him walking out. She should have turned on her heels.

But she didn't.

She stood, frozen, her eyes mapping the multiple scars scattered over the tanned skin of his back, seeing the muscles actually ripple as he opened a cupboard and searched for something. She saw the raised, mottled flesh - wounds from knives and bullets and burns - and felt her heart start to clench just as he stilled.

He stilled.

She stilled.

And he turned his neck, his blue eyes locking with hers.

Her breath hitched.

She saw the extensive scars on his torso as he turned to face her, the flesh permanently bruised and tainted. What kind of hell had this man been through? She took in his tattoos, some of which she couldn't make out the shape of, took in the scars, took in the impeccable muscles, coiled, tensed under the skin, his chest rising and falling evenly as his eyes watched her. Morana held his gaze, trying to hide the odd sensation in her chest as she watched him, knowing she was failing from the shift in his gaze.

He took a slow step forward, deliberate, measured, his eyes studying her sharply. Morana held her place, not backing down an inch, holding his gaze. By now she knew these games of control, and though she shouldn't, she played them.

He took another step, the towel hanging on his hips by a knot, his abs completely bare to her eyes, a trail of hair disappearing into the edge of the fabric. Morana noticed it all without removing her eyes from his, her heart pounding, fists clenched as she stood at the top of the stairs.

Another step and he stood mere feet from her, the muscles in his body tight, tensed, controlled. His eyes were clear, his pupils slightly expanded. And seeing the pupils she realized this, whatever this was, was affecting him too. As much as he kept it under wraps, he couldn't control those physical reactions. For some reason, that made her feel better, knowing she wasn't the only one with a loss over her bodily responses.

It also made her pulse spike higher.

They stood in tensed silence, their gazes locked. The silence was rife with something, heavy with a kind of anticipation she could not understand, almost as if they were facing off at the edge of a cliff, a breath away from plunging down. Her stomach was in knots, a bead of sweat rolling down her cleavage to between her breasts, the conditioned air cool against her heated skin. The sound of rain splattering against the glass mingled with the blood in her ears, her own breathing seeming loud to her even as she tried to control it, to not let him see anything at all.

Another step.

She tilted her neck back, her back arching as her feet moved of their own accord backward, completely forgetting that she stood at top of the stairs. She felt her balance tip a second before gravity hit her, her hands reaching out to hold onto something and finding purchase against the warm, solid muscles of his arms. Even as she steadied herself, Morana felt his hand slip to the back of her neck, cupping her nape as he pulled her back from the edge and upright, with nothing but his hold on her neck.

Heart thudding, her hands full of muscles she'd never felt against her palms, Morana looked up at him, while he looked down, his hold on her neck firm but non-threatening, a sort of almost edge to the grip she couldn't place.

Inches.

Bare inches.

Blood rushed through her body, small currents running down her spine from where he held her neck, her breaths coming faster even as she tried to keep it under control.

His own chest rose and fell and little faster, his breaths washing over her face, the scent of musk and something woodsy wrapping around her in the close proximity.

The sudden ringing of her phone broke the daze.

Morana blinked, shaking herself mentally, clearing her head. Pulling her hands away from his arms, she brought out her phone from her pocket. His hand remained in place.

She looked down at the caller id and froze.

Her father.

Ice filled her, cooling her overheated systems her completely. The fracture in her control repaired as she straightened and pulled away from his grip. His fingers flexed once before he loosened his hold, the imprint of his touch searing her skin, the ghost of sensations assaulting her flesh. The nape of her neck burned.

Without a word, she turned away and hurried down the stairs, every response in her body back under her rigid control, like it always was except with him.

Exhaling deeply once she stood in the kitchen, Morana picked up the call and stayed silent.

"You slipped your detail," her father's cool voice came through her line, and Morana sat down on a stool rigidly, keeping her face clear of expression and voice even.

"I said I would," she responded without a flinch in her tone.

"Who was the biker?" her father asked, anger restrained in his voice.

Morana wasn't surprised his goons had reported the man who'd helped her escape. "What biker?" she asked.

There was a pause. "When are you returning?"

"I'm not," Morana informed him. "Not tonight." Maybe not ever.

Another pause. "Where are you?"

Morana took a deep breath. "Since you cannot seem to grasp it, I'll spell it out for you, father. I am not a dog you think you can leash. I'm an independent woman, and if I say I'm not returning tonight, that's it. I know it's not out of care that you ask."

"Your independence is an illusion I've let you sustain, Morana," her father spoke in chilling tones. "I will find out who he is. And I will have him killed."

For the first time in the conversation, Morana felt a sliver of amusement. She hated Tristan Caine, but the thought of him facing off with her father somehow didn't seem like the best course for her father. And she should've felt bad about not rooting for her own flesh and blood. All she felt was cold.

"Good luck, father," Morana spoke and disconnected, putting her phone on the counter, her body slumping as soon as she took a breath.

She felt him behind her and turned.

He stood in loose sweatpants and a black t-shirt, watching her rather speculatively. Morana felt her hackles rise.

She raised her eyebrows. "What?"

He stayed silent for a beat before heading to the big refrigerator. "So, your father pimps you out to his friends and tries to leash you," he spoke, the heavy disgust in his voice clear. "What a man."

Morana grit her teeth. "Pots and kettles. Did you forget the number of times you tried to control me, Mr. Caine? I can remind you if you like," she spoke, her tone deliberately polite.

He stilled on his way to the refrigerator. "I'm nothing like your father, Ms. Vitalio."

"That's actually not true," Morana commented. "You both try to control me and threaten to kill me. What's so different?"

"You don't want to know."

Morana tilted her head, her eyes narrowed. There was an undercurrent of something beneath the heat in that statement. She tried to put her finger on it, but it completely escaped her, much to her frustration.

"Actually, I think I do."

Tristan Caine turned back to the refrigerator and for some reason, she got the sense that he was biting his tongue to keep from speaking.

Okay.

"So, who drugged me at *Cyanide?*" she asked, ready to demand some answers.

"One of the bartenders," he replied, pulling out frozen chicken and vegetables from the freezer, and setting them on the counter. Morana felt the surprise hit her yet again, seeing the ease with which he moved around the kitchen, as much ease as he would in a field of bullets. She saw him pick up a chopping board and knife.

He cooked.

Tristan 'The Predator' Caine cooked. Would wonders never cease?

Ignoring the odd sensation in her chest, she focused on the questions.

"Why did he drug me?"

The knife stopped above a slice of chicken, hovering in the air as he looked up at her. His jaw clenched, that familiar hatred she'd seen in his eyes so many times flashing before he reined it in. He'd been keeping it under control today for some reason.

Baffled, Morana played with her phone, waiting for an answer.

The elevator doors slid open just as he unclenched his jaw to speak. People had the worst timing!

Dante came walking into the area, his tall, muscular body encased in a dark suit, his hair slicked back. His dark eyes came to her, before flickering to Tristan Caine, some kind of silent look passing between them, and back to her again.

"Morana," he spoke, coming to stand beside her as she tensed. "I apologize for being unable to meet you. Something very urgent came up at the last second."

Morana studied him, her eyes narrowed. He seemed sincere enough. She nodded. "That's okay."

"I heard you were attacked. Are you alright?"

Morana raised her eyebrows even as his concern seemed genuine. And then she remembered what Amara had told her about the two men being protective of women.

She nodded again. "I'm fine. But I need my car tomorrow."

Dante smiled. "Tristan arranged for the repairs already."

Her eyebrows hit her hairline as she turned to the other man. "You did?"

He ignored her, his eyes on Dante. "Should I get ready?"

"Yes."

Another silent look.

Tristan Caine nodded and walked around the counter, heading towards the stairs.

Dante turned to her, his dark eyes genuinely concerned. "My apartment is two floors down. I know you said you didn't want to work with him, so if you'd like you can stay there for tonight. I won't be home and it will be empty."

She saw Tristan Caine stop on the stairs before she could speak, his entire body tensing as he turned to face Dante, his eyes cool.

"She stays here," he growled.

*Growled.*

Morana blinked in surprise as the edge in the tone. It sent a shiver through her. She'd have thought he'd be glad to have her out of his hair.

Dante spoke up from beside her, addressing the man, a hand in his pocket. "It's a better option. You will return later and I won't. She can stay comfortably till morning."

Tristan Caine didn't blink away from his blood brother, and another look passed between them.

"Tristan..." Dante spoke, his voice slightly worried. "You don't..."

Tristan Caine turned his eyes to her, the force of his gaze knocking the breath out of her lungs.

"You won't come to any harm tonight," he told her, the conviction in his voice hard. "Stay."

Before Morana could blink, much less digest the words, he was gone.

And Morana sat exactly where she had been sitting minutes ago, completely stumped.

Rain.

Drops beating against the glass in a musical, melancholic symphony. There was something about the sound of rain that sent pangs through her chest.

Morana lay curled on her side, listening to the sound of raindrops hitting the glass, the urge to feel them, to see them, overwhelming her.

She was all alone. In the room. In the apartment. In her life.

Swallowing, she got down from the bed in the darkened room, and slowly walked towards the door, her heart heavy in her chest for some reason. Opening the door, she looked out into the completely darkened living area and walked on quiet feet towards the glass wall that beckoned her on a level she hadn't realized she had.

The faint light from outside filtered through the wall almost ethereally. She walked, closer and closer to the glass, seeing the raindrops splash against the glass and slither down.

Morana stopped a step away from the glass, watching her breath steam it slowly before it disappeared. The clouds hung heavy in the night sky, the lights of the city twinkling on the right, glittering like gems on a fabric of obsidian, the sea on her left for as far as she could see, cresting and falling with the storm.

Morana stood on the spot, drinking in the view, her throat tightening.

She had never seen rain like this. Never felt this freedom in her eyes. Her views from her window had ended in manicured lawns and high fences, beyond which nothing could be seen. She felt her hands rise of their own accord, the profound need in her heart so acute, for something she knew she could never have, for something she hadn't even known she'd needed.

Her hands hesitated an inch from the glass, her heart bleeding. She slowly pressed them down. The cool glass felt solid against her palms. She stood there for a long moment, aching, only a wall of glass between her and certain death. She watched the city in a way she'd never seen it, the city she had lived her entire life, the city that was still a stranger.

Her hands slid down the glass as she sat down on the floor right against it, cross-legged, and leaned forward, her breaths steaming the glass repeatedly.

Thunder crackled in the sky, a split of lightening bathing everything in brilliant white before disappearing. Droplets hit the glass in tandem, trying to break it like bullets, trying to reach her but unable to. She sat behind that wall, longing to feel those droplets on herself, longing to let them sear her, but unable to. And wasn't that her life. Longing for things she couldn't reach, things that tried to reach her and came up against a wall. A glass wall. Where she could see everything, know exactly what she was missing, drown in her awareness even as the glass couldn't break. Because just as it did now, breaking the glass meant death.

And lately, Morana wondered if it wouldn't be worth it.

Her lips trembled, her hands pressed against the glass, seeing the tears fall from the sky and slide down the walls in defeat, and felt one slip from the corner of her eye.

And felt him in the room.

She should have turned around and stood up. She knew she definitely shouldn't give him her back, should not leave herself vulnerable. But in that moment, she couldn't get herself to move her eyes from the view and her hands from the glass. She couldn't get herself to tense.

She felt tired. Exhausted deeper than her bones.

And the fact that he'd told her she wouldn't be harmed told her she wouldn't be. She'd seen enough liars in her life to recognize a man who wasn't. He'd made no secret of his hatred for her, and that, conversely, was the very thing that told her that for this moment, she could believe his word.

So, she didn't tense, didn't turn, just waited for him to leave.

The back of her neck pricked as he watched her, and she felt him move. She didn't know how she knew. He made absolutely no sound, his feet completely silent on the floor. But she knew he'd moved.

She sat there in silence and saw his feet in her periphery.

She didn't look up. He didn't look down. The silence continued.

Morana kept her eyes on the raindrops, her heart pounding as he folded his legs and sat down a foot away from her, his eyes looking out.

Morana glanced at him from the corner of her eye, seeing his unbuttoned shirt teasing a strip of flesh she'd seen earlier, his weight resting on his palms that rested on the floor as he leaned back on them.

She caught sight of a small scar and felt her heart ache. She'd never really given a thought, in all the injustice that happened to women, to what happened to men in their world. She knew that power and survival were the two ultimates but never wondered about what the price of it was. Were the scars on him a norm or an anomaly like he was? Were they the price of being that anomaly in a family that valued blood? How many had been inflicted by enemies? How many had come at the hands of the family? Was this the cost of him coming to where he was in their world? What kind of a toll did it take on men? Was that why most of them were so detached? Because that became the only way to deal with the pain? Was that what had happened to her father? Was he detached because that was how he'd coped all his life, to keep his power?

Questions lingered in her mind, along with the memory of the gashes she'd seen across the flesh of the man beside her. She might hate him, but she respected strength. And his body, she realized, was more than a weapon. It was a temple of strength. It was a keeper of tales –

107

tales of his survival, of things she couldn't even fathom in this ugly, ugly world.

Morana thought about Amara, about the torture she had resisted and survived for days at the hands of enemies, and realized how truly lucky she had been in comparison. She'd never been abducted, never been tortured, never been violated like so many other women in their world. And she wondered why. Was it because of her father? Or some other reason?

"My sister loved the rain."

The softly spoken words, in that husky, rough voice of whiskey and sin, broke through her thoughts.

And then the words sank in, stunning her. Not just because it was something supremely private he'd shared with her, but because of the deep, deep love she could hear in his tone.

She'd not thought him capable of the kind of love she heard in his voice, not for anyone. And that's what stunned her. Morana didn't turn to look at him, didn't even glance at him as he didn't at her, but her hands pressed into the glass, surprise coursing through her at his words, even as it confused her.

She swallowed, her heart pounding. "I didn't know you had a sister," she spoke in the same soft tone, never looking away from the view.

Silence.

"I don't anymore."

And the flat tone was back. But Morana didn't believe it. She'd heard that warmth, heard the love. Even he couldn't snap back to that detached mode that quickly. But she didn't call him out on it for some reason.

They sat in the complete darkness, facing the sky and the city and the sea, facing the quick droplets that fell in sync with heartbeats, the silence between them not thick but not brittle either. Just silence. She didn't know what to make of it.

Her mouth opened before she could think about it.

"My mother loved the rain."

A pause.

"I thought you had a mother."

A familiar knot constricted her throat. "I don't anymore."

She felt him glance at her then, and turned her head, her eyes locking with deep, deep blue. Something dark flashed in his eyes again and he looked away.

Morana swallowed. "Why did you want me to stay here?"

He sat there, not tensing, not looking at her, his gaze outwards. Silence.

"Dante was right. I could have been safe, comfortable there," she told him quietly.

"You are safe and comfortable here," he told her in an equally quiet voice, the words heavy with meaning.

"For tonight."

"For tonight."

Morana looked back out the window, seeing the rainfall, hearing it clap against the glass as she sat a foot away from him.

They sat in that utter darkness, with a kind of silent truce that she knew would lift the moment the sun came out, a silent truce they would never acknowledge in the light of the day, a dark stolen moment against a glass wall that she would remember but never speak of.

She would remember it because, in that moment, something inside her shifted. Shifted utterly, because in that moment, the enemy, the man who hated her more than anything, had done what no one had ever done.

In that moment, the man who'd claimed her death had given her a glimpse of life by doing something he probably didn't even realize he'd done.

In that moment, the enemy had done what no one had ever even tried to do for her.

He had made her feel a little less lonely.

The moment would be over when the sun came out.

But for that silent moment, something inside her beyond her own understanding, even as she hated him, shifted.

## cornering

Indecision was weighing her down, where her own emotions were concerned.

Her father hadn't called again.

Not once.

Morana didn't know why that worried her, but for some reason, she couldn't shake the feeling that something was going to happen. Something she was not going to like by any means. She wouldn't anyway, not if her father was perpetrating it.

Taking a deep breath, and shaking off those thoughts for later, she opened the door of the guest bedroom and walked out into the penthouse.

After the previous night, had she been any regular girl in any other world, she wouldn't have known what to expect. But her normal wasn't regular, which was exactly the reason she knew what to expect.

She walked out of the guest bedroom, knowing she was alone in the penthouse. He'd left as soon as dawn had struck, and so had she, retreating into the guestroom for the remainder of the night, a few hours ago.

They hadn't spoken a word after that initial conversation, but she knew, as she walked towards the kitchen, that whatever silent truce had existed with those fragile raindrops had disappeared along with the rain. The sun shone brightly in the sky, the light cutting through the glass wall and lighting up the entire room, every dark inch of space touched with fire, the conditioned air keeping away the heat. The view, that gorgeous view, lay bare before her eyes, the sunlight glinting off the water at one end and climbing over the buildings at the other.

Hopping up on the stool she'd been sitting on the previous evening, she thought of preparing some coffee for herself then thought better of it. The truce was over. She'd already been drugged once. She wasn't a fool enough to be again.

The sound of the elevator opening made her turn quickly, her hand resting on her handbag, where her gun resided. Her grip on the bag eased slightly when she saw Amara walking towards her, her tall, curvy body encased in tan slacks, a red top, and green silk scarf, her dark, wild curls falling around her beautiful face, a small smile on her lips.

"Good morning, Morana," the woman nodded, her forest-green eyes bright.

Morana relaxed slightly and nodded back. "Amara."

Amara smiled and pulled open the fridge. The familiar manner with which she moved around the space as she got glasses from cabinets irked Morana for some reason. She grit her teeth and turned away, looking out at the view.

"Would you like some juice?"

Morana turned back to see her holding up some orange juice in her hand, her head tilted in a query. She hesitated and Amara smiled. "It's not drugged, don't worry."

Mentally shaking her head at herself, Morana nodded.

"I cannot blame you for worrying, though. Not after what happened at the club," Amara kept on speaking, pouring out the cool liquid in two tall glasses, her voice that same soft timbre it had been, making Morana's heart clench, her mind racing with questions about this woman who'd shown her only kindness. What was it like for her, knowing she could never speak above a whisper? Did it hurt if she spoke louder? Did she carry physical scars too? How badly had she been tortured?

Morana blinked the questions away, more pressing ones rising in her mind.

"Did you get back to the club safely that night?" she asked as the other woman sat across from her, her elbows on the table.

111

"Yes," Amara replied in her soft rasp. "Tristan was there. I was safe."

Coming from a woman who'd been tortured as a girl, that one statement told Morana a lot. She filed it away for later and continued with the questions.

"Do you know who got in the SUV after you and Mr. Caine made it to the club?"

Amara frowned slightly, her lips pursing. "No. Did something happen?"

Morana sighed, shaking her head. There was no point in telling her the story if he hadn't. Had he told Dante? Or had he omitted information again?

"Although," the woman mused, her dark eyes blinking in memory, "now that I think of it, Tristan did hurry back out when he saw the SUV going again."

Morana watched Amara take a sip from her glass, and satisfied that it was fine, she took a sip from hers. The sweet, cool drink washed down her throat, tingling her senses as she sat straighter, her eyes on the other woman.

"You're incredibly brave, you know," Amara spoke in that hushed voice of hers, a smile on her lips.

Morana blinked in surprise, before feeling herself flush slightly. "Um, thank you, I guess."

The other woman chuckled at her awkward response, completely relaxed in the space. "Tristan is an intimidating man, all on his own. And he goes out of his way to intimidate you more. The fact that you spent the night alone at his house tells me a lot about you. Although being the only child of a man as reputed as your father... I don't know why I'm surprised. You're strong. I admire that."

Flushing harder, even as she tried to keep it under wraps, Morana cleared her throat. She'd never received any kind of compliment on anything besides her intelligence. And getting one now, about something so rooted in who she was, was unsettling, to say the least.

Ready to change the topic, she took a deep breath and –

"Do you live here?"

– wanted to disappear into thin air.

Amara choked a little on her juice, her eyes widening before she burst out laughing, the sound soft but genuine. "With Tristan? Good lord, no!"

It bothered Morana that she relaxed at that.

Amara continued chuckling. "That man is territorial about his space. Very territorial. I once entered his room without knocking, he almost glared the life out of me!"

Everything inside Morana stilled with the information.

She had entered his room without permission yesterday. She had stood, right on the edge of his space, and he'd seen her. Except he hadn't glared. He'd been affected.

Words, his words, from weeks ago filled her mind.

*'I have territory that is mine. Don't ever invade it.'*

Had those just been words in an attempt to assert his control as she'd thought, or something more?

Amara's voice broke her out of her thoughts.

"Tristan doesn't allow people into his space. Everyone who knows him knows that."

Morana blinked, still reeling from questions about the incredibly baffling man. "Then why did he let me, of all people, stay here?" Why had he insisted that she stay? Why had he growled like that when Dante had been ready to offer her his apartment?

Amara's eyes sharpened slightly, a smile on her lips. "It's curious, isn't it?"

Morana stayed silent. Amara shook her head. "So, to answer your question, no, I don't live here. But I live nearby."

Her curiosity piqued. "You don't live in Tenebrae?"

Morana saw Amara's eyes shadow as she looked away, out at the view. An air of pensiveness hung around her shoulders as she sighed, the sigh wrenched from deep in her soul.

"I can visit my family there, but I haven't been allowed to stay."

Interesting choice of words.

"Why?" Morana asked before she could stop herself.

Amara looked at Morana, her dark eyes pained, carrying dark burdens even as her lips smiled wryly. "Some things are better left

113

unanswered, Morana. My home is there. My mother still serves the Maroni household. My roots, everything I am, everyone that I love - it's all there. But I'm cursed not to stay."

Morana blinked, feeling her heart ache for the woman. Amara had a home, a loving place where she could never live. Morana lived in one place but didn't have a home. And in that moment, she felt the woman's pain.

Before she knew it, her hand was crossing the space between them, taking hold of Amara's and squeezing softly. "I'm sorry."

Morana saw the surprise in the other woman's eyes at the gesture, even as she squeezed her hand back, her expression soft, grateful.

She shrugged. "I just miss home sometimes. That's why I get so happy when Tristan or Dante visit."

"You must have friends here," Morana mused.

"Not really," Amara looked down. "I'm here for work, mainly. Plus, it's not my city. I have limitations."

Morana wanted to tell her to give her a call sometime. She wanted to tell her she didn't have any friends either. She wanted to tell her she would love to be friends with her own brave self.

But she couldn't.

She had the words, on the tip of her tongue, ready to tumble out. She had that need, so, so deep inside her, to know someone, to have a friend, to share her life and stories with a person. But actions like that could have consequences, not only for her but for Amara too. She had been banished by her own city and sent here. Morana couldn't get her thrown out, or killed.

She bit her lip and pulled back her hand, clearing her throat, looking out from the glass wall inside her, reaching but unable to touch.

The sound of the elevator opening saved her from any awkward silence.

Morana turned again to see the newcomers, her eyes falling on Dante and Tristan Caine walking in, both tall, broad, incredibly handsome men. She saw Dante falter for a second as his eyes fell on Amara, but he continued approaching them, dressed in another sharp suit. The man beside him, on the other hand, strode in gracefully, drawing Morana's eyes. Again.

114

She could feel her stomach knot as her eyes locked with his, those sharp blue eyes looking magnificent in the sunlight, his tight, muscled body in a simple t-shirt and cargo pants, telling her wherever they had been, it had been informal enough for him to go casually.

"I see you've made yourself comfortable in my kitchen, Amara," he spoke, in that whiskeyed voice of his, to the woman behind her even as his eyes stayed on hers.

"Just in your kitchen," Amara responded, her voice soft but perky.

Dante walked to the glass walls, his hands in his pockets, and looked out at the view, completely ignoring everyone in the room. Morana observed the other man, sensing the tension between him and Amara. She'd sensed it before as well.

Curious, she looked back at Tristan Caine, only to find him rifling through his cabinets, his eyes coming to hers just as hers went to him.

He looked at her.

Her heart stuttered.

He looked away.

Her heart started.

Closing her eyes at her own stupid reactions, Morana cleared her throat, turning towards Dante, where he stood against the wall.

"Did you find anything at the warehouses?"

Dante didn't turn but spoke loudly. "Not at the one here. But there were certain... oddities at the ones in Tenebrae."

"Oddities?" Morana leaned forward, interested.

"That warehouse had been owned by one of our local competitors a long time ago," Dante informed her, his profile in the sun sharp. "Except for the equipment my men found belonged to another gang. We can't figure out who'd used it yet."

Morana narrowed her eyes, the wheels in her mind churning. "What would it mean for Mr. Caine if the codes were to be used and he was to be framed?"

Dante turned around, his eyes hard on hers. "It would mean his death, Morana."

So she could rule out Tristan Caine playing a mastermind game and framing himself. Unless the man was on a suicide mission.

115

"You'll know of any developments the moment they occur," Dante promised her, and Morana nodded, refusing to turn towards the other man.

Amara cleared her throat. "I'd actually just come to give these to you, Morana."

Morana looked at the counter, to find her car keys resting there. Her car, her baby, was fixed. Her eyes flew up to lock with Tristan Caine's. He wasn't looking at her.

Morana nodded, her heart accelerating, and jumped down from the high stool, hitching her handbag over her shoulder and grabbing her keys.

"I should leave now," she muttered, looking around once.

Dante gave her a polite nod, to which she nodded back, knowing they'd be in touch.

Amara smiled at her. "I hope we meet again, Morana."

Morana swallowed. "Me too."

And then she turned around, without a word to the owner of the penthouse, without a look in his direction, without an expression of the gratefulness she was feeling. She walked towards the elevator, with quick, sure steps, her eyes going to the view outside one last time, memorizing it, etching itself into her memory like the previous night had been etched on her soul.

No one spoke a word behind her. The tension caressed her back as she entered the elevator, her heart pounding, her palms sweating.

Taking a deep breath, she turned to press the button, and found her eyes locking, for one last time, with magnificent blue ones, where he stood in the kitchen, watching her.

Morana pressed the button, their gazes locked.

And the doors closed.

Something was wrong.

The moment she breezed through the mansion doors, the deep, deep sense of foreboding settled into her stomach.

She shouldn't have returned. She should have taken her fixed, amazing car and hightailed it to someplace other than this mansion. But she hadn't. Because Morana Vitalio was many things but she wasn't a coward. And if she was going to die, she was going to die knowing that.

Gritting her teeth, she parked the car in the spot and got out, her eyes roving over the new wheels. How had Tristan Caine gotten it repaired overnight, on a stormy night? Were his connections that good?

Shaking her head, and shoving that baffling man out of her thoughts, Morana took in the beautiful, sunlit lawns, the gorgeous driveway and the stunning mansion.

And felt nothing but more foreboding.

She was going to leave. The moment the codes were found, she promised herself, she was going to run away and disappear, change her identity, make a life for herself, just like she wanted. She was going to go someplace far, far away and make friends without hesitation, meet men and have fun, and live without death dangling every day over her head.

The moment the codes were destroyed, she was leaving everything behind.

Feeling the strength seep into her with that decision, Morana started towards her wing, intending to head straight to her room, the eyes of her father's men following her, when she saw the man in question sitting outside in the gazebo, with two other old, gruff men, discussing business.

He saw her enter and motioned for her to come to him with his fingers, a gesture that irritated her to no extent. Morana would have loved to show him her own finger and stride up to her suite, but he was with other people, and she knew defiance like that, especially after last night, might push him too far.

So, gritting her teeth again in a handful of minutes, Morana walked over to where he sat, the large canopy of leaves overhead providing shade for everyone seated.

Her father looked up at her, his eyes completely neutral, not a flicker in them. "We are dining out tonight at *Crimson*. Dress accordingly."

117

Morana nodded and waited for him to say anything more. He raised his eyebrows and dismissed her with another flick of his fingers.

Hands clenched in fists, she turned away and walked up to her suite, locking the door firmly behind her.

Then, she sat down on her bed.

And thought.

This was off. She'd expected him to be angry or even taunting. She'd expected him to be indifferent like he had always been. But this... it almost seemed manipulative. His calm, after she'd spent the night out, was troublesome. It wasn't a good calm. And for some reason, her stomach was in knots, and not of the good kind. Not the knots she liked.

*'Your independence is an illusion I've let you sustain.'*

Taking a deep breath, Morana stood up and headed towards the bathroom, the knots only getting worse with each step.

*Crimson.*

Her lips were crimson. The blood rushing inside her body was crimson. The blood she wanted to see come out of the other man's nose would be crimson.

Clenching her jaw, Morana sat in the restaurant, on the table in the corner that was always reserved for her father, dressed appropriately in a black sleeveless, backless dress that flared out in a skirt from her waist. The only notable thing about it was the simple split on the side. Four other men sat around the table, excluding her father.

Her father had not spoken a word to her throughout the day, and while it wasn't out of the ordinary, it was out of the ordinary after the stunt she'd pulled. It hadn't been an ordinary day. Usually, she drove her own car to the dinners she attended. Tonight, her father had simply told her to get inside his town car. She'd almost protested when he'd given her a silencing look.

"It is important we arrive together," he'd told her.

Morana had bitten her tongue and gotten in the car.

And now she sat, realizing why her father had wanted them to arrive together. It wasn't just dinner. It was a *humiliating* dinner.

One of the men, a handsome man in his early thirties, sat beside Morana, trying for the third time to get his hand under the split in her dress. The first time she'd thought it had been an accidental brush. The second time she'd brushed his hand aside with a stern look in his direction. This time, though, her temper spiked.

She took a hold of his hand in her grip and bent his fingers backward.

"Touch me again, and I will break your fingers."

Silence fell upon the table at her words. Her father glanced at her, raising an eyebrow. She waited for him to reprimand her or the man. He just turned away, engaging the others back into the conversation, like a guy ten years her senior hadn't tried to molest her under the table.

Morana threw the man's hand away from herself in disgust. She leaned back in her chair, taking a deep, controlled breath, anger invading her bones.

"The Outfit is here."

The words of one of the middle-aged men at the table broke through her crimson haze.

Her father nodded. "I know. Security is in place."

On cue, for the first time, Morana looked around the restaurant to realize her father was right. The place, the entire place, was crawling with security. Both theirs and the Outfit's. Men in plainclothes sat alert at tables, weapons concealed but obvious against their clothes, the threat of an outburst hanging violently in the air. Civilians, seemingly aware of whatever was going down, were tensed and finishing their meals as quickly as they could. The staff walked around on eggshells and nervousness dripped from every tray.

Morana let her eyes wander and take in everything, trying to locate the table of the Outfit, but unable to see the two men she recognized anywhere in the restaurant.

But her nape prickled.

She could feel eyes on her.

His eyes.

Hungry eyes.

Her breath hitched. She didn't know how she knew it was him. She didn't want to think about how she knew it was him. But she knew. It was the same gaze she'd seen in his territory. The same gaze she could feel in hers.

Picking up her glass of wine, she let her eyes roam covertly over the space again, trying to pin where he sat. She couldn't, which only meant their table was behind her.

She didn't turn. Turning would mean acknowledging not just him, but the Outfit, and with her father behaving the way he was, she stayed in position.

But she felt those eyes caress every inch of her exposed back, felt her nape prickle in awareness as her body buzzed with sensation, imagining him, sitting somewhere, devouring her with those blue, blue eyes. He would be in a suit, like the ones she'd seen him in. A suit that would hide his scars and tattoos, and highlight his muscles. Morana swallowed, keeping her eyes down, her entire body rushing with heat just thinking about him.

She shouldn't be thinking about him.

But god help her, she couldn't stop.

Closing her eyes, inhaling softly, she quickly brought her phone on her lap and opened a window, typing a message, her hand hovering on the 'send' button.

He could see her. He *was* seeing her. And she was at a disadvantage. Nodding, on the tail of that thought, she hit 'send'.

Her heart started to pound, indecision warring with grit, unable to understand why she'd sent him that message.

*Stop staring.*

Her inbox glowed with a new message. Heart hammering, Morana pressed on it.

**Tristan Caine:** *No.*

No. Just no? How eloquent.

*Me: Your funeral. My father might see and kill you.*

A message came back almost immediately.

**Tristan Caine:** *I highly doubt it.*

*Me: And why is that?*

**Tristan Caine:** *He barely raised a finger at the dick pawing you. He won't kill me for staring.*

Morana felt her face flush, humiliated anger washing over her, anger that turned into fury as she realized the truth in that statement. She was just a piece of property that one man could touch and others could watch to her father. Her body almost trembled but she grit her teeth.

*Me: He's a guest. You're not.*

There was a pause before the reply came.

**Tristan Caine:** *So he can touch you and I cannot?*

Her heart stopped. Before pounding with a vengeance. He'd never spoken to her like that.

*Me: This conversation is over.*

She locked her phone. And unlocked it again.
New message. She swallowed.

**Tristan Caine:** *Chicken.*

Morana stopped, blinking at the screen for a second before anger infused her again. Chicken? Who the fuck did he think he was? He was clearly baiting her, and she'd be damned if she took it.

Before she could lock her phone, he was typing again.

**Tristan Caine:** *I dare you.*

*Don't. Don't take the bait,* Morana kept on repeating.

**Me:** *To do what?*

Long pause. Heart thundering, she waited, careful not to seem too engrossed.

**Tristan Caine:** *To show him even half the wildcat you are.*

Morana locked her phone away. She wouldn't rise to the bait. She absolutely was not going to fall for that. She was a grown woman and not a toddler. There were men with weapons ready to rain bullets on everyone and she could not trigger them.

But she could feel that stare on her back, zinging across her skin.

*She wasn't going to rise to the bait. She wasn't going to rise to the bait. She wasn't going to rise to the bait.*

And the asshole groped her thigh again.

Everything she'd been feeling all day, all the confusion, the anger, the frustration, the heat - everything mingled together. Her fingers were wrapped around the man's hand before she knew it, and she snapped his wrist back hard, not enough to break a bone but enough to give him a serious sprain.

"You bitch!"

He cried out loud, cradling the hand to his chest, his handsome face twisted in agony as the entire restaurant went silent. Morana felt multiple eyes on her, felt a few weapons pointed at her. She ignored them all, rising from the table.

"Morana," her father ground out, his voice hard.

"I warned him to keep his hands off," she told him aloud, every inch of her body aware of the climbing tension. "He refused."

The tension climbed. No one spoke.

"She's got fire, Gabriel," one of the men on the table hooted, his eyes crawling over her exposed skin. "I wouldn't mind getting burned."

"You're welcome to die," Morana spit back at him.

Her father didn't address the man, but her. "Go cool yourself down."

Disgust plastered all over her face, she picked up her clutch and turned towards the corridor that led to the washrooms, not sparing anyone a single glance, her body trembling with rage.

She'd almost turned the corridor when her eyes locked with his.

Her step slowed, as she took him in, that dark suit and open collar he always wore out before her disgust with the entire male population filled her. His eyes were watching her, completely blank of any look. The moment she let her disgust show, his eyes flared with something. She turned before she could linger and read what.

Entering the restroom, she placed her hands on the clean granite counter, watching her own self in the mirror, the cubicles at the other end empty.

What was she doing there? In the restaurant, in her life? Why was she even doing anything? Her father didn't care one wink about her. Nobody did. And it made her angry.

She was angry because a strange man had groped her right in front of her father and he hadn't said a word. She was angry because she'd messaged the man she hated and he'd prodded her to act rather than anyone else. She was angry because she'd left that glass wall and rainy night and yet something inside her completely refused to leave it.

She was *angry*.

And she could see it. On her flushed face, on her trembling body, on her heated skin.

She was angry. God, she was so angry.

The door to the restroom opened, and Morana looked down, hiding her eyes from whoever had entered. The last thing she wanted was a casual chitchat with some clueless woman.

She washed her hands and pressed the cool water on her cheeks, waiting for some sound behind her as the other woman moved about. There was no sound.

Stilling, her body alert, she looked up slowly, to find her eyes ensnared with blue, blue ones.

He was there, in the ladies' room, in a restaurant filled with men and women of both their families and guns and weapons ready to be fired. Was he *insane?*

Morana turned on her heels, heading towards the door, the rage inside her kindling, only to find him blocking her path.

"Get out of my way," she spit out, in no mood to deal with him.

"So you can go out to your father and that dickhead?" he goaded, his voice washing over her in a way she completely did not want in that moment.

Gritting her teeth, she tried to sidestep him, only to fail. The anger simmered.

"Get. Out. Of. My. Way," she enunciated, every word hard, her tone frigid.

He didn't budge.

And she *let it out.*

Her fingers circled his neck before she could blink, and she slammed her entire body into his. He fell a step back against the door, not because of her strength (she knew well enough to know not to fool herself into that), but because he wanted to. His eyes blazed on hers as he tilted his head, uncaring that she could strangle him. Her fingers flexed on those corded muscles, warm muscles, and the urge to let out all her anger, for some reason, assaulted her. Because whatever the reason, he was honest about his hatred of her. She appreciated that honesty. She needed that honesty.

But she was on the edge. On an edge she hadn't known she'd been walking. She was tiptoeing now.

"I asked for one simple thing," she ground out, her mouth trembling. "I told you to stay away from me. You agreed. You gave me your word. Then why is it that I find you everywhere I turn? I'm warning you, right now, I won't give a damn about the codes. You all can die for all I care. You. Stay. The. Fuck. Away. From. Me."

124

Before she could even blink, her front was pressed against the door, the hand that had been on his neck twisted behind her back firmly but not painfully, her other palm pressed flat on the wood as he pressed into her back, her completely bareback, the buttons of his shirt rubbing against the exposed line of her spine with each breath they took. A woodsy, musky scent she knew was him wrapped all around her as his other hand pressed on the wood beside her own. Her body shook as she turned her face sideways, her forehead brushing against the scruff of his chin as he leaned down, his lips lined against her ear.

Her heart thundered in her chest, blood pounding in her ears. Heat infused her body, the scent, the feel, the sensations heady.

"Get one thing straight, right now, Ms. Vitalio," he murmured right against the shell of her ear, that voice – that voice of whiskey and sin – rolling down her spine in waves, spreading throughout her body, pooling low in her belly. The sensation of those lips made her chest heave against the wooden door. The wooden door that was the only barrier between them and a restaurant full of people, including her father, who wouldn't hesitate to kill either of them.

That knowledge sent another thrill through her. That knowledge that for some reason, this man made her feel like a dangerous woman; that knowledge that for some reason, she knew this man wouldn't let anyone else kill her. And she stood inside with him pressed to her, not an ounce of remorse for betraying her father inside her. The thrill was all that there was.

"I will stay away when I want to," he whispered. "Not because you or anyone else tell me to. But I've never forced a woman, and I won't now."

Morana bit her lip, realizing he wasn't touching her anywhere except where her hand was behind her back. He wasn't touching her, and she felt on fire.

"We've been honest so far, Ms. Vitalio," he murmured. "I'll be honest now. I despise you but I want you. Fuck it, I do. And I want you out of my system."

The crude way he spoke made her breaths heave faster. He continued.

125

"Your father's men are right outside this door this very second. You want me gone? Just say the word."

Morana stilled, her head turning towards the wood, her breaths rapid in the confined space.

"You need to make a decision."

Holy fuck. How was she supposed to make a decision with her brain fried? God, she wanted him. She'd had sex once, with Jackson, mostly out of rebellion, but it hadn't been something she'd wanted to repeat anytime soon. There hadn't been even a quarter of the heat just locking gazes with this man had. She'd never felt so heady, so carnal, so, so utterly wanton in her own lust.

And that was the crux of the entire problem. She hated him, everything he had done and every word he'd said. She wanted to kill him someday. But her body wanted him. And she wanted him out of her system. Just once.

Her father was right outside. His men were right outside. The Outfit was right outside.

Tristan Caine was inside. Behind her.

She wanted him inside her.

Morana closed her eyes, raising her free hand to the top corner of the wooden door.

And she locked it.

Decision made.

# *silencing*

**B**reaths.

She could hear his breaths, right against her neck, blowing softly over her ear, heating the skin it washed over. Her neck tingled. Blood rushed over the spot, igniting it with a flame she was unfamiliar with, his exhale kindling it, higher and higher, just across that expanse of skin. Her heart stuttered, her fingers pressing harder into the wood, her trapped arm wanting to squirm. She barely contained the urge, standing still except for her heaving breasts, her fingers tingling with the need for touch, for sensation, hungry for contact with warm male flesh she could feel behind her, not pressing into her but so, so present.

She turned her face towards his.

Breaths.

A scent of scotch and chocolate, mixed in a heady concoction she wanted to taste on her mouth. Her eyes flickered down to his lips, tracing them with her gaze, seeing the ripe fullness of it, making her teeth want to sink in them, test their plushness, their softness. Her eyes went to the scar at the corner of his lip, peeking out from under his scruff, making her tongue heavy, wanting to lick it, to taste it, feel it. Her gaze lingered on the scruff around his mouth, wondering if it would scratch against her skin, itch, or maybe burn, leave the marks of his devouring for the world to see, red and pink skin burning with the memory of his hunger.

The world definitely couldn't see.

And neither could she later.

No. She wanted him, but she wanted him out of her system more. This was a one-time thing, and she wanted absolutely no memories of it, ever. Not once that door opened and she walked out on her heels. She wanted to get to her codes and get the hell out of this life. She wanted this just to be a thrilling memory in her past. Nothing more.

Turning her eyes up, she locked her gaze with those magnificent eyes, the blue darkened to just a rim on the outside, telling her he was serious about this, not faking anything. He was aroused, very aroused. His breaths were heavy, deep, controlled but his eyes were blazing with such intense lust and hatred, that familiar hatred that she didn't even blink at anymore.

"Keep your mouth away from me," she told him in a low voice.

His face remained completely passive, only an annoying eyebrow hiking up. "I had no intention of bringing my mouth anywhere near you."

Morana grit her teeth, the residual anger burning deep in her belly. She didn't know why it offended her, given she had suggested it, given she wanted it, but she was offended and it made her angrier. This was just a quick fuck. There was no point in complicating it.

"Just your cock then," she told him crudely, unabashedly, her body flaring with fury and desire, mingling in a way she couldn't tell which was which anymore.

He let her hand go, his eyes narrowing slightly, but he didn't move. "How much experience do you have?"

The question fuelled the fire even more. If he thought she was telling him anything about her sexual history, he was more deluded than she thought. Her hands fisted beside her before she knew it, her spine straightening.

"How badly do you want to get punched?" she growled out, her voice barely low enough to not be heard outside the door.

He didn't say a word, that amalgamation of lust and hate pure blaze in his eyes, his head tilting to a side as he kept his eyes on hers, his face completely bland of any expression.

Morana waited, for a word, for a move, for a wrong breath to tip her over and murder him. She was that close.

128

He didn't do a thing. Not a thing.

Just watched her with narrowed eyes.

And that tipped her over.

"Go fuck yourself," she spit out and turned to the door, to open it and leave, humiliation churning through her stomach on the tail of everything else. She was trembling. Trembling. Trembling like her body couldn't contain anything anymore, as though she was a bomb ticking to its doom, ready to take down everything and everyone around her. Oh, if she was a bomb, she wanted to explode and take down this asshole first. Or maybe her father. And the creep at the table. It was a freaking line. And wasn't that her jolly life.

She almost turned to the door when in a split second, it happened.

His hands gripped her waist before she'd taken one step, picking her up with a kind of strength she'd never experienced, making her heart fall to her knees. She barely contained a yelp at the sudden movement, but the moment her feet were off the floor, he moved her like she weighed nothing more than a cushion, and put her on the granite counter in front of the mirror.

The cold granite hit the overheated skin of ass suddenly, making her hiss, the counter hard against his not-so-gentle deposition.

Her dress bunched up against her upper thighs in the motion, the cold granite against her exposed flesh making her shiver. His hands left her waist and the moment they did, she put her hands flat on the counter, a little behind her to maintain her sitting position and keep her balance. The action made her breasts push outwards, her legs slightly spread from the way he'd deposited her, with her dress almost above her thighs. She felt a flush crawl over her face at the wanton picture she made, never having displayed herself so carnally to anyone.

Her gaze locked with his as he stood two steps away from her, his eyes sharp on hers, before slowly going down her neck, her cleavage, her heaving breasts to the top of her thighs, all the way down to her toes in a slow, languid perusal. Her breasts got heavier, nipples hardening unabashedly as heat pooled even heavier in her belly, her breaths hastening.

She did her own perusal, her eyes roving over that hard, male chest she'd felt pressed against her so many times in the muted yellow lights in the room, the chest she'd seen bare just a day ago, the suit covering the hard muscles as the open collar exposed a strip of delicious male flesh that made her want to lick it, from the line of his pecs to the vein running at the side of his corded neck, right up to that chin, then that scar, and the mouth. God, why couldn't he have been some old, ugly, pot-bellied bastard with bad breath and worse smell and creepy eyes and a squeaky voice? But he wasn't. He was who he was, and she let herself see him, her eyes drifting lower and lower to below his waist.

And her breath hitched.

The front of his trousers bulged out, unashamed and unapologetic, tenting the fabric in a big way. Big. Bigger than Jackson. Much bigger.

And she felt a frisson of fear cool the lust. Fuck what had she gotten herself into? She'd never had sex like this, she was inexperienced and he was big, and he hated her.

Her eyes flew up to clash with his, doubts filling her.

Before she could blink, he closed the gap between them, his hands going straight to her thighs, parting them wide as he stepped between her legs, his face inches from hers, his eyes still holding that mix of sheer lust and utter hate, more than hate for just her. Was it for himself? For wanting her? Because lord knew she hated herself for wanting this. Wanting him.

His hips snapped to hers, her dress bunching up even higher, and her breath locked in her throat. She felt him, pressed into her, right against her core, his hard, hard erection rubbing deliciously against her bundle of nerves. And she was wet. Getting wetter with every rub of his length against her. At this rate, she'd leave a wet spot at the front of his pants, and that just wouldn't do.

And then another thought struck her.

"You have a condom, right?" she blurted out before she knew it. Even though she had measures, she could ride him bareback but she didn't trust him an inch, and she so did not want him spilling inside her.

He stilled, anger flaring in his eyes.

She grit her teeth, her fingers pressing into the cold granite. "Don't think for one second you're getting anywhere inside me without one."

One of his hands came up, circling the front of her neck like she had circled his moments ago. His grip was firm, just on the edge of threatening but not quite into the territory yet. He tilted her head up by pressing on her neck – his big, rough hand warm against her already hot neck – and a shiver traveled down her spine, suddenly making her realize how easy it would be for him to snap her neck. She'd seen him snap necks as normal people blinked. He could kill her, right there, in the ladies' room of one of the poshest restaurants in town, and given his strength, she knew she wouldn't be able to stop him.

Her anger crackled.

"Do you?" she demanded, keeping her fear locked deep inside her, never blinking away from his hypnotic gaze.

"Are you a virgin?" he asked, his voice soft, lethal, whiskey over her senses, making her heady. And it was a sensible question. For once.

"No," she told him, raising her eyebrows, daring him to utter a word.

He didn't speak.

But he put his other hand right between her legs without preamble, his fingers pushing aside the fabric of her panties and diving straight into the core of her.

Her back arched.

A current zinged through her body, making her toes curl in her heels, the scent of her own arousal wafting up to her, making her even wetter. One of his hands circling the front of her neck, the other plowing into her folds expertly, his eyes holding hers captive.

Morana realized in that moment how much control he was exerting over her, how much control she was giving him. And with the realization came a wave of hatred and rage. Her body might betray her, her mind wouldn't.

Removing one hand from the counter, resting her weight on the other palm, she placed it right over his bulge, gripping it like he was gripping her neck, squeezing once. His hips thrust towards her sharply, barely missing the edge of the counter as his eyes flared with temper. He knew what she was doing. He'd made her vulnerable. She'd made him. Bingo.

His fingers never penetrated her, just kept circling round and round, completely avoiding her nub, just straying around her opening, sending currents of pleasure and such deep, utter need through her she would

131

have begged had it been anyone else. She barely controlled anyways, biting her lip to keep the whimper of need from escaping, refusing to give him the satisfaction.

Her fingers tightened over his length in response, and a low sound rumbled in his chest, barely heard because of their proximity. Had he been anyone else, she would have taken a moment to admire the control he had over himself. He felt big in her palm, bigger than her hand, bigger than she could hold all at once, and her walls clenched with desire as hunger for flesh gnawed at her. Her breaths came out in soft pants as her heart thundered, completely beyond her control now.

And he stopped.

Removed his hands.

From both her neck and her folds.

She'd kill him, truly kill him, if he stopped now.

He removed his wallet from his pocket, his fingers glistening with her essence, the sight of her own desire on his rough digits, the realization that his fingers had been there, sending another wave of unchecked heat through her body. At this rate, she would combust before he even got inside her.

He pulled out a condom, tearing the wrapper with his teeth. Morana didn't look down as he unzipped his trousers. Neither did he.

And suddenly, before she could take another breath, his hand came back to her neck, this time the back of her neck like it had at the penthouse, his other on the granite beside hers.

She felt the tip of his erection brush against her clit, and her breaths quickened, the realization that she was doing this, with him of all people, thrilling some deep-rooted part of her. She wanted this. She hated it, and she was mad at herself for it. But she needed this.

She needed him to rut against her and make her explode, not like a bomb but like a woman, so, so badly. God, she needed to scream her lungs out as he fucked her like his eyes promised every single time he'd looked at her, like they had promised since they'd met. She needed to feel wanton, sexed-up. And she hated it. Hated that need. Hated him for making her need like a desperate maniac.

A rapid heartbeat passed.

And suddenly, he thrust inside, burying himself to the hilt in one stroke.

A cry left her mouth before she could stop it, the burning sensation, her own wetness lubricating him, his big size spearing into her depths in that one stroke, making her breath catch, her heart hammering as the pressure of his presence filled her. He pulled out before she'd even felt him completely, hitting back in, *hard*, without waiting for another breath. This time she bit her lip, hard, containing her cry of pleasure as sensations assaulted every inch of her skin, the fire rising to a crescendo inside her body as her breasts bounced once from his hard thrust.

He pulled out again before she'd even acclimated to his size, bending his chin down to his chest, hiding his face from her.

She deliberately closed her eyes, not wanting to remember his face when he felt every inch of her walls squeezing him like they were, her body unable to hide any reaction from his. She didn't want to see the gloating triumph or the smirk or worse, genuine pleasure. She didn't want to see anything but stars behind her eyelids as he pulled her apart.

He pulled out, snapped back again.

Currents traveled up and down her body, her breaths coming faster and faster, her heart beating wilder and wilder, the smell of sex and his woodsy scent filling the restroom quickly. She got wetter and wetter with every thrust, wetter than she'd ever been before, wetter than she should have been, barely containing her moans of pure bliss, her body going in a state of nirvana.

The sounds of their rapid breaths and barely contained sounds filled the room. Her blood pounded loudly in her ears. Her palms ached from being pressed so hard into the granite. Her back arched as her spine curved, legs hitching higher on his hips to get a better angle as he got into the rhythm of the movements, quick, fast, hard, his hand hard on the back of her neck the only other place he touched her.

And then another sound penetrated her lust induced daze.

A knock.

*Fuck.*

Her eyes opened, flying towards the door as he stilled, turning his neck towards the door as well, his erection completely still inside her for the first time, throbbing like an electric wire with a pulse. Her walls clenched tightly around him as she felt him completely filling her more than she'd ever been filled, so, so tight a fit she felt like a custom made sheath around his blade.

The knock came again, making her blink, making her realize where she was – in a restaurant full of people with weapons, men of the mob, and her father, his enemies, just a door outside.

Someone actually stood a few feet away, just separated from them by a thin wooden door. And she sat there on a counter, fucked up, with Tristan Caine throbbing inside her.

Holy expletives.

"Ms. Vitalio?" a man's voice penetrated her consciousness, making her eyes widen slightly on the door. "Your father has asked you to come out."

Oh lord.

She was close.

So close.

The door was close too.

Ah…

She saw Tristan Caine turn his face back towards her, his face blank, his eyebrows raised. Nobody seeing him would believe he was standing in a restroom, buried balls deep inside her, getting harder by the moment. What did the man seriously eat?

Her eyes locked with his, and he tilted his head to the door, telling her to answer silently.

She took a deep breath, an action that caused her inner walls to spasm around him, shooting heat up her spine.

And Tristan Caine pulled out suddenly, thrusting in just as hard.

*Holy…!*

Her mouth opened instinctively to cry out loud at the suddenness of the movement, and his other hand clapped over her mouth, muffling the sound. Her eyes widened on his, *stunned.*

Had he just covered her mouth? *Actually covered* her mouth?

Her father's man was right outside the door, waiting. Right outside the door. Was this man insane?

As though in answer, he snapped his hips into her sharply, the angle hitting a spot inside her that made her eyes roll back into her head even as sounds tried to escape her, muffled against his large hand. His pace increased suddenly, becoming more rapid than it had been, becoming faster than she'd thought a man could possibly ever move, becoming so quick he was in and out of her before she could even breathe.

If she'd been incoherent before, she was barely lucid now. The friction, the pressure of his hips pistoning into hers, the sheer thrill of being fucked while her father's man stood outside the door, her mouth covered and neck held made heat singe through her.

Her hands were moving away from the granite counter and holding on to his shoulders before she could stop herself, her nails digging into his hard, hard muscles as his hand on her neck held her weight, like it had in the penthouse, the sheer strength in his body making her try to flex her hips and match his pace. But she couldn't. He moved so fast, so quick, she was just pinned to the spot, letting him move in and out and in and out of her without doing anything except breathe, her walls clenching and unclenching at a pace that couldn't match his ardent hips.

It was basic, primitive, carnal.

It was heated, wild, insane.

But it was making her scream against his hand and see stars behind her closed eyelids.

Her nipples hurt, scraping against her the fabric of the dress, needing touch so badly. She wanted to grab his hands and push them on her breasts. She wanted to pull her dress down, pull his head down and make him suck her aching nipples. She wanted to feel the lash on his tongue against her hungry breasts, feel the rasp of his tongue, feel the wetness of his mouth as his hips moved into hers like a machine.

But she couldn't. She dug her fingers into his flesh.

God, she hated him. But he was good at this. Very good.

The knock came again.

Awareness slithered down her spine even as she curved it, her breasts rising and falling rapidly as a bead of sweat rolled down her cleavage, her hands tightening on his shoulders, his flexing on her neck.

And then, he suddenly bent his knees, thrusting upwards, and her mind blanked. *Blanked,* feeling the force of that thrust down to her bones. Her teeth clenched, the coiled heat in her belly winding tighter and tighter and tighter. He speared her again and again, and her toes singed with the sudden roar of heat, traveling up and up her legs and spine to where he held her neck, starting from where he drilled and drilled and ending where his hand rested, the coil curling and curling and curling even as the heat spread through her limbs.

And suddenly, with one more thrust, her body locked, everything exploding, behind her eyelids in pure, sheer black, inside her body with a consuming fire she'd never felt, outside her skin in a clenching of muscles as her neck tilted back, her hips lifting off the counter from the sheer power of her orgasm, her mouth opening in a silent scream for a split second under his palm. His hips kept moving, in and out and in and out, hitting that spot again and again and again.

It was too much. She tried to shake her head, her body screaming in ecstasy, but his hands didn't let her move.

He kept moving.

She kept exploding.

And she bit down on his hand before she realized it, trying to find some purchase of the intense currents of pleasure zapping all her senses, making her wail and whine and whimper in her throat as she bit and bit and bit on his hand, drawing blood.

The knock came again.

The taste of copper and rust filled her mouth. He didn't remove his hand. She didn't remove her teeth.

And he thrust in, one last time, before stilling, expanding inside her before flexing his hips in reflex, exploding into his own orgasm, her walls quivering around him in stunned aftershocks. His own small, shallow thrusts spurred more from them, milking her as she milked him for all he was worth, his hand tight on her neck, a low rumbling sound the only sound from him. His breaths were rapid, quick, and shallow like his thrusts, her own matching his.

She was done. *So done.*

She couldn't feel her limbs. Couldn't feel her face. Couldn't even feel her teeth.

She'd never felt this.

Her eyes remained closed, her breaths rapidly moving through her, feeling him soften inside her slowly.

"Morana?" her father's voice invaded her fried brain.

As did the ice.

"Stop sulking like a child and come outside," her father ordered from the other side of the door. "You've been in there very long."

Morana grit her teeth as Tristan Caine pulled out of her, the motion almost making her want to moan. He removed his hands from her, his face towards the door as he disposed the condom and tucked himself in his trousers again, his back to her. Morana sat on the counter for a second, gathering her wits, before sliding down. Her legs trembled in her heels. Her knees were weak, her inner thighs burning and the center sore, bruised, used. Truly fucked.

She straightened herself, turning towards the mirror, and barely contained a gasp. Not a single hair was out of place on her. No handprints around her neck. Except for her bunched dress and flushed skin, there was no sign at all that she'd been involved in anything physical, not even a sprint let alone sex.

Blinking her shining, blown up eyes, she straightened her dress, pressing on the creases till it fell over her body like it was supposed to, like it had been the entire night. She took a deep breath, letting her skin settle slightly until just a slight shiver down her exposed spine was any indication of disquiet.

She became aware of him a second after she was put together, her eyes flying up to his in the mirror, taking him in. Like her, there was nothing on him indicative of what he'd been doing. She swallowed. And tasted the residual copper and rust.

Her eyes drifted to the hand where she had bitten him, shock filling her system as she realized it was the same hand he had cut with her knife at her house. The hand had been healing. Her teeth had done some damage.

She bit back the automatic apology that came to her lips, and pressed them together, steeling her spine.

"Ms. Vitalio," the goon's voice came loudly. "Your father demands you to return to the table."

Yeah, well. He could stick it up his ass.

She didn't reply but turned around to face Tristan Caine, deliberately keeping her face blank.

"Not as experienced as you wanted me to believe, Ms. Vitalio," he said quietly, so quietly she barely heard him.

But she did. And the rage that had disappeared after the explosion returned, not just at him, but herself. She'd let him toss her on a restroom counter, for goodness' sake. A *restroom* counter. She'd let him take her hard and fast and quick. She'd let him cover her mouth and muffle her sounds while her father's man had been right outside the door, in a place where her father had been dining along with so many enemies. She'd let him make her come so hard her teeth had clenched.

And she'd enjoyed it. She'd wanted it. Every. Single. Second. Every. Single. Thrust. She'd wanted it, and she'd not wanted him to stop. Had her mouth not been covered, she would have been screaming. Had he not covered her mouth, she would have been crying out for him. And he hadn't even touched her. Their clothes had stayed completely in place. She hadn't wanted to touch him.

Good lord, what had she been thinking?

One time.

Just one time.

This was done. Completely. She wanted to leave. She wanted him gone. She didn't want a single reminder of her own flesh's depravity. This was messed up, more messed up than she'd thought it would be.

Regret and anger burned through her, along with hatred for herself.

And she saw it all mirrored in his gaze in one split second of clarity before he masked it again.

He was hating himself too. He was regretting too. He was angry too.

Good.

The worst part was, even as everything burned in her body, so did desire, as unsated as it had been when she'd walked into the room. What had been the point of it all if she felt no satisfaction whatsoever?

Without a word, she turned towards the door and took her first step.

And almost buckled down, the heaviness between her thighs almost knocking her to her knees. She was sore. Goodness, she was *sore*. One step and she remembered the fullness of him, the feeling of having him inside her, the sheer bliss. One step.

How the fuck was she supposed to walk out into the restaurant?

The same way she walked into her house every day.

Steeling her spine at the sobering thought, she passed him, the memory of pleasure resonating with every single step, the wetness perpetual around her sore walls, somehow hungry for even more.

His hand caught her arm just as she passed him, and she turned her head sideways, looking up at him, raising her eyebrows silently.

"Break his arm next time," he said quietly, his blue eyes magnificent, the sheer power in them making her heart pound.

His words sank in.

She snatched her arm back, a sneer curling her lips. "Touch me again, and I will break yours."

"Once was more than enough, Ms. Vitalio."

Her hackles rose. "I'll tell that to the notch on my bedpost, Mr. Caine."

Without waiting for his response, she strode towards the door, not giving a fuck about how he would escape the ladies' room. He had come in; he could go out.

Unlocking the door, she pulled it open, to find two men waiting for her towards the end of the corridor.

Not glancing back where she could feel his eyes on her back, she walked towards the men, her head high. Her stride was steady even as the soreness between her legs throbbed with each step, reminding her again and again of exactly what she had done and let be done to her, reminding her of the man who'd done it, reminding her of the pleasure she hadn't wanted to feel but had, and to what degree. Every single step. Her throbbing core spasmed on air, getting hungrier. She'd just had the most mind-blowing orgasm, and she felt anything but sated. What was wrong with her?

The men started walking behind her, their guns hidden under their jackets, stance alert.

Morana entered the main eating area, her eyes falling to the Outfit table at the other corner, her eyes meeting Dante's. He knew. His gaze told her he knew exactly what she'd been doing, and where his blood brother was. But she saw no judgment, no trepidation, and no pity in his eyes. Just tiredness.

She looked away before she could linger, heading towards her father's table, her face clear of all her emotions and turmoil.

Without looking at anyone, she took her seat rigidly, her lips pursed, her thighs clenching tightly to keep the throb to a minimum. She was aware of her father watching her, and she looked up, challenging his eyes. The creep beside her glared at her.

Her phone vibrated.

She broke the gaze and looked down at it.

**Tristan Caine:** *How many notches does that bedpost have?*

Her jaw almost dropped at the audacity of him. How dare he?

She quickly typed a reply, memories – of friction, of heat, of pleasure – flooding her with more and more rage.

**Me:** *All you need to know about my bedpost is simple.*

**Tristan Caine:** *And that is?*

**Me:** *You'll be on it just once. Been there. Done that.*

She waited for his reply. It didn't come.

She felt his gaze on her back, her nape prickling, and deja-vu hit her like a train wreck.

This was exactly where she'd been almost an hour ago. Exactly where she'd been. Same place, same people, same plots.

Except she had changed.

She didn't want to admit it, but she had. Something, very, very tiny, had shifted infinitesimally within the hour, with her acceptance of her desire, her locking of the door, her opening her legs for him. She didn't want to admit it, but it had. And she'd die before she let anyone else know it. Least of all him.

The table broke up finally, people getting up and turning to leave, shaking hands with her father. She stood up as well, standing as tall as she could in her heels, ignoring the ache in her belly and south, one hand holding her clutch and phone, the other beside her hips.

140

The creeper turned to her, taking her free hand and bringing it to his lips before she could blink. Morana felt her skin crawl, even more than it had earlier when he had been trying to grope her thigh. It was just his lips pressing into the back of her fingers, a gesture so many men had repeated at the end of so many dinners, and while they'd always disgusted her, this felt more intense, more.

She could feel *his* stare boring into her exposed back, the man who'd fucked her minutes ago a few feet away, the man she hated, while the creeper kissed her hand. His gaze burned on her back, on her neck, on her spine.

*'Break his arm next time.'*

The stare intensified. She tried to pull her hand back. The man didn't let go.

Her father looked around the room. The stare never left her back. Was he trying to start a war? He needed to look away!

The entire restaurant was on edge, everyone on alert, hands hovering over weapons, tension ratcheting higher and higher as her father's men headed towards the main door.

The creeper finally let go. She picked up a napkin from the table and wiped her hands, insulting him, and her father blatantly.

"I hope we meet again soon," the man told her.

"Sure, if you want another sprain and some broken bones," she said, her words loud enough for people to stiffen.

His gaze lingered. Her body throbbed.

She started walking towards the door with the party, keeping her gaze deliberately averted from the table in the corner, the table from where she could feel his gaze searing her, watching her every move like a panther watched a doe – still, quiet, waiting.

Her phone vibrated in her palm. Turning her eyes away, she peeked at it quietly as the men walked.

She saw the message and everything came rushing through her – the anger, the desire, the hate, the regret – mixing together in a concoction she barely even recognized anymore.

Her breath hitched.

Her body buzzed in memory on his rough hands and thrusting hips, hips she could still feel against hers, blue, blue eyes staring into hers, with the same emotions mirrored back for the split second the mask cracked.

She saw the text, and her stomach dropped, her heart pounding.

**Tristan Caine:** *Apparently, you're not out of my system, Ms. Vitalio.*

Her father stopped her before she'd processed it, his dark eyes cold, icy on hers.

Her stomach dropped again, for an entirely different reason.

"What were you doing with Tristan Caine?"

## *falling*

Panic hit.
Her heart stopped.
For a split second.

And then it kick-started with a vengeance, thumping wildly, the ache between her legs throbbing with every mad thud.

Keeping her face clear of all expressions, keeping her body completely still, not showing even the hint of the rampage inside her, aware of her father's shrewd eyes sharp on her for any indication of guilt, Morana raised a quiet brow.

"Who's Tristan Caine?"

Her voice stayed steady; her insides shook.

Before her father could respond, the other exit of the restaurant at the end of the street opened and Morana saw her father's eyes turn to it. Steadying herself, not to make any moves that could give her away, she turned along with him and saw the men of the Outfit walk out the door, towards the other end of the lot where their cars were parked. Four men exited in a file before Dante stepped out, his huge body that was his namesake athletic in his suit. Morana saw him turn and stare at her father.

Her father nodded once, in that polite warning way reserved for enemies who were in his territory and he couldn't do a thing about it.

Dante nodded back, all tiredness from previously gone, in that polite way that gave her father the finger.

Morana resisted the urge to smile at the way it riled her father.

Dante's eyes shifted to her then, for a second, and he nodded to her, in the way she'd always seen him nod at her. Morana didn't nod back, but standing there with the realization that her enemy was more respectful of her than her own father stung.

Dante moved from the door and Tristan Caine walked out, his animalistic body contained inside that suit, flexing with his steps as he strode with four other men on his heels. He stopped to talk to Dante, presenting her with his profile. Keenly aware of her father standing right beside her, Morana averted her eyes and pretended to check her phone, her heart pounding everywhere in her body, from her chest to her ears to her core. Everything throbbed. She throbbed.

And then his eyes came to her.

Again.

Fuck.

She contained a shiver. Barely.

And then his eyes left her.

She held her breath, and when it didn't return, she looked up at her father, to find him watching Tristan Caine with narrowed, angry eyes.

Curious, she followed his gaze to the man who'd been between her legs just minutes ago and blinked in surprise.

Tristan Caine was holding her father's angry glare without blinking, one of his eyebrows raised, his lips curled in a small sneer that was as fake as her British accent. What was he doing?

She got her answer a second later, understanding the game. It was a game of dominance. And there he stood, asserting his dominance in her father's territory, completely unruffled. And she knew, deep in her gut, it was about her.

She'd never felt so alive and never wished she could be more dead than she did at that moment.

"Get in the car," her father spit out angrily, pushing her arm towards the town car. At any other time, Morana would have dug her heels and argued. But not right then. Right then, she practically bolted to the car and got inside, needing to get away from the situation that could explode at any time. Her skin sizzled with the tension hovering in the air and she got in the vehicle without sparing him one glance.

Her father followed, shutting the door and telling the driver to pull away.

Morana grit her teeth and looked out the window, resisting the urge to clench her hands into fists as her father watched. Slowly, her heart calmed down and the shaking inside her stopped as she closed off. She'd been dealing with her father for many, many cold years. She would deal with him now. Ignoring the ache in her body, keeping all and every thought and memory of *him* at bay, Morana sat straight and just kept her eyes on the fleeting scenery –poised, calm, collected.

Her father didn't say a word for the entire ride. Not that she'd expected him to. No. All the cool he lost would be in private, not in front of his men where she could insult him again. His reputation was much, much more important than hers.

It was a short journey from the restaurant to the mansion. It was long with her knowledge of what was coming.

The minute the property gates appeared and the car slid into its spot, Morana got out of the vehicle and started walking towards the monster of a mansion, closed behind high fences and weapons that could turn against her at a moment's notice.

She almost reached the stairs to her suite when her father's voice boomed from behind her.

"He couldn't keep his eyes off you."

The words, the memory of that gaze lingering on her skin, stroking her naked back, caressing her flesh made her falter on the third step. She quickly recovered before the falter could be noticed and kept her voice cool.

"Isn't that why you doll me up?" she asked, her heart hardened over years of disappointment and hurt.

"He was gone from the place. You were too. And then he comes back and can't keep his eyes off you?"

Morana ignored his harsh words that evoked rough, physical memories, and kept climbing up.

"What were you doing with Tristan Caine?"

Her father followed after her, for the first time in her memory. He never came to her suite. It had always been summons for her.

Morana reached the landing and turned to him, gritting her teeth, the anger in his voice fuelling the cold inside her, the wheels in her head turning.

"I was having sex with him," she told him, her eyebrows raised in challenge.

She saw his arm come up to hit her, hover mid-air, and drop back down.

Her heart pounded, the cold, cold ice in her heart seeping deeper as she stood her ground.

"Tell me the truth," he demanded, his jaw clenched and eyes mad.

"I told you," Morana insisted, prodding him. "I was having wild sex with him in the bathroom with you right outside."

Her father sighed. "No, you weren't. You're not that kind of a girl. I raised you better."

Morana scoffed a laugh at that. "You didn't raise me at all." She was exactly that kind of girl. The heart of the daughter in her – the young girl who'd never won either her father's love or approval – ached. Morana hardened it again.

Her father narrowed his eyes. "What about the man on the bike? Who was he then?"

Morana smirked. "Oh, I slept with him too."

Technically, she had.

"Enough!" her father glared at her, his voice cutting, his accent deepening in the anger. "If you think I will not bring a doctor to have you checked, you are mistaken."

How dare he?

How fucking *dare he?*

Her blood boiled.

"I dare you," Morana snarled, her lips curling in a sneer. "You even think of bringing a doctor to violate me, I'll shoot her in the head and anyone else who comes near me."

"I've given you too much independence," he grit out, his dark eyes raging. "Too much. It's time it's put to a stop."

"Try to lock me in," Morana clenched her teeth, her voice lowering, her eyes glaring at the man who had spawned her, "and I will dump a heavy file on you right in the FBI's lap and serve you up like meat."

Her father gritted his teeth.

"Oh, I'd die too, but I'd take you down with me," Morana told him, uncaring about her own death. "Keep your nose out of my business, or I'll put mine in yours. And you wouldn't like it, *Daddy.*"

The sarcastic emphasis on the word couldn't be missed. The threat lingering in the air couldn't be missed. The utter, black rage in her father's eyes couldn't be missed.

"You should have died," her father spit out, the words like bullets to her chest.

What? What was he talking about? She couldn't ask.

Morana turned to leave but he gripped her arm tightly, swinging her around. "I'm not done!"

The sudden motion made her totter on her heels. Before she could blink, her right ankle twisted and her left overbalanced at the edge of the landing, her entire body moving backward. Deja-vu suddenly flashed through her, of the moment she'd been tipping over the stairs at the penthouse and Tristan Caine had gripped her neck and prevented her fall. Her father was gripping her arm, and she kept her heart from pounding.

And then it happened in a split second.

In that split second, Morana knew the stark difference between her father and Tristan Caine.

His grip loosened.

Deliberately.

She fell back, her eyes widening.

Down the stairs.

Down and down and down and down until there were no more steps to fall from.

It was over in a series of mere seconds.

It was over before she could realize it had started.

And then it began.

Every single bone started to hurt. Every single joint started to ache. Every single muscle started to pain.

Morana lay there, on the cold marble floor, as cold as the house, as cold as the man who stood at the landing, his face an odd twist of remorse and iciness. She didn't know whether her body hurt more or her heart, all those shattered hopes splattered on the cold floor beside her. But she knew, in that moment of utter betrayal of the worst kind, in that moment of finally letting go of the little girl she'd held on to, she knew this was a good thing. Because she knew there was no hope now. Not anymore.

Slowly sitting up, Morana bit back a sharp cry of pain as her ribs protested, removing her heels from her feet and threw them to the side.

As fluidly as she could, she picked up her clutch from the ground where it had fallen with her and stood up on wobbling legs. Her teeth dug into her lips as she locked the pain away for later. Without another word, another glance, picking up all her dignity as sharply as she could, Morana took a step towards the door.

Sharp tendrils of pain shot up her legs, up her spine. Her body was making her feel each and every stair she had tumbled over. The ache between her legs that had been the highlight of her night was buried under all the other painful sensations.

Bruised, battered, she walked out of the house on bare feet, keeping her spine straight and not sparing anyone any glance, her rigid frame screaming for her to relax and let her skin breathe.

She didn't.

She stifled the groans and let her skin turn blue, angry welts appearing all over her arms and legs and back, the gravel of the driveway cutting the skin of her feet. But she kept walking to her car, her only friend in this world of pain, and pulled out the keys from her clutch, thanking heavens she always kept it with her.

Throwing the clutch and her phone on the passenger seat, she got inside, the action resonating in every single bone in her body, muscles she didn't know she had hurt.

But she clenched her jaw, keeping every sound at bay, her eyes flooding with tears that rolled down her cheeks, burning the skin of her cheeks where the marble had cut.

Pulling out of the driveway without sparing the cursed house a glance, she drove out into the road in the deep night, the moonlight bathing the way, trees lining on either side as she just drove and drove, away and away, her tears torrential.

A sob escaped her throat, rapidly followed by another, and another, and another till they became uncontrolled, the noises loud in the silence of the car, mingling with the familiar purr of the engine.

She drove mindlessly, trying to keep all thoughts at bay, everything inside her breaking with each sob. She didn't know where to go. She had no friends, no people who cared about her, not one place she could go to when she needed to stay. She could go to a hotel but with the battered clothes and bruised skin, the police might become involved and that couldn't happen. She couldn't go anywhere public. Not even a hospital.

No one tailed her as she drove. Why would they? Her father had dropped her. What if she had broken her neck? What if she had died? Did she really not matter at all?

It was a few minutes of her harsh thoughts before Morana realized where she was heading – the penthouse.

Subconsciously, she had steered her car towards the penthouse. Why? That was the last place she could go, should go. Especially after the night. Especially as she was.

And yet, she didn't hit the brakes.

She was two minutes away and over the bridge, and even as she knew she shouldn't go there, she continued to drive.

What would it mean? She was going to him. He had told her she wasn't out of his system, and in all honesty, neither was he out of hers. But they were still who they were and their hatred hadn't gone down.

She remembered those glass walls, remembered that truce for one night as he'd sit beside her, an almost decent man. Could that truce prevail again? Should she even ask for it? Because she was not her best, neither physically not emotionally. And yet, as the building came into view, as the guards waved her in, recognizing her from before, Morana parked her car and sat in silence.

The comforting scent of her car, the sounds of her own breathing made her calm down a little.

But she didn't take a step out.

She couldn't.

She wanted to move, to walk, to get out. She couldn't.

Wiping her tears from her cheeks even as more escaped, Morana sat in the car quietly in the darkened area, her chest heaving with sobs. Sitting there, she let herself cry, let herself weep in a way she'd never allowed herself to do. She cried for the girl she had been, the girl who had died after the fall today. She cried for the lost hopes she'd been clinging to, for the lost dreams of maybes. She cried because she had no one to give her a shoulder and hold her as she cried because she had to wrap her arms around herself and hold herself together, in the basement of her enemy. She cried.

The sound of the elevator dinging had her wiping her tears. She looked up, alert. She didn't want anyone to see her even as a part of her wanted someone to.

Swallowing, she watched as Dante walked out in the suit he had been in at the restaurant, his phone held up to his ear, his voice low as he talked to someone. He headed to a black SUV two cars away from her, and she saw him still as he spied her vehicle lingering innocently in the lot.

"Morana?"

Shit.

Morana quietly opened her car, berating herself for not even knowing how bad her face looked with the injuries. She got out and closed the door, and saw Dante's eyes take her in, from head to toe, his eyes widening slightly in concern.

"I'll call you back," he spoke into the phone, his voice hardening as did his eyes, anger flashing through them.

Morana remembered what Amara had told her, about the two men being protective of women. She remembered Dante offering her comfort when she'd had to stay the night. And tears welled up in her eyes again, because that comfort, that concern, was a stranger to her.

He took a step towards her, still keeping his polite distance, his handsome face twisted in anger.

"Who did this?"

It touched her. The fact that he was the enemy and yet he wanted to hurt the culprit. It touched her *deep*.

Morana gulped.

150

"I fell down the stairs," she spoke quietly, her voice shaking just a bit. She really, really hoped he didn't ask her what she was doing there. She didn't have an answer.

He searched her eyes for a long moment before his eyes softened. "I will be away for the night. You can go upstairs and rest, Morana."

Morana felt her grip tighten on the car door handle, her lips trembling. She shook her head. "No. I'm okay. I'll go stay with some friends."

The fact that he didn't call her out on the obvious lie, that her presence there of all places was the indication that she had no friends, gave him a point in her books.

She shook her head again, and he cursed. "Tristan's up there."

Her eyes flew to his, her heart pounding. She didn't know why but it did. Anger burnished her.

Why? Why the hell did it matter? Why was her stomach in knots over it? Why had she come here of all places?

"Look," Dante's gentle tone broke through her spiraling thoughts. "Just let me call Amara. Stay over at her place if you're not comfortable at mine. You're hurt and Amara won't hurt you."

Morana was coming undone at his genuine concern. Unraveling bit by bit.

Her lips trembled but she shook her head. As tempting as the offer was, she couldn't drag Amara into this mess, not knowing that she couldn't protect herself, not knowing her history. Perhaps that's why she'd come here. Because she knew he could protect himself, that he had dragged himself into her mess. In a way.

"It's okay," she told him, opening her car door, ready to leave. "I'd really appreciate it if you didn't tell anyone" – him – "about this."

Dante stared at her for a long moment, before suddenly moving towards the private elevator with a loud "Fuck it!"

Morana watched, shocked, as he typed in the code and looked at her, tilting his head towards the open door.

"Go up."

Morana stood rooted to the spot, stunned.

"Morana, I don't have all night and I cannot leave you like this," Dante told her quietly, his eyes beseeching. "Please go up to the penthouse and rest."

She was the enemy. She was the woman his blood brother hated for a reason he knew of.

And yet...

Swallowing, she locked her car and moved towards the elevator on aching legs, her heart beating hard.

She looked up at Dante, her lips trembling. "Thank you," she whispered, meaning every single syllable from her heart.

Dante nodded.

She entered the familiar elevator and pressed the button. The doors closed on Dante's face. The mirrors stared back at her.

And Morana gasped.

Her dress hung off her shoulders, her hair a mess around her face, her cheeks cut and knees abraded, the skin of her hands and legs and shoulders turning bluer by the second, her lips swollen from her own bites and eyes puffed red from the tears.

She looked like a wreck. No wonder Dante had let her in.

And Tristan Caine was up there.

And she was going up.

What the hell was she *doing?*

Nerves attacked her, her chest constricting as panic hit.

*No. No. No.*

She couldn't let him see her like this. She couldn't enter his territory, not like this.

Heart hammering in her chest, her phone clutched tightly in her hand, keys digging into her palm, Morana raised her hand and let her finger hover over the button for the parking, ready to hit the moment the elevator stopped. She was going to turn her tail and go back to her car and go to some seedy motel if she had to. But she was going back. She was not letting him see her like –

The elevator stopped, the doors sliding open.

He stood right at the entrance, waiting.

Morana hit the button for down quickly, before he could see her.

The doors started to close.

Her heart thundered.

She hit the button again.

The doors kept sliding shut.

*Almost there.*

And just when they almost closed, his hand inserted itself in between.

Morana bit her tender lip, her heart pounding, pressing her back into the mirrored wall, her body aching, her lungs unable to draw in a deep breath. The long-forgotten ache between her legs throbbed at the proximity to its perpetrator, her eyes glued to the large hand that forced the doors apart again. She could see callouses on his long fingers, the ridges and hard lines. The hand was wrapped in a bandage from when he'd bled on her, from tonight when she'd made him bleed.

Her heart picked up pace seeing that hand.

And then the doors slid apart.

She straightened her back, her ribs hurting from the action, and stood as tall as she could, which didn't amount to much on her bare feet.

He came into view. Shirtless.

She gulped.

*Blue.*

Blue eyes locking onto hers, making her breath catch, before moving down her cheeks, down her neck, to her breasts and hands and legs down to her bare feet. And standing there as his eyes took her in, Morana realized the utter difference between his perusal from earlier at the restaurant and the perusal right then. This perusal was heated but not with hatred. It was heated with fury. Sheer, utter rage that made his eyes blaze as they roved over every single inch of her skin, before coming back up to her eyes.

Morana didn't know how that made her feel. She was so used to the other kind of heat from him, this was putting her off-kilter, more than she already was. She let her eyes take in the bare muscles of his torso, the muscles she'd ogled the other day right in the apartment, the sight of his scars and tattoos as much a shock as it had been then, along with those magnificent muscles under it. But it was the still unbuttoned jeans that, combined with him waiting for her, made her realize he'd thrown clothes on quickly and woken up from rest in the buff.

The sight of his blue, angry eyes made her take a deep breath, her body sapped of energy even as she stood there.

His nostrils flared, lips pursing, and he took a step to the side while holding the elevator doors back, the silent invitation to enter clear.

Swallowing past the lump in her throat, Morana took a few steps into the dark living room illuminated by gorgeous moonlight, the stunning, clear view of the city and the sea making her breath catch for a moment.

She heard the elevator ding upon closing, and stilled, her heart stopping for a second as realization dawned upon her.

They were alone.

Completely alone.

And she stood in his living room, and he was somewhere behind her.

What was she supposed to do? She couldn't curse him, she couldn't thank him and the limbo between the two urges tired her.

Morana held her breath, waiting for him to move.

He did. Towards the guest room.

Morana tracked his movements with her eyes, watching his muscles flex as he moved his body, his frame tensed, coiled. She would have appreciated the raw beauty of him had her own body not been aching, had her own heart not been bleeding.

He disappeared into the room for long moments while she stood pinned to the spot, not knowing what to do. Then, he came out, keeping his eyes away from hers, heading towards the stairs that led up to his master bedroom.

And then, he vanished into his room.

Morana heard some sounds, angry sounds, of doors opening and slamming shut, and headed towards the guest bedroom on slow steps, sapped of all energy, her shoulders slumping.

So, he wasn't the most hospitable man. Nothing she didn't already know. But at least he hadn't turned her away. She wasn't sure if she would have been able to take that humiliation tonight, on top of everything else.

The moment she entered the bedroom, she blinked. The bathroom door was open, steam billowing out from a full tub while a large black t-shirt and drawstring pants lay draped over a chair, the sheets on the bed turned down.

Morana stood there in the doorway, blinking back the sudden tears welling up in her eyes, her heart unable to understand the man. He hated her, she had no doubts. He had claimed her death and he had tried to fuck her out of his system. He had not spoken a word to her, not even looked at her, and yet, there lay the evidence of a kindness that was completely at odds with everything she knew about him.

Pursing her lips, she picked up the clothes and headed to the inviting bathroom, closing the door behind her but finding no lock. Shaking her head, she looked around the large room, the brown and cream tiles a comforting sight for the sore eyes, the tub sunken in a block of deep mahogany granite, two towels on a stand beside it. Morana shoved her dress off her body and onto the floor along with her underwear, turning sideways to look into the mirror above the sink.

Blue and purple crisscrossed all over her torso, the sides of her ribs tender.

Her father had done that. Without raising an arm, without actually abusing her, he had punished her. And she was seeking refuge with a man like Tristan Caine. How messed up was her life?

Closing her eyes, she dipped her toe in the warm, perfectly warm water, before slowly gripping the edges and sitting down in the tub.

A groan left her the moment she did, tears of pleasure at the intense relief of having such warmth envelop her muscles flowing down her cheeks. She leaned back against the tub, relaxing into the water, closing her eyes, and forgetting, for one brief moment, about everything.

Her phone buzzed beside her.

Peeking with one eye, she opened the message and blinked in surprise.

**Tristan Caine:** *Do you need a doctor?*

Why hadn't he asked her himself?
Surprised, she typed back a response.

**Me:** *No. I'll be out of your hair in the morning.*

She waited for a response after that. It didn't come.

Shrugging, feeling oddly conflicted but deciding to leave all the thinking for the morning, she stayed in the tub until the water cooled, and then slowly, languidly rose. Her body hurt even more, and yet, the knots in her muscles were relaxed after the bath. Quickly drying herself off, Morana pulled on the borrowed clothes. The t-shirt hung on her small frame, almost to her knees, the scent of something musky wrapping around her as she walked out to the bedroom.

The sound of voices drew her towards the closed door, voices coming from the open kitchen.

"You have a plane for Tenebrae in an hour, Tristan," Dante's voice came through.

Morana's heart sank. She didn't know why it did, and it made her angrier. Why did she care?

Tristan Caine stayed silent. What was up with him?

Morana heard Dante sigh. "Look, I would have gone, but father specifically asked for you. You know when he summons..."

"I'm not his dog," Tristan Caine grit out.

"Neither am I." Dante's voice hardened. "But we have innocent people to watch over. So, go to Tenebrae. I'll handle stuff here in the meantime."

Tristan Caine didn't say a word, and Morana retreated back into the comfortable bed, sliding into the sheets and switching the lights off.

Her phone buzzed again.

**Tristan Caine:** *How much of that did you hear?*

Morana swallowed.

**Me:** *Enough to know you're leaving.*

**Tristan Caine:** *Relieved, are you?*

**Me:** *Doesn't bother me either way.*

There was a pause for a heartbeat before another message came.

**Tristan Caine:** *There are painkillers in the drawer.*

Morana looked at the message for a long time, before closing her eyes and going to sleep, no worry in her heart. If Tristan Caine killed her in her sleep, it'd probably be a mercy.

It was the sound of some kind of crash blaring through the apartment that woke her up.

Morana sat up on the bed suddenly, all the aches in all the muscles coming back tenfold as a groan left her, her eyes blinking into the dark. How long had she been asleep?

She looked at the clock beside the bed and blinked. Eight hours. She'd been asleep for eight straight hours.

The door to her room suddenly opened, and Tristan Caine stood there, his eyes blazing with such strong fury that she trembled. Wasn't he supposed to be in Tenebrae?

"Give me your car keys," he growled.

Morana blinked, her hand automatically going to her clutch before she stopped. "Why?" she asked, slightly suspicious.

"Because your car has a fucking tracker and your father is tracking it here as we speak."

Morana felt her jaw drop, before she got down from the bed, his clothes hanging loosely on her. His eyes never took in the clothes or any other part of her body. He just stood there, all harsh lines and hard angles of a man, his hand held out as he waited for the keys.

Keys to her car.

Swallowing, Morana turned the keys over, her stomach tying itself up in knots, biting the urge to ask him what he intended to do with it. Tristan Caine turned away without a word and handed the keys over to Dante.

The other man looked at Morana, his face hard as well, before he nodded at her and left. Morana stood in the doorway, lingering, with no clue of what to do or say as she watched Tristan Caine, in a sharp dark suit that hugged his body, making calls on his phone. He didn't look at her again, not once, just like last night.

She stayed silent for five minutes, a million thoughts running through her head. Could the Outfit be installing a tracker in her car instead? Could they be exploiting this as an opportunity? Could they be using her too?

She shook her head. If the Outfit had wanted to do it, it could have been done while they had gotten her car fixed. And Dante, or he for that matter, had not faked that outrage last night at the sight of her injuries. She could still feel her tender, bruised skin, and pain in her body. It would be a long time before she healed completely.

But why wasn't Tristan Caine in Tenebrae? Last she'd heard, he had to be there.

And she had to get out of there – of the apartment, of the life. She'd had enough. Codes be damned, she had to leave and go someplace far, far away.

But she needed her car. *Damn it.*

The sound of his phone ringing made her clear her thoughts.

"Yes?" he spoke, crisp, cold, completely unlike the man who'd pinned her against the door and propositioned her.

Morana took a deep breath, realizing that she was sore between the legs too.

"Fuck! Stop him. I'm on my way."

He was out before she could utter a word.

Morana blinked and went to stand beside the window, looking down. She could see tiny, little cars at the end of the road. She could see three other vehicles leave from the building and reach them.

"Morana," Amara's voice came from beside her as the other woman joined her. Morana looked up, surprised she'd missed the woman coming in.

"Amara," she nodded, watching as the woman took note of her injuries, her eyes compassionate.

"I'm sorry."

Morana swallowed, looking back out the window.

"What's happening?" she asked, curious and worried.

Amara took a deep breath. "Your father came looking for you. He tracked your car here."

It hit her at that moment, watching it from the glass wall.

It had been a setup.

She had been a pawn and she'd fallen exactly with the plan.

Her father had been testing her, seeing where she would go. That was why he'd insisted she leave her car behind for dinner, why nobody had been tailing her. She should have suspected something, but her own grief had blinded her. And she had come straight here. To Tristan Caine. To the biker. Fuck.

It hit her at that moment, watching the two sides stop at the road, that she belonged on no side of the line. She belonged nowhere, not with her father and certainly not with the other man who was reputed in the mob for being the predator.

What was she doing?

Panic hit her chest. She couldn't stay.

"Amara, do you have your car here?" Morana asked quietly, feeling the other woman's eyes turn to her.

"Yes."

"May I borrow it?"

"What for?"

"I need to leave," Morana clenched her hands to keep the panic at bay. "I have to get out."

The other woman blinked in understanding. "I can't let you go, Morana. Especially not with the situation as it is right now. It could turn into a blood bath. And Tristan would never forgive me."

That snagged her attention. Morana looked at the woman sharply. "You know why he hates me, don't you?"

Amara nodded. "Yes, but it isn't my story to tell."

"What can you tell me?" she asked bluntly.

Amara tilted her head to the side. "How much do you know about the time the Alliance ended?"

Frowning, Morana tried to recall. "Not much."

"Look it up. That's all I can tell you."

Morana sighed, knowing the woman wouldn't divulge any secrets. She even admired that.

Keeping her eyes on the scene below, Morana saw the cars turn back and return to the building, and straightened her spine, picking up her phone.

*Me: I need my car.*

*Tristan Caine: For?*

Morana raised her eyebrows but replied quickly.

*Me: Leaving.*

*Tristan Caine: Where exactly do you plan on going?*

She had no idea, but she sure as hell wasn't telling him that.

*Me: I'm leaving the city. I have a friend I've spoken to.*

*Tristan Caine: Unspeak to your friend. If I'm not leaving this city, you sure as hell aren't.*

Morana grit her teeth, her anger burning in her gut again.

*Me: You don't get to decide that, Mr. Caine.*

Morana walked towards the couch, dropping her body onto it, glaring at the elevator as her phone buzzed again.

*Tristan Caine: We have unfinished business, Ms. Vitalio.*

*'Apparently, you're not out of my system, Ms. Vitalio.'*

His words rattled her mind. Last night. It had just been last night. It seemed like a lifetime. Deliberately misunderstanding his words, Morana typed a response.

**Me:** *I'm done with the codes.*

He obviously wasn't because if he was framed, his neck was on the line.

The elevator doors opened just as her phone vibrated. Morana looked up to see him enter the room, his lithe, muscular body fitting right into the sunlit apartment, his blue eyes finding hers, the energy in them burning her. Blue locked with hers, the color beautiful in the bright sunlight, shining and focused, right on her.

Morana took a deep breath and broke their gaze, looking down at the text he'd sent.

**Tristan Caine:** *I wasn't talking about the codes.*

**Tristan Caine:** *I meant **our** business.*

Her heart thumped. She didn't look up, aware that he stood just feet away in the room, talking to Amara. She didn't need this. Not right now. Not on top of everything else.

**Me:** *We are done. Is my father is gone?*

**Tristan Caine:** *With more bruises on his face than yours.*

Morana's eyes flew up, locking with his.

He'd *hit* her father? *Was he insane?*

And seriously what was she doing? Predators scented injured animals and attacked. He'd attacked her father.

And yet, there she was, in the den of the deadliest predator, one who had told her in no clear terms that she was his prey and his prey alone. There she was injured, bleeding, and vulnerable in so many ways. Yet, she'd never felt safer.

161

Panic hit.

## *running*

**M**orana Vitalio was not a woman easily scared. She'd been brought up in a house full of snakes. She'd seen and observed those slimy beings since before she had learned to walk. And she'd never feared them. Not when she'd seen their guns. Not when she'd seen the mayhem they were capable of with her own young eyes. Not when she'd seen the bright color of blood splattered on the pristine white walls, only to be covered up within the day.

She hadn't been scared when her own life had been on the line with the codes, nor when her father had let her fall down the stairs with the possibility of her breaking her neck.

No. Morana Vitalio was not scared of death.

But she was scared of Tristan Caine, even though she didn't want to admit it.

She watched him move about the kitchen with the natural grace of a predator - lithe, sure and completely certain of its victory- the jacket of his suit hanging on a chair while his white shirt stretched taut across his back, the sleeves rolled up over his muscular forearms as he moved the frying pan with one hand and added the seasonings with the other. She sat on the same stool she'd been sitting in the last time she'd spent the night in the penthouse mere days ago. Lord, it felt like a lifetime.

Back then, she'd seen his body in motion and harbored a minuscule root of feminine appreciation for such beauty. Now, she marveled. Because she knew, intimately, how that body moved inside her. She knew how he felt inside her, knew how he pulsed inside her.

And that's all she knew. Because that was all she'd allowed herself to know. And for some reason, it had only fuelled her hunger.

She watched the muscles in his back flex and wondered what they'd feel like if he was above her. She watched his hands moving the pan skilfully and wondered what they'd feel like playing with her body, caressing her skin. She watched that taut, taut ass of his and wondered what it'd be like under her teeth.

Heat pooled in her belly at her erotic thoughts. Squirming uncomfortably on the stool, her blood heated and her body bruised, Morana moved her eyes away from him to the two other people sitting in the room, far away from each other. Amara scrolled through her phone a few stools beside Morana, and Dante watched the spectacular setting sun from the floor to ceiling windows, sitting on the other side of the room while Tristan Caine cooked silently.

The tension in the room, between each and every one, was choking her. It was fucking unnerving. And she was not used to it. This awkward silence – because she knew they had to talk but couldn't in her presence because there was some weird stuff going on between Amara and Dante and the other two people in the room knew it. Also because there was some weird stuff going on between herself and his majesty, and the other two knew about it too. Everything was just weird. Yet, weirdly comfortable in a way it shouldn't have been.

"What should I tell father?"

Dante's quiet voice broke through the silence like a whip, his dark eyes trained on Tristan Caine's back.

Tristan Caine turned off the stove, the smell of something hot and spicy permeating the air, making her mouth drool while she closely observed him for even a minute reaction. She got none.

He continued transferring the food into a big serving bowl, his hands that had held a knife to her throat and a gun to her head once carrying on the domestic task with such ease she envied it. Amara stood up to pick up glasses from the cabinet and in silence, they set the table in a way they'd done a hundred times.

Her envy notched up. She tamped it down.

And all this time, while she knew he'd been aware of every single move of hers, he hadn't looked at her once. Not once. Not since coming in after punching her father hours ago.

It shouldn't bother her. It did. And she hated it.

Finally, he took a seat at the table and started serving some kind of chicken into four plates, not extending an invitation to her but clearly telling her she wouldn't be starved. That was something, she supposed.

Sliding down from the stool, Morana felt her newly bruised muscles protest against the movement as she limped her way to the chair farthest from the man, which happened to be the one beside Dante and sat down. She saw Tristan Caine's eyes flicker from her chair to Dante's once before he dug into his food without any preliminaries, and Morana picked up her fork to load some delicious smelling chicken on it.

She almost had the fork to her mouth when her eyes fell to his throat, exposed by the open collar of his shirt, his Adam's apple bobbing as he swallowed, working that piece of food in a way that made the blood rush to her head. What the hell was wrong with her? It had been yesterday. Just yesterday they'd fucked on a bathroom counter in the restaurant. Her body wasn't supposed to be reacting like this, at least not so soon.

Forcing herself to remove her eyes from his corded neck, she raised the fork to her mouth and took a bite.

And nearly moaned.

Spices burst forth on the tongue, curling around it, invading her senses, the taste rich and the food succulent. It didn't taste like he'd cooked it in under an hour in his home. It tasted like something chefs tired over for an entire day before serving the customers. Had she not seen him prepare it from the scratch, she'd never have believed he had cooked it. So, he was also good at cooking too. Figured.

Keeping her reaction under the lid, she quietly proceeded to eat, ravenous, her body realizing how long it had been since she had fed it. She was nearly halfway through the meal when Tristan Caine looked at Dante and spoke, continuing the conversation from before.

"About what?"

Dante chewed on his bite, his handsome jaw working the food before swallowing it, briefly glanced at her and Amara before looking at the other man. "About everything."

Tristan Caine didn't blink. "Tell him what you wish to."

Dante dropped his fork down, steepled his fingers and took in a deep breath of control.

Morana watched the interaction with fascination.

"She can't stay here," Dante announced in a quiet tone, his voice unapologetic.

Tristan Caine just raised an eyebrow.

"You know what I mean, Tristan. It's dangerous for all of us to harbor her here," Dante looked at her again, his dark eyes flickering with a hint of regret before he turned away again.

"I understand last night was dire and I wouldn't have let her leave in her condition myself. But this is the light of the day. We can't have this mess with the codes, the stuff happening at home and Vitalio running his mouth, accosting us of kidnapping and god-knows-what his daughter."

Morana's breath hitched. Dante was right. She hadn't even thought about all the riot her father could create. All the war they'd wanted to avoid, all in her name.

"He doesn't know she's here," Tristan Caine informed the table. "He tracked her car but he has no proof."

Dante scoffed. "And that punch to his face? You know how well that's going to go with father."

Tristan Caine shrugged. "He invaded on our turf without warning or permission. He knows the rules."

Dante sighed. "We can get her to a safe house. But she can't be here."

Oh, no way in hell. God, this was bad. She didn't dare look at Tristan Caine, not sure what she would find in his face, not sure what she wanted to find.

Swallowing, she spoke. "Look, I just need my car and I'll be out of your hair–"

"She's not leaving," Tristan Caine interrupted quietly. Too quietly.

Dante sighed again. "Tristan, this is insane. You can't keep her here like this. You need to tell her —"

"And you need to leave."

Morana did a double-take at the sudden lethal harshness in his voice. Tristan Caine still didn't look at her, just stared evenly at his blood brother, his face giving no indication whatsoever of what was going on in his head. Dante stared back just as evenly, a silent conversation happening between the two men that raised the hair on the back of her neck – a conversation about her. They were clashing over her and she had no idea why. What did Dante know that he wanted Tristan Caine to tell her? What the hell was going on?

She wanted to ask but the testosterone level climbed higher as both men sat immovably, the silence so thick she could hear her heart pounding in her ears, the food completely forgotten. Morana never removed her eyes from the two men, trying to weasel out any hint from any movement but nothing.

The tension just notched.

Until Amara spoke, in that soft voice of hers. "Dante."

Morana looked at her and saw her shake her head in warning once. So, they both knew.

Dante abruptly got up from the table and headed towards the elevator, before Amara pushed her chair out as well, briefly touching Tristan Caine on the shoulder. "He's not wrong, Tristan."

Tristan Caine looked up at the woman, a brief moment of understanding passing between them. "Neither am I."

Amara smiled sadly at him before turning to her, her eyes warming. "Tristan has my number. Call me if you need anything, Morana."

Morana smiled tentatively at her, a little unsure and Amara moved away, walking out to a waiting Dante by the elevator.

And Morana watched, completely confounded.

What the hell was going on?

It was dark outside, the sun long-settled below the horizon. The city lights twinkled in the distance and Morana took a deep breath, and looked down at her half-empty plate. She slowly started eating again, without glancing up at the man she was alone with now.

The man who was looking at her. Finally.

She could feel his stare over every inch of her body in his line of vision. She could feel the caress of his eyes over her exposed skin and feel the heat rising in her body and pooling in her core, just from his eyes. She did not like it. Unable to pretend it wasn't grating over every nerve in her body, Morana dropped the fork and looked up, only to find those fierce, magnificent blue eyes pinning her to her chair.

She didn't like this. She didn't like it at all. She needed to push her chair back and get to the guest room. She needed to lock the door and get away from this man.

Because he scared her. She didn't know anything about him. Nothing. Not his past, not his present, not his future. She didn't know any reason for anything he did and that made him the unknown. The unpredictable.

And it scared her.

Because she had no idea if he would kill her or protect her in his next breath.

There were too many things going around them, between them. He'd hit her father. He'd not gone to Tenebrae when he was summoned. He was harboring her in his home when, as Dante said, it was very, very dangerous. But he was also the man who'd repeatedly told her he would kill her.

She blinked, trying to clear her head but his eyes refused to move from hers, his jaw tight, the scruff littering the line of his jaw longer than it had been in the morning.

Heartbeats and breaths quickening, the look in his eyes so predatory she felt like a meal on the table that he was going to devour any moment.

Fuck. This was supposed to be done. That was what the restaurant had been about. He should've been just done, not looking at her with that hateful hunger. Naked hunger unleashed on her in a way she'd never seen before. In a way that made her hungry. In a way that made the hunger gnaw at her skin.

She needed to close him up. Shut the shutters over those eyes and contain that look.

She needed to do something fast.

Suddenly remembering what Amara had been telling her earlier, Morana broke the silence.

"When did the Alliance end?"

And it worked. His eyes flared momentarily, with something that was such an intense mix of hatred and pain she couldn't differentiate between them.

And then his eyes blanked. Completely. Just blue orbs looking at her with quiet consideration. No emotion.

She wasn't sure she liked it any better.

"Twenty years ago," he spoke quietly, watching her.

Silence.

"Oh," she said dumbly, then zipped her lips shut, not knowing what more to say.

His eyes narrowed slightly as he leaned back in his chair, folding his muscular arms across his chest, the fabric of his shirt stretching over his biceps, the hint of a dark tattoo visible under the white material.

The silence stretched. Morana, already shaken over the events of the past twenty-four hours, finally gathered the strength to push away from the table and clear the dishes, carrying them to the kitchen, aware of his eyes on her back. She rinsed them hastily and stacked the plates in the chrome dishwasher, drying her hands on the towel and turning to find him still observing her.

She had so many things she needed to know, so many things to ask. But the past day had played havoc on her, and for some reason, she didn't think she could take another confrontation right now. Not until she replenished her reserve.

"Thank you for the meal, Mr. Caine," she spoke and turned to the guest bedroom, not giving him the chance to respond.

He didn't utter a word. Just tilted his head to the right.

Unnerved, Morana ran off into the room, not even caring about being obvious, and leaned against it, her heart battering her chest, her blood running hot. Why was she running now, when she never had before? Why was she letting him get to her now when she hadn't before, not to this extent at least?

Before she could think, she quietly locked the door and went to the bed, sitting down and staring at the wooden floor.

Dante was right. She couldn't stay there anymore. Damn the codes. Damn her father. Damn everything.

She was done.

She had been done for a long time. And she needed to get out.

Because the more she stayed, the more she realized her plan had backfired. He wasn't out of her system. She could feel him sinking his clutches deeper and deeper into her.

And that was scarier than an impending mob war.

Morana sat silently on the bed, her eyes on the locked door, her hands gripping her phone, waiting.

Waiting to be certain he was asleep before making her move. Staying here – in this apartment, in this city, in this country – was foolish. She didn't know what her father thought anymore, whether he believed she was with the Outfit or not despite tracking her car there, but she certainly didn't care anymore. Not for him or whatever he was hiding. Not for the hopeful girl she had been. Not for the codes that may or may not be discovered sometime. She knew it was incredibly selfish of her in a way, but she just couldn't do it anymore.

She'd already used her hidden bank account to buy herself a one-way ticket to the other side of the globe, where she would be completely anonymous. She needed to go there, away from this world, away from her father, from this mob, from *him*. She had to go so she could give herself a chance for something better, for happiness. Maybe find someone who made her heart race and her blood heat. Someone who understood her in her silence and protected her because he wished to. Someone who challenged her on every level and treated her as an equal.

Morana groaned at her thoughts. She shook her head, trying not to think of the man sleeping upstairs. And she was certain he was sleeping. It was 2 in the morning and there hadn't been a single noise in the house for over an hour.

It was time to move.

Slowly standing up, she moved towards the door as silently as she could and took a deep breath. Opening the latch quietly, she stepped out into the darkened space, her eyes going to the beautiful twinkling view of the city from those gorgeous windows.

Morana felt a pang shoot through her heart. It felt odd leaving this place with the knowledge she would truly never return. Especially odd considering she'd just been here only for two nights. She'd not felt this when leaving the house that had been her home for more than two decades. There was a memory here, a glimpse of a man she loathed and didn't. A memory of not being alone.

Shaking off the feeling, her chest tight and heart constricting, she moved towards the elevators on quick, slow steps, the ache in her muscles just a lingering presence, keeping her ears open for any noise. It was only her own breaths and the ambient sound of air conditioning.

Typing in the code in the keypad, Morana waited for the doors to open, her throat taut with an emotion she had never felt in her life. She was going to leave everything known behind – this place, this world, even her car. God, how she'd miss that car. It had been a loyal friend to her for so, so long. And when she'd needed it the most, it had brought her here, to safety.

The doors swished open and Morana stared at the mirrored panel staring back at her, her stomach in knots as she realized that despite everything, Tristan Caine had made her safe for both nights that she'd been in his territory, both times when she'd been at her most vulnerable. He could have taken advantage. He could have turned her over to her father. He could have simply refused to take her in. But he hadn't. He'd sat down with her in silence and watched the rain that first time. He'd run her a bath and given her clothes and fed her this second time. He'd gotten her car repaired and refused his own summons to Tenebrae. And he'd punched her father in the face.

She didn't even know who he was anymore.

She didn't know who she was with him.

But it didn't matter because she was leaving. Yet, she couldn't, not without clearing her conscience.

She knew she couldn't see him face to face or he'd never let her leave, nor would she want to. Which was why she unlocked her phone and opened the messages, taking a moment to read over their last conversation.

*'We have unfinished business, Ms. Vitalio.'*

Yes, they did. But there would be no finishing it.
She quickly typed out a message and hit send before she could stop herself.

**Me:** *Mr. Caine. Thank you. I wish you well.*

Before she could allow herself second thoughts, she stepped into the elevator and pressed the button for the doors to close. The panels slid shut. Her reflection stared back at her. Messy hair pulled back in a ponytail, an over-sized white t-shirt and a pair of black leggings that Amara had brought to her along with soft ballet flats. She held nothing but her phone and her wallet in her possession. Although she didn't have a plan on how she'd get to the airport if her car wasn't in the parking lot, she wasn't stressed. She'd planned on hot-wiring it. Maybe she could just walk far enough over the bridge to get a cab, but she didn't think her legs would cooperate much there.

Ignoring the tempestuous jolts in her stomach and her sweaty palms, she waited with bated breath as the doors finally opened and she exited into the empty parking lot, rows of cars standing eerily as two overhead lights lit the huge area.

She looked around for a few seconds and spotted Tristan Caine's muscular bike, her heart skipping for a second before she forced her eyes to move, seeing her car a few feet down to the left. She made her way towards it quietly.

She'd not taken more than two steps before the sound of a door bursting open shot through the silent lot like an errant bullet, piercing straight through her heart and making Morana grind to a halt as she jumped to look towards the door.

The stairwell door.

Framing a very large, very muscular, very infuriated Tristan Caine.

A half-naked Tristan Caine, much like he'd been when she'd come to him last night, pinning her to the spot with those blue eyes.

A thrill shot down her spine, dread and terror and excitement washing over her in waves.

Adrenaline crashed through her system. Fight or flight. She knew she couldn't fight him right now, shouldn't fight him unless she wished to lose. Flight it was.

Without waiting for another beat, she turned on her heels and started running towards her car, not daring to even glance back to see if he was closing in. The blood rushed too loudly in her ears and her heaving breaths made it hard for her to listen to the sound of his footsteps but she didn't even stop to take a breath. She just kept running at full speed, giving it all she had. Her legs hurt from the sudden exertion, her heart beat madly to keep up but she ran like her life depended on it. It did.

Three cars down.

She was three cars down when two hard arms closed around her, pulling her flush against a warm, naked chest, stopping her in her tracks. She struggled wildly, her body wriggling against his to be set free, but the arms remained like bands around her, her head fitting under his jaw, her toes coming off the ground in her effort to jump away from him.

"Let me go!" she yelled at him, turning her head and biting down on his taut bicep, thrilling at inflicting that small injury on him.

She felt his chest rise sharply on an inhale against her back, his cock coming to life against her moving spine as he leaned down closer, putting his lips close to her ear, his whiskers brushing against the shell and sending heat straight to her core.

"You wish me well, do you?" he murmured softly, his lips almost touching her skin yet not, making her body ache for that touch. "Don't you know not to run away from predators, sweetheart? We like the hunt."

His words made her insides clench with a forbidden thrill even as she struggled against him, trying to escape while a part of her felt electrified.

"Unless you want me to lay you out right on that bloody car of yours and fuck you, stop moving."

Morana stilled, her breasts heaving against his arms as a small part of her told her to move her hips, daring him to carry out his threat.

No, this wasn't supposed to happen. Not again. Never again.

Swallowing down her confused emotions, she spoke quietly. "Let me go."

His nose nuzzled against her head, inhaling deeply. "I told you we have unfinished business."

"I don't care," she grit out, her teeth clenched against all the sensations overwhelming her inside and out.

There was a second of silence before he spoke.

"We've never lied to each other, Ms. Vitalio. Let's not start now," he murmured in that deep voice of his, the whiskey and sin rolling over her skin like a lover's caress, making her want to roll back her eyes and lean against him.

Her jaw clenched.

She turned her head again and bit him on that bicep. Again.

Before she could do more, he turned her around and pulled her flush against his body. Her heaving breasts pressed against his chest, his erection nudged against her belly, arms around her almost in the intimate hold of a lover rather than a foe. His magnificent blue eyes bore into hers with an intensity that both startled and somehow reassured her.

He didn't say another word, not for a long time, just looked at her with that singular focus, his jaw tight, his skin warm against hers, his breath fanning over her face. His lips hovered just an inch from hers, that musky scent of his surrounding them in a deadly cocoon.

He slowly brought up his right hand and gripped her jaw in his palm, his fingers and thumb on her cheeks, not painfully but firmly. Tilting her head all the way back as her heart pounded in her chest, the two conflicted sides of her fighting inside herself about the small space between their mouths. Her hands trembled beside her as she clenched them into fists to control the shaking of her body.

"Mind that mouth of yours, wildcat," he spoke softly, lethally, erotically in the space between their lips, the movement almost making them touch. *Almost.* His voice dropped lower, his eyes glued to hers. "It makes me want to reciprocate. And you don't want my mouth anywhere near you, remember?"

Morana felt her heart thud, her chest rise and fall rapidly. "It wasn't a damn kiss. I bit you."

One side of his lips quirked up even as his eyes heated. "Doesn't matter. I get my mouth on you, and you'll never be the same."

He leaned closer, impossibly closer, his lips right there, *right there*, but still far away, his hand on her face keeping her from moving both forward and back.

"Choose wisely, Ms. Vitalio."

Before Morana could blink, he smoothly took a step back and let go of her face, inclining his head towards the open elevator, waiting for her to move without saying another word.

In that moment, when he stepped back and gave her the space to choose, between so, so many things, Morana realized that no matter how much she wanted to escape, she could not. She was so entwined into the mess she had created, she wouldn't have been able to go away for long without her conscience poking her. She was so curious, so lured by whatever this bizarre thing between them was, this thing that made her feel safe for the first time in her life even as he promised to kill her, that she could not leave.

She couldn't run.

He wouldn't let her.

Morana gulped and took the step, slowly walking towards the elevator, aware of his vigilant presence behind her, telling her silently that he wouldn't let her go. Not yet. And for some asinine reason, it thrilled her. She wondered if she'd sent him the message subconsciously because she'd been aware of this. Had she?

She didn't know.

That was exactly why Tristan Caine scared her so much. Not because he was killing her – the 'her' she had known her entire life.

She admitted the truth to herself as she stepped into the elevator that would take her up again beside him.

Tristan Caine terrified her, but it wasn't because of the death he was bringing her slowly, the death he would bring her one day, the death he raised in her.

No.

It was the *life*.

# connecting

*'The more you know, the less you do.'*

Morana remembered reading that quote somewhere a long time ago. The words had stuck to her brain, but she'd never truly understood it. Being a certified genius, she'd always believed knowledge was the ultimate power. It was her thirst for knowledge which had made her bold enough to step out of her defined norms, time and again. It was this very belief that had led her into putting in everything she had and making those codes she'd come to dread so much.

Knowledge was power, but in the wrong hands, it was a weapon.

The Alliance had ended twenty years ago. Twenty-two, to be precise.

Two days after her laughable escape attempt, two days of living inside the guest room like an actual guest and not someone despised, the seething mess of Morana's emotions were finally calm.

For the first time in a long, long time, Morana felt in control. She felt she was seeing things clearly and logically again, not letting her emotions run roughshod over her in raging waves. Whether that was because she'd come to face and accept some facts about herself or because Tristan Caine had been largely absent from his own house doing god-knew-what for the two days, Morana just knew her cool, composed head was back and she was grateful. She didn't like feeling off-kilter, uncontrolled by her own body.

And though his absence and lack of pursuit did confuse her to some extent, she'd learned not to put too much thought into what he did or didn't do. The fact was, she was the daughter of Gabriel Vitalio who'd never returned to her prison of a home after leaving. She was taking refuge in the enemy's camp instead. The fact was, that the said enemy had punched her father in full view of his people in his territory and refused to return back to his own when summoned. The fact was, knowing her father, she was getting antsy because he hadn't reacted to any of it.

That wasn't like him. Her father made statements; he retaliated in a way that set examples. To let Tristan Caine get away with something like this wasn't in his DNA. That was why Morana was a little worried, this silence from her father more unnerving than anything else, like the calm before the storm. And in their world, a storm could mean anything from a dead body to a street war. It wasn't a soothing thought.

As for Lorenzo Maroni, she didn't know how he would react. From what she'd heard of the man, his hands were even dirtier than her father, and Dante had seemed worried about his reaction. But then again, what did she know? Maybe refusing his summons was a normal thing in the Caine-Maroni relationship. If Tristan Caine wasn't worried about it, which she didn't really know if he was, she wouldn't give it much thought either.

Her objective thoughts were focused on two very important things - finding the codes, and end of the Alliance.

Now that she was level-headed and mostly alone in the huge penthouse with the gorgeous view, Morana had a plan. She and the Outfit brothers had been focusing on trying to find the codes and then subsequently destroying them, but from their success so far, it didn't seem very plausible in the near future.

So, she changed the plans and decided she was going to write a new set of codes, and create a software that would completely undo the effects of the original codes the moment they were initialized. Although she wasn't really clear on how she was going to go about it, she knew she had both the capability and the incentive. And since Tristan Caine had been a ghost in his own house, Morana called Dante after waking up to discuss this with him.

As she sat curled on the plush couch in the living room in more clothes that Amara brought for her yesterday, she watched the sunlight dance with the tall peaks of the buildings. It filtered in through the windows and warmed her, warming the entire apartment with its soft glow, Morana let her mind drift to the other thing she needed knowledge about.

The Alliance. Or rather, it's demise.

The Alliance had been in place for so long, peaceful and beneficial to both the families involved, so why exactly had it ended? What had happened twenty-two years ago that had led to the end of one of the most lucrative associations in mob history? There hadn't been any wars. Morana had researched for those and the last known war between the two families had been more than fifty years ago. It was the end of that war that had created the Alliance. For almost three decades, it had worked well.

So what had happened?

More importantly, what did that have to do with Tristan Caine hating her? How did everyone else know about it? She hadn't even known much about the Alliance, which was surprising considering she'd grown up listening to everything her father and his men had talked about. She'd known of the Outfit and its people through word of mouth. She'd known of the many players around their area through those conversations. So why had she never known of the Alliance? Had they purposely never mentioned it in front of her? Or was she imagining things? Why would her father hide from her the very thing that made his enemy despise her?

Morana picked up her phone and logged into her personalized search engine, continuing reading her old research on the topic quickly. She prayed for some good leads as she combed through the content.

The sound of the elevator opening jolted her from her search, making her hastily lock her phone. She looked up to see Dante's huge form walk smoothly out the doors, his body in one of those pristine dark suits she'd come to associate with him. Morana tilted her head, considering the man, realizing she'd judged him a little too quickly in the beginning, her own prejudices covering the reality.

Just like Tristan Caine and her, Dante wore a mask on the outside. Being in his company for a few days, seeing the way he had reacted to her bruised body that night, what he'd done despite his misgivings, Morana had warmed to him. Though he was still the enemy, he had been good to her so far. And that was more than she could say for her own father.

Shaking off her thoughts, Morana waved at him and he strode forward to take the chair opposite her, his polite smile in place even though his dark eyes were less guarded than usual. Guess he'd warmed to her too.

"So, what is it you wished to discuss with me, Morana?" he asked in that same cordial tone he'd always used with her.

Morana played with her phone as she asked, already knowing the answer. "Do we have any leads about the codes?"

Dante shook his head. "No. There's been a situation in Tenebrae, and everyone's been busy handling that."

Morana frowned. "That situation with the fake dealers who were pretending to be Outfit?"

"Yes."

Morana pondered on that for a long moment, the wheels in her head turning rapidly. "Do you think it could be connected?"

Dante's brows furrowed in confusion. "What could be connected?"

Morana sighed impatiently, leaning forward on her elbows, her mind racing as the dots started to make an odd kind of sense.

"All of this! Don't you think it's weird? The timing of it all? Someone pretends to be Mr. Caine and steals the codes from me, taking the extra efforts to frame him should the codes be used. Also, enough to get my attention, which had I not been me would've meant the attention of my family. And then someone pretends to be the Outfit where you guys used to do business and takes the profits while framing you for the losses. Really, what are the odds?"

How could she not have seen this before? There was a clear pattern. There was one person or one group doing all of this, one mastermind.

But who were they trying to frame - Tristan Caine or the Outfit? Was it personal or was it bigger than that? And how did she figure into all of it?

Dante sat in stunned silence for a whole minute, absorbing what she'd said, the implications of what she'd said going through his head at breakneck speed. She could feel it even though his face refused to betray a thought. He and his blood brother were certainly alike in that regard.

"Could it be your father?" Dante finally broke the silence, asking the most obvious question.

Morana shook her head. "No. Had it been him, he'd have just ordered me to give him the codes and never let the whole Jackson-is-my-boyfriend-thing happen. That would hinder his greater agenda of getting me married to some asshole who wants a pristine, virginal mob bride."

Dante's mouth flattened in a hard line, his eyes dimming slightly. "That's how this world works, Morana. I wish it didn't. I'd give anything for it not to, but that's how it is. You are truly lucky you could escape. Not everyone is."

Morana looked at him, her heart softening as she remembered what Amara had told her in similar words.

Taking a deep breath before she could respond, he pinched the bridge of his nose, clearly done with whatever emotion he'd expressed. "Okay, so we have to consider the possibility, which is large, that these are all connected events and not isolated like we had been treating them to be. Thank you for that. Anything else?"

Morana shook off her own gloomy thoughts and inhaled. "Yes. I'm going to write a failsafe software that will prevent any consequences of the original codes since we can't get it and destroy it. So this software will undo anything that one does once I initialize it."

Dante raised his eyebrows. "Will it work?"

"In theory, it already does. Writing it is going to be a bit of a job though."

He nodded. "Great. If that works, we'll all sleep much better."

Morana bit her lip, her hands wanting to wring each other for this next part. "But, to write this, I'm going to need my own stuff. My laptop and hard drives, mainly. Which, by the way, is still in my office. In my suite. In my house. Which I left a few nights ago."

Dante nodded, standing up. "It'll be handled. Do you need anything else?"

Morana shook her head. "Thank you. I'm good."

"Good. Call me if you think of anything else."

With another polite nod to her, he strode out towards the elevators just as the doors opened, and Tristan Caine, in a suit without the tie, walked out, coming to an abrupt stop upon seeing Dante.

So, the ice between them had not cooled since the disastrous lunch. Good to know.

His eyes never moved in her direction from the other man, and Morana forced herself not to move, not to attract his attention, not to allow him to influence her emotions. She liked her level-headed self a lot, thanks very much. And this man made her want to scream like a banshee on crack, which although wasn't the most enticing imagery, was very appropriate.

It also helped to know that first – he had avoided her for two days – and second – that he usually never addressed her as long as there were other human beings in the room. She didn't know his policy on cats or puppies so far. So, she was safe from her banshee self for a little while longer, and if all worked the way it had been, he'd be gone and she'd be rational.

"We need to talk, Tristan."

Not the most inviting of statements. But at least Dante's even voice cut through the tension between the two men enough to make her look up at them – two tall, broad, handsome men who were as lethal as men could be.

"Yes, we do," Tristan Caine replied, the warning in his tone clear for her to hear, warning for Dante not to open his mouth with her ears glued to them. As if. She rolled her eyes and turned back to her phone, aware of both men leaving the apartment and getting into the elevator. The doors closed with a soft 'ding', and Morana felt the tension she hadn't been aware of seeping in leave her body on a loud exhale.

So, new codes out of the way till she got her stuff, Morana unlocked her phone and got back to researching the mysterious break of the twenty-two years ago Alliance.

Morana woke up abruptly, disoriented, her neck in an odd position on the back of the couch, her legs numb and curled under her, her hair sprawled all over the place as her hands held her phone, lost somewhere on her lap. She straightened her neck, a dull ache throbbing where she'd given herself a crick, her eyes going to the gorgeous windows, to see dusk settle across the city in a fiery embrace, losing itself to the dark velvet of the coming night. The twinkling lights of the city and the cool waves of the sea on the opposite side were a cool contrast to her senses.

This was a view she'd been seeing for the past few nights without fail, these windows becoming a part of her since that rainy night in a way her car was. And yet, she didn't think she'd ever tire of watching this same thing over and over and over again. It wasn't just the beauty of it all. It was more than that. It was the memory of what had accompanied this beauty, the memory of a sad, lonely night that hadn't been so lonely anymore.

Would she have felt the same way about these windows had that memory not been there? Or would they have been like the windows of her own house? Just windows. Yet, every time she looked their way, every time she saw the city, saw the sea, saw the stars and the limitless sky, her breath caught in her throat.

Just as it was at the moment.

She suddenly became aware of her surroundings as sleep drifted further and further away from her mind.

The lights were still off, only the glow from the outside world penetrating inside, seducing the shadows inside, the sound of her own breath lingering around her in the stillness.

But she knew she wasn't alone.

He was there. Somewhere in the dark. Watching her.

She didn't know where he was, didn't turn her head to feel him in those seduced shadows, didn't do anything but sit still, letting him watch, letting herself thrill in being watched. It was twisted. It was wrong in so many ways. It had never felt so right.

And this, right here, was exactly what she didn't understand about herself, about them. This need to give and seek attention from each other while loathing it. This thrill that shot through her even as she knew it shouldn't. This heightened awareness inside every pore of her body as soon as he came into the vicinity.

Had it been like this since that first night in Tenebrae? Or had it happened later? Where had she lost her body, her senses to his? At what point had being watched by someone in the dark from behind become not something threatening but thrilling? And only by him, because Morana knew, was it someone else, she'd be running for the knife.

Her heart pounded in the silence, as she stayed unmoving, barely breathing, nerves stretching tighter and tighter with every single breath, her nipples hardening under the constraining fabric of her bra, heat pooling between her legs. Good lord, she was ready to combust and she didn't even know where he was. Didn't know how he was affected. She was going to change that. Make sure he got as affected as she did. She wasn't going to be burning alone, not if she could help it. If he afflicted her with this insane lust, the least she could do was return the favor.

He liked to watch? She'd give him a fucking show.

Trusting her instincts, which had worked pretty well for her so far, Morana slowly uncoiled her body from its slumberous position, stretching her arms above her head and her legs out before her, arching her spine, playing his game. She was caught unawares by the sudden rush of blood to her sleeping legs, the sudden million pinpricks bursting across her skin.

A moan of relief escaped her lips unbidden before she could call it back, and she suddenly tensed.

That one sound in the silence had been loud as a scream. It hadn't broken the tension. It had thickened it.

Morana could feel his eyes drift leisurely, heatedly all over her, examining her with a scrutiny that should have been disturbing but wasn't, would have been disturbing but wasn't. The thickened silence hung over her like a thunder cloud. She held her breath, her heart pounding, for the lightning to split the air between them, for the thunder to roar in her body, for the electricity to singe them and leave its mark.

She waited.

His eyes never moved away even as she felt his movement in the room, the air snapping around him, changing around her. Was he stepping closer? Or farther? Would she feel his breath on her skin, or feel the empty caress of the air?

She waited, her nerves stretched so taut she was afraid she would snap.

The sudden vibration of her phone on her thigh made her jump, her heart thumping against her ribs. Aware of his eyes on her, Morana picked up her phone with slightly unsteady hands and unlocked the screen, blinking at the message.

**Tristan Caine:** *Meet me in the parking lot in 5 minutes.*

Morana could've spoken. She could've talked and asked him why. But she didn't want to break this silence, this moment where she was sitting in the dark alone being watched by him from the darker shadows.

**Me:** *Planning to make me go somewhere, Mr. Caine?*

**Tristan Caine:** *On the contrary, I'm planning to make you come somewhere, Ms. Vitalio. 5 minutes.*

Her breath caught as she read the message, the dinging of the elevator loud in the quiet of the penthouse, telling her he'd left her alone and stepped back. Knowing he was gone, Morana put a hand to her racing heart, feeling its hard thump under her fingers, her breasts heavy and heaving as she inhaled and exhaled, regularizing her breaths.

Was she really going to do this again? Let him do this again? That time in the restaurant had been to get them out of their systems. It had failed spectacularly. Would this time get him out? And just in case it didn't, would she let him fuck her again? At what cost? She wasn't foolish enough to delude herself into thinking it won't deepen whatever connection they already had. Could she risk it? Maybe she was overthinking it. Maybe they'd get themselves out of their systems, and Morana would develop the counter codes and leave everything peacefully with closure.

Another incoming text interrupted her thoughts.

***Tristan Caine:*** *If you're scared...*

He was baiting her. Why?

***Me:*** *Of what?*

***Tristan Caine:*** *Come and see for yourself.*

What, was he parading around naked in the lot with whipped cream smeared over his man parts?

***Me:*** *You use 'come' a lot, you know that?*

***Tristan Caine:*** *Women are usually grateful in all sorts of ways.*

Morana scoffed, trying not to let the image of him tangled with some gorgeous woman, multiple women, get to her. It didn't bother her. *Not. At. All.*
Standing up and straightening her clothes, she slipped her feet into her flats and headed for the elevator, typing all the while.

***Me:*** *You actually let them speak during sex? Outside of a restroom? How classy.*

The elevator doors slid open and she got inside, looking back at herself in the mirror, at her tousled hair and the tank top that tended to slip her shoulders. The jeans Amara had loaned her was slightly loose on her, the hem folded back to accommodate her shorter height. She looked like a little hipster who'd burst into a song and dance at the drop of a hat, like in a music video.
Scoffing, she pushed her phone inside her pocket, straightening the strap of her top, and walked out when the doors opened. Dante and Tristan Caine stood together, talking in quiet tones beside his bike. It was her first proper glimpse of him since the afternoon, and she was

surprised to find him wearing not the suit he'd been wearing during the day, but well-worn jeans that hugged his ass in ways she could envy, and that black leather jacket of his. She was surprised because it meant he'd been in the apartment longer than she'd realized. It meant he'd let her sleep without disturbing her, and she didn't know what to make of that.

Dante looked at her, gave her a small nod and headed to his car, dialing someone on his phone.

And then, Tristan Caine took one handle of that beast of a bike, swung one leg over it, the muscles of his thighs flexing under that jeans in a way that made her insides roar with feminine appreciation. He settled his ass back on the seat, picking up a helmet from behind him and finally looking at her with those piercing blue eyes. It was only then that she noticed a second helmet on the seat. A smaller, more feminine helmet.

Fuck.

He was taking her out on his bike? His bike? The sacred, holy bike? The bike he actually enjoyed riding?

"If you're done gaping, Ms. Vitalio, we're on a clock," his rough, low voice rasped over her, breaking her out of her stupor, his eyes locked on her.

Morana gulped and walked forward, apprehension curling in her stomach along with excitement, eyeing the beautiful black and red chrome monster, the seat higher than her waist. How in the world was she going to climb onto it?

She picked up the smaller helmet, aware of his gaze on her. It wasn't new and it was clearly feminine. Who did it belong to? Or was it like the common helmet for any and all females climbing the back? For some reason, the idea did not sit well with her.

"Who's is this?" she blurted out before she could stop herself, berating herself the moment the words left her lips.

Tristan Caine raised an eyebrow at her but stayed silent, and suddenly, a horrible, horrible thought occurred to her. Was there someone he was supposed to be with back in...? She shook the thought off even before it could complete. No. What little she knew of him, from what she'd seen and heard, Tristan Caine did not mistreat women. She was the only exception and even with his hatred, he'd given her sanctuary when she'd needed it to lick her wounds and heal.

Had there been someone else, he wouldn't have pursued her as sexually as he had.

Morana was certain of that.

This was exactly why she took a deep breath and put on the helmet, looking up at him, to find him staring back at her with an inscrutable look.

"You might want to remove those glasses," he commented, his lips in a completely straight line.

Pulling them off wordlessly, she floundered for a second, wondering where to put it to keep it safe, before tucking one ear-handle into her cleavage, letting the glasses hang off her tank top. She looked up to find those blue, blue eyes watching her exposed skin unabashedly, before leisurely stroking over her neck, her mouth, and halting at her eyes.

They stayed that way for a moment before he turned back to face the front, his lithe, graceful body moving as he kicked the bike off the stand. He started it with a powerful thrust, waiting.

Morana felt an odd kind of excitement filling her.

She'd never been on a bike. Only ever in her car and her father's.

Her first time on the back of a bike, with Tristan Caine.

Morana took in a deep breath, putting her feet on the stand and her hands on those broad, muscular shoulders for support, swinging her leg over. She settled onto the seat, her legs spread wide and held that way by his hips in between them. The beast of a bike rumbled underneath her, sending vibrations up and down her spine, vibrations into her core, making her bite back on a gasp.

"You'll need to hold more than my shoulder if you don't want to fall," his voice rumbled over the noise of the engine.

She didn't want to.

But she did too.

Morana hesitated, but slowly placed her hands on the sides of his jacket, feeling nothing but tight, packed muscles beneath the leather, her fingers flexing against the warmth of his flesh.

"And keep your leg off that big rod on the right."

She'd already figured that one out for herself.

After a second, the bike rumbled under her as he pulled out of the spot, the vibrations quickening against her flesh as the bike picked up speed, pressing her flush against his massive back.

Dear Lord, how was she supposed to survive an entire ride like this?

He pulled down his visor and throttled the engine once before pulling out of the lot, exiting into the quiet street in front of the building, turning left once on the bridge, flying across it.

The world sped by faster and faster, becoming a blur she could not see without her glasses, the motion of the bike smoother than she'd thought it would be. The wind whipped through her free locks, sending them careening wildly into different directions as her breasts flattened completely against him, her body plastered to his as she gripped him around the stomach, his abs rock hard against her palms. The bike purred under her like a content beast being stroked seductively by his lover.

And she had to admit it, Tristan Caine rode the bike well. Really well. He maneuvered around crowded areas expertly, gave it free rein in the open road, all the while in complete control of the monster. Not for one second did she feel worried about breaking her neck, and she should have as they raced across the almost empty freeway way beyond the speed limit. She should have worried when she felt the gun he'd tucked into the back of his jeans press against her stomach. But she didn't.

All she felt was free.

Wild.

Exhilarated in a way she'd never been before.

Was this the high he got every time he climbed his bike? Was this the freedom he tasted that was so elusive in their lives? Was this the wildness he felt beat like a pulse through his blood?

Morana tilted her head back, feeling every caress of the wind over her skin, feeling a rush so profound she couldn't even explain it to herself. So she didn't. She let herself go, let herself have this, let herself be free in a way she had never believed was possible.

Removing her arms from around him, she tightened her grip on his hips with her thighs and raised her hands above her head. Some switch inside her had flipped. She knew he wouldn't let her fall, or he already would have, on the many chances he'd had to destroy her. She knew he would destroy her, but not today. Today, for the first time, she got to be no one but a girl on the back of a man's motorcycle, if even for a moment. Today, for the first time, she was just a woman with no past and no future, just this endless road with this man, this freedom, and this life.

She couldn't contain the loud shout of pure exhilaration rushing through her lips, the loud scream announcing to the world of her joy, letting the man controlling this bike know she was enjoying it. She was not inhibited about it.

Morana spread her arms, closing her eyes, feeling the wind rub against her, feeling him rub against her, feeling the bike rub against her.

She yelled even louder - unashamed, unbound, unchained.

She let herself feel deeper - uncaring, unhinged, unabashed.

It was just a bike. It was just a ride. It was just a man.

It just *was*.

It was almost an hour later that reality intruded.

Tristan Caine turned from the main road onto a dirt lane she'd known all her life, and for the first time in an hour of bliss, her heart started pounding again. Her fingers flexed against his abs as she saw the massive structure of the Vitalio mansion loom behind the wrought iron gates.

What the hell?

He stopped the bike on the side of the property, nearer to her wing than the gates. He parked behind thick bushes that were tall enough to hide them from the view.

The sudden quiet under her thighs contrasted starkly with the buzz that coursed through her body, setting her senses on high alert, only the sound of nocturnal creatures penetrating the area around them along with her own blood pounding in her ears.

Slowly, she removed her fingers from his stomach and her arms from around him. She pulled back enough to give him the space to get down. He did one of those leg-over-the-handle moves that she'd only seen on Sons of Anarchy, and was standing on solid ground within minutes, waiting for her to disembark.

Morana removed her helmet and handed it over to him, pulling her glasses from between her breasts and putting them on her nose, blinking at the world suddenly coming into focus. She found his intense blue eyes on her, just watching her as she threw her leg around the bike and hopped down.

Big mistake.

The sudden standing position made her knees crumple beneath her just as hands gripped her low on her hips and pulled her upright, her hands landing on his hard chest for support as blood rushed to her legs.

"You enjoy riding," he said softly into the space between their faces.

Morana watched the moonlight play with the shadows on his face. His scruff hid his cheeks while his eyes seemed even bluer, focused on her with the same expression she could feel pulsing inside herself – sheer, undiluted exhilaration.

"You enjoy making me ride," Morana shot back just as quietly.

His lips twitched for a second, his eyes drifting to her mouth for a long, heady moment, before the veil came back over his face and he took a step back, leaving her standing on thankfully steady legs.

Taking out his phone, he pressed it to his ear and spoke, "Now," before hanging up.

Morana raised her eyebrows. How eloquent.

A moment later, a chunk of the wall of the property came away. A man with a thick beard stood on the other side in a guard's uniform, nodding respectfully at Tristan Caine.

He had spies in her father's house?

Of course, he did.

That was how he'd gotten inside and climbed her wall so easily all those weeks ago. God, that was so long ago. She'd been so different then, in so many ways.

Morana looked at him, taking him in, and realized how much she'd changed since then, and how much he had to do with it.

"Clear?" Tristan Caine asked the guard, his voice cold, lethal.

The man nodded. "Yes, sir. You can go straight to the wing. Nobody will bother you."

Holy... okay. That was a first. Another first.

Morana watched, stunned, as Tristan Caine entered the premises, telling her with his eyes to follow him.

He was breaking into her father's house.

She was breaking into her father's house.

Her father - the most dangerous man on this side of the country.

*Not right now,* a voice whispered inside her head as she watched the man beside her. He moved with that stealthy grace of his as the guard disappeared somewhere in the shrubbery, the moonlight their only guide across the trees that lined the property.

Morana's heart thudded erratically in her chest. This was beyond anything she'd ever imagined she would do. Yet, there she was, following the enemy's footsteps as he wove his way in and out of the green, intruding on her father's property to retrieve something of hers.

Watching him weave his way over that made Morana realize just how well he knew this property. Better than any enemy should know. She wondered if her father had any idea at all.

Morana saw the window of her bedroom come into view minutes later. Were they going to do the crazy climbing thing he'd done the last time? Because she couldn't fly, and she sure as hell did not have those biceps to hold her while she dangled fifteen feet off the ground. She wasn't the biggest fan of heights either, something she could not let him discover or he'd probably kill her by throwing her off a high cliff. She'd rather die by a plain gunshot to the head. Vertigo sucked.

Shaking off her gloomy thoughts, Morana swallowed, her palms sweating, heart racing. Without thinking, she placed her hand on his back.

He stilled completely, turning around to pin her to the spot with those magnificent eyes shining in the moonlight.

She blanked.

Tristan Caine, in motion, was beautiful. But Tristan Caine, in utter stillness, could not be described.

She didn't even try.

"How are we getting inside?" she whispered, keeping her voice as low as she could, the fear of discovery, of execution, not just hers but his making her antsy.

"Through the door."

Before Morana could utter a word, he wrapped his long, rough fingers around her wrist. Pulling her behind him, they across the empty patch of grass on quiet feet, his longer strides making her work double to catch up. They ran across the clearing, in clear view of anyone who happened to look their way.

Her heart in her throat the entire time, fear and thrill fighting for dominance in her body, Morana ran faster than she'd ever run, still so much slower than him, his hand pulling her along the only thing to keep her from stumbling at the speed.

They reached the side door to her wing, the one beside the stairs, and he clicked it open. Slipping inside, he pulled her along in one smooth move. In silence, awed by the fact that they'd made it without discovery, they walked in the dark hallway that opened up to the staircase.

The same dreaded staircase her father had all but pushed her down from.

Morana came to an abrupt halt at the foot of the stairs, the memory of her disillusionment crashing through her body, the same bruised body that had only just healed at the hands of the enemy. Her father had not known whether she would live or break her neck in the fall. He'd just let her go, and lay a trap that she had fallen for hook, line, and sinker in her emotional state.

She wasn't emotional now. No. She was logical, calm, and rational where he was concerned.

For some reason, the emotions inspired by the man beside her were much greater in intensity than the one inspired by these stairs, affording her that calm. And for the first time, she was grateful for it. She didn't want him to witness that, to witness her being any more vulnerable than she had already been when it came to her father.

Without another word, constantly aware of his scrutiny of her, she quickly climbed up the stairs, knowing he was right behind her even though she could not hear him. She'd never thought she'd walk these steps again, and it seemed surreal to be doing so not only stealthily in the dead of the night but also with the man who'd vowed to kill her. She needed to keep reminding herself of that, even as she felt things change inside her. There was a reason he hated her enough to take that vow, and until she discovered it, she could not, would not let all her guards down.

She made her way hastily to her suite, unlocking the door and heading towards the study where she kept her equipment, ignoring any nostalgia inspired by her small haven. Opening the door, she stood for a moment on the threshold, looking around the little heaven she had created for herself in this strange place. She remembered every countless night she'd spent working here, remembered the dreams she'd had of getting away from it all in here.

That girl seemed so different from who she had become. That girl with hope and dreams and the fire to make it.

She didn't even know who she was any more in so many ways. Had she lost the fire somewhere along the way?

"Get what you need."

Whiskey and sin. Molten lava and dancing flames.

No, she hadn't lost the fire. It just lay dormant inside her most days. And what she couldn't figure out was why him. Why not Jackson, or any of her father's men, or even Dante for that matter? Why this man with the voice of sin and the body of a sinner? He called her fire forth like a mage and she did not understand it.

Morana nodded to acknowledge his words and quickly hurried about, picking up her laptop from where it still lay on the desk. Opening the bottom drawer, she pulled out her hard drives, dumping them all in a small backpack from the desk. Taking a quick inventory, realizing she had everything she needed, Morana looked about the room one last time, memorizing it, and swallowed down the lump in her throat.

He was watching her, and she needed to be cool.

Inhaling deeply, she turned to him, only to find him leaning against the door casually, like he owned the place. Those focused blue eyes observed everything that crossed her face while his own remained carefully blank. Morana felt her heart start to stutter in that familiar way it did with him, the fire flooding her bloodstream, igniting every cell it touched.

This was not the place for this. If there was ever *not* a place for this, it was her father's house.

"All done?" he asked quietly, his voice even but tone heated with something her body recognized and called back to.

She nodded.

He let her take the bag and moved out of the suite as she followed, her warm body not giving her the luxury of emotions at that moment. They went down the stairs, the house dark and quiet, and she didn't know whether her father was in or not. Nor did she care.

Opening the side door, he escaped out first, pulling her behind him as they stayed in the shadows, walking towards the tree line.

Suddenly, a group of guards came around the corner, talking among themselves, their guns relaxed on their shoulders.

Morana halted in her tracks, her mind blanking as fear filled her veins, and she turned around to run for cover the exact moment a hand pulled her roughly and pushed her face-first against an alcove in the wall at the side of the house. Heart hammering in her ears, blood rushing around in her body with a vengeance, Morana stayed completely still, overwhelming sensations crashing over her as the scent of leather and musk permeating all around her as she took in a few deep breaths, becoming aware of many things all at once.

His arms trapped her against the wall, hands flat beside her head as his body completely covered hers from view, his large form curled over her in a way that was not protective but something else entirely, something she could not define. His breaths brushed over her ear, his scruff rasping against the skin of her neck as he tucked his head in to make them merge even deeper into the shadows.

But it was his body against her back, his tall, hard, lethal body against her small back that made her knees shake.

Her breath caught in her throat.

He did not move.

His erection pushed into her back.

He did not move.

The guards' voices faded away.

He did not move.

The fire pooled in her belly, low between her legs, making her instinctively arch against him.

Then, he moved.

He pushed the bag off her shoulder to the ground, the strap of her top falling down to her elbow with it. His hand traced her bare skin with a rough finger. Breaths hitched, Morana closed her eyes, feeling the calluses on his hand rub deliciously against her soft skin, the goosebumps scattering all over her arms, making her nipples pebble, making her breasts hurt as heat licked between her legs.

He hadn't touched her like this the last time. He hadn't breathed against her neck like this and rubbed his jaw over the spot against her shoulder, all the while keeping his mouth away from her. His hand slowly moved around her neck, leaving her breasts untouched, unattended like last time. She wanted – no, *needed* – him to touch them. She needed him to tug on her nipples, and give her that sweet pleasure she knew her body was capable of. She needed to rub them against his thumb, and create that delicious friction she could feel pulse inside her core.

She needed his hands on her breasts.

But his hand closed around her neck, in that hold she'd come to recognize, firm but not tight, as his lips moved right next to her ear.

"Did you feel me inside you the next day?" he whispered against the soft skin of her shell, the whiskey in his voice going straight to her head, his words going straight to her core. Her walls clenched in the memory of that hard, fast fuck on the restroom counter.

Morana bit her lip, not giving him her response verbally, even as her hips pushed back against his. She felt his cock slip against her ass as she stood on her toes, the erotic friction making her behave like a cat in heat rather than the smart, rational woman she'd been until moments ago.

Her anger at herself though, her regret for letting this happen again was much less than what it'd been a few days ago. She didn't know what that spoke about her, or even what it meant, but for now, she embraced it, her head falling back against his shoulder as she ground herself on him, with her front pressed to the wall.

His hand tightened around her throat, his hips thrusting against her as his other hand slipped inside her jeans, her panties, homing in straight on her sweet spot. Her mouth fell open on a pant as he buried his digits knuckle deep inside her.

"So fucking wet for me," he growled in her ear, his hips pushing forcefully against her ass. His fingers worked on her front, the hard brick wall rubbing against her breasts, scraping against her nipples, making her walls quiver every time his fingers slipped in and out. His thumb rubbed over her clit.

"Fuck if I'm not hard for you," he spat, his hatred, his desire, his possession seeping from his voice into her body. Her heartbeats pulsed everywhere she felt him. His scent, his warmth, his touch surrounding her, imprisoning her, invading her in a way that made her blood so hot she felt like a ticking time bomb waiting to explode.

His hand moved against her, inside her, as he moved behind her. The dual assault coiled the heat tighter and tighter into her belly, her spine tingling, arching, and pulsing with electric sparks of pleasure as she bit her lip to keep her pants contained.

Before she could question it or stop herself, Morana slipped a hand behind her, cupping him through the fabric of his jeans. She squeezed him hard as he cursed into her ear, his fingers speeding up impossibly inside her.

"Not – fucking – here."

He gave her clit one rub, then another right before he pinched it hard, and simultaneously covered her mouth with the other hand. Muffling her noises like before, he pushed her over the edge as she came all over his fingers, panting loudly, her breasts heaving. Every single beat of her heart throbbed everywhere in her body.

She throbbed. She pulsed. She clenched. She quivered.

His fingers remained inside her for a few moments, milking out her orgasm as much as they could before he pulled his fingers out of her pants, wiping them over his jeans and picked up the fallen bag while surveying the area.

And Morana just stood there – speechless, stunned – looking at the wall.

The wall of her father's house. The wall of the same house where her father lived. The wall of the heart of his territory.

And Morana had let Tristan Caine make her come like a firecracker, against that very wall, out in the open while guards patrolled the area, while he remained completely under control.

Fuck.

*Fuck.*

What was wrong with her? What was wrong with him?

This was the restaurant all over again except much, much more twisted. No, this wasn't a proper fuck, and yes, it had been the mother of quickies. Still.

The worst part though? She didn't feel an ounce of remorse.

A hand closed around her arm and turned her around, making her face those blue eyes still heated with the lust of an animal who'd caught the scent of blood, the hunger in them so intense her still-hot body pooled with molten lava, ready again. Just with his eyes.

He leaned forward, his breath whispering across her cheek, his scent engulfing her as his lips lined against her ears.

"Next time, I'm going to see how loud you can scream, Ms. Vitalio. I'm going to make you so sore you won't know if it's from the screaming or the fucking."

This man needed a leash for that dirty, explicit mouth.

Morana rolled her eyes even as her heart stuttered, his words settling into her inflamed body.

"You give yourself a little too much credit."

"Say that when I can't still smell you on my fingers."

She could too. And the fact that this knowledge aroused her while it shouldn't have made Morana purse her lips, the reminder of his control and the lack of hers like a slap to her senses.

She straightened herself, pulling the bag over her shoulder, and gave him an icy glare. "Can we leave?"

His eyes narrowed slightly at her tone and he considered her for a long moment, his fingers flexing on her arm before he nodded. Turning, he pulled her towards the tree line. They walked in silence for a few minutes, Morana contemplative.

They were almost at the property wall when her phone suddenly vibrated with an incoming message in her pocket.

Ignoring it, Morana focused on getting to the hole they had entered through, seeing the guard waiting for them there. Morana reached the opening and climbed out of it, walking towards the parked beast of a bike, not willing or ready to think about what had just transpired inside.

She focused instead on the smell of the earth, the light from the moon bathing the house of horrors in clean white while watching Tristan Caine speak quietly to the guard.

Remembering the earlier message while she waited beside the vehicle, she pulled out her phone and unlocked it.

Unknown number.

Frowning, Morana clicked open the message, to find a multimedia image attached and no text. She clicked on the image, her brows furrowing as she made out the scanned picture of some old newspaper article.

Morana tapped on the picture and zoomed in, the words becoming clearer on the screen and read.

## The Count of Missing Girls Shoots Up To 25

*Tenebrae, July 8, 1989: In a ghastly turn of events that have shocked the city, 25 little girls between the ages of 4 and 10 have been gone missing in the 2 years. However, this is only the tip of the iceberg. Sources reveal that these are only the open and reported cases the police are working on.*

*The latest victim is the 6-year-old Stacy Hopkins (above), who went missing right from the sidewalk while her mother turned the corner at Madison Avenue. It is unclear as to who is to blame. While some believe this to be the work of organized crime groups, some have even talked of the occult. Most of the girls, from what our sources revealed, had gone missing from right under adult supervision...*

Morana read the entire article describing the gruesome details, not understanding why someone had sent this to her. Who had sent it? And why? Had it been sent by mistake? It must have been.

Bothered about what she'd read but ready to put it out of her mind for the moment as Tristan Caine walked towards her, Morana almost locked her phone when something on the screen caught her eye. A tiny little note was handwritten in the corner with the headline.

*Check the article from July 5, 1998.*

An article dated twenty-two years ago.

# deciding

She couldn't decide if she was really, really brave or really, really stupid.

Maybe an odd combination of both.

Honestly, there were times when Morana wasn't particularly proud of herself, even while she wanted to pump her fist in the air and jump in glee. The reason for that was simple – sometimes, Morana did things in her recklessness that she knew she shouldn't but still when she succeeded in doing them, she wanted to preen.

Right then was one of those reckless moments that made her want to preen.

She contained the urge. *Barely.*

The reason for both her stupidity and her bravery was five cars down, driving a huge black SUV, the vehicle so huge she was easily able to keep her eye on it from so far down the lane. Not a good vehicle for covert operations at all. But since it worked in her favor, she liked it.

After returning back to the penthouse from her old house with her stuff, Morana had locked herself in the guest room and gotten to work on the new set of codes, while also running a background check for the newspaper article some mysterious person had sent her from over thirty years ago. Tracking the said mysterious person had been impossible despite her numerous tries, telling her the one thing she'd needed to know about him or her – he or she knew computers. *Really* knew computers, for having evaded her.

And it made her wonder if they hadn't been related to the original theft of the codes.

She'd mulled over a lot of possibilities while doing the work. Thankfully, the owner of the apartment hadn't bothered or interrupted her at all. Not once in the thirty hours that she'd been working tirelessly on the codes - not for food, or drinks, or just plain staring.

Nothing.

And honestly, after getting the article, she was grateful. Because there were things going on, things she had no idea about. She needed some answers before getting in deeper than she already was. Her stray thoughts had been evident enough for him on the ride back to the apartment, and he'd withdrawn himself.

For nearly thirty hours, Morana had worked on the base for the new codes. She actually made a whole lot of progress, but it wasn't that which had sent her down the path to recklessness. Oh no. It had been the article, or rather, the background search.

Trying to find something on the Alliance had resulted in absolutely nothing. But trying to find about the series of kidnappings in Tenebrae thirty years ago had yielded more results and gruesome truths than she'd been able to digest.

It had been a series of forty-five abductions (at least those known to the public). Abductions of young girls from their homes or parks that had spanned over a period of ten years. The missing girls were never found, not one. Since they had been abducted sporadically over the years, it had been hard for the police to gather much evidence.

Morana was smart enough to connect some dots, yet she had no clue how that was related to the fall of the Alliance. She didn't even know *if* it had something to do with it. For all she knew, the person behind the article could've been a lunatic or just a prankster.

Yet, she knew in her gut it was connected.

She had since the moment she'd seen the article and the note. The note had led her to the last article reporting the disappearance of a baby Jane Doe.

Morana had tried, after catching up on some much-needed sleep, to try and talk to Amara about it. It had been the beautiful woman after all who'd given her the first clue. But the moment she'd brought up the kidnappings and the Alliance, Amara had stiffened and zipped her lips tight. Morana knew it was because of the loyalty she felt towards Tristan Caine, but it had only frustrated her. Dante would've been as helpful as a goat, and asking Tristan Caine alone would've either resulted in her pressed against the nearest flat surface or dead.

And she wanted answers. Not his fingers wreaking havoc on her, or his knife slicing her skin open.

Just answers.

Which was why, under dire circumstances, her brain had come up with a plan after exhausting every single option (short of alien abductions). The plan was simple in theory - find out something about Tristan Caine, something to hold over his head (because that man's closet of skeletons could accommodate a small country, she was certain), and then blackmail him into giving her the truth.

Or die. But at least she'd go down knowing she'd tried her best to find out the truth.

In theory, it was a good plan. In execution, it was reckless.

That was exactly the reason she'd been ready and dressed inside the guest room this morning, waiting for him to leave so she could follow him out. Her car, her beautiful baby, had been waiting for her, purring under her as she'd started it. Happy to be back inside it, she'd told the guard at the gate that she needed some computer stuff. After he opened the gates, she had pressed down on the gas, shooting out into the road like a bullet, whizzing past the other cars to catch up with the one Tristan Caine had taken.

She'd been following him for almost an hour, at a very safe distance where she was sure he couldn't spot her in the rearview mirror, occasionally admiring his driving skills. The man maneuvered the big SUV almost as well as he did that beast of a bike. For some reason she didn't want to explore, she was partial to the bike.

The hard sun shone relentlessly down on the road as she followed him out of town. The city was slowly left behind for more and more countryside as she carefully kept her distance, knowing how observant he was.

He drove on the highway for almost ten minutes before turning onto a dirt road off to the left, disappearing behind the line of trees that shrouded the path.

Morana stopped her car, the sun glinting off the hood as the cool conditioned air brushed over the skin of her bare arms. Biting her lip, she waited for the SUV to get far enough away so she could follow. The fact that she couldn't actually see the vehicle anymore made her jittery.

She slowly restarted the car, hovering on the edge of the turn, palms slightly sweaty because she had no idea what he would do if he discovered her tailing him. But it was too late to turn back. She was already on the reckless path, might as well follow through. Plus, answers.

The moment the other vehicle would've been nothing but a dot in the distance, Morana turned slowly onto the dirt road. Her car went over the bumps roughly as she drove through at snail's speed, his choice of vehicle suddenly making sense to her. But that made her wonder –how did he know the areas around her city so well like a resident? Could it be something as simple as GPS?

She grit her teeth, following as inconspicuously as she could, her whole body jarring over the bad road and shushed her mind, storing random thoughts away for later.

Almost after five minutes of driving at a speed slower than her car was capable of, an old barn came into view. It stood tall and abandoned under the high sun, the woods around it concealing it from the view of the highway.

The SUV came to a stop outside it, and Morana quickly maneuvered her car behind some trees on the side of the path, hiding it completely from view behind the thick foliage. Taking her gun out from her bag, Morana opened the door noiselessly and got out, tucking the weapon at the small of her back in the waistband of her jeans, silently crouching down beside a tree to watch the scene.

She saw Tristan Caine's muscled form fold itself out from the driver's side, his eyes hidden behind dark shades as he removed the jacket of his suit and threw it in the car. Without missing a step, he shut the door, the fabric of the white shirt clinging to the muscles she knew were harder than they looked. He started walking towards the main entrance of the barn, disappearing inside.

Morana waited for a beat, adrenaline flooding her system as she quietly made her way to the building, still crouched low, looking around to constantly check she wasn't being watched.

The door was partially open.

Without making a sound, she slipped inside carefully, blinking once, then twice, to let her eyes adjust to the dark as muffled voices reached her ears.

Eyeing a pillar right near the entrance, Morana slid behind it. Looking out, she was careful to stay low in the shadows while the sunlight filtered in through the high windows, the beams lighting the center of the empty space.

Tristan Caine stood in the center, four tall men surrounding him as he stood still, just watching them.

Gripping the pillar with her hands for support, she leaned slightly closer, the voices becoming clearer as they echoed in the cavernous space.

"Last I knew, Doug ran across the ocean without finishing his end of the bargain. Where is he now?" Tristan Caine asked calmly, in a quiet voice that made a shiver run down Morana's spine. He spoke as though he wasn't surrounded by dangerous looking thugs with weapons while he had absolutely none.

One of the men laughed, shaking his head. "Why do you want Doug?"

"That's my business," Tristan Caine replied in the same voice, his body still but alert, his eyes never moving from the men.

"You wakin' up old skeletons, Caine," the man she assumed was the leader of the group warned. "There's a rumor running 'bout you. 'Bout 'dem missing girls."

Morana held her breath.

Tristan Caine sighed.

*Sighed.*

"You want to walk out of here, tell me where Doug is," he informed them, slowly unbuttoning his shirt at the sleeves and rolling them up those forearms, the hint of his tattoo coming out from under it, a tattoo she had yet to see in detail.

The two men behind him exchanged looks, before suddenly pulling out their knives and throwing it right at his back.

Morana covered her mouth to stifle her gasp, her heart pounding as she watched in disbelief. Tristan Caine dropped down to his haunches without turning back even once, as though he'd been aware of every single movement the entire time, the knives missing him completely and falling down with a clatter.

Before the others could even react, he was on his feet, punching one guy right in the throat, breaking the bone with a loud snap, while kicking the other out simultaneously with his foot.

The other two came at him, one with a gun that he disarmed in seconds while breaking the guy's wrist, and choking the other man with an arm wrapped around his neck.

The man passed out.

Taking the gun he'd divested the leader of, Tristan Caine shot him right on the knee caps, on both of them, the sound of the gun loud in the barn. Morana watched in silence, swallowing down her nerves, as he sat down on his haunches in front of the bleeding man, and tilted his head to the side casually, his hands draped lazily over his knees.

"Where's Doug?" Tristan Caine asked again.

The man blubbered in pain, cursing everything to hell and back. "Don't know, man."

Tristan Caine pushed the gun into the wound and the man screamed so loudly Morana felt herself flinch.

"Don't know, I swear," the man blubbered. "Swear. Just know he visits the *Saturn* backroom every Saturday. That's all I know. I swear."

It was Saturday.

Tristan Caine considered him for a second, then nodded, dropping the gun beside the man and standing up.

Without a care in the world, he walked towards the door, a few steps from where Morana was hiding, her blood rushing to her head, looking at him in awe. It wasn't just awed because of how quickly and smoothly he'd handled four big armed men without a weapon on himself, or at how casual he was about walking away from an injured man with a gun by his side.

She was in awe because watching him, right at that moment, she understood exactly who he was.

*The Predator.*

Always the hunter, never the hunted. He could not be hunted. He could not be tamed. He could not be destroyed. That kind of unbreakable aura was so, so tempting to her.

She should have been disgusted. She should have been exasperated. She should have been horrified. But she was enthralled because she could remember every single time she'd seen her father shoot a man; she could remember the way the blood spurted from the flesh, coating itself on his fingers as he'd tortured a man. Growing up the way she had, she'd seen men make others bleed, seen them covered in blood, seen them bathe in it.

To her, as horrifying as it was, it wasn't the presence of blood that was odd.

The fact that Tristan Caine had extracted information from a man, made him bleed but hadn't let that blood even touch him was odd.

Morana looked at his hands from her hiding place, looked at him as he made a phone call and spoke too quietly for her to hear, only one thought going through her head after witnessing the scene she had, in contrast to the countless others in her memory.

His hands - his big, rough hands that touched her so intimately - were clean.

*Saturn.*

She'd heard about the place of course, but never really seen it. Never wanted to see it.

It was a casino in East Shadow Port that was frequented by many mobsters – like a neutral ground for members of different families to hold a meeting in her father's territory. As far as she knew, every city had one *Saturn* – and that casino served only one purpose, to let men meet without shedding blood in other's territories. On the face of it, *Saturn,* like every other casino, was flashy – all the glitter an invitation for innocent tourists and civilians to spend their money and try their luck in.

After knowing where Tristan Caine would be headed, Morana had made a quick stop on the way at a boutique. Buying herself the first flashy dress she saw – a very silver, very short number that showed way more skin than she was comfortable showing. But she was pressed for time, so she changed in the dressing room and ran out to her car, stashing the silver heels on the seat beside her.

Pressing down on the accelerator to get to the casino quickly, she cursed her need to wear a dress to get inside the place because that meant no gun. No gun meant bad things. She even slept with a gun - at least when she wasn't drifting off to sleep on strange couches.

Morana inhaled deeply, eyeing the dark SUV where it was parked innocently, and pulled her own car into the lot.

It was already getting darker outside, the sun fading away to give room to the moon, the air chilly as she crossed the lot to the main door, shivers racing down her spine, not entirely due to the cold.

The guard looked up as she approached, eyeing her in a way that was all too familiar, thanks to her father and his choice of dinner companions. It was exactly what she needed at the moment. Her spine straightened, her teeth gritting as she passed the guard by, wishing for the hundredth time she'd had her gun instead of the small butterfly knife in her bra.

Clenching her jaw, she cleared her mind of everything but getting to the back room, so she could spy in peace and entered the casino.

Bright lights and a plethora of colors assaulted her eyelids, the sound of music and laughter drifting about everywhere, along with the voices of the dealers and the slot machines pinging.

Morana stood still for a moment, fisting her hands beside her, taking it all in. She wasn't used to such crowds, and her experiences with such a large number of people had not always been the best. No. She preferred her computer and her solitude, maybe a few people.

*The dinner with Dante and Amara and Tristan Caine at the penthouse had been nice*, a voice whispered inside her. Awkward but nice.

Morana hushed the voice, not willing to hear whatever it had to say, shaking off her musings. She started walking towards the back of the large but overcrowded area. The closer she got, the more clearly she could see a narrow corridor of some kind, with a single red curtain at the end.

Assuming it was the room the man had referred to, Morana looked around to make sure she wasn't being watched, then made her way to the corridor. Once safely there, she stood at the curtain, trying to listen hard for any sounds, but heard nothing. Hesitating for a second, she pulled the curtain away slightly, peeking around it, and saw a simple wooden door with a keypad on the side.

Bingo.

Stepping into the small area, she pulled the curtain back in place, concealing her from everyone outside, and checked the keypad out. She knew her father's security, having installed a lot of it herself. She knew if she cracked the lock, there won't be any alarms of any kind. The keypad was complex, but not uncrackable, not for her at least.

Pulling her lip under her teeth, Morana concentrated completely on the lock, undoing it in a matter of seconds.

The minute the lock opened, a hand grabbed her roughly from the back.

Morana's hand instantly went to the knife she'd hidden but a gun pressed into her ribs, stilling her.

She turned slowly, looking at an older man her height, his face cruel and harsh, especially under the dim lighting by the curtain.

"What are you doing here?" the man demanded, his hand shaking her in a way she knew would leave bruises.

Morana opened her mouth to make up an excuse when the man's eyes fell on the open lock. Shit.

"Well, well," he leered at her with interest. "You want to get inside, little girl? Let's get inside."

Shoving her hard through the door, he pressed the gun into her side, ordering her to move. Morana didn't try to struggle. In a place like that,

208

she knew it would be futile, that she'd have her own knife in her back before she'd even turned around properly. Being smart about this was the only way to make it through.

Fuck.

The dark room at the back of the casino was lit up with multi-colored lights that should have made it look cheap and flashy but had the opposite effect instead. Unlike the outside, there were no female servers in there. That was the first thing Morana noticed. No women at all and that told her something very important – whatever was going on here was highly private and highly important. It was only under those circumstances that women servers were refused at a gathering.

Okay, then.

Morana let her eyes take it all in. There was a huge round table in the center of the room, with dangerous-looking men around it. There was a single gun smack in the middle of the table, within the reach of each and every man.

And seated right across from the entrance, facing the door and every other person in the room, sat Tristan Caine.

His eyes flicked up towards her as the man dragged her in by the arm, and Morana's heart pounded hard in her chest. Not just because she'd been discovered, but because she had no idea how he would react to this, to finding her here where he was doing whatever he was doing, which was something important by the looks of it.

His face didn't flicker one bit.

No spark of recognition in those magnificent blue eyes, which seemed even bluer under the lights. No twitch in his jaw muscle at any attempt to control his expression. No movement of his body.

*Nothing. At. All.*

And yet she could feel the heaviness of his gaze upon every inch of her exposed skin. It went over the slip of her dress, over the hand strangling her upper arm.

God, how she admired that amount of self-control. How she envied it.

She kept her raging emotions completely off her face as well, easily enough, and tried to hide it in her eyes too, but wasn't sure she managed completely. But no one knew her there, including him for all intents and purposes.

Standing still, she removed her eyes from him and scanned the room (something she should have and would have done first as soon as she entered an unknown environment before she'd met him, and she hated how deeply he was affecting her common sense). There were a total of six men, including him, all wearing expensive suits and groomed hair, a few smoking cigars, all in their forties or fifties perhaps.

He was the youngest man in the room, and yet he emanated the most dangerous air, even in his stillness. Or perhaps that was because she'd seen what his stillness held, what it'd done in the afternoon.

The man holding her arm jerked her forward, and she grit her teeth, the urge to punch the asshole in the nose making her fist clench. She swallowed it down.

"Found her lurking behind the door," he informed the room in his rough voice. "Anyone know her?"

Everyone stayed silent.

*Watching.*

Morana stayed silent.

*Waiting.*

The man holding her arm turned to her, his face just a little above her. "What were you doing, girl?"

Morana stayed silent.

"What's your fucking name?" the man spit out.

Morana glared up at his attempt to intimidate her, knowing she couldn't let her real name be known, not in a crowd she didn't know, in a casino in her father's territory, and especially not when Tristan Caine stayed quiet. That told her enough for the moment.

"Stacy," she finally said the first name that came to her mind.

The man raised a skeptic brow. "Stacy?"

"Summers," she supplied sweetly.

"Well, Ms. Summers," the man bit out, his voice harsh, his tone gleeful. "You see this room? Here's where we play. But it's not for money. For information."

Ah. That made sense.

"There are only two ways you leave when you come to this room," he grinned, his tobacco-stained teeth gleaming in the red light evilly. "You play and win, or you leave with a bullet in you."

Dead or alive. Nice. Very mob-like.

Morana raised an eyebrow, looking pointedly at the gun on the table, her mind racing. She didn't know what the game was but she did know that if she refused, the gun digging into her ribs would go off in a second, lodging the bullet very, very close to her heart. Plus these men were playing for information. If there was something she wanted more than freedom from this world, it was information.

"I'll play," she informed the man in a saccharine tone of voice, completely hiding her nerves.

She saw the disbelief flash on the man's face momentarily before he pushed her into an empty chair, right in front of Tristan Caine.

Morana sat down, her back to the door. It was a vulnerable position. Anyone could enter and shoot her in the back.

But she looked up and saw Tristan Caine watching her, watching the door, watching everyone in the room without moving his eyes from her, and she felt her insides relax minutely. If there was one thing she knew for a fact, it was that this man would not let anyone else kill her. Her death was his, and only his. And looking at him, seeing not Tristan Caine but *The Predator*, she believed it with every fiber of her being. That was also the reason why she could not relax. Because she did not know this man. She'd met him once when he'd pushed her own knife against her throat back in Tenebrae. She'd met him when he'd threatened her on top of her car. Since then, she'd seen only terrifying glimpses of him.

But he was completely in his element now, any trace of the man who'd taken her riding on his bike, given her refuge in his territory, or cooked meals while she'd watched, completely gone.

She realized in that moment how much she'd come to know Tristan Caine without really knowing him. And how much she did not know this man leaning back in his chair, casual, composed, like a sleeping panther, crouching down, readying itself for the strike.

He would've realized by now how she'd ended up there. That made her stomach knot. She didn't know how he would react, didn't know if he would kill her right at this table or take her somewhere to torture her first.

Her heart hammered in her chest as she kept her eyes on him, her spine straight and every sense in her body on high alert. She was in a jungle of predators and the deadliest was watching her.

The slimy man, who'd dragged her in, loaded the gun at the center with one bullet and put it back on the table, within the reach of every arm, taking a step back.

That was the precise moment Morana realized the game.

There was one bullet.

Her stomach sank.

*Fuck, fuck, fuck, fuck.*

She was dead. She knew she was dead. There was no way she was going to live this game through.

"The rules are simple, Ms. Summers," the man informed her. "You pick up the gun, ask a question. The man does not answer, you pull the trigger. Empty shot, you ask another question. Man don't answer, shoot again. But he can ask back, and you don't answer, you eat the bullet."

Morana knew of this game. She'd heard her father and his men when they'd played it at the house. She'd spied on the games when she'd been a little girl. There were six slots in the gun, and six questions to go between a pair. If she survived all empty shots, she could ask other questions. But so could the other man.

The older man beside Morana picked up the gun, pointing it at an even older man smoking a cigar, the back of his hand wrinkled with age.

"Where is the next shipment going?" the first man asked forcefully. Morana watched as Cigar Guy blew a thick swirl of smoke into the air, refusing to respond.

Morana watched the procession, a bead of sweat rolling down her spine.

Without further ado, the first guy pulled the trigger, but the shot went empty. Cigar Guy stubbed his cigar in a tray and pulled the gun towards himself.

"When did you start licking off Big-J's shoes?"

The first man pursed his lips as Cigar Guy pointed the gun to his chest and shot.

The loud boom echoed in the room and Morana barely stopped herself from flinching, only years of hearing the sound allowing her to keep her composure as the first guy coughed blood and went limp, his eyes lifeless.

*Oh god.*

This game was like counting shots, instead of counting cards. She was good at the latter but she had no idea about the first. Looking across at Tristan Caine, she could tell by the easy way he sat that this wasn't the first time he'd been to a game like this. Hell, she'd be surprised if anyone had actually questioned him. The fact that he sat there told her he'd never lost.

She didn't want to play. But she knew there was no better time to get information out of Tristan Caine.

She eyed the gun sitting in the middle of the table, loaded again with a single bullet, her heart thudding, and shook herself.

Fuck, she wasn't a coward.

Steeling herself, she leaned forward and gripped the gun in her hand, letting her palm familiarize itself with the weight, and pointed it at the man sitting across from her, completely still.

The room had gone dead silent – so silent that she could have heard a breath catch. It told her what she'd been suspecting was correct – no one pulled the gun on Tristan Caine. Yeah, well, no one dry humped him against the wall of their father's house either.

Clearing her face of all emotions, knowing her voice would be steady even as her legs trembled under the table, she pinned him with her eyes and spoke quietly, not knowing if she'd get the answer. She didn't want to think about pulling the trigger and killing him, and she definitely did not want to look into it, not for now.

"Tell me about the Alliance."

His blue gaze pinned her to her chair, not a flicker of anything anywhere on his face as his body stayed relaxed, the suit of his jacket parted to reveal the shirt stretched taut across his chest. The collar was parted to reveal the strong line of his neck. Morana watched the vein on the neck, not seeing it flutter or give any indication of distress. It just lay against his skin, kissing his flesh, taunting her for all of his control.

"It's been dead for twenty-two years," he spoke quietly, his voice even, tone neutral, like he was discussing the weather with no gun pointed at him.

Morana grit her teeth, knowing she couldn't shoot because he had answered, yet told her nothing she didn't know.

Clever.

She placed the gun on the table just as he extended his hand and took it from her, his fingers brushing her, sending tingles up her entire arm.

She saw his eyes take in the bruise on her upper arm, where the brute had grabbed her roughly before he leaned back again. Keeping his hand on the gun, he let it stay on the table. Morana knew, having watched him in action, that he could have the gun up and shooting her dead before she could blink. He was deceptive that way. Dangerous.

"Why are you here?" he asked, his voice leaving no inflection of anything for her to read.

Morana felt a little smile on the inside. He wasn't the only one who could play on words.

She raised her eyebrows, tilting her head to the side. "For information."

She saw his one eyebrow notch up slightly, before he slid the gun across the table to her, his hands on the arms of the chair.

Morana picked up the gun, pointing it at him again, aware of all the eyes on them, all the men watching the game shrewdly.

"Why did it end?" she asked, her skin crawling from all the stares of the man, knowing their eyes were lingering on places she'd rather they not see.

Tristan Caine spoke, his eyes never straying from hers. "Mutual interests weren't so mutual anymore."

Seriously?

She hadn't risked her neck for this. He needed to give her something.

Mulling over the next question in her head, her senses alert, she slid the gun across the table, where he stopped it with his hand, keeping a casual palm over it, that huge, huge palm covering the entire gun.

He considered her for a second in silence, before tilting his head to the side, his mouth curling deliberately in the imitation of a smirk even as his eyes remained blank.

"How do you like to be fucked, Ms. Summers?"

Her breath caught in her throat. Shae was aware of the lewd men in the room who started laughing around her. She felt her body flare with anger, the blood rushing through her system in a tornado as her chest tightened, her fists clenching under the table.

And through the haze of red, she saw something that suddenly gave her pause.

His eyes.

Those magnificent blue eyes – not laughing, not cruel, not even heated. Just completely blank.

His face was cruel. His eyes were not.

Clarity returned suddenly with a rush. He was goading her. Trying to throw her off her game. Deliberately doing the one thing she'd been pretty obvious about enraging her. She was handing him the gun to shoot her with.

Morana blinked, taking a small breath to cool herself and deliberately curled her lips up in imitation of his. She let her body remember the time his fingers had been inside her, his breath hot on her neck, his cock pressing into her back.

She gave him a heated look from under her lashes and murmured in a low, sexy, just-fucked bedroom voice.

"Like I'm going to feel it every time I walk."

Something flared sharply in his eyes for a second before it was gone. She'd have missed it had she blinked. But she hadn't blinked. She'd seen it, and she knew he'd be remembering the question he'd asked her against the wall of her father's house. The question she hadn't answered for him.

One of the older men with a wicked mustache whistled loudly before speaking, "Come home with me tonight, baby. You'll feel it for the next month."

Everyone chuckled. *Fucking bastard.* She was fucking another asshole at the moment, so her schedule was full. Tristan Caine didn't react to any of the men, just slid the gun back to her.

Six shots. Six questions. This was her last one.

Morana thought the question over for a minute, before wording it carefully.

"What happened to break the Alliance?"

She should have known he wouldn't answer if he didn't want to.

"The two parties disagreed on matters but didn't want a war. Alliance ended."

Morana exhaled, closing her eyes for a second. She'd lost her chance. She'd lost the one chance she'd had to make him answer some questions, and exposed her hand in the process.

She slid the gun back to him when suddenly, her heart started pounding.

It was the last shot. The last question. And something told her he wouldn't waste it.

Morana felt her heart hammer in her chest as, for the first time, he picked up the gun, leaning back in his chair, completely relaxed yet ready to launch into action in a second, the barrel pointed at her chest.

His intention to shoot her in the heart became clear if she gave an answer he didn't like.

Her hands shook as she held them together, keeping her jaw locked tight, her gaze trapped in his blue one.

"What do you know about my history and Alliance?"

Morana felt her throat lock.

She knew.

Oh lord, *she knew.*

She knew his sister had been one of the girls gone missing.

She'd figured it out pretty quickly into her research, knowing it had been twenty-two years ago, which would've made him eight. What she didn't know, however, was what that had to do with the Alliance.

But as she looked at him, looked at the men around the room – all older than him, all afraid of him, respectful of him, of The Predator in a world where reputation mattered more than lives, none of them knowing a thing about Tristan Caine – Morana's heart clenched.

He'd shared the memory of his sister with her on that rainy night. He'd volunteered that memory, on a lonely night, just a lone man with a lone woman, giving her a truce, a respite for a few hours.

216

He had the gun pointed at her heart, and his eyes remained hard and cold, but Morana knew she could not die knowing she'd betrayed the one beautiful, powerful memory she had. He'd given her something incredible that night, something that her soul was so immensely grateful for, and she could not rape that for her own means, could not repay that small truce from him despite his hatred, with this betrayal.

He'd cracked a small light for her. She couldn't suffocate it.

Heart clenching with fear, the decision made, Morana held her breath and closed her eyes, remaining silent.

*Silence.*

There was utter silence.

No sound except her own blood rushing in her ears. Nothing except darkness behind her shut eyelids.

She was aware of every single man in the room holding his breath as they waited for the bullet to pierce her heart, aware of the blood throbbing in her body. She realized in that moment of facing death – the very death she'd been contemplating mere days ago – that she didn't want to die. She didn't want to die, not when she'd started living for the first time in her life, because of the very man holding the gun at her chest.

Her heart beat in staccato, taking as many beats as it could before it was forced to stop, her shaking hands clenching the arms of the chair, sweat rolling down the line of her spine.

She waited a breath.

Two.

Another.

And suddenly, the loud bang made her flinch –

Her heart stopped –

– right before her eyes flew open on a loud intake of breath. Her teeth grit in pain as fire burned down the length of her arm, flames licking along her flesh as agony seared through her.

Morana looked down at the blood soaking the fabric of her dress, not over her breasts, where she'd expected to see it, but on the outside of her arm.

She'd been shot on the outside of her arm.

Right on the where the bruise had been.

The bullet wasn't even in her arm.

It was just a graze.

He'd not killed her. Not even injured her severely.

Her eyes flew to his, to find something completely unreadable in his eyes, his gaze heavy and intense with something she had no name for. She recognized the fury, the hatred, but there was something else, something *so live*, something she didn't recognize. It pulsed between them, making her realize how utterly controlled he had been, and suddenly, the dam had burst.

His eyes held her ensnared, the blue ferocious in that foreignness. Her breathing stuttered, eyes on his, disbelief washing over her because he'd been pointing to her chest. The rule of the game was to answer or die. And yet, she was merely grazed on her bruised arm.

One of the men would kill her because they played by the rules. She couldn't be allowed to leave alive after everything.

Yet she knew, she would. Because he'd decided she would live. Because he had shot her, and the men couldn't argue with that.

Their eyes remained locked over the table, his hand holding the gun loosely and hers pressed down on her bleeding upper arm, her stomach in knots.

She should have felt angry. She should have felt betrayed. She should have felt hatred.

She should have felt relieved to be alive. She should have felt shaky at the close call. She should have felt uncertain about what was to come.

She should have, could have felt so many things…

But as she sat there, watching him, after she hadn't spoken a word in this jungle of hunters to make him seem less than deadly, she was surprised at herself. Morana didn't feel a single one of those emotions.

It almost made her want to smile.

*Almost.*

She should have felt a lot of things, yet what she felt was a change.

Something changed in the moment she chose to kept silent instead of speaking, forfeiting her life, and he chose to shoot her in the arm instead of her heart, sparing her life. Something between them changed, just like it had on that night in the dark, this time in the middle of a crowd of lethal men.

She felt the connection between them that she'd tried to deny so very hard, felt it roll itself round and round, deepening, thickening, choking every shadow it encountered in her mind, strangling every bit of uncertainty.

She'd chosen to not betray him to these people. He'd chosen not to let her die.

She didn't want to think about it. Didn't want to think of the implications. Didn't want to acknowledge their connection that just kept folding itself over and over between them, something fundamental had shifted with her both their decisions.

Because she realized, she wasn't the only one reckless between them.

Things, while the same, had changed. Inadvertently, tonight, they'd both decided.

# *stripping*

She was bleeding.

A drop of blood slid down her arm.

Morana turned her head and watched in slight fascination, as the drop rolled over the curve of her elbow, leaving a fresh streak of red over her skin. Her eyes followed the lone drop as it traveled down smoothly, down the back of her hand, down her empty ring finger, right to the tip. It hung on the precarious edge, teetering, trembling in the slightly cool conditioned air, fighting gravity with all its little might to keep clinging to her skin.

It lost.

The drop lost the battle with a force that was much stronger than itself – a force it did not even understand – and fell to the clean floor of the elevator, splattering in defeat, marring the clean white lines with its crimson.

Another drop took its place and joined its brother on the ground.

And another.

Morana stared at the drop of blood for a moment, her arm throbbing where the gash from the graze was open, the entire evening and the consequence of it finally sinking into her mind slowly.

That she had made it out of the casino alive was a miracle in itself. That she had made it out alive with nothing but a graze was a bigger miracle.

But now, in the privacy of her own mind, when the adrenaline had left her body cold and logic had rooted itself, Morana swallowed. Because there, on that seat in the dim casino, she'd made a choice, a choice that she'd had no idea she would make until that very moment. And her choice had incited a decision in the man who'd become the bane of her existence. Had it been a private choice, known only to herself, she wouldn't have fretted so much. It would've been disconcerting for sure, but knowing that the knowledge of her choice lay solely within her would've been much better.

But it wasn't so. Not only had her choice been obvious to him, his had been obvious to her as well, and she couldn't imagine he liked it any better than she did at the moment. Frankly, she had no idea what the hell that could even mean.

The elevator doors opened, jolting her from her thoughts, and Morana took a deep breath, stepping out into the living room, the skyline of the city glittering like colorful diamonds outside the huge windows. Keeping her hand elevated to staunch the flow of blood, she walked straight to the kitchen, dumping her bag and phone on the counter, and pulled out the clean dish towel from the rack. Turning the faucet on, she wet the towel, and slowly cleaned the area, hissing at the slight pain the pressure caused, before pressing the towel hard down on the arm.

Pain shot up her shoulder, down to her fingers, and she grit her teeth, breathing evenly as the pain subsided into a low throb, the flow of blood already lessening.

Keeping the towel pressed on her arm, looking out the windows, Morana let her mind drift to that moment in the casino, that moment after he'd shot her. That moment when the man who'd brought her in had protested that she hadn't taken a bullet, much to the agreement of the other men present.

Morana remembered the way Tristan Caine had smoothly looked at the man and just raised an eyebrow, leaning back into his chair. She remembered the way the quiet in the room had become tensed, how she'd held her breath, not knowing whether these people would let her go.

And then Tristan Caine had spoken, without removing his eyes from the man behind her.

"Leave."

It'd taken her a moment to realize he'd been speaking to her. But for once, she hadn't wanted to sit around and argue with him. Picking up her keys, Morana had moved her chair back, watching the entire time, not the people in the room but The Predator, as he'd watched the others, his quiet gaze daring anyone to make a move to stop her.

Not one man had moved.

Heart in her throat, she'd walked out quickly and sprinted to her car, not allowing herself a single moment to even think about what had happened. The drive to the apartment had been short and now, standing inside the safety of these walls, Morana didn't have a clue as to what was going to happen.

What had happened in the casino after she left, she couldn't imagine. A part of her wondered if the six men had confronted Tristan Caine. Another part of her was in awe of the power he actually held in the mob.

Hearing something and seeing something were two completely different things. And having seen the genuine fear in the eyes of men much older and more experienced than her father, for the first time, it dawned on Morana, *truly dawned,* who she was dealing with.

A shiver ran down her spine.

Those men back at the casino had dealt with blood and grit all their lives and they feared Tristan Caine. Morana couldn't even fathom the kinds of things he must've done to perpetuate that fear at such a young age.

In hindsight, she could see how incredibly foolish she'd been, sneaking up on him to kill him. After her stunt today, she didn't know if he was going to come back and finally kill her, or get rid of her, or send her back to her father with a neat little bow.

God, she was so completely out of her element.

And it scared the shit out of her.

The sudden sound of the elevator's opening made her start.

222

Her heart picked up the pace.

*He was here.*

It took an effort not to bolt to the guest bedroom and lock the door. For the first time, she was so utterly confused she wanted to run. Instead, spinning on the spot, she turned to face the elevator doors head-on.

And felt her breath caught in her throat mid inhale.

Tristan Caine stood there in the semi-darkness, his jacket missing and sleeves rolled up, his legs braced apart as the shadows playing over his hard face in the light from outside.

But it wasn't that which made her breath catch. No.

It was his eyes.

Blue, magnificent eyes.

*Blazing* eyes.

A frisson of something slithered down her spine, making goosebumps erupt all over her arms, her heart exploding in her chest as the hand holding the towel to her arm dropped down. The towel fell from her slack grip to the floor, and Morana couldn't remove her eyes to even look down to see if her wound was still bleeding.

She stayed still, eyes on him.

He stayed still, watching her.

*Silence.*

And then he took a step forward.

Her feet moved back.

His eyes flared at her involuntary action, his next step slower, more deliberate.

Heart pounding, for the first time since meeting him, Morana couldn't stand her ground.

Her legs moved back on their own, something deep, deep inside her bringing forth all her survival instincts as he approached, some deep-rooted sense of self-preservation made her feet move before she could even process the action.

Eyes pinning her own, his next steps somehow seemed more aggressive, his lithe body fluid in his movement, the clothes of civility doing nothing to mask the animal in him, emphasizing it even more.

Everything inside her rebelled at the thought of being preyed upon, yet she couldn't stop her feet from going back, her chest heaving slightly, her hands shaking, whether in fear or thrill or something else she didn't know. Her emotions were an indistinguishable mass of *something* and *everything* in the moment.

Morana took a last step back, feeling the counter separating the kitchen and the dining area at her back, the cool granite top pressing against the base of her spine, sending small shivers coursing through her body. She clenched her jaw, her pulse beating with vengeance in her body, throbbing everywhere as she kept her eyes on him.

*He would stop a few steps away.*

But he didn't, just kept stalking, his body loose but controlled.

Morana pressed deeper into the counter.

He needed to *stop.*

He didn't.

And for the life of her, she couldn't voice the single word, not as his eyes bore into her, glimpsing at things she never even knew existed inside her.

He stepped right into her personal space, so close she had to tilt her head back to keep their eyes locked, so close that the tips of her breasts brushed against his hard torso as she inhaled, a current zapping through her core even as she leaned away, half bent over the counter.

His eyes glittered as the shadows danced over his face, making him look even more dangerous than he was, his magnificent blue eyes with their pupils blown wide, telling her he was not in control right now, not like he'd been the entire day that she'd tailed him.

God, she needed control. She needed to *breathe.*

Making herself focus on the dull throb in her arm, Morana broke their gaze, averting her eyes, and turning her face to the side.

Her face hadn't even turned halfway when his hands shot out, planting themselves on either side of her on the counter, caging her in completely. His chest pressed into her breasts, not completely but enough to make the friction of their breathing drive her mad, the warm heat of his solid muscles a contrast to the cold granite at her back, his breaths brushing lightly over the top of her head.

Her heart thudded, pulse fluttering like a bird caged suddenly, her fingers curling into the counter beside her, gripping the cold slab, the urge to press her palm flat against the moving, hard chest acute. The desire to taste the tempting scent of that musk he always smelled like was on her tongue, even more profound.

What the hell was she even thinking of having those thoughts, especially after tonight?

Her jugular had been exposed to him for a long time, but more because of circumstances rather than choice. Not tonight.

Her heart rebelled.

Suddenly, she felt his hand on her neck, the entire hand cupping her jaw from under as he turned her face towards his.

Inches.

Mere inches.

His breaths brushed over her face as her eyes latched on to his again by some inner compulsion she couldn't understand, his eyes searching hers feverishly, blazing while his face remained hard and cold, the dichotomy in the man both annoying and fascinating her in equal measure.

Tilting her head back completely, he took the final step to close the distance between their bodies, his semi-hard erection nestling against her stomach as her breasts completely flattened against his torso. Her nipples pebbled in response, her spine curving over the counter. She kept her hands beside her, gripping that slab, keeping her lips shut with deliberate effort, determined not to break the silence between them, not to give in in at least one way.

But it wasn't really a competition, because in the next breath, he spoke, his whiskeyed voice washing over her lips.

"I don't know whether to snap your neck or fuck the life out of you," that voice washed over her senses, so low it made her want to roll her eyes back into her head and wantonly lay back on the counter.

His words sank in.

Morana straightened her spine, the move bringing her face infinitely closer to his, their bodies pressed to close she could feel every indentation of every ab across her own body, feel the cut of muscles he was using to intimidate her.

Morana glared at him, her eyes narrowing, her blood heating from both anger and arousal.

"You want to touch me, Mr. Caine?" she spoke in an equally low voice. "You tell me the truth."

His face shut down so fast Morana would have missed it in a blink. All the anger, all the *everything* that had been on his face? Gone. Just like that.

His eyes remained on hers, the blaze contained but not gone as his fingers tightened on her jaw, pulling her up until she had to stand on her toes to accommodate.

He leaned down, his lips almost in line with hers as his eyes pricked her like cold chips of ice, his jaw clenched so tight the scruff seemed even more pronounced.

"Don't. Ever. Try. To. Fucking. Control. Me."

Morana felt her body tremble at the fatality in his voice, the tone making it evident it had been the wrong thing to say. She had no leverage over him. Absolutely none. And to think that his lust would work as one had been a long shot anyway.

No one could hold anything over this man to make him do something he didn't want to.

Had someone ever tried that, though? The way he'd reacted, with such icy vehemence, certainly implied that.

But playing with fire as she did on a regular basis these days, Morana smirked slightly, and deliberately ground her hips into his, rolling it in one smooth motion. She felt his respond automatically, thrusting into her stomach, *hard*, her core clenching in need as his breath ghosted over her mouth. Her lips tingled as wetness flooded between her legs, her nipples squashed against his rock hard and incredibly warm abs, her body alive, so fucking alive with sensations.

Trying to keep it cool, smiling intently, she brushed her nose over his, in a mockery of the intimate kiss, and spoke over his lips.

"Then I suggest you control yourself, sweetheart."

The corner of his lip twitched ever so slightly, right above that delectable scar, his hips rocking into her one last time before suddenly, he was moving away. Already halfway across the room, his trousers tented evidently, his stance shameless as he scrutinized her.

Feeling like she'd just lost a game she'd had no idea they'd been playing, unable to understand what in him made her behave like this, like

226

a wanton thrill-seeking animal. Morana swallowed and turned towards the guest room, walking away as quickly as she could without making it seem like she was running, which she totally was.

She felt his eyes on her retreating back all the way till the room and kept her head averted, shutting the door behind her, shutting his eyes out.

Taking her first deep breath in what seemed like minutes, Morana shook herself and walked to the bathroom, closing the door behind her even though it didn't have a lock. He'd never entered this room before though, so she wasn't really worried about him doing so. For all his high-handed ways, he seemed to have a thing for her privacy, something she couldn't help but wholeheartedly approve of.

Stripping her bloodied dress off, Morana let it fall to the floor with a 'plop' and looked up at the mirror to check her arm.

The bleeding had stopped, as had the pain. It was just a gash that throbbed, nothing a few butterfly bandages and some sleep wouldn't cure. Deciding to take a shower first and then go to the kitchen to wrap it up, Morana walked to the glass stall at the end of the cozy bathroom and turned the knob for warmth.

She stepped under the spray, letting the warm water slide over her, feeling the sweat and grime of the day go down the drain along with the exhaustion, careful to keep her wounded arm away from the spray. Eyes closed, head tipped back, she let the water wet her dark hair, caress her muscles as she let go of the breath she'd been holding the entire day. Her mind replayed what had happened outside, what she'd almost wanted to happen.

She'd seen him. Eyes ablaze, body trembling with that thin control, his aggression, his physicality, his focus – all on her. She'd seen him and like every other time, something in her had responded to that wild animal call. Only this time, it had been louder than ever before, more ardent.

A shiver ran down her spine even as the hot water slid down her skin –

That was when she felt it.

*His eyes.*

She stilled, her barely calm heart picking up pace again as the water sluiced over her body. She was suddenly aware of the gush, of her entire being aware of the man standing at the glass door.

227

The man who'd never once entered the guest bedroom. The man who now leaned against the shower stall casually, watching her with the steady, ready eyes of a panther. The man who barefoot but still dressed in those clothes.

That was the precise moment she realized, looking down at his feet that – for some reason that made her nipples pebble – that she was naked. Completely naked. For the first time, she was nude to his eyes.

She didn't like it, didn't like the way he was watching her without her layers, no glasses, no clothes, nothing.

Stripped.

She felt *raw.*

Exposed.

Bleeding.

And he stood there, scenting her blood, watching her.

She'd asked him to control himself, and yet, there he stood, sporting the exact same bulge in his pants.

Morana breathed in, biting the inside of her cheek and moved her head up to face him, keeping her face clear of all thoughts and raised an imperious eyebrow.

Uh-oh.

Her eyebrow hit her hairline; his hand hit the glass stall.

And then he *moved.*

Straightening from his position, he stepped inside the stall, shrinking the previously big shower to something much smaller. His tall, broad frame dwarfed the walls and the ceiling. Steam swirled around him, clinging to his body, and dampening the fabric of his shirt. Morana watched, enthralled, as a drop of water condensed on his tight neck, right beside that infuriating vein, and rolled down his skin, into his now completely transparent shirt.

For the first time, in this close proximity, Morana saw with clarity the shadows of his tattoos littered amongst his numerous scars.

There was no way she was going to stand naked in front of him while he was still covered. No way.

Before he could make a move, Morana put her hands on the damp collar and tugged at his shirt forcefully, ripping the buttons off, sending them scattering on the floor, a strip of flesh bared to her eyes just as his hands came up to grip her wrists, his eyes inflamed.

All that cool control she'd witnessed five minutes ago... *evaporated.*

With bare feet, he stepped under the spray with her, pushing her back into the wall and turned her around. Her front was pressed into it, much like it had been at her father's house.

Her heart thudded in her chest so rapidly she could feel her pulse in her ears, his body not pressing into hers but there, *right there,* hovering behind her. He was so close she only needed to lean back a little to touch his skin, the urge to do that so intense she brought her hands up to the wall and stayed still.

And for the first time, she felt his hands, on her bare skin.

His rough, big hands on her skin.

Sucking in a sharp breath, Morana felt his hand grip the back of her neck as the other one moved down the line of her spine, in a gentle touch meant to lull her into a false sense of security. It only managed to wind her up tighter instead, the water falling sideways on them, on the side of her good arm while the wounded one remained dry.

Morana knew she could stop him if she wanted. Except she didn't want.

Somewhere along the way, she'd become so okay with wanting him, so okay with this lust she could feel coursing through her blood, that she was fine admitting it to herself. It didn't make her hate herself any less, but the heady rush of sensation as his rough, calloused hands moved over her made her desire it.

She felt him lean down, his lips brushing over the shell of her ear as he whispered softly into her skin, his hand wandering down to the base of her spine, slowly drifting down to her ass with surety.

"This body belongs to me, Ms. Vitalio," he murmured in a low voice, the whiskey and sin combining to make her head tip back over his broad shoulder as her stomach clenched.

"This body is mine," she retorted, unable to recognize her own voice dripping in sex.

He continued, like she hadn't spoken, cupping her ass. "I'm a territorial man. And this has been mine since the moment you locked that bathroom door."

"That was one time," she informed him, even as she knew there was no stopping them now.

"Then let's make it a second, shall we?"

Morana could feel the anger simmering in his body behind her, the rage he'd been controlling, hear the shake in his smooth voice.

The hand on her ass dipped lower, his fingers brushing over her nether lips, before entering her with a certainty that made her close her eyes, the rough abrasions on his fingers rubbing her deep in the most delicious ways, wetting her even more than she'd been.

She heard the sound of his zipper going down and the tear of that condom before his leg spread hers wide apart. His hand moved to the base of her spine and pressed down, making her push her hips out and lean her weight on her arms against the wall.

Morana looked at the wall in front of her, her breasts heaving and heart pounding in anticipation.

She felt his arms cage her in like earlier and watched in fascination as his hands came to rest on the wall a little above hers to the side. Morana looked at their hands, so close and so apart, comparing the differences, the similarities. Both pairs of hands excellently talented in their respective fields, yet his was dark, rough, with veins and long, wide fingers, with blunt nails and a smattering of hair at the back. Hers looked so much paler, smoother, so much smaller, the tips painted a bright green.

Seeing their hands together like that, watching the thick forearms alongside her delicate wrists, something fluttered in the pit of her stomach.

No. She didn't like that. Didn't want that at all.

Morana closed her eyes, shutting the view, but the image was imprinted on her brain.

Gritting her teeth as anger filled her, anger at being unable to shake off something as trivial as their hands side by side, something so stupid, Morana pushed her hips back, wanting him to just get it on.

She felt the tip of his cock prod at her opening, and she inhaled deeply, her heartbeat erratic, the water pouring down over them from the side.

With complete, utter ease, he slipped into her slowly, inch by deliberate inch, making her breath catch in her throat at the sheer size of him. Fuck, she'd forgotten what he felt like inside her, filling every empty ounce of space, spearing through her walls in a way she hadn't thought possible, making her back arch even more to take in all of him. She'd thought he would thrust in like he'd done at the restaurant and be inside.

He didn't.

Instead, he pulled back a little, before pushing in again, easing into her, making her feel, truly feel every inch of him.

Morana hung her head as her palms pressed into the wall, her body lifting on her toes to allow some leverage, her hips pushing back into him.

He entered her to the hilt, her walls clamping down on him, the new angle penetrating her in ways that made her see stars, pressing into spots inside her she hadn't been aware of.

And all this time, she kept her eyes deliberately closed, feeling him inside her but not feeling his torso against her back, aware of the distance between their bodies.

She was glad for it.

Because at the restaurant, it had all been easy to explain to herself, to blame it mainly on the fact that she'd been defying her father right under his nose with his enemy. There, having him pressed into her had been an act of rebellion. But in the shower, there was nobody she could blame other than herself, having him close a desire she didn't want to define.

He pulled out of her suddenly, making her acutely aware of her body, and thrust up inside her, hard, all traces of gentleness gone. Morana sucked in a breath, curling her hands into fists on the wall as pleasure shot through her core right down to the tips of her toes, her legs trembling with the effort to keep standing.

"You do something like that again, I'll fucking shoot you in the heart."

His guttural voice made her shiver even as her walls clenched around him.

"I decide when you die."

Morana huffed a laugh that got strangled in her throat. "You're crazy."

Without a pause, his hips started snapping into hers rigorously, rolling on every thrust in a way that made her bite down on her lips to keep her moans to herself, sweat beading upon her brow, her breasts heaving as her head neck arched, her hair floating down her back in a tangle of wet strands.

"No. I'm *fucking* crazy."

She moved back against his ardor, the friction inside her walls making her squeeze her muscles around him as the tip of his cock rubbed over that spot inside her over and over again. His hips never paused, the rhythm never breaking, and her jaw slackened as heat coiled deep in her belly. It was a snake coiling tighter and tighter around its prey, squeezing the very life out of it with such brutal strength, ready to sink its fangs in divine ecstasy.

Morana shook all over, her lips swollen from her own nipping teeth in an effort to keep her sounds to herself.

He'd had his hand covering her mouth the last times he'd made her come, muffling all the noises she'd made and in a convoluted way, granting her the freedom to let out all the noise inside her, knowing it wouldn't be heard.

There was no hand muffling her response this time, and try as she might, moans escaped from deep in her throat as she felt him move in and out of her, over and over and over again, her legs trembling and hands aching but hips moving with his. She tried to bite the noise down, but couldn't, not completely.

Suddenly, she felt him shift on his knees, changing the angle of the penetration. A low growl rumbled from his throat as he thrust in with such force her mouth parted on a loud moan, all sense, all control of her body lost to her as her vision blackened. The shaking in her body intensified, as did his movements, aggressive, fervent, but so removed from her body, not touching her anywhere except where they were joined.

Morana wanted to lean back into his solid mass, let him support her weight because her body felt too slack to do so anymore, have his palms cover her breasts and his face turn into her neck. She wanted every bite, every nibble, and utter dirty, dirty words into her ear as his cock sliced her open.

Her fingers dug into the wall with the effort not to do any of that as pleasure rocked over her body, washing over her with such suddenness she was stunned by its intensity, unable to hold back her scream that started as a moan and got increasingly louder. He pushed in, hitting that sweet spot inside her, over and over again, with such precision her head lolled into the wall, her body slacking completely against it as her orgasm snapped inside her. Her heart raced so hard she could feel it throb in her toes, in her core, in her fucking teeth. Her body shook all over, her walls clamping down on him, milking him, as he thrust in a last time and stilled, his breathing loud behind her.

They stayed standing like that, him caging her in without touching her and her trembling against the wall in bliss.

The sound of water penetrated her pleasure induced haze first.

She stood alone, despite him still being inside her. Her body had been sated but she could still feel something hungry gnawing inside her, trying to claw out and find satisfaction. She kept tamping it down. Would it ever be enough? Would anything ever be enough?

It was as he slipped out of her, as her heart stuttered to a quieter beat, that she realized the water had gone cold, flowing against her back because of the space between their bodies.

Acutely aware of him behind her, Morana remained standing the way she was, not moving, not turning, not certain she wanted to face him at that moment. This had been the first time they'd been together physically just with themselves, no external factors into play, and it had been just as removed, if not more. It made something inside her chest feel tight before she shook it off and agreed. Distance was needed.

She opened her eyes, only to see those hands, clenched into fists against the wall – tight fists that made his arms shake.

"Why?"

One word.

Guttural.

Spoken in that low voice. The voice that shook. Asked so, so many questions in that one word. She understood some of them.

Why had she not sold him out when she'd had the chance? Why was she still not out of his system? Why was this mad lust not sated despite their bodies having found completion? Why had she followed him? Why...

There were many other questions in there, questions she didn't understand, questions she was certain he wasn't even aware he'd asked.

Why?

Why was this happening? Why did she feel this connection to the one man she should run away from? Why did he make her so alive when he'd told her he wanted her dead? Why hadn't he killed her yet?

Why?

*Why?*

Morana looked at his fists, swallowing down the sudden wave of emotions inside her, and replied softly, with one word.

"Why?"

*Silence.*

For long, long moments, she felt nothing but his breaths at her back, saw nothing but his hands beside hers, so close yet so far.

And then suddenly, he pulled back his hand and punched the wall above her hand, hard.

"God damn it!"

Morana stood utterly still, stunned at the way he went at it.

Once, twice, thrice.

*"Fuck!"*

Such utter frustration bled from his voice. Such *pain*.

He kept cursing until she heard nothing but foul words. Pained words. Aggravated words.

He kept punching the wall until his knuckles cracked until the wall dented and plaster became smudged with red.

And through it all, through that entire display of rage, he never touched her, not once.

Despite her answer having triggered this, despite his desire to kill her, she remained untouched.

*"Motherfucker!"*

And it was over as soon as it had begun.

Before she could blink, she was completely alone in the stall, his body gone from behind her, his hands gone from beside hers.

Morana stood there, breathing hard, just watching the place where his hands had been.

The once smooth white wall beside her hands was cracked, fissures appearing in small grooves in it, the clean white space painted crimson.

She swallowed, her eyes latching on to a drop of blood sliding down that wall, leaving a streak on scar behind it, marring the pristine white.

A drop of blood rolling down.

He was bleeding.

# *trembling*

She went to bed later that night, after taking care of her wound, lying down silently, trying to understand what had happened, when her phone chimed.

It was a message, from an unknown number, with a multimedia file attached. Morana looked at it, her heart picking up as she sat up in the bed and saw the number.

It was the same number which had sent her the article; the same number she'd been unable to track.

Taking a deep breath, uncertain of what she would find next, Morana tapped on the multimedia icon, to find a folder. Squinting, Morana looked at the small fonts, reading the name of the folder.

*Luna Evelyn Caine.*

Her breath caught. With shaky hands, Morana clicked on the icon and found out why he was bleeding.

She couldn't stop trembling.

Something had moved inside her again, shifted, been replaced, been awakened and deadened. Turmoil coiled in her belly like a hungry beast salivating for food.

Morana closed the bedroom door behind her and stepped out into the pale morning light that flooded the living room. Her eyes looking out the tall windows, she took in the sun that was barely out in the sky. The clouds were roiling along the horizon, headed towards the city, giving the skyline a majestic albeit morose backdrop as the wind whipped the sea into currents.

It was barely four in the morning, and she hadn't slept a wink the entire night. Hadn't even tried to.

And it wasn't because of her arm.

It was because of what she'd discovered.

Morana didn't know who the anonymous man or woman was, or if it was even a single person rather than a group, who had sent her the article a few hours ago, but they were resourceful, finding things she hadn't even had an inkling of, from sources she hadn't known existed.

Personal things.

Things that had twisted her stomach into knots and made bile rise in her throat.

According to the information in the folder titled 'Luna Evelyn Caine', Morana had found out, to an extent, truths that made a whole lot of sense but she had never known about.

She'd already known about the girls who'd gone missing never to be found again in Tenebrae and nearby areas about twenty years ago. She'd also known that Tristan Caine's baby sister had been one of the missing girls.

What she hadn't known were the speculations about the kidnappings. How the authorities had suspected one, or maybe two people working together, with no clue as to what purpose. But the anonymous source had given her enough evidence – which she'd pored over for hours – to make her realize it had been much bigger than one or two men. It had been the work of a group of very strong, very powerful people. What for, she didn't know. What could young, little girls ever get anyone if not ransom?

There had been enough lewd details to make her want to be sick, but still, it hadn't been that which had brought her to the edge.

It had been about her.

The fact that she'd been one of the little girls too.

She'd seen her own photograph staring back at her, her chubby cheeks wet with tears as she sat along with two other little girls.

One of whom had been Luna Caine. Dark red cap of hair, just a little older than her, rosy mouth, bright green eyes sparkling with tears of her own. There had been another toddler in the picture between them.

Three girls in the picture.

Twenty-five girls gone missing.

And Morana was the only one to have been found.

How? Why? Why only her and nobody else?

Legs shaking, Morana collapsed onto the stool in the kitchen, staring out the window, trying to remember something, anything from years ago.

She couldn't.

She'd tried for hours to think back, to recall even the tiniest detail of being abducted, but she'd come up absolutely empty with only a mild headache to answer for it. Was it because she'd been barely three years old at the time, or because she'd buried the memory like people did sometimes? Could she even do that?

And was that why Tristan Caine hated her so much? Because she'd come back while his sister hadn't? She'd lived life while his sister probably hadn't? Was that why?

Her hands were trembling. They'd been trembling all night and no matter what she tried, it just wouldn't stop.

God, she was breaking down.

Why had her father never told her about it? When it had been a part of serial disappearances? Why hadn't anyone told her? The Alliance had mysteriously ended around the same time and someone had sent her this?

Her head hurt.

The sudden sound of a throat clearing made her jump in her seat. She turned around quickly to see Tristan Caine standing at the foot of the stairs, without a shirt but in unbuttoned jeans, his hair sticking up like he'd run his fingers through it repeatedly, his eyes slightly red.

Either he'd been crying or he hadn't slept either.

She'd bet her degree it wasn't the former.

His face was his usual neutral, controlled mask as he took her in, his eyes lingering for a split second on her shaking hands before coming back to hers.

God, she couldn't do this. This intense eye contact game they played. She just couldn't do it right now, not with the way she was barely keeping down the scream that had been building in her throat. It wasn't a scream of fear, or devastation, or desperation. Not even frustration, truly. It was trapped somewhere between them all, bouncing from one to the other while they laughed in her face.

She turned back to face the window.

"Did I hurt you?"

The question, asked in that low, rough tone, caught her off guard.

Keeping her back towards him, her hands knotted together in her lap, Morana scoffed deliberately. "Why do you care?"

Silence.

He still stood exactly where he'd been. She was so completely attuned to his movements that her body tensed with awareness, spine straightening and shoulders rolling back even as she kept her gaze at the skyline.

"Did I hurt you?"

Low. Rough. Again.

"You did shoot me," Morana pointed out with a lightness she didn't feel.

Before she could take another breath, he was suddenly beside her, his fingers on her chin, the calloused edges pressing into her, his hold firm but gentle as he turned her to face him.

Morana blinked up at his sleep-deprived, yet magnificent blue eyes boring down into her, his warm musky scent even more prominent, not a hint of his cologne anywhere, his Adam's apple bobbing once as he swallowed in her peripheral vision.

"Did I hurt you?" he asked again, his voice barely a whisper, his breath warm on her face as his eyes scanned hers.

She knew what he was asking. He'd not hurt her physically in the shower, he knew that too. It was another kind of hurt he wanted to know about, another kind of hurt which frankly, she hadn't even considered in the light of the information that had flooded her.

So, she thought about it as he waited for her answer. She thought about how she'd felt when he'd seen her naked, how she'd felt when she'd pulled him closer, how she'd felt when he'd asserted the intensity that was as much a part of him as that limb holding her.

How had she felt? He'd been surprisingly possessive and unsurprisingly angry. In the light of the day, she could understand why. Not to say she agreed with a lot of shit that he'd said, but she could understand the anger. She felt for that pain.

But was she hurt?

She was thicker than that.

"No," she told him quietly.

He waited a beat, blinking once before pulling back, dropping his hand and stepping towards the stairs without another word.

Morana looked at his retreating back, the beast in her chest clawing tighter and tighter until she thought it would choke her, and before she could even think about it, the words left her mouth.

"I know about your sister."

Morana watched as he ground to a stop suddenly. He stilled, his arm on the railing, the muscles on his scarred back bunching, one lone muscle by one as he completely coiled his body, the action of his naked skin visible to her eyes. Her words were louder than bullets fired between them, confirming his worst suspicions and revealing her hand.

She didn't know if she should have told him or not. She hadn't even thought before speaking.

God, she was tired of thinking, of trying to decode every damn thing.

She swallowed, her bravado making her slowly get to her feet, her need to know, to finally know if that was why he hated her so acute it tightened every air cavity in her chest to the point of pain.

Because if he hated her for being alive when his sister most likely wasn't, she really didn't see any way forward for them. And looking at his back, at the multitude of scars littering his flesh like a lover's kisses, after witnessing that moment of utter pain and agony bleeding from him not hours earlier, she wanted a way forward.

240

She clenched her shaking hands into fists.

"I know she was taken and never came back."

He didn't move.

Didn't even breathe.

His back remained completely motionless.

Her heart clenched for him, for the pain he must have felt, still evidently felt. She remembered the softness with which he'd spoken of his sister.

Biting her lip, she took a step closer to him. "I know I was taken too."

Another step.

"But I came back."

Stillness.

"And she didn't."

Such *stillness.*

The air heavy between them, like it had been chafed too much, rubbed raw and had swollen in pain.

Morana closed the distance between them on shaky legs, until she stood beside him, and looked up into his face, placing a hand on his scruffy chin like he'd held hers just moments ago. He turned his face towards her, a clean slate wiped of all expression, his eyes vacant, dead, just looking out at her.

"That's what you hate me for, don't you?" she whispered in the air between them, her voice wavering slightly. "Because I was found and she wasn't?"

His lips trembled for a split second before they were pursed again, a movement so minute, so quick, so real she'd have missed it had she not been standing so close to him.

His jaw clenched.

Morana let his chin go and looked down. "How can you even stand to look at me? God, how can you let me stay here when you hate me for..."

"I never hated you for that."

Barely a whisper but the words reached her.

Her eyes swung up to his. His were still devoid of all emotions.

But she knew he was telling the truth. A man like him, who'd made his hatred so honest since the beginning wouldn't lie about it when blatantly questioned.

"Then what do you hate me for?" she asked softly, all her speculations, confusions, crashing a hard death.

The light in the room dimmed even more, shadows elongating as the clouds took over the sky.

He broke their gaze, looking away.

She waited for him to take a few breaths, waited for him to look back at her, waited for him to speak. He didn't.

Anger flooded her veins with surprising speed.

Grabbing a hold of his bicep, she shook it, tried to shake it, gritting her teeth. "Tell me, damn you! Tell me why you want to kill me. Tell me why you didn't when you could have. Tell me why you're so bothered with hurting me when you promise me my death with every word that you speak. *Tell me!*"

She was yelling by the end of her tirade, shaking his arm, her anger, her confusion, her frustration, her desire, all warring in a way she'd been so unfamiliar with before she'd met him, a way that had become her bedside companion now. She'd been abducted along with twenty-five other little girls, including his sister, and nobody had returned but her. She'd never been told this, never even had any indications, but clearly, it had been important enough for the anonymous person to tell her. And even though it could have been an understandable reason for his hatred, it wasn't a reason at all.

What the fuck was then?

His blue eyes speared hers, a spark of anger in them giving them sudden life. His free hand came up to take a hold of her wrist as he pulled her hand away from that taut bicep, pulling her closer until suddenly they were nose to nose, his chest rising and falling as rapidly as hers, her heart pounding with a vengeance as she glared at him.

"I don't owe you a fucking thing," he growled inches away from her mouth. "I do what I do. Only I need to know the reasons for it."

Morana growled back. "Not when they affect other people, which in this case happens to be me."

"Not my problem."

She narrowed her eyes. "It is if I start believing you're just full of shit and hot air. You're losing your touch, *Predator*."

His lips curled slightly at her sneering tone even as his eyes bore down upon hers with unwavering intensity, without a hint of amusement.

"You forget I haven't really touched you at all."

Her breath hitched even as she understood his deflection. He released her hand and climbed the stairs three at a time, his taut ass flexing as Morana watched him disappear back inside his room, once again leaving her without any answer at all.

Morana closed her eyes, inhaled deeply, and walked to her room, deciding, once and for all, that she was going to get some answers from somewhere no matter what she had to do. She needed those answers to keep hold on her sanity, which she could feel slipping away with multiple epiphanies sinking into her – the realization that she'd been a part of something so horrific at such a young age; the realization that only she had been lucky enough to have been recovered; the realization that everyone had deliberately kept her in the dark for some reason.

Her bed was a mess from tossing and turning all night. Quickly making the bed, she dressed in dark jeans and the first top she could find from Amara's collection. Putting on flats, she knotted her hair on top, adjusted her glasses, grabbed her keys and her gun, and walked out.

Tristan Caine was in the kitchen, surprisingly dressed and freshly showered from the looks of it. He didn't look up at her as he whipped eggs efficiently, his wrist moving at a quick speed, and she didn't stop on the way to the elevator, not sparing him another glance.

"Going somewhere?"

Duh, asshole.

She stayed silent and kept walking, her keys digging into her palm.

"The guards won't let you out until I say so."

The words stopped her in her tracks. Rage flooded her system as she whirled around to skewer him.

"I didn't get the memo that I'd been promoted to a prisoner," she spoke in a cool voice, completely at odds with the riot inside her.

His face remained blank as he placed the bowl on the counter and leaned against it, crossing his arms over his chest.

"I've treated you as a guest here, Ms. Vitalio, we both know that," he pointed out evenly. "You've had the access to your beloved car. You've had the freedom to come and go as you please. But yesterday, you changed the equation. You followed me the entire day, putting not only your life on the line but mine. Not just once, but repeatedly."

He pushed away from the counter and started walking towards her slowly, his arms still crossed and face hard, the shadows playing on his face, the longer scruff and stiff look making him seem even more intimidating than he was.

"Do I need to remind you we're on the cusp of war here?" he grit out, blue eyes sparking fire. "Just because your father hasn't retaliated yet, don't think he wouldn't. I insulted him on his territory, not only by hitting him but by letting you stay here. That's not considering your wild codes out there that need to be found."

He wasn't wrong. But Morana didn't utter a word, letting him speak as he stopped a few feet from her.

"So yes, I've explicitly told the guards not to let you out unless I say so, because if your pretty neck is wrung before the codes are found, all of us are screwed."

Her heart stopped for a second before picking up pace again. "Is that why you didn't kill me back at the casino? Why you haven't killed me yet?"

He tilted his face to the side, expression blank. "Of course."

A pinch of hurt curled inside her heart but she shoved it away, knowing this man had more layers to peel than a stubborn onion, and she couldn't see them with teary eyes. She narrowed her gaze and focused on his eyes, seeing them without her own emotions clouding them.

Her lips curled as she shook her head, turning away to leave before he could say anything, pressing the button for the elevator. "Tell the guards to let me through. Otherwise either they'll get hurt, or I will. Dealer's choice."

The doors swished open and she stepped inside, pushing the button for the parking and finally looking at him again.

"Oh, and keep telling yourself that's why you didn't kill me, Mr. Caine. You might get some decent sleep."

His eyes flared and the doors closed, shutting him out, the mirrored panels reflecting her own form.

Morana looked back at herself, at the smug smile on her face, and realized, that after a few minutes with the infuriating man, her hands had finally stopped shaking.

She was in the graveyard, lying on the grass, looking up at the cloudy sky.

This was *her* place.

Morana had discovered this small little graveyard right beside the airport by accident a few years ago. It was closed off from the runway by a huge fenced wall. When she'd stumbled upon this place while driving around, she'd become addicted to the peace and quiet immediately. The ground had shaken beneath her feet and she'd looked up, to see the belly of a monstrous plane just a few feet above her head, taking flight. Something so, so much bigger than she had made her feel so small beneath it. That had been the moment she'd been hooked.

She'd come to this place countless times since then. Just to lie back on the grass and see plane after plane leave every five minutes, the noise rumbling everywhere in her body, the seclusion of this place making it just hers. This was where she thought the best. She'd made a lot of brave decisions for herself here, and in the insanity of the past few weeks, she'd forgotten how much she missed this place.

Lying on the soft grass now, Morana felt the tell-tale rumble in the ground and smiled up at the cloudy sky, folding her hands on her stomach as the rumble grew and grew until her entire body shook with the ground. With a roar, the nose of the plane came into view, followed by its underbelly, so vast and so close above her she could feel it in every pore, the noise deafening.

She kept her eyes glued to the plane as it soared higher and vanished from sight, leaving behind utter silence.

Making her feel alive and then leaving her with the dead. Quite literally.

Morana chuckled at her own thoughts, before sobering, sorting out the mess her head had been for days, dividing and categorizing her problems into three neat stacks.

The first stack was the codes. Although she'd almost written the sister program that would render those codes useless, it wasn't that which worried her. Someone had hired Jackson, while pretending to be Tristan Caine, to woo and get her to make the codes, framing the other man without his knowledge. Had she not confronted him at his party, he probably wouldn't have found out until it was too late.

But who, and why? The person clearly knew Tristan Caine enough to want to frame him but how did they know about her? The only people who knew about her expertise were people who were into programming, and not many of them were found in the mob. Except within the span of a few weeks, she'd encountered two such people. Clearly, her anonymous source was an expert in finding things digitally, things even she hadn't been able to find.

Could the two be related? And what did it all have to do with the Alliance?

The second stack was Tristan Caine. Even as everything inside her shied away from wanting to take a close look at whatever she felt about him, she forced herself to do exactly that. Denial wouldn't do her any good.

She desired him, she'd admitted that much. Not just a quick fuck against a wall as they didn't look at each other. She wanted him to stroke her back like he'd done last night for a few seconds. She wanted, for once, for him to hold her breasts and not just make her wet with his fingers. She wanted to be able to caress that jaw and feel the scruff rasp against her palm. She wanted to feel the scars under her tongue. She wanted to trace those tattoos with her fingers. She'd desired him before and still did. Yet, her hunger was not appeased, not satiated, and it had been dumb of her to think one time would have been enough.

She felt alive with him, she knew that too. But despite the casino incident, and last night when emotions had been running too close to the surface for both of them, and this morning when he'd needed to know if he'd hurt her, Morana, for some reason, felt safe with him. It was a stupid thing to feel with a man like him, but she couldn't understand it.

The moment she'd entered that casino and seen him, something in her had relaxed. The moment she'd left her father and come to him, something in her had collapsed. The moment she'd let him see her naked, something in her had snapped. He'd seen her vulnerable multiple times and nuzzled her jugular instead of ripping it out. He'd seen her feisty so many times and had fed her fire instead of dousing it. He'd seen her as her and despite everything, he'd not exploited that, like her own father had done so many times.

She couldn't ignore these things. She knew he was a complex man, a harder puzzle than anything she'd ever encountered. She knew he hated her, and if it wasn't for being alive in place of his sister, it had to be much, much worse. Something he refused to talk to her about. Why?

And, if it was worse, where did she even go forward with him? And yes, she wanted to. She didn't know where, but somewhere.

Another vibration startled her, but she realized it was too soon and too small to be another plane. It was her phone.

Morana pulled it out of her pocket and looked at the screen.

The third stack was calling her.

Daddy dearest.

Morana stared at the screen, her hand hovering over the green icon.

She hadn't spoken to him since that night. Any illusions she'd ever carried had been shattered not just by her fall, but by him using her as bait, never once asking for her. Now that she'd found out about the kidnappings, her own and others, she knew she had to talk to him.

And yet her thumb couldn't come down.

The screen died.

Another plane went.

The screen lit up again.

Morana took a deep breath and swallowed, making sure her voice remained completely even, and pressed on the green icon, putting the phone to her ear.

"You've settled quite well as his whore, Morana," her father's voice came out, cold. "I had such plans for you."

Morana grit her teeth but spoke with a deliberate smirk. "I'm sure you haven't called to get the details of my scandalous sex life, father. Oh, I forgot to ask, how's your nose?"

Silence.

Score 1.

"I know you're out of the building alone," the man informed her. Ah, the ever-faithful spies. Of course, he had people watching.

"And?"

"You've been branded a traitor, Morana. This territory will no longer be safe for you. You'll be hunted and brought to me for justice, if not killed immediately."

Morana shook her head. "You care too much about your reputation to do that to me, father. Your name is everything to you. A daughter sleeping with the enemy? Oh, you'd bury the news so deep into the ground it'd never see the light of the day."

She paused, taking a deep breath. "Isn't that why the news about my kidnapping was never known?"

Morana heard her father's breaths catch.

He waited a beat, then ground out, his accent more pronounced. "That fucking vermin! He was a good for nothing brat then and he's a good for nothing brat now. What did the shit tell you?"

Interesting.

Morana blinked up at the sky, seeing the clouds rolling in overhead, the wind picking up pace.

"What do you think?" Morana bluffed, keeping her voice controlled, seeing what else she could glean. "I know, father."

She heard his breaths on the phone, deep breaths, clearly trying to control his agitation.

"You know everything?"

"Yes."

"Then, you're right," he spoke finally, his voice so cold it sent a shiver down her spine. "I do care about my reputation. I have worked too hard for too many years to let this get in the way."

Morana frowned, trying to piece together everything her father said.

"You've known for a while now, haven't you?"

She continued to bluff. "Yes, I have."

"You should have died," her father repeated the words from the other night. "At least I wouldn't have had to deal with you all these years."

Morana stayed quiet, letting him talk.

"You've spurned me, shamed me, and now you know the truth about us. You've not only signed your death warrant, Morana. You've signed his too."

Her mind spun, not just because of the severity of the threats but because of what he'd said.

'Truth about us?'

To whom was her father referring?

"Starting now, you're dead to me."

The line went dead.

Morana looked at the phone, another hard shiver wracking her body, goosebumps erupting all over her arms.

She looked around, seeing the secluded area for the first time as not the safe haven it was but the perfect spot to dispose of a dead body. Her senses went tingling with dread.

Urgency hit her suddenly.

She needed to get back to the penthouse, to safety. *Now.*

Pocketing her phone, she stood up quickly and started walking towards the gate of the graveyard a good distance away, beyond which her car stood waiting for her. Hastening her steps, she kept her senses vigilant, looking around and over her shoulders, seeing nothing but graves and grass and trees at the far edge on this side of the fence in the utter quiet.

The wrought iron gate came into view, and Morana could see her car a little beyond that.

Releasing a sigh of relief, she sped up to a jog and exited the graveyard.

It was perhaps because she was on alert for anything out of place combined with the absolute silence that she heard the little beep she would have otherwise missed as she neared her car.

The sound came again, like a whip cracking on the ground before meeting flesh, making her heart pound as blood rushed through her body in a tsunami.

Stopping exactly where she was, Morana dropped to her knees and leaned over to look under her car, her hands scraping in the dirt and her body ready to jump and run if what she suspected was true.

It was true.

A small black box was hooked under her car, a red dot of a light blinking on it with every alternate beep. Since there was no timer, it meant that it was controlled remotely. Which meant someone had been watching and waiting for her to come near enough.

Heart in her throat, adrenaline flushing her system, Morana pushed back and stood, turning and running back towards the graveyard without wasting a breath. Blood pounded in her ears and the muscles in her calf burned. Little pebbles got under the sole of her flats but she continued to run, feeling a stitch on her side, just as the ground beneath her feet started to rumble.

Oh god, not now.

With a burst of speed, not looking back even once, just as a plane roared into the sky, a hot gust of wind blew into her from behind, forcing her onto the ground. Heat seared her back as she fell on her front, the breath knocked out of her, the exposed skin at her neck and arms singed as the fabric tore at her back.

Panting, Morana rolled onto her back, wincing with pain as she put pressure on the sensitive skin, the wound in her arm bleeding again, dirt coating her skin, as she looked back at the gate.

A sob broke from her chest.

Her car.

Burning in flames.

*No, god, no.*

The sight seared itself into her vision, the tall flames of orange licking the red of her car, sucking its life away, turning it into charred black right before her eyes.

Tears escaped her eyes as she looked at the one friend, the one constant she'd had for so long, be brutally murdered, pain and rage suffusing her with every passing moment. That car had been her freedom, her escape, her companion. That car had held her when she'd shouted songs at the top of her lungs and when she'd broken down in tears, delivering her to safety.

250

That car.

*Her car.*

Morana looked at it, sobs bursting from her chest. Her father had done this. His men had done this.

For one long minute, she stared at the burning mass of metal, mourned it for one long minute. Then, she buried the pain deep inside and let the rage take over.

The men had to be nearby, to make sure she was dead, and to get the proof for their boss.

Standing up, she wiped under her eyes and pulled out her gun from her waistband.

They wanted death? She'd deliver it on a fucking platter with blood on the side.

Wiping the remnants of all tears, Morana let the heat infuse her, and crouched down, creeping slowly towards the road from the inside, clearing her mind of all thoughts, all pain in her body ignored.

After a few minutes of nearing the edge, the black SUV her father's goons used came into view, parked a good distance away.

Morana stayed crouched low, recognizing them.

Two men. Only two men sent to take care of his daughter. But two of his closest men.

Too bad.

The men stood beside the vehicle, their gazes on the burning wreck where they thought she would be.

She needed to take them out, make an example of her own, and send her father a clear message. Nobody messed with hers and got away with it unscathed. *No one.*

She knew she couldn't shoot one without alerting the other, and her body couldn't handle a fight injured if she was spotted. It needed to be quick, efficient. Narrowing her eyes, Morana pointed the gun at the vehicle, at the gas tank to be specific, getting a clear shot from her vantage.

Her hand shook slightly, but she steadied it.

*Set an example. Tell Daddy Dearest to fuck off.*

Taking a deep breath, Morana closed one eye, took her aim, and fired.

The SUV was intact one second, blown up the next. It wasn't like in the movies at all. It was done and over within seconds. She watched even as her arm recoiled as the same flames licked the vehicle and her father's men along with it. She dropped down on her ass, exhausted, on the cold ground, feeling no satisfaction, nothing but emptiness.

She sat there, hidden from view, behind two gravestones, wanting nothing more than to go to the penthouse and sleep. But she couldn't go. Not without a car and not when her father's other goons could very well be nearby.

With shaking hands, she put the gun down and pulled out her phone, tears streaming down her face again.

She knew she could call him. She somehow also knew that he would come.

She wouldn't. She was a mess, again, and she couldn't make it a habit to let him help her. But then, who could she call? She had no one.

Opening up her contacts, Morana stared at the third number right near the top, a number she'd acquired just recently, and swallowed, hitting call before she could think about it.

She pressed the phone to her ear, pulling her knees up towards her chest and stared unseeingly at the ground as it rang.

She bit her lip, deciding to hang up just as the call was answered and a soft, raspy voice came over.

"Morana?"

She could hear the surprise, the worry, the concern wrapped in that one little word, and it tipped her over.

"Amara," Morana spoke, her voice quivering. "I didn't know who else to call."

"I'm glad you called but are you alright?" Amara's soft tones were rife with concern.

"Not really."

"Are you hurt? Tell me where you are, I'll be right over."

"I'm... I'm okay," Morana hiccupped. "I need your help. And I'd really appreciate if you didn't tell anyone about this, please."

"Don't worry about that," came the immediate reply. "Just tell me what I can do."

"I need you to pick me up."

Morana told her the place, told her to be careful and make sure she wasn't followed.

"I'm ten minutes away. Sit tight, okay?"

Morana nodded, her lips trembling. "Thank you."

"Anytime, Morana."

She put the phone down and away beside the gun and leaned back against the gravestone. Her back hurt, her skin sensitive from the blast but thankfully not burned. She stared up at the sky.

So, that was that.

Her car was dead. And she'd murdered someone, two someones, for the first time.

She'd never thought she had it in her. Even though she'd never balked at hurting guys trying to hurt her. She'd never given much thought to if and when she would murder people, not in protection but in hatred, in vengeance. She had. She had retaliated, and she felt no remorse. She felt nothing. Not right now. Maybe she would later, but at the moment, she was nothing but one giant ball of empty.

At least the stack with her father had crashed and burned. She knew exactly what he wanted to do, knew he would try to do it by any means, and she needed to be prepared.

Her phone buzzed with an incoming text.

Morana tilted her neck to see it flash on the screen.

**Tristan Caine:** *Tsk tsk, wildcat. You should have at least allowed me another punch at your father before you signed on my death warrant. Now I have to take the liberty myself. Where's the fun in that?*

Morana read the text, a laugh bubbling out of her as she hit reply. How did he even know? Had her father done something? Besides blowing a bomb with the intent of killing her, that is?

**Me:** *Damn. I know right? I asked him how his nose was, though.*

**Tristan Caine:** *That must have been colorful.*

**Me:** *He used a lot of cuss words for you.*

253

**Tristan Caine:** *No gentleman, him.*

Morana smiled, shaking her head.

**Me:** *You're one to talk, mister.*

**Tristan Caine:** *I told you I wasn't a gentleman that very first night.*

Morana remembered that conversation that first night in Tenebrae, at the mansion, with her knives at her throat and him pressed into her front.

**Me:** *Yes, you did. It's a good thing I'm not into gentlemen. Gentlemen can't handle me.*

**Tristan Caine:** *I don't think anyone can handle you. Not if you don't want to be handled.*

Morana read the message, her heart thundering. That was probably the nicest, most empowering thing anyone had ever said to her – that she was strong enough to handle herself, that she chose who she allowed to handle her. It was especially surprising, considering the kind of world she'd lived in.

**Me:** *Funny, I was going to say the same thing about you.*

Amara's incoming call filled the screen. Morana picked up and quickly directed her towards her location. Another message waited for her, a message that sobered her up completely, bringing back what she'd managed to forget for a few blissful seconds.

**Tristan Caine:** *I think my guards are afraid of you.*

She read the message once. Twice. It was written in the same teasing tone that she couldn't imagine talking to him blatantly in, but the answer in her heart was slowly eating at the emptiness.

*Me: They should be. After all, I just blew up a car and killed two men in cold blood.*

She put her phone away before he could respond and saw Amara emerge from behind the trees. The other woman, as gorgeous as she was, was dressed in a rumpled shirt, jeans, and a printed scarf around her neck, her hair tied in a lopsided ponytail, as though she'd dressed in a hurry. That fact warmed something inside Morana that someone had dropped whatever they'd been doing to come for her.

Something heavy lodged in her throat as she saw her come closer and raised a hand, waving her over.

She saw Amara's step falter as the other woman took in Morana's appearance. Between the dirt on her skin and her disheveled hair, the slightly torn and dirty clothes and the invisible neon sign that hung over her head screaming *'she's miserable'*, she was pretty sure Amara knew something quite drastic had happened.

She finally stopped in front of Morana, and without a thought to dirt or grass or whatnot, dropped down on her ass, leaning back against the headstone opposite hers. Silently, without asking a word, the other woman rummaged through her handbag and brought out a sealed bottle of water, handing it to her.

Morana took the cap off, put the bottle to her mouth and chugged down the water with thirsty sips. The cool drink flowed down her throat, making her groan in bliss. She hadn't realized how thirsty she'd been until she tasted the delicious water.

After she'd had her fill, Morana washed her hands and splashed some on her face, taking deep breaths, trying to clean herself as much as possible.

"This is quite pretty for a graveyard."

Amara's soft words made Morana look up at her. Seeing the concern in her dark green eyes, Morana took a deep breath.

"It is. The best view is on the other end of it, though. Near the gate."

Amara's eyebrows hiked up. "I don't think you mean the burned vehicles."

Morana chuckled. "No, I don't mean the burned vehicles. But we have to talk about them, don't we?"

"Only if you want to, Morana," Amara's rasp made the words even sweeter. Morana was pretty sure, by this point, she was more than half in love with Amara. It was impossible for her not to love her.

And after everything she'd done for her, she deserved a friend. As did Morana. Everything be damned, she was going to make a friend.

Just because she'd lost everything known to her didn't mean she couldn't find something beautiful in the unknown.

With that thought, Morana cleared her throat. "I've discovered a lot of things about myself and the people around me recently, Amara. And nothing is what it appears to be."

The other woman tilted her head for her to continue without interrupting once.

Morana smiled slightly at that.

"I know about Luna," she told her, watching her eyes widen slightly. "I know about all the disappearances and about the victims. I know I was one of those babies too, the only one to have been found."

Amara swallowed visibly, nodding. "Yes, you were. Not everyone knows it though. It was kept very quiet."

Morana nodded back, not pushing. "I know those kidnappings have something to do with the Alliance, maybe even my own abduction. And I know he doesn't hate me for being alive and here when his sister isn't."

Amara's eyes filled with a sheen of tears as she bit her lip. But she didn't utter a word, and for some reason, that loyalty made Morana respect her even more.

Morana continued. "I know my father doesn't care one iota for me. Something bigger than me is going on, with the codes, with everything. I know it. I know my own father put the hit on me, bombed my car and almost killed me. But I don't understand why. Why did he do that?"

Amara swallowed, her deep green eyes shining with sincerity. "I'm so sorry."

Morana nodded. "I just killed two men, and when I had nobody to turn to, I decided to put my faith in you. I just want you to know that if you decide to reciprocate, I wouldn't betray you."

She paused, then stated plainly, her heart clenching. "I don't have anyone to betray you to, Amara. The man who's supposed to protect me wants me dead, and the man who's supposed to kill me offers me protection. Convoluted as that is, I wouldn't betray that act of kindness. I've not known a lot of it, and what little I have has come from you and Dante and him. I cannot betray that."

She took a deep breath. "But the fact is simple – I don't know who Tristan Caine was. Who he is. Help me understand him. Help me fight."

Amara leaned her head back, staring up at the sky for a long moment. Morana gave her the time to mull things over, before the other woman spoke again, in an even softer tone of voice.

"I know why he hates you, Morana. Not because he confided in me. He doesn't confide in anybody. He doesn't let anyone even close to him. As lonely as all of us are, he's the loneliest of us all."

Morana's heart clenched as the memory of a rainy night and glass windows filtered through her. She watched in silence as a tear streaked Amara's cheek as she continued speaking.

"Dante knew the truth because he's the heir. And in a moment of trust, to ease the helplessness of seeing his brother bleed but being unable to do anything about it, he told me. And I swore to him on my life that Tristan's truth would never escape from my lips."

Morana heard the unsaid 'but' hovering in the air between them. She bit her tongue, not willing to break the moment.

Another tear ran down Amara's face.

"I see how he looks at you. Despite knowing about you all my life, I never thought he'd be as he is with you."

"How is he with me?" the words escaped her softly before she could think about them.

Amara didn't look down at her, kept staring at the clouds overhead, her lips curling slightly.

*"Alive."*

Morana felt something pass through her heart. A current, a zap, a something.

"There's no other word for it. That's why I don't believe he can truly ever hurt you. Because after tasting life, you don't really ever let it go, do you?"

No. She hadn't.

His insistent words from the morning came to her.

*'Did I hurt you?'*

Was Amara right?

Morana stayed quiet, contemplating.

"I like you, Morana," Amara finally looked down at her, her eyes determined but pained. "I would love nothing more than to have you as my friend. Which is also why I believe I should warn you. Knowing Tristan, knowing why he holds that hatred so close to himself, he will inevitably hurt you. Not because he wants to, but because he doesn't know any other way to be. He's lived for twenty years without feeling an ounce of affection for anyone but Dante and I. And only an ounce. We know it, and we accept it. Are you sure you'll be able to?"

Morana blinked, her heart pounding. "What are you asking me, Amara?"

Amara took a deep breath. "I want you to know the reasons, Morana. I want you to know, woman to woman, friend to friend but also because you're the only one I think can save Tristan from himself. To do that, you need to know the truth. To do that, you need to understand and accept that it will be anything but easy and Tristan himself will be the biggest roadblock in your path."

Her hands shaking slightly, Morana inhaled deeply, pondering Amara's words.

"The truth will change the way you understand him, Morana. It will change things for you, but it won't change things for him. Do you still want to know?"

God, this was a mess.

To know or not to know, that was the question.

Ignorance is bliss, they said. Sorry, ancient philosopher, ignorance sucked.

But once she knew, she could never go back. They could never go back. How would it change things between them? How would it change things between their families? And if he decided to be rid of her because she'd found out the truth and he hadn't wanted that, what then?

She could leave this all behind and go away.

No, she couldn't. Not anymore. Not until she knew everything about herself that she hadn't known existed.

The conflict inside her, the worry, the anger, the curiosity, all tangled together in a knot lodged right in her chest, making her breaths heavy and heart sore. Twisting sensations ran amok in her stomach, as Morana closed her eyes, took a deep breath in, and nodded.

"I want to know."

With those words, she sealed her fate. She knew she wouldn't be the same again.

With those words, she leaned back and opened her eyes, her hands trembling again as Amara, slowly, softly, began to talk.

# *fearing*

*Tristan, 8 years old.*
*Tenebrae City.*

He was scared.
*He wasn't supposed to be here.*
Tristan knew he was breaking a rule even as he pushed himself as high as his small toes would allow. His short body leaned against the pillar as he tried to look into the dining hall at the big house. It was a big space, with tall lamps at every corner of the room, lighting the area brightly, side tables scattered close to the walls. There was a long brown table in the center, with twenty chairs on each side and two at the heads of the table. The walls were the same stone the big house was made of, the name of which he couldn't remember, and the curtains were deep blue in color. Tristan liked the color. He liked the room too.

He'd only been inside the house twice before, both times when the Boss had been holding some party. His mother had helped organize everything. Tristan was keen to see this dinner meeting, while his dad protected the Boss.

It was a very important job, Tristan had been told enough times. Which was why his mother always left him out in the garden to play and never let him in the house. The two times he'd sneaked in, he'd just roamed around the large halls and escaped back, scared someone would see him and complain.

Tristan was old enough to know that if the complaint ever reached the Boss, he would be in big trouble. The Boss didn't kill little boys, or so he'd heard, but he did punish them as he saw fit. Tristan didn't want to be punished.

Though he'd sneaked in before, it had been a very long time since he'd entered the house. He really should leave, but his feet remained glued as he watched the hall. At first, his break-ins had been out of curiosity. This time though, it was for information.

Nobody told him anything since he wasn't old enough to be told adult things. That didn't mean he didn't know.

He knew.

He saw.

He heard.

He *felt*.

So much pain. So much guilt.

His baby sister was gone and it was his fault. Her protection had been his duty; her safety his responsibility. It had been seventeen days and not a clue about her.

Tristan still remembered the night so clearly it was a vivid picture in his head. He remembered tickling his little Luna as she giggled in that sweetest voice, laughing with him in her white pajamas with red hearts on them. He remembered her big green eyes, looking up at him with such innocent love, such devotion it always made him feel funny in his chest. He remembered checking under her bed and hugging her good night, remembered that soft baby smell of hers as she gripped his hair in a tiny fist.

She was the most beautiful baby sister in the world. Tristan had vowed the first moment he had seen her pink scrunched face and held her tiny body in his thin arms that he would always keep her safe. He was her big brother, after all. That's what big brothers did. They protected their baby sisters at any cost.

Yet, that night, he had failed. He didn't know how, but somehow he had.

Her windows had been locked – he'd locked them himself. And the only way to enter her room was through his. Not even his mother could get through the door without him waking up to check on his sister.

That night he'd hugged her good night like any other night.

And in the morning, her bed had been empty.

The windows had been locked. He hadn't woken up once during the night. It was as though she'd vanished without a trace, and somehow, he'd slept when she'd needed her big brother. He had failed her.

The hole of her absence was eating at him. He just wanted her back. He wanted to smell that baby smell on her skin and hear her giggles and just hold her. He missed her *so* much.

Tristan wiped the tears that fell down his cheeks quietly with his long white sleeves. His father had taught him to never cry. He was a big boy and if he wanted to be powerful, he could never cry.

Tristan tried. He tried really hard not to.

But every night he would look at the small empty bed across his room, and the tears would come down. Every night he would hear his father shouting accusations and screaming at his mother in pain, and the tears would come down. Every night he would hear his mother try and calm his father down with so much hurt in her own voice, and the tears would come down.

Everyone was crying these days. He just made sure his parents never knew he did too. He washed away all evidence in the morning and was really quiet about it.

No one knew he closed his eyes and whispered prayers every night for his little sister. He prayed for her to come back. He prayed for her to be safe and warm and fed. He prayed for her not to miss him too much.

He prayed so much, and he was so tired of praying.

The need to do something, anything, pushed at him.

And while no one told him anything, he had sharp ears. He'd heard his father shout at his mother last night, about some conspiracy that had taken away Luna and many other baby girls from the city. It had made him angry, to realize that there were other big brothers feeling the way he was, helpless and hurt. Tristan had listened to it all, looking at the rain outside the window, remembering how happy it had made Luna.

He had hoped for her happiness again.

But seventeen days was a long time without a word, and while he would never consider the possibility of anything bad happening to her, he knew his parents did.

262

And then his father had mentioned the girl - the girl who'd been found.

The only girl to have come home.

That was why Tristan had sneaked in.

Tristan had come to see the girl. He had come to see the one who had come back while his Luna was still lost. He just wanted to see her, maybe learn something about what had happened to his sister. He wanted to know if she had been with her; if she'd seen Luna.

As Tristan lurked behind the pillar, he let his eyes roam around the hall, watching the people, observing them. There were ten men in total, including the guards and one woman.

His father had always told him to remember faces. Faces in their business, he'd taught little Tristan, were secrets. And secrets were weapons that could be used someday.

His mother had always told him to read eyes. Eyes, she'd said, were windows to the soul. That was why Tristan knew that his baby sister had the purest soul of anyone he'd ever met. That was how Tristan knew his father's soul was getting blacker each day Luna wasn't found. That was how Tristan knew his mother's soul was dying under the weight of all the pain.

Tristan took his time, watching both faces and eyes of the people around the table, not looking at the security that flanked all around the circular room. His eyes went straight to his father.

David Caine stood beside the chair of the Boss, a tall, lean man with his hands clasped behind his back – hands that Tristan knew were shaking. They'd been shaking for a long time, and it had only gotten worse in the past few days. Not allowing that thought to bother him, he let his eyes drift down to the Boss.

The Boss – his actual name was Lorenzo Maroni but Tristan's father called him Boss – sat at the head of the table on one side. He wore the black suit everyone in the family wore, his face covered in beard and head covered with short hair, his eyes dark.

Tristan remembered the first time he'd met the man. He'd been sitting outside in the garden while his mother had been organizing another dinner when the Boss had walked out. Tristan hadn't known who he'd been at the time. He'd just looked at the tall, big man, at his dark eyes and a hard face, and he'd disliked him in an instant.

The Boss had held his gaze. "I eat people for looking at me like that, boy."

Tristan hadn't said anything, just disliked him even more for it.

The man had smiled then, a bad smile. "You're not like other little boys, are you?"

"No, I'm not," Tristan had said, narrowing his eyes.

The man had observed him closely, then walked away after that and Tristan had run back to his bench, never to meet the Boss again since then. He'd never understood why his father worked for a man with dark eyes and a hard face.

Tristan studied the man now, as he smoked a cigar, a gun sitting on the table before him, the metal glinting in the bright lights of the room. A few other men had their guns out as well.

That didn't bother Tristan. Guns never had. His father had taught him how to hold a gun, and though he'd never fired one, Tristan liked guns. He liked the feel of it in his hands. One day, he was going to have his father train him in shooting them properly and he would own a collection of them.

One day. After Luna was home safe.

Moving on from the familiar faces of the family, the men Tristan had only ever seen in passing with his father but didn't know the names of, he turned his neck to look at the other end of the table. That was where the guests from outside the city were.

He scrutinized them closely. The man at the head of the table was big, bigger than the Boss but not bigger than his father, in a dark suit like everyone else and a short beard. Tristan stared at his face for a long moment, memorizing it, and looked at his eyes.

Something heavy settled in his stomach.

He didn't like this man. He didn't like this man at all.

His face was regular and his eyes were dark, but there was just something about them that would have scared any other boy his age. It only made Tristan dislike the man even more.

Yet, it wasn't him who held his attention a moment later.

It was the woman, sitting beside the bad man in a pretty blue dress, holding a baby.

Tristan felt the breath rush out of his chest.

She was so *small.*

So much smaller than Luna. Wearing a pink dress, her head sparsely sprinkled with curly dark hair, Tristan could only see her back as the woman held her.

Had she been with Luna? Had she been with his sister, sat with her, cried with her?

How had she been found? Why only she and no other girl?

The questions never left his mind as he watched the little bundle in the woman's arms, everything else forgotten. She was wiggling like an inquisitive little worm, trying to get away from the woman he assumed was her mother. Tristan remembered when Luna used to do that, the noises she'd made in her little chest in frustration, the happy laugh that had bubbled out of her upon release.

This baby was making the same noises. Tristan could hear her across the room.

"Just put her on the table, Alice!" the bad man's voice made Tristan's eyes narrow in focus.

He saw the woman, Alice, hurry to sit the toddler on the table in a way that she could see the room with her back to her mother.

Tristan looked at her face, feeling the same flutter in his chest he'd felt the first time he'd seen Luna.

She was beautiful – rosy cheeks chubby on her pink face, little cute legs folded on the wood of the table, pink mouth opened in a small 'O' of wonder as she looked around the room at all the people. But it wasn't that which Tristan found so beautiful. It was her eyes. Big, pretty eyes the color of wheat and grass mixed together. Those eyes were blinking at people, at things – clear, sweet, pure. Untouched by the evil around her.

Tristan hoped his sister was the same way. He hoped he would see her like this one day soon. He hoped he would kiss her little fingers and blow raspberries on her tummy again.

Another tear left his eyes.

And then something happened.

265

He didn't understand how. He didn't understand why. But suddenly, the little girl's eyes came to him beside the pillar in the shadows, found him.

She tilted her chubby little head in wonder.

And then she smiled.

A completely toothless, completely adorable smile that just knocked him in the stomach.

Tristan felt his own lips move.

He felt himself smile for the first time in days since Luna had gone missing.

The baby flapped her chubby arms wildly, wiggling on the table, her giggling cackles loud in the room.

"I'm glad to see little Morana is well."

The Boss' voice erased the smile from Tristan's face.

Morana. A pretty name. Tristan saw the baby turn towards the sound of the voice, and tilt her head again. He didn't like it. He didn't like how they'd put her on the table along with so many guns. He didn't like how the room was full of men with dark eyes and they were all looking at her.

It made him want to pick her up and leave the room like he did with Luna when men came to their house. He didn't like anyone seeing his baby sister with their dark eyes. He didn't like anyone seeing this baby with those dark eyes either.

But he stayed quietly hidden.

"You wanted to see her for yourself, Lorenzo, here she is," the bad man spoke from one end of the table to the Boss at the other end. He leaned back in his chair, his hand on the table. "Now, can we get to business?"

Tristan grit his teeth at the man's tone.

"In a second," the Boss said, putting out his cigar, the smoke curling around him. Air swirled around the room from the overhead fan, spreading the smoke around.

"Alice," the bad man spoke to the woman. "Take Morana and leave us."

"Leave the baby," the Boss drawled out as the woman stood up. She hesitated for a second, but then turned around and left the room. The door closed behind her. The little girl, Morana, completely oblivious to everything, put a piece of her pink dress in her mouth and started chewing on it.

The Boss's voice broke the silence. "Since only your daughter has been found from all the missing girls, you will do me the courtesy of answering some of my man's questions, won't you, Gabriel?"

There was something in his voice Tristan didn't understand – like he was speaking in riddles.

The bad man raised his eyebrows. "Who has these questions?"

The Boss' eyes gleamed in the lights from around the room. "My head of security. His daughter has been missing for a few weeks."

Tristan inhaled deeply as his father stepped forward, coming closer to the table as the bad man, Gabriel, nodded at him.

"How did your daughter go missing?" Tristan heard his father ask in his cool voice. He'd never understood how his dad could shout and scream at home like he did and yet stay so composed outside the house.

Gabriel indicated to the door from which the woman in the blue dress had left. "My wife took her to the park and lost her. We didn't know she'd been taken until she wasn't found for four days."

The men near the Boss' side straightened as his father nodded, stepping closer to the table. "And how did you find her?"

"We didn't," the bad man, Gabriel, said. "She was dropped outside our gates at night."

Just like that?

But why?

Apparently, his father's thoughts were on the same track.

"So, she's taken and four days later, delivered to your doorstep?" his dad asked, his voice losing its cool and resembling the tone Tristan had heard for so many nights. "How convenient."

The bad man glared at his father. "Are you implying something?"

"Damn right, I am," his dad responded, walking right to the table.

Leaning down, his father's face shone in the lights, the look in his eyes scaring Tristan.

Tristan looked at his face, looked at the bad man sitting at the edge of his chair, looked at the baby between them, and his gut dropped to his knees. She needed to get away before his father started his shouting and the bad man responded.

"I've looked into you, Gabriel Vitalio," his dad spoke, his voice edging towards the blackness in his eyes. "I've looked at the things you have done. So many girls gone missing, and not one is returned. Yet, when it's your child, she's sent back to you gift-wrapped. It only means two things – you either scare them, or you know them. Which is it, huh?"

Gabriel Vitalio whipped his head towards the Boss, his eyes angry, his men on edge and their fingers on their weapons. "Is this why you invited me here, Lorenzo? For this?"

The Boss laughed. "You know exactly why I invited you, Gabriel. We're done."

"You really want me to air our dirty laundry here? I've got you by the balls and you know it, Bloodhound."

The Boss leaned back in his chair and chuckled even as his eyes remained dead. "Look around you, Viper. You're in my city. My territory. My house. Surrounded by my men. With your inner circle here."

As though on cue, all the Boss' men trained their guns on Vitalio's men. Tristan swallowed, watching.

Gabriel Vitalio breathed in deeply. "Even if you break our deals, you can't kill me. I have my own territory and fail-safes in place."

"I know. I may not kill you, now," the Boss said. "But I can do to you what we did to Reaper."

Gabriel Vitalio went silent.

"You fucking bastard."

Tristan's eyebrows went up on his head. Who was Reaper and what had they done to him?

"As I said, we're done, Viper. That means my head of security can roll you in the mud for all I care. If you're not the ally, you're the enemy."

"You're stupid to think you can threaten me into silence, Bloodhound," Gabriel Vitalio said in a low voice. "I can burn your empire with the things I know."

"Then be ready to burn with me."

Quiet.

Tristan didn't understand what they were talking about but he held his breath as he took in the whole room. The two men glared at each other across the table, the tension so heavy in the air Tristan felt goosebumps on his arms. He rubbed them softly, trying to cool himself down.

Maybe he should leave. Just let the grownups talk. His father was there. He would find out whatever he could about Luna.

But Tristan didn't move.

His eyes kept returning to the little baby smack in the middle of the men, the baby who had perhaps been the last of them all to see his sister. The baby who was curiously inspecting a spoon she'd grabbed with her hand.

Biting his lip, he stayed put.

It was his father's voice that broke the silence, his harsh words directed at the bad man. Viper.

"Where are the girls?"

Viper grit his teeth. "How the fuck should I know?"

His father didn't like that answer.

In the blink of an eye, his father pulled out his gun and pointed it right at Viper's head, while the Boss sat back, watching the show.

Viper's hand inched towards his pocket. His father shook his head. "Don't move an inch."

Tristan held the pillar with his hand, his muscles tightening instinctively. Without moving his eyes from the scene, Tristan quickly bent down to his sock and took out the Swiss knife he'd stolen from his father's stash one day, just in case he had to protect Luna. The knife felt slightly heavy in his small hand but Tristan held it, ready to fight if need be.

His father turned to the bad man and spoke in that loud tone that made Tristan flinch, the knife slipping in his hand, cutting across his palm. The pain exploded on his skin but he bit down on his lip, not wanting to give away his presence to anyone, wiping the tears streaking across his cheeks.

"I know you know, Gabriel Vitalio. I know that you know something. Spill it now, or I won't be responsible for what happens."

Viper chortled. "You poor bastard, you have no idea what's going on, do you?"

Tristan wanted to punch the man in his face. Forget his bleeding wound, he wanted to hit the man and break his nose. His sister had disappeared and the man was laughing? When his own daughter had just returned?

Tristan hadn't known men like this. He never wanted to know men like this. Men who could laugh with such evil.

He shuddered.

His father shoved the gun deeper into the man's face. "Tell me! What do you know?"

The man chortled. "You want me to tell him, Bloodhound? Want me to tell him why you want to break the Alliance so bad?"

Tristan looked at the Boss, who'd stilled.

"Remember Reaper every time you think of opening your mouth, Viper."

The other man bared his teeth but stayed silent.

Tristan's father snapped his fingers. "What does that have to with my daughter?"

Viper shrugged.

And then Tristan's father moved.

Before Tristan could blink, his father pulled his hand and shifted the gun, pointing it right at a small, chubby face and bright hazel eyes studying the gun in fascination.

Tristan couldn't breathe.

His father's shaking hand steadied, his eyes becoming completely black.

"You don't tell me what I want to know," his father said quietly, "she dies. Your daughter for my daughter."

Tristan could only watch the scene in horror but stopped himself from thinking bad thoughts. His father was just bluffing. He was trying to find everything about Luna and playing the other man. Yes. That was it.

Maybe, Tristan could help him if Viper did something.

Swallowing down his nerves, stepping out from behind the pillar, Tristan stayed in the shadow, looking around.

His eyes landed on the gun lying towards his right on the small table against the wall. Without any thought, Tristan placed the knife gripped in his bleeding hand quietly on the wooden surface and picked up the gun. He didn't know what kind it was, or how many bullets it had. But it was heavy in his small, shaking hands. It was heavy.

Yet, Tristan raised up his thin arms, pointing the gun at Viper, unlocking it like his father had taught him to do. He was ready to shoot the bad man who didn't realize what a miracle he'd received when his daughter had come back to him. He would do anything, give anything away to have his sister back with him.

He wanted his sister back so much.

His father missed her too. That was why he was bluffing. That was why he was trying to get information in any way he could. Tristan understood that.

He just kept his hands steady even as they started aching, the bleeding gash on his palm throbbing.

Gritting his teeth so he wouldn't make any noise, Tristan kept his eyes on the scene from the shadows. He saw the Viper's eyes move to the Boss, saw the Boss shake his head ever so slightly, saw the man lean back again.

"I can't tell you anything," he said aloud, his voice controlled. "Do what you want to do."

Blood rushed through his ears. The Boss' men kept their guns on Viper's men while his father kept his own gun pointed to the head of the little girl. Tristan understood his father's motivation but he was unable to understand how these other men could do what they were doing, and why nobody else standing there did a thing to stop them.

How could a man do that to his own daughter?

Tristan swallowed, waiting for his father to lower his weapon and do something else.

He didn't.

His heart started thudding, the gun shaking in his trembling hands.

Why wasn't he putting his gun down?

Why wasn't he moving away from the baby?

Why wasn't anyone else doing something?

"Last chance, Vitalio," his father said softly.

Viper shook his head.

The Boss spoke. "Leave it be, David."

*Move the gun, dad,* Tristan urged in his head, his lips trembling.

His father shook his head. "His daughter for my daughter."

*Move away, dad.*

He shouldn't have been here.

He shouldn't have sneaked in to see this.

He couldn't understand.

He didn't understand.

Oh god, why wasn't his father moving away?

He was so scared. He was so, so scared.

He wanted to leave.

But his feet wouldn't move. They wouldn't *move.*

He tried to swallow his whimpers as his heart started to hurt. He just wanted to go home. He just wanted to sleep in his bed. He just wanted his sister back. He wanted to go home.

But his shoes were stuck to the ground.

*He shouldn't be here.*

Oh god, he was so scared.

His heart pounded so hard he could hear it in his ears, his stomach heavy.

His entire body started shaking, his arms trembling, bleeding, hurt.

His father cocked the gun, unlocking it.

Tristan started to cry, unable to stop his tears anymore. He loved his dad so much. But why was he doing this? He didn't understand. This wouldn't bring Luna back.

His breathing became heavy.

Tristan watched his father's finger hold the trigger and saw his muscles move, and he knew with sudden certainty that his dad was going to pull the trigger.

This wasn't a bluff. This wasn't a game. It was life and death.

Tristan looked at his father's face and saw nothing. No hint of the face he had when he looked at Luna. No hint of any softness.

Tristan waited.

*Inhale.*

*Exhale.*

*In.*

*Out.*

His father's finger flexed.

*In.*

*Out.*

The finger started to pull.

Tristan whimpered, terrified.

And before he even understood, he pulled the trigger.

The force of the hit pushed Tristan down to the ground, the gun still gripped in his arms as the loud sound of the bullet broke through the hall, accompanied by curse words and screams, and the crying of the girl.

Oh god.

The sudden onslaught of noise became white as Tristan looked back at the table, only to see the little girl with splattered blood on her face.

Without a thought, his mind silent, completely silent, Tristan walked out into the fore, straight to the girl who was getting red in the face from her cries. Hands trembling, Tristan wiped the blood off her soft face, forgetting his own bleeding palm.

Instead of cleaning her skin, he marred it even more with his own blood.

His dad was going to punish him so badly for this.

Ready to apologize for hitting him, to accept whatever punishment he gave out, Tristan turned to the side.

His heart stopped.

*No. No. No. No. No.*

The gun dropped from his hand, clattering loudly in the suddenly silent hall.

Tristan shook his head.

*No. No. No. No. No.*

His father lay there on the floor, his eyes open, staring up at the ceiling, his body motionless.

With a hole right in the center of his head.

The hole from a bullet.

Something lodged in his chest.

"You killed your own father?"

273

Tristan heard the Boss' voice. He heard him ask, heard the words, but kept looking at his dad, denying it in his heart.

*No. No. No. No. No.*

"That's his father?" someone else asked.

"How could he aim from there?"

"How did no one know he was here?"

"He's ruthless for a kid. Can you imagine what he'd be like?"

Words.

About him.

Rushing all around.

Over him.

One word.

On repeat.

*No. No. No. No. No.*

"The next course is ready when–"

It was the sound of his mother's voice that pulled Tristan's head up.

Oh god, *what had he done?*

Tristan saw as she came to a stop in the doorway, her eyes on him.

"Tristan, what are you doing here?" she asked, her eyes angry as she came towards him. Turning to the Boss, she started speaking, "I apologize for him, Mr. Maroni. He's just a kid. He doesn't know what he's doin–"

Her voice cut off abruptly as her eyes fell on his father, the words choking in her mouth.

Tristan saw as her hands came up to her lips, tears streaking down her cheeks as a sound escaped her chest. His jaw started to hurt from the way he'd clenched it.

"Who?" her mother's voice wavered on the word.

The Boss stepped forward towards Tristan. "Your son."

His mother's eyes snapped up to his, disbelief etched on her face. Tristan let her watch him silently, watched the disbelief change in horror as she saw the truth on his face. The horror he saw in her eyes killed something inside him. His jaw trembled as he stepped towards her, wanting to rush into her arms and have her tell him everything would be okay.

She jerked back from him, her mouth agape in terror. "Get away from me."

Tristan stilled.

His mother looked at him for a long time, shaking her head. "Why?"

"I.. it..." the words stuck in his throat, lodging there, unable to escape.

She took a step back. "You lost your sister. Now, you've killed your father. My husband. My daughter."

Tristan clenched his hands to keep from reaching out to her, not uttering a word. There wasn't anything he could say.

"My son was a sweet boy," his mother whispered almost to the door now. "You're not him. You're like *them*. Monsters."

. Something broke – damaged beyond repair in his chest.

"I don't want to see you again," her voice cracked as she stepped through the door from whence she'd entered. "You're dead to me."

She left.

Tristan stood there.

Alone.

Without his baby sister.

Without his father.

Without his mother.

Only with men who looked at him like they would eat him alive.

And a baby who had stopped crying.

A baby who, a few minutes ago, had been nothing to him. A baby for whom he'd murdered the father he'd loved so much.

Tristan looked at her – her eyes swollen from crying, the colors in them shining and twinkling; her little mouth rosy and soft; her chubby face smeared with his and his father's blood.

The flutter he had felt in his chest minutes ago was gone. In its place was something else instead. Something he'd never felt before. Something he didn't understand. Something twisted and ugly and alive, taking root inside his chest as he watched her breathe, because of him. Something poisonous bleeding its way into his heart, paralyzing it, deadening it, until he couldn't feel it anymore.

Until he could feel nothing but the poison. Until he could see nothing but her face with his blood.

He had spilled his father's blood to protect her.

His mother had called him a monster. She'd been right. He'd become a monster, more evil than all the men in the room, in one second.

All because of *her*.

Because she'd made him choose.

And he had nothing.

No one.

*Nothing.*

Nothing except this feeling in his chest. He latched on to it, looking at her face, etching it to memory. He looked at her eyes, seeing her soul forever tainted with his blood.

As of tonight, her life was his. He'd given up everything so she could live.

*Her life was his.*

He didn't know what he would do with it. But it was his.

"Come with me, boy."

The Boss's voice reached him. No. Not the Boss. He'd been the Boss to his father. And his father was dead.

Tristan Caine was dead too. In his place, someone else was born. Someone who looked up at Lorenzo Maroni and the gleam in his dark eyes dispassionately.

He kept quiet, everything inside him detached except for the strange, bitter sensation he felt when he looked at the girl. The men around him were considering him, all bigger than he was, with heavy weapons and the power to scare him.

He wasn't scared anymore.

This was the last time, he vowed to himself, that he'd be scared. Never again.

He was going to become the scariest of them all.

Saving her had destroyed him. One day, he vowed as he watched a man pick up the little girl and take her away, his blue eyes on her, he would collect his debt.

# *choosing*

*Morana.*
*Present Day.*

S he didn't know this, this coiled knot of emotions in her chest.
It just hurt.
Everything hurt. Every-fucking-thing.
Her trembling hands, her trembling lips, her trembling heart. All of
it.

She couldn't breathe. The air was trapped somewhere in her chest,
close to her bleeding heart. Her throat was tight, locked down; a weight
settling low in her stomach as the noise from the airplane flying
overhead filled the death in the graveyard.

The airplane came and went.

And it still hurt.

*She hurt.*

In a way she'd not thought herself capable of hurting. In a manner
she'd never known a person could hurt.

Eyes stinging, Morana blinked rapidly, years of training herself not
to shed a tear in front of anyone not allowing her the liberty to let a
single drop fall. But would it have stopped at a single drop? Would it
have stopped at all when the weight on her chest seemed to get heavier
and heavier with each passing breath?

She wanted to screech until her throat pained as her heart did. She wanted to become hoarse until the sound faded away into the nothingness inside. She wanted to scream but couldn't find her voice.

She was innocent.

Completely innocent.

She had done nothing wrong except exist.

Yet, her very existence made her want to weep. Her very existence made her want to break bones.

She existed because of him. She was innocent but he had been innocent too. She was innocent, and yet she was stained with blood.

His blood.

The blood of his father.

The blood he had shed to save her; the blood he had marked her with trying to clean her.

People who knew the story thought he'd made a claim in that gesture. But she knew, she knew he'd just been a sweet boy trying to wipe the blood off the face of an innocent baby.

Pain and rage, hate and turmoil, compassion and heartbreak, amalgamated inside her in a knot she could feel in her throat, transfused in her blood that beat in every inch of her body, came together in a way she couldn't distinguish one from another, didn't understand which was directed at whom.

She closed her eyes, her body starting to shake, unable to bear the conflict inside her very soul.

"Morana."

Amara's broken voice made her eyes flutter open. Unlike herself, the other woman was crying openly, the pain in her eyes reflective of her own. Morana owed the other woman so much, so much she couldn't even begin to comprehend it, for simply telling her the truth that had been stymied from her at every turn, for breaking her vow and putting her faith in her.

"Do you want me to stop?"

Morana shook her head immediately, her voice lost within her, tangled in the mass of emotions assaulting her, her jaw hurting from how hard she kept clenching it. She needed to know. She needed to know everything there was to know about him, her soul hungry for the knowledge that it had been denied. She needed to know, to understand him. She'd been locked for years from the truth and he had always been the key.

She needed to know.

Wiping her cheeks with small hands, her nails painted a green that matched her unusual eyes, Amara continued, her voice trembling like a leaf in the wind.

"I met Tristan when Mr. Maroni brought him to the house that day..." her beautiful, swollen eyes glazed over, lost in the memory she was speaking of, making Morana grit her teeth harder at the image of the aftermath.

"He was wearing this white long-sleeved t-shirt, splattered with drops of blood, one entire hand completely bloodied, his hair a mess. He was just two years older than I was but he seemed so much older. His eyes... god, his eyes, Morana... they were so *dead*," Amara shuddered, looking into space, goosebumps erupting over her arms.

She rubbed them slowly. "Mr. Maroni told everyone he would be staying at the compound. He talked about Tristan but Tristan just stood there, not moving, not reacting, his eyes moving over everyone. But he didn't look at anyone, he looked right through them... as though he was seeing nothing... It was so terrifying coming from such a young boy."

Morana tried to find the congruence in what Amara was telling her what she'd seen for herself. She'd seen him look that way at other people – at the men in the casino, at the people in the barn, at the crowd in the restaurant. She'd even remembered him looking that way at her that first night in Tenebrae when he hadn't known who she'd been, and her own knife had been pressed against her neck by his hands.

Now that she knew, she realized he'd evidently never, not since then, looked at her with nothing. There had always, always been something in those blue eyes of his. He'd always looked at her, in that intense way that seared her.

Amara's voice broke through her thoughts, a gust of cool breeze lifting a strand of her dark hair, chilling Morana.

"I remember asking mama about him that night. Nobody in our world knew why an outsider had been brought into the family, more so to live on the compound. That had never happened before. But a few days later, there were rumors."

Morana wrapped her arms around herself, a chill settling in her bones as she waited for Amara to continue.

"My mama told me she'd heard whispers among the servants about him. The servants always knew what happened at the compound, but they never spoke of it because of fear – for their families, for themselves, some even from loyalty. But they did talk among themselves, and Tristan had created quite a stir. Mama told me about those whispers, about how he'd murdered his own father in cold blood in a room full of men, about how dangerous he was, about how they said he was going to be the most feared of all men when he grew up. She told me to keep my distance from him. Everyone did. And I'm ashamed to admit, I kept my distance, shunned him like everyone else because of course, I was a little scared."

"You were just a child," Morana spoke up before she could help herself, her voice rusty and small.

Amara smiled sadly, fidgeting with the hem of her top. "So was he, Morana. We all forgot that so was he."

Morana swallowed the lump in her throat, gripping her top with her fingers.

"Him being such a terrifyingly silent boy just fed the wariness everyone felt for him even more. People talked about him, and I'm certain he knew, but he never uttered a word. Nothing. The first time I actually heard him speak was years after he'd come to live there."

Shaking her head, as if to shake off the memory, Amara continued. "Mr. Maroni had sworn his men to silence about Tristan's truth – not out of the goodness of his heart, if he even has any, and not because he wanted to protect the boy. Oh no, it was so that the man Tristan would become one day would owe him."

The disgust in Amara's voice seeped into Morana, her heart shuddering. The depth of cruelty in her world astounded her. Even though she'd known how brutal their world was, this still managed to catch her off guard. There was no place for innocence here. None. What a little boy had done out of instinct had cost him everything. Not because someone wanted to get revenge against him, or because someone wanted to kill him for themselves. No, but because someone wanted to simply exploit him. He should have been loved and protected. More importantly, he should have been forgiven. Instead, his crucible had only begun at the hands of the people who'd taken him under.

"Fuck," she whispered, not knowing what else to say, the one word encompassing the entire situation perfectly.

"Yeah. As if that wasn't enough, he was kept away from all the other children in the family, in a separate wing," Amara reminisced, another tear trailing down her cheek, her raspy voice trembling. "During the day when other kids went to school outside the walls or played until their time came to be trained, he was locked in the compound with private tutors. Maroni's best men trained him, tortured him, and he never said a word. Mama said she heard his screams sometimes in passing when she went to the wing. All of us did at some point. But never heard his words. And after a point, the screams just stopped."

Morana closed her eyes, rage infusing her blood, the urge to kill all those people, the need to kill all those people, to destroy them as they destroyed a child, so acute it became an ache in her heart. She remembered the deep, mottled scars she had seen all over on his body, the burn marks on his back. How many of those had been inflicted by these people? How many when he'd been just a boy? How many had taken him to the brink of death? To the brink of insanity?

A tear made its way down her cheek – a tear of pain, of anger, of compassion – before she could stop it. She let it roll down, taking a deep breath to calm her racing heart.

She opened her eyes. "Go on."

Amara sighed softly, her face etched in remorse. "I'll never forgive myself for ignoring him back then. I know I was just a child, but even back then, I knew it shouldn't have been happening like that. I knew it wasn't right. And yet, I did absolutely nothing to help him, not in any way. And I wonder sometimes if maybe a kind word, a selfless gesture, a hand of friendship would have made things a little better for him…"

Morana didn't say anything to that. She couldn't. Not with the rage she was feeling.

Amara swallowed, evidently struggling with something before she sucked in a breath and continued. "I saw him around the compound for years. I'd be wandering around the quarters, playing with the other children not under training, or helping my mama, and I'd catch glimpses of him over the years."

Rubbing a hand over her drained face, she went on. "He was always bruised. He walked with a limp sometimes. Sometimes, he could barely walk. And even then, nobody dared pity him, or talk to him. It became clear within years that he was lethal. His silence fed that even more. People within the family shunned him for being an outsider and people outside shunned him for being on the inside. He belonged nowhere. And while nobody messed with him, nobody talked to him either."

"Wh-what happened then?" Morana stuttered, barely able to get the words out, her heart clenching for the boy he'd been, wishing she could've known him back then. She'd been so alone growing up too, surrounded by people but nobody to talk to. Maybe, she could've extended that hand of companionship, surreal as it would've been. Maybe, they could've helped each other feel less lonely.

Maybe...

Amara smiled slightly, breaking Morana's thoughts, her entire face softening. "Dante happened."

Morana frowned, not understanding.

Amara shook her head, grinning softly, her beautiful eyes glistening. "A few years later, Mr. Maroni started Dante's training with the same men who'd trained Tristan for years. They both trained in the same place sometimes. There had already been talk about Tristan taking over the family when he grew up, and Dante was the obvious heir, being the oldest son and all. It didn't help that Tristan barely acknowledged anyone, much less spoke to anyone. Dante would try to talk to him and Tristan would shut him down so fast... he was that way with everyone. Only spoke when spoken to, and most of the time, not even then. Dante wasn't used to not getting his way. It created a lot of tension between them."

She could imagine.

"Then one night after training, Dante lost it. Got in Tristan's face. Tristan tried to walk away, and Dante punched him. Tristan broke his jaw."

Amara paused. "He broke the jaw of the oldest son of Lorenzo Maroni, the Boss of the Tenebrae Outfit."

Morana felt her eyes widen, the implications making her breath hitch, a shiver running down her spine.

The wind swirled around them, bringing stray, fallen leaves on their laps.

"Was he punished?" she asked in a whisper, afraid of the answer.

Amara's responsive chuckle surprised her as she shook her head again. "Mr. Maroni called everyone to the mansion. All the staff was there too, watching quietly. Anyways, he created a big scene, demanding the culprit, demanding who had broken his son's jaw. He took it as a hit to his honor or something."

Morana leaned forward, her breaths picking up. "Then?"

That little smile on Amara's face remained. "Dante never spoke up or even looked in Tristan's direction – he already hated his father. But Tristan did. I remember how stunned I'd been when Tristan stepped forward without hesitation. There was no fear in that boy. None at all. I mean, I'd seen grown men cower before Lorenzo Maroni and him... anyways, Maroni tried to threaten him subtly..."

The wind picked up. Morana shuddered. This just kept getting better and better.

"... and that was the first time I heard Tristan's voice."

Morana raised her eyebrows, heart pounding. "What did he say?"

The look of awe on Amara's face, even at the old memory, matched the wonder in her voice. "God, I still remember it like it was yesterday. Mr. Maroni threatened Tristan, thinking he'd feel obliged, maybe scared, maybe respectful – God knows what he was thinking – and Tristan... he got nose to nose with Mr. Maroni and told him – 'You ever put a leash on me, I'll fucking strangle you with it.' "

Morana blinked, stunned. "He said what?!"

Amara nodded. "You ever put a leash on me, I'll fucking strangle you with it. Word for word."

She tried to wrap her mind around it as astonishment flowed through her. "How old was he?"

"Fourteen."

Morana sat back, feeling the wind knocked out of her.

Amara nodded, as though she understood completely. "He was fearless, Morana. That was the first time any of us had seen a boy shut the Boss up. That was also the moment Dante decided he was completely Team Tristan. And when his father told him the truth about Tristan to make him stay away, it only made Dante more adamant to befriend that boy."

Stealing in a quick breath, Morana asked, "So they became a team?"

"Hell, no!" Amara retorted, shaking her head in fond memories. "Dante was always a charmer on the outside. He could seduce you in one breath while planning a million ways to kill you in the next, and you wouldn't even know. Tristan didn't trust him an inch, but he couldn't shake him off either. Dante was, still is, deceptively stubborn. And though he was the oldest son with responsibilities, Dante went against his father repeatedly by sustaining his association with Tristan. Maroni wanted them to compete. They basically gave him the finger. Over the years, they just sort of fell into this relationship – they're not really friends or brothers, but they'd not have anyone else on their side in battle. It's complicated with them."

Morana stayed silent, digesting all of it.

Twisting the cap off the bottle in her hand, Amara took a sip of water, swallowing slowly and leaning back against the headstone, quiet for a long moment as Morana soaked up everything.

"I was taken a few years later," she spoke quietly into the space between them, her voice husky, eyes dulling with the memories. "Tristan was the one to find me."

Morana started at that.

Amara nodded. "Yeah, he found me and left me with Dante while he took care of the men who'd kept me captive. It was after I was found that I truly interacted with Tristan. While I was recovering, he became… more present, I guess, without being obvious about it. I didn't know back then that it hit too close to home for him. He was being protective of me. Not obviously, and never with people around, but he just… became a presence in my life. He never talked much but the fact that he looked at me, listened if I talked said it all. That's why I know he's incredibly protective of women and children. I've seen him be that way for years now."

It was dawning on Morana – his deep-rooted need to protect. The fact that he'd survived all of what he had and not rid himself of that need to protect said more about him than anything ever could, more than he could ever show.

"He's never trusted anyone, Morana," Amara continued, her voice tinged with sadness. "He's never had much of a reason to."

"He trusts you and Dante," Morana reminded her.

Amara smiled sadly again. "Only to an extent. He lives behind his walls, all alone, dead to the world. We're allowed to come close to that wall but never behind it. That's why he's so feared. Everyone knows he's got nothing to lose. His weaknesses were exploited out of him. Now? No weak spots. Nothing. I've never, in all the years I have watched him, seen him be anything except deadly. He's not happy. He's not sad. He's not in pain. He's just made himself nothing..."

Memories came to Morana in a rush.

*'Did I hurt you?'*

His sleepless eyes, the intensity of his question, the stillness in his body.

The rage in him when she'd come to him hurting. The heat in his eyes when he'd fucked her in his mind. The curses in the shower when he'd cut himself open, bleeding in pain.

Amara was wrong - he wasn't nothing.

He *felt*.

He felt so deeply he didn't let himself feel.

He felt so deeply he feared his own reactions to it.

Or had it all been a trick to manipulate her? To make her compliant for his vengeance?

A loud clap of thunder rang across the skies, startling her.

Morana looked up, surprised to see the sun was low on the horizon, hidden behind thick, dark clouds roiling over each other. The wind rushed through the graveyard, whipping the leaves on the trees in a frenzy, whipping her hair around her face, whistling through the columns, making her aware of the dried blood on her arm from where the gunshot wound had opened in the blast.

Borrowing the bottle of water from Amara wordlessly, Morana tore a relatively clean piece of fabric from the bottom of her shirt, cleaned the wound the best she could with the limited water she had, and wrapped it in the cloth to keep it from bleeding again. The bottle nearly empty, she handed it back to the other woman, aware that she was being watched by her quietly.

She needed to be alone.

She needed to be by herself to even begin to process everything she'd learned. She needed time to herself, to grasp the magnitude of how intertwined they had always been, how defined they'd both been – him more so than her – by their pasts. But more importantly, she needed time to figure out her future, their futures, or if they could even have one.

Taking a deep breath and shoving the heaviness in her throat back down, Morana looked Amara in the eyes.

"I just… I need..." she scrambled for words, not really sure what to say.

She saw the other woman's eyes soften as she nodded, pushing herself off the ground to kneel. Picking up her spacious bag and putting the bottle inside it, Amara stood up, hitching the bag over her shoulder, brushing her backside to get the grass off.

Morana remained seated on the hard ground, leaning against the headstone, and looked up at the tall woman, the light in the sky falling right on the scar across her slender neck. The scar she'd received when she'd refused to rat on her people at fifteen. Morana had never clearly seen it before – because of scarves or makeup or shadows – but it was naked to the eye now, a thick, jarred white line of raised flesh going right across her throat.

Morana looked up at her beautiful eyes before she could stare. Amara had come to her with her scar exposed, showing a kind of trust Morana had never felt before, and she wouldn't let it down by making her feel conscious.

"I can't even imagine how hard this must be for you, Morana," the beautiful woman spoke softly in her raspy voice, the voice that had somehow started to soothe Morana. "Just give me a call if you need me."

Was this what friendship was like?

She didn't know. Tears threatening again at the kindness this strange woman had shown her repeatedly, at the hard truth she'd brought to light despite being bound by her own word to someone she loved, at dropping everything to come to her aid at one phone call – Morana was alien to these. But heaven help her, she was going to try.

She swallowed, trying to keep her lips from trembling.

"Thank you, Amara," a whisper escaped her, wrenched straight from the bottom of her soul. "Thank you... for everything."

Amara sniffled, wiping her tears, smiling. "I'm just happy to have you. In my life and especially in Tristan's. He's... he's spent twenty years in pain without acknowledging it. I love him, Morana. He's like a brother I never knew I had. And he's been through so much, so alone... just..."

Morana inhaled at her hesitation, waiting for her to continue.

Amara took a deep breath. "I can understand if it's too much for you... if he's too much for you. Frankly, I'd be surprised if he wasn't. Just – if it is too much – just don't give him hope if there's none. He never shows weakness. He doesn't expect anyone to stay with him, stay for him. That's a reason why he doesn't trust anyone. So, please, this is my only request to you, Morana. Please don't encourage him to trust you if you're going to leave in the end."

Blowing out a breath of air, she brushed a hand through her dark hair. "I told you all this because you needed to know the truth about yourself and about him. Do what you need to do, Morana. I won't deny a part of me hopes it's what he needs too, but just in case it isn't, do what you have to do for yourself and please don't hurt him."

The lump in her throat grew until her vision blurred.

She closed her eyes and nodded. "I need to... process. It's a lot."

"I know. I'll leave you be."

"Just don't... don't tell anyone about this for a while, please."

"Okay."

With one softly murmured word, Morana heard Amara's footsteps grow distant as she left her alone in the graveyard with the dead.

Morana closed her eyes, tilting her head back against the stone.

Death. So much death.

287

In her past. In her present. In her future too? Was that what she was moving towards? Did she want to go forward like this? Knowing she'd done nothing wrong? She'd just been a baby. She didn't even remember a thing, for fuck's sake!

And yet, a part of her, deep in her gut, heavy in her chest, rooted in her heart, was bathed in pain – pain for the boy he'd been, pain for the man he'd become, pain for everything he'd lost.

It had been twenty years.

How had he survived?

Her eyes opened.

She knew.

He'd survived through sheer will, for her.

She pictured all the scars she'd seen on his body, all the scars she had yet to see. She pictured him, the young boy who'd lost everything, getting nothing but pain, scar after scar, day after day, year after year. For twenty years, he'd had nothing, absolutely nothing, except what he believed she owed him.

Her life.

He'd lived for her life. He'd held on to his life for hers. And while her heart bled for him, while she understood him, was that what she deserved? Was it right for her to stay with a man who'd vowed to collect his debt one day? Could she live with a sword like that hanging over her head?

She couldn't.

Morana looked down at her fingers, dirty fingers, and let herself be absolutely, utterly honest with herself. No more denial. She let herself reflect on every moment she'd spent with him – from that first moment of that knife against her neck to that last moment of his text message telling her he didn't believe anyone could handle her if she didn't want to be handled. In the short span of a few weeks, she had changed. She had rebelled against that change, feared that change, but it had been uncontrollable.

She had changed.

And she couldn't believe, not after the honesty she had witnessed in his eyes, time after time – about his lust, his hatred, even his pain – that he hadn't changed somewhere too. While the boy he'd been might want her life, might still want to hold on to the debt in his mind, the man he was only wanted her.

That was his weakness.

He wanted her and he'd made it obvious. He wanted her and that was the reason she was still alive. He wanted her and that was why he'd protected her, sheltered her, saved her, time after time, from her own father.

This want was his weakness.

And she had two choices before her – she could exploit that weakness and battle with him to turn him, or she could expose her own throat and put her faith in him, her trust in him, to not rip it out.

Every single survival instinct she'd honed for years protested just at the thought of the second option. Yet, there was this tiny voice deep inside her, telling her this was the only way forward. In the last few weeks, he'd always acted in reaction to her choices. She'd have to be the one to act first.

Everything else aside, the bottom line was she was alive today because he'd chosen to save her. And she couldn't leave, not without giving him some closure. She owed him that much for her life. Running away wasn't an option anymore. Her life mattered everything to him. He was making it matter to her again.

She had killed two of her father's men. She'd killed in the rage and vengeance she'd felt for twenty minutes for her car.

He had harbored that rage inside him for twenty years.

God, this was a mess. And she wasn't even allowing herself to think of her father or Lorenzo 'Asshole' Maroni and all the shitload of mess with the Alliance. Her brain couldn't sustain so much together.

Taking a deep breath, she looked up at the now dark sky as another flight went overhead loudly, the clouds stark gray against the black backdrop of the night.

She needed something. If she was going to expose her own weakness, her own vulnerability, she needed something, anything at all to tell her it wasn't the worst mistake of her life. Anything to tell her that everything she'd experienced so far wasn't manipulative on his part and wasn't construed by her in her head.

A noise from near the entrance gates suddenly slithered through the empty silence.

Morana stilled.

It was late, later than she'd realized.

Heart pounding, she palmed the gun beside her quietly, forcing her hands to stop trembling. She wouldn't be able to make any decision if she ended up dead. And she couldn't die like this – not after surviving her father's attempt, not after learning the truth, not after the twenty years Tristan Caine had spent wanting closure.

Raindrops clung heavily to the clouds, the crackle of lightning loud in the wind. Morana could feel it in the air, the heavy rain that would drown her tonight. It was already dark, the sun strangled below the horizon by the night, and she realized how very secluded she was.

Standing up as quietly as she could, the wind chilly on her bare arms, Morana quickly moved out from behind the headstone and crouched, heading towards the blast site near the gates where the noise had come from. Staying in the shadows, grateful for the dirt that kept her shoes from making any noise, grateful for the clouds that hid the moon and provided cover, she crept ahead, her own eyes acclimated to the dark behind her glasses, letting her see mostly clearly.

Finally coming behind a tree with a clear view of the gates, Morana pressed herself against it, leaning outward slightly, just enough so she could see whatever was going on.

Two stocky men in suits were rummaging around the vehicle she'd blown up – clearly her father's men. One had a phone pressed to his ear while the other was looking around, smoking a cigarette, the orange glow of the tip a burning point from her vantage.

Keeping the gun ready in her hand, Morana just stayed put and watched.

And then, her heart stopped.

He was there.

Somehow, someway, he'd found her place.

Her surprise lasted only a moment, her heart heavy with the knowledge she didn't have before. Amara had been right. Knowing the truth would change things for her, but it wouldn't change things for him – she would have to do that herself.

Heart racing, her body acutely aware in a way it was only in his presence, senses alert, Morana watched as he smoothly got out from the black SUV he usually drove, his body encased in a suit, his usual open collar closed with a dark tie. His clothing told her he'd been somewhere important, somewhere out, and he'd come straight here.

Why?

The two men raised their arms to point their guns at him.

He shot one in the knee before the vehicle door was even shut.

The man dropped to the ground, shrieking in pain as his partner aimed straight. Morana didn't even wince. She'd seen enough of him in action to know he wouldn't be getting a single scratch.

Slamming the door behind him, he sauntered forward slowly, his entire body tight, agile, fluid in its unhurried movement, a flash of lighting giving him a deathly glow before shrouding him in black.

And then his voice, that voice of whiskey and sin, spoke in death.

"Where is she?"

Silence.

Her heart started to pound erratically, thundering in her chest. Without conscious thought, Morana pressed herself deeper into the bark of the tree, holding it tightly with her fingers until her knuckles turned white, her eyes glued to the man who would decide tonight if he would be her life or her death.

Her throat locked, suddenly wanting to call out to him. She strangled the urge.

Her father's uninjured man didn't say a word; he just kept his gun trained.

*"Where. Is. She?"*

He didn't threat. Didn't bluster like she'd seen a lot of men do.

He didn't need to though. The three words were wrapped in so much death it was hard to miss.

Evidently, her father's man, the one whimpering on the ground, thought so too. "We just got here. The blast took out both cars. Let us go, please. We have a family."

Morana watched as he suddenly stilled, his eyes going, for the first time, to the burned remains of her car.

For a moment, nothing moved – not the wind, not the leaves, not the men.

*"Where the fuck is she?"*

Thunder split the sky; winds became chaotic, making his tie and open jacket flap against his hard chest, his gun arm pointing straight at the other man, the imminent death in his voice making her flinch.

But his eyes remained on her car.

Something tightened in her chest.

"We don't know. We were told to come check on our guys."

He turned to the men, lowering his gun, no movement on his face.

"Leave. Now. You turn around and come back, you die."

The man who was standing nodded, putting his gun away as he helped the injured guy up and towards their own car. Within minutes, they were in the vehicle and driving away, the bright taillights disappearing, leaving everything back in the darkness.

He'd let them go.

Morana moved slightly out beside the tree, unable to understand him, the beating of her heart vicious, the rush of blood hot through her veins.

Dust slowly settled.

She watched him take a few steps towards the pile of charred metal that had been her beloved car, and come to a stop.

The gun dangled loosely in his hand at his side.

He stood before the bombed remains of her car, his back to her, the jacket of his suit clinging to his muscles as they tightened, before flapping in the onslaught of the wind.

Morana stood quietly against the tree in plain sight and watched him from behind, wanting to see his reaction, needing to see his reaction. Because if she was going to gamble with this man, she needed to know her cards.

She hadn't spoken to him since that last text she'd sent him. Her phone had been switched off, and she'd made Amara promise to give her some time alone to figure things out. She'd been missing for hours, and she needed to see his reaction, not in front of those men, but his reaction alone. Because even though she hadn't figured anything out, if he gave her even a sliver of hope, she knew she wasn't going to run away. For once in her life, she wanted to stay.

His back moved as he breathed, his hands clenched beside him as he kept looking at her dead car. The darkness clung to his frame, only the flash of lightning illuminating him brightly for split seconds before leaving him standing alone in the dark again in the graveyard.

Thunder roared in agony.

The winds lamented.

Morana swallowed the pain rising in her chest but didn't make a move, knowing instinctively that even a tiny motion would make him aware of her.

So, she just kept watching him, waiting for him to do something.

He did.

He touched her car.

Stroked it.

Just once.

But he did.

He did it when he thought no one was watching.

He did it when he thought he was completely alone.

Morana blinked at the stinging in her eyes as she saw his big, rough hand move across the charred remains tenderly, the sliver of hope expanding to a fragment now.

She knew.

She had seen.

And she was going to fight him, fight for him, like he'd fought for her. She was going to gamble. She was going to throw herself off the cliff and hope he would catch her. Because she didn't see how they could move on if she didn't do it. Lord knew, he wouldn't.

Gulping in a deep breath, she took a step forward in the darkness, her eyes on him.

For a moment, nothing happened.

It was silent. It was dark. It was vacant.

She stood in plain sight now, enough so he could just turn his neck and see her.

But nothing happened.

Heart pounding, Morana swallowed, her own gun in her hand, and took another step forward.

He just took a deep breath, his back expanding, the fabric of his jacket stretching across those scarred muscles but he didn't turn.

And suddenly, Morana knew that he knew that she was there.

He knew she was standing behind him, watching him, and he didn't turn.

God, he wouldn't make this easy on her. Well, she wasn't going to make this easy for him either.

She walked another step forward, then another, and then another, watching his back muscles tighten with each one of hers, his body coiling.

Deja-vu hit her, from that very morning, when she'd confronted him about his hatred for her, about his sister, and the fact that she'd been one of those missing girls.

*'I never hated you for that.'*

No. He never had. Not for that.

Had it just been that morning? Just a few hours? It felt like a lifetime.

But she had incited a reaction from him.

Taking another deep breath, closing her eyes momentarily and calling upon all the strength inside herself, Morana threw herself off the cliff.

"I know."

Two words.

Piercing the silence between them like bullets.

Hovering in the air between them.

He didn't turn around, didn't move, only his back stretched once as he took in a heavy breath. Her hands ached to feel those muscles, feel those scars under her fingers. She clenched them into fists.

His own gun hung loosely by his side, his other hand going into his trouser pocket. Yet, he didn't turn, didn't face her, didn't acknowledge her.

"I know…" she bit her lip, "Tristan."

Hushed. Everything hushed.

He stilled even more, impossibly.

She stilled even more, reflexively.

The air between them stilled, dangerously.

She knew she'd crossed an invisible line they'd both repeatedly acknowledged but never toed. She knew that by calling him by his name, she'd ventured into territory unknown. And it scared her. So much, she stood trembling against the now calm gales, her hands balled into fists by her side as she kept her eyes glued to his back, waiting for a reaction.

It came.

He turned.

Lightning split the sky.

And in that momentary light, his magnificent blue eyes found her, imprisoned her, burned her.

Her throat locked, heart pounded, blood beat hard in her ears.

Her breath started coming faster, until she was almost on the verge of panting, because he stood a few feet away from her, cutting a lethal form in the darkness that enclosed him, wrapped around him like a lover, wrapped around her like a foe.

And he uttered not a word.

God, he wasn't going to give her an inch, not unless she forced him to. And she would force him to. There was no other way, not now, not for her, not for him, not for them.

With that knowledge deep in her heart, she closed her eyes once, gasped in another breath, and forced herself to at least appear somewhat calm.

"Thank you," she began quietly, her words, though soft, loud in the silence of the graveyard.

She couldn't see his eyes clearly, so she didn't know how he reacted to it. She was almost going into this on blind faith and hope.

So, without waiting for his reaction, or give herself more time to panic, she started to talk.

"Thank you, for saving me," she spoke to his hard, motionless form. In a way, it was better that she couldn't see him. It made this much easier of sorts. "Not only in the past few weeks but twenty years ago."

His fingers flexed on the gun.

"I know it came at a cost nobody should've had to pay, least of all a young boy, and I'm so, so very sorry for all of it."

Only the movement of his chest.

In. Out.

Her own breathing synced with his.

Okay.

"But I'm not going to discuss it, not like this and not when you don't want to. We'll only speak of it when you are ready because it's your story."

And now came the tricky part.

Allowing the blast of anger to shoot through her veins, Morana took a step forward, her fear mingling with the rage inside her.

"You hate me, loathe me, for something I never did. While I can understand that – I completely understand it – I cannot live with it. Not knowing that I was innocent," she sucked in another breath. "But you did save me, and my conscience won't allow me to move on without giving you a chance for closure."

The scent of incoming rain permeated the air, along with the scent of night blooms that grew wildly in the area. Morana drew in the scent, taking strength from the memory of another rainy night that had triggered the change in her.

Wetting her lips, she spoke, keeping her voice as firm as it could be while her insides shook.

"So here's the thing, Mr. Caine." She won't call him by his name again, not until he gave her the right. "I have made my decision – for good or bad. Now, it's time for you. I'm giving you the chance to kill me, right here, right now."

A beat passed.

With that aforementioned strength, she threw the gun she had in her hand, the gun that had been her savior for so long, very deliberately to the side.

His own stayed right in his hand, his eyes burning on her.

Morana pushed forward, gathering courage as the words came to her. "My father already tried to off me and if I die tonight, none would be the wiser. They'll all think I perished when the bomb went off and all the responsibility would lay at my father's feet – not you or the Outfit.

Nobody would ever need to know you even came here or that you were involved. No blame would ever go to Tenebrae. No mess. No foul. Nothing."

The wind whipped her hair around her face, touching her all over before it reached him, caressed him, making his jacket flap against his torso.

Thunder roared through the sky again.

Morana waited for it to quieten before continuing.

"As for the codes," she spoke, unable to stop now, wondering if anyone had ever made arguments for their own death like she was, "we both know you can get other computer experts, so that's not the main issue. You'd never get a better opportunity to kill me. You know it, I know it. This would stay only between us and the dead that are buried here. So, point that gun at me one more time and aim for my heart. Shoot me. Find your closure. Find what you've been looking for, for twenty years."

His hand didn't move, even as his fingers twitched. The silence, though her ally as she delivered her words, was undoing her, bit by bit.

She took a step closer to him, still keeping many feet between them, to cover for her shaking body.

"But understand this," she kept speaking, in the same firm tone, thankful it didn't quiver. "This is the only chance I'm giving you to kill me. After this, should you choose not to, this will never come up again. After this, you'll need to let go of the idea that you're killing me. After this, you never, *ever* threaten me with my life again."

The hand in his pocket came out, his fist clenching and unclenching.

That small outward movement gave her fortitude.

"You deliver my death or you let it go. Either way, you need to make a choice, as I've made mine and come to peace with it. Because if your choices affect my life so deeply, if a choice you made two decades ago is defining my life right now, then I'll make you choose again. This time, not as a boy but as a grown man."

And then the tremor in her voice came out, her jaw clenching as her voice broke. "Because I sure as fuck will never, *ever* let you think you'll kill me again. This is the only chance you'll ever have."

Her instincts were raging inside her. "So, choose."

Her palms started sweating.

She saw his grip on the gun tighten, his arm starting to move, and she closed her eyes.

The noises around her seemed louder in the utter darkness behind her lids. The sounds of creatures doing their nightly rituals, the sound of wind rustling through the leaves, the sound of her heart pounding in her ears.

The scents were more acute as well. The scent of the heavy clouds in the air, the scent of her own fear permeating her skin, the scent of the wildflowers in the night. The storm brewing outside, the tempest breaking inside, combining, colliding, capturing.

*Was he pointing his gun at her?*

Her chest grew heavy.

*Was he thinking it over?*

Lead settled in her stomach.

*Was he about to pull that trigger and end her misery? Was her last act on earth going to be putting her trust in the wrong man, yet again?*

Her heart thudded.

Should she have just run away and lived her entire life with the regret of never knowing, never exploring the possibility between them? Could she have lived better without offering him a semblance of closure?

Her body started trembling.

Seconds, minutes, hours. Suspended between them. Between his choice and hers.

Memories, moments, an entire history. Stuck between them. Between his choice and hers.

Questions, doubts, fears. Settling between them. Between his choice and hers.

*Silence.*

She was coming undone, bit by bit. She was fraying apart at the edges, bit by bit. She was imploding in on herself, bit by bit.

She needed him to make a choice. She needed him to choose her like he'd chosen her years ago. She needed him to choose her – because, after the day she'd had, her father trying to kill her like her life was worthless, she needed him to choose her, not for her life, but herself.

Silence.

A change in the air around her.

The scent of wood and musk.

The warmth of a breath over her face.

And then she felt it.

Lips.

Soft, tender lips settling upon hers.

Her heart stopped.

It fucking stopped as her stomach bottomed out.

Her gasp got stuck in her throat as her lips started to tremble against his, her eyes stinging, her heart full.

She didn't dare open her eyes, fearful that this would stop, that he would stop. She didn't dare open her eyes, fearful that the moment would be shattered never to be realized again. She didn't dare open her eyes, fearful of the tear that hung on the threshold of her lashes.

She didn't dare *breathe*.

And he brushed those soft lips against her, before settling again.

She squeezed her eyes shut, her breaths hastening, fingers curling into her palms to keep from touching him since he wasn't touching her, even as she tilted her head back as far as it would go, letting his lips lock with hers better.

A cold drop of rain fell on her cheek. Thunder rent the sky.

She parted her lips, feeling the shape, the make, the beauty of his. He captured her bottom one, sucking on it lightly before brushing her lips again.

The rain came down, drenching them both within seconds.

She let go of that tear in her eye, letting it mingle with the rain, the tremors of her lips evident against his. His mouth pressed onto hers more firmly, no other parts of his body touching hers. The scruff around his lips chafed across hers in a way that sent her flesh tingling, wondering about places his mouth could go and how that delicious scruff would feel, making her sway forward slightly.

Morana tilted her head instinctively to the side, her hands shaking as fire rushed through her veins from that minimal contact of his lips.

He kissed her – softly, simply, expertly.

He kissed her – until her knees turned to jelly and heat invaded her belly.

He kissed her – without his tongue, without his hands, without his body.

Just his lips – soft, firm, present – on hers.

It was the most beautiful kiss she could have ever dreamed of, the most untainted she'd ever imagined from him, with a softness she'd not thought him capable of. With his intensity, with his blazing eyes, the silent promises had been of devouring.

This wasn't devouring.

This was savoring.

He was savoring her lips, memorizing her taste, introducing himself to her so much more intimately than he ever had. Her toes curled even as her heart clenched, pulse throbbing all over her body.

The rain poured all over them, the scent of wet earth rising and mingling with the scent of him, invading her senses, burying itself under her skin, making her breasts heavy and a flame ignite deep in her core.

He kissed her for long, long moments – as chaste as kisses could be, yet she felt it down to her soul.

And then, she felt the cool tip of his gun, stroking over her face, the metal kissing her wet skin from temple to jaw.

She pulled back slightly, just an inch, to find those magnificent blue eyes on her in an inferno, his shadowed face wet, lips a little swollen, stark against his scruff.

Her eyes drifted to the big gun in his large hand, surprise filling her as she saw his knuckles – the skin freshly broken over them, raindrops streaking down over the tumefied flesh. The contradiction – of him in his suit and tie while sporting bruised knuckles getting drenched in the rain – thralled her. Who had he been hitting so hard before coming here?

He put a little pressure on her jaw with his gun, demanding that her eyes return to his silently.

Morana obliged, aware of his finger on the trigger and the gun at her jugular.

And yet, she'd given him the choice.

He traced her swollen mouth with the tip of his gun, once, before settling it back under her jaw.

He looked down at her face for long moments as she kept her head tilted up, his weapon underneath on her neck, their bodies wet and close but not pressed to each other. The cold wind and water sizzled over her heated skin, running down her hot breast, the contrast erecting her nipples almost painfully. Her heart started beating faster than it already was, the need inside her, for so many things, coming to the fore. His eyes caught it, the fire in them singeing her, inflaming before her very own.

Before she could blink, his mouth was upon hers, prying her lips open with his tongue, flicking her tongue in a movement she felt between her legs. Clenching her thighs together to relieve the throbbing, she closed her eyes and went up on her toes, instinctively allowing him more.

And then, he *devoured* her.

Fulfilling every promise his eyes had ever made to her.

He devoured her in the rain, with his gun beneath her jaw.

He devoured her while tasting like the whiskey and sin she heard in his voice.

He devoured her without touching another inch of her body, stroking her tongue with his, tasting her so thoroughly her legs weakened, her hands catching onto the lapels of his jacket to keep herself upright, not touching his skin like he wasn't touching hers, yet letting him support her.

Electric.

There was no other word for it.

It sizzled. It sparked. It consumed.

His scruff rasped over her wet skin, lips meshing together as heat infused her, and she knew she would carry the evidence of that burn around her mouth later. She wanted that evidence. She wanted him to look at her reddened flesh tomorrow and feel the heat in his body like she would every time she saw it. She wanted him to look at her swollen lips and remember the invisible line he crossed with her. She wanted him to look at her and remember that first kiss in the rain.

Holding onto his wet jacket, she sucked on his tongue, inviting him deeper, and got her lower lip nipped in response, the gun kissing her skin, sliding down from her jaw, down the slope of her neck, down her cleavage, to stop between her breasts.

It stopped above her heart, making it jump out of her chest even as he kept ravaging her mouth, all his heat, his intensity, pouring over her along with the rain.

A shiver ran down her spine, her fingers fisting the fabric of his jacket, her lips trembling against his, and he pulled back.

Morana opened her eyes, stunned at the force of that kiss, stunned at her own reaction, stunned at him.

She saw his lips, swollen, wearing the evidence of her wild mouth, and her skin heated, her nipples pebbling even harder, even with the gun pressed to her heart.

His jaw clenched, a vein popping on the side of his head as his eyes pierced hers for a long moment. She held his gaze, never blinking once, the water sluicing down their faces as they stared at each other.

He stayed unmoving for a beat, then two, their lips hovering right next to each other, neither making the move, their eyes on each other before he closed his eyes for a small second.

He closed his eyes, for that small second.

His Adam's apple bobbed above the knot of his tie, for that small second.

And then his arm went down.

A breath Morana hadn't known she'd been holding escaped her in a rush.

He stepped back, not looking into her eyes again, leaving her to be kissed by the cold rain and chilled air, his jacket falling out of her grip as he bent down swiftly to retrieve her gun from the muddy ground.

Standing back up to his full height, his white shirt plastered to his torso, wet skin and ink peeking underneath the transparent fabric, making Morana swallow reflexively, he extended her own gun back to her. Morana let her eyes rove away from his chest to his red-knuckled hand that was making her heavy gun look small.

She took it from him silently, her fingers brushing his, sending tingles up her arm.

He didn't react, as was usual with him.

He also didn't look into her eyes, which was unusual.

He just turned on his heel and headed towards his huge vehicle, the rain pelting down on his imposing figure in the utter night, after kissing the breath out of her.

*'I get my mouth on you, you'll never be the same.'*

His words came back to her. He'd been right.

Morana looked down at the gun he'd picked up for her and handed back to her.

She'd wanted something. He'd given it to her, in a way only he could. He'd not uttered a word. But he'd made his choice. So had she.

Taking a deep breath in, Morana swallowed, stepping forward.

And she followed him into the dark.

*To be continued in **The Reaper**, coming in July 2020.*
*Thank you for reading this book. If you've enjoyed it, please*
*recommend it to a friend and leave a review.*

## About the Author

With stories in her veins and words in her blood, RuNyx began her writing journey online five years ago. Since then, she has devoted her life to story-telling and made a career out of the same. She believes that the best of stories come from the best of conflicts, and has made it her mission to find love in the darkness.

Connect with her on her Twitter, Instagram, and Tumblr. She loves to hear from her readers. To stay updated about upcoming books, sign up for her newsletter.

*The Reaper* will release worldwide in July 2020.

CPSIA information can be obtained
at www.ICGtesting.com
Printed in the USA
BVHW091432301221
625230BV00010B/685